FRANKENSTEIN

A Kaplan SAT Score-Raising Classic

Also Part of the Kaplan SAT Score-Raising Series:

Dr. Jekyll and Mr. Hyde:
A Kaplan SAT Score-Raising Classic

Scarlet Letter:
A Kaplan SAT Score-Raising Classic

The Tales of Edgar Allan Poe:
A Kaplan SAT Score-Raising Classic

War of the Worlds:
A Kaplan SAT Score-Raising Classic

Wuthering Heights:
A Kaplan SAT Score-Raising Classic

FRANKENSTEIN

A Kaplan SAT Score-Raising Classic

By Mary Shelley

New York

Editorial Director: Jennifer Farthing
Editor: Caryn Yilmaz
Production Editor: Caitlin Ostrow
Production Artist: John Christensen
Cover Designer: Carly Schnur

Published by Kaplan Publishing, a division of Kaplan, Inc.
1 Liberty Plaza, 24th Floor
New York, NY 10006

Printed in the United States of America

November 2006
10 9 8 7 6 5

ISBN-13: 978-1-4195-4224-4

Library of Congress Cataloging-in-Publication Data is available.

Kaplan Publishing books are available at special quantity discounts to use for sales promotions, employee premiums, or educational purposes. Please email our Special Sales Department to order or for more information at kaplanpublishing@kaplan.com, or write to Kaplan Publishing, 1 Liberty Plaza, 24th Floor, New York, NY 10006.

How To Use This Book

Not only is Mary Shelley's classic novel, *Frankenstein*, filled with chills and thrills—it's also filled with SAT words! Now Kaplan makes it as easy as 1-2-3 for you to learn these vocabulary words as you read the story.

On the right-hand pages you will find the tale of *Frankenstein* with selected words **bolded** throughout. These bolded words are frequently found on the SAT. On the left-hand pages Kaplan defines these SAT words, as well as gives you the part of speech, pronunciation, and synonyms for each word—everything you need to know to improve your vocabulary and to ace the SAT.

Some of the most challenging vocabulary words found in *Frankenstein* aren't likely to appear on the SAT, but we thought you might want to learn those, too. That's why we've underlined them throughout the text and added their definitions to a glossary at the end of the book. After all—you never know where they might pop up next! In this edition you will also find an index of all SAT words at the end of the book.

So what are you waiting for? Start reading!

Volume I

FOREBODING (fohr boh dihng) *n.*
an omen, prediction, or presentiment of upcoming evil
Synonyms: anxiety, dread, premonition, augury

FERVENT (fuhr vehnt) *adj.*
passionate, intense, zealous
Synonyms: vehement, eager, enthusiastic, avid

DESOLATION (deh suh lay shuhn) *n.*
barren wasteland; sadness, loneliness
Synonyms: bleakness, devastation, ruin; despair

DIFFUSE (dih fyooz) *v.* **-ing,-ed.**
to spread out
Synonyms: scatter, disperse

PERPETUAL (puhr peht chyoo uhl) *adj.*
endless, lasting
Synonyms: continuous, constant, ceaseless, eternal

BANISH (baan ish) *v.* **-ing,-ed.**
to force to leave, exile
Synonyms: expel, deport

LETTER I

To Mrs. Saville, England.

St. Petersburgh, Dec. 11th, 17– .

You will rejoice to hear that no disaster has accompanied the commencement of an enterprise which you have regarded with such evil **forebodings**. I arrived here yesterday; and my first task is to assure my dear sister of my welfare, and increasing confidence in the success of my undertaking.

I am already far north of London; and as I walk in the streets of Petersburgh, I feel a cold northern breeze play upon my cheeks, which braces my nerves, and fills me with delight. Do you understand this feeling? This breeze, which has travelled from the regions towards which I am advancing, gives me a foretaste of those icy climes. Inspirited by this wind of promise, my day dreams become more **fervent** and vivid. I try in vain to be persuaded that the pole is the seat of frost and **desolation**; it ever presents itself to my imagination as the region of beauty and delight. There, Margaret, the sun is for ever visible; its broad disk just skirting the horizon, and **diffusing** a **perpetual** splendour. There—for with your leave, my sister, I will put some trust in preceding navigators—there snow and frost are **banished**; and, sailing over a calm sea, we may be wafted to a land surpassing in wonders and in beauty every region hitherto discovered on the habitable globe. Its productions and features may be without example, as the phaenomena of the heavenly bodies undoubtedly are in those

SATIATE (say shee ayt) *v.* **-ing,-ed.**
to satisfy
Synonyms: sate, cloy, glut, gorge, surfeit

ARDENT (ahr dihnt) *adj.*
passionate, enthusiastic, fervent
Synonyms: intense, vehement, fervid

INDUCE (ihn doos) (ihn dyoos) *v.* **-ing,-ed.**
to persuade; bring about
Synonyms: prevail, convince, lead, effect, occasion

CONJECTURE (kuhn jehk shuhr) *n.*
speculation, prediction
Synonyms: postulation, hypothesis, supposition, guess

ASCERTAIN (aa suhr tayn) *v.* **-ing,-ed.**
to determine, discover, make certain of
Synonyms: verify, calculate, detect

DISPEL (dihs pehl) *v.* **-ing,-ed.**
to drive out or scatter
Synonyms: disband, disperse

AGITATION (aa gih tay shuhn) *n.*
commotion, excitement; uneasiness
Synonyms: disturbance, restlessness, anxiety

ARDOUR or ARDOR (ahr duhr) *n.*
passion, enthusiasm
Synonyms: intensity, vehemence

NEGLECT (neh glehkt) *v.* **-ing,-ed.**
to ignore or disregard, to be negligent
Synonyms: overlook, skimp

INJUNCTION (ihn juhnk shuhn) *n.*
command, order
Synonyms: directive, behest, mandate, edict, decree

undiscovered solitudes. What may not be expected in a country of eternal light? I may there discover the wondrous power which attracts the needle; and may regulate a thousand celestial observations, that require only this voyage to render their seeming eccentricities consistent for ever. I shall **satiate** my **ardent** curiosity with the sight of a part of the world never before visited, and may tread a land never before imprinted by the foot of man. These are my enticements, and they are sufficient to conquer all fear of danger or death, and to **induce** me to commence this laborious voyage with the joy a child feels when he embarks in a little boat, with his holiday mates, on an expedition of discovery up his native river. But, supposing all these **conjectures** to be false, you cannot contest the inestimable benefit which I shall confer on all mankind to the last generation, by discovering a passage near the pole to those countries, to reach which at present so many months are requisite; or by **ascertaining** the secret of the magnet, which, if at all possible, can only be effected by an undertaking such as mine.

These reflections have **dispelled** the **agitation** with which I began my letter, and I feel my heart glow with an enthusiasm which elevates me to heaven; for nothing contributes so much to tranquillize the mind as a steady purpose—a point on which the soul may fix its intellectual eye. This expedition has been the favourite dream of my early years. I have read with **ardour** the accounts of the various voyages which have been made in the prospect of arriving at the North Pacific Ocean through the seas which surround the pole. You may remember, that a history of all the voyages made for purposes of discovery composed the whole of our good uncle Thomas's library. My education was **neglected**, yet I was passionately fond of reading. These volumes were my study day and night, and my familiarity with them increased that regret which I had felt, as a child, on learning that my father's dying **injunction**

PERUSE (puh rooz) *v.* **-ing,-ed.**
to examine closely
Synonyms: scrutinize, inspect, investigate

EFFUSION (ih fyoo zhuhn) *n.*
an emotion expressed without restraint
Synonyms: profusion, feeling, expression

NICHE (nihch) *n.*
best position for something; recess in a wall
Synonyms: alcove, cranny, crevice, place, station

CONSECRATE (kahn suh krayt) *v.* **-ing,-ed.**
to declare sacred; dedicate to a goal
Synonyms: sanctify, devote

RESOLVE (rih sahlv) *v.* **-ing,-ed.**
to determine or to make a firm decision about
Synonyms: solve, decide

INURE (ihn yoor) *v.* **-ing,-ed.**
to harden; accustom; become used to
Synonyms: habituate, familiarize, condition

DERIVE (dih riev) *v.* **-ing,-ed.**
to obtain from a source
Synonyms: infer, deduce, arise

ENTREAT (ehn treet) *v.* **-ing,-ed.**
to plead, beg
Synonyms: beseech, implore, importune, request

RESOLUTION (reh suh loo shuhn) *n.*
a firm decision
Synonyms: determination, will, explanation

FLUCTUATE (fluhk choo ayt) *v.* **-ing,-ed.**
to alternate, waver
Synonyms: swing, oscillate, vary, undulate

FORTITUDE (fohr tih tood) *n.*
strength, stamina
Synonyms: endurance, hardiness, toughness, courage

had forbidden my uncle to allow me to embark in a seafaring life.

These visions faded when I **perused**, for the first time, those poets whose **effusions** entranced my soul, and lifted it to heaven. I also became a poet, and for one year lived in a Paradise of my own creation; I imagined that I also might obtain a **niche** in the temple where the names of Homer and Shakespeare are **consecrated**. You are well acquainted with my failure, and how heavily I bore the disappointment. But just at that time I inherited the fortune of my cousin, and my thoughts were turned into the channel of their earlier bent.

Six years have passed since I **resolved** on my present undertaking. I can, even now, remember the hour from which I dedicated myself to this great enterprise. I commenced by **inuring** my body to hardship. I accompanied the whale-fishers on several expeditions to the North Sea; I voluntarily endured cold, famine, thirst, and want of sleep; I often worked harder than the common sailors during the day, and devoted my nights to the study of mathematics, the theory of medicine, and those branches of physical science from which a naval adventurer might **derive** the greatest practical advantage. Twice I actually hired myself as an under-mate in a Greenland whaler, and acquitted myself to admiration. I must own I felt a little proud, when my captain offered me the second dignity in the vessel, and **entreated** me to remain with the greatest earnestness; so valuable did he consider my services.

And now, dear Margaret, do I not deserve to accomplish some great purpose. My life might have been passed in ease and luxury; but I preferred glory to every enticement that wealth placed in my path. Oh, that some encouraging voice would answer in the affirmative! My courage and my **resolution** is firm; but my hopes **fluctuate**, and my spirits are often depressed. I am about to proceed on a long and difficult voyage; the emergencies of which will demand all my **fortitude**. I am required

SUSTAIN (suh <u>stayn</u>) *v.* **-ing,-ed.**
to support, uphold; endure, undergo
Synonyms: maintain, prop, encourage, withstand, confirm

not only to raise the spirits of others, but sometimes to **sustain** my own, when theirs are failing.

This is the most favourable period for travelling in Russia. They fly quickly over the snow in their sledges; the motion is pleasant, and, in my opinion, far more agreeable than that of an English stage-coach. The cold is not excessive, if you are wrapt in furs, a dress which I have already adopted; for there is a great difference between walking the deck and remaining seated motionless for hours, when no exercise prevents the blood from actually freezing in your veins. I have no ambition to lose my life on the post-road between St. Petersburgh and Archangel.

I shall depart for the latter town in a fortnight or three weeks; and my intention is to hire a ship there, which can easily be done by paying the insurance for the owner, and to engage as many sailors as I think necessary among those who are accustomed to the whale-fishing. I do not intend to sail until the month of June—and when shall I return? Ah, dear sister, how can I answer this question? If I succeed, many, many months, perhaps years, will pass before you and I may meet. If I fail, you will see me again soon, or never.

Farewell, my dear, excellent, Margaret. Heaven shower down blessings on you, and save me, that I may again and again testify my gratitude for all your love and kindness.

Your affectionate brother,
R. Walton.

DAUNTLESS (dawnt lehs) *adj.*
fearless
Synonyms: unafraid, courageous, valiant, daring

ASSAIL (uh sayl) *v.* **-ing,-ed.**
to attack, assault
Synonyms: beset, storm, strike

SUSTAIN (suh stayn) *v.* **-ing,-ed.**
to support, uphold; endure, undergo
Synonyms: maintain, prop, encourage, withstand, confirm

DEJECTION (dih jehk shuhn) *n.*
a state of depression or melancholy
Synonyms: grief, sadness, low spirits

CAPACIOUS (kuh pay shuhs) *adj.*
large, roomy; extensive
Synonyms: ample, commodious

AMEND (uh mehnd) *v.* **-ing,-ed.**
to improve or correct flaws in
Synonyms: adjust, emend, ameliorate, rectify, revise

ARDENT (ahr dihnt) *adj.*
passionate, enthusiastic, fervent
Synonyms: intense, vehement, fervid

EXECUTION (ehk sih kyoo shuhn) *n.*
1. the act of performing or carrying out a task
Synonyms: accomplishment, achievement
2. the act of putting to death
Synonyms: killing, capital punishment, murder

LETTER II

To Mrs. Saville, England.

Archangel, March 28th, 17—.

How slowly the time passes here, encompassed as I am by frost and snow; yet a second step is taken towards my enterprise. I have hired a vessel, and am occupied in collecting my sailors; those whom I have already engaged appear to be men on whom I can depend, and are certainly possessed of **dauntless** courage.

But I have one want which I have never yet been able to satisfy; and the absence of the object of which I now feel as a most severe evil. I have no friend, Margaret. When I am glowing with the enthusiasm of success, there will be none to participate in my joy; if I am **assailed** by disappointment, no one will endeavour to **sustain** me in **dejection**. I shall commit my thoughts to paper, it is true; but that is a poor medium for the communication of feeling. I desire the company of a man who could sympathize with me; whose eyes would reply to mine. You may deem me romantic, my dear sister, but I bitterly feel the want of a friend. I have no one near me, gentle yet courageous, possessed of a cultivated as well as of a **capacious** mind, whose tastes are like my own, to approve or **amend** my plans. How would such a friend repair the faults of your poor brother! I am too **ardent** in **execution**, and too impatient of difficulties. But it is a still greater evil to me that I am self-educated, for the first fourteen years of my life I ran wild on a common and read nothing but our uncle Thomas's books of voyages. At that age I became acquainted with the celebrated poets of our own country; but it was only when it had ceased to be in

DERIVE (dih riev) *v.* **-ing,-ed.**
to obtain from a source
Synonyms: infer, deduce, arise

DROSS (drahs) (draws) *n.*
waste; something base, trivial, or inferior
Synonyms: garbage, remains, rubbish

RETAIN (rih tayn) *v.* **-ing,-ed.**
to hold, keep possession of
Synonyms: withhold, reserve, maintain, remember

ENDOWMENT (ehn dow mehnt) *n.*
a natural gift, ability, or characteristic of someone
Synonyms: talent, quality, attribute

AMIABLE (ay mee uh buhl) *adj.*
friendly, pleasant, likable
Synonyms: affable, convivial, amicable, agreeable, genial

AMASS (uh maas) *v.* **-ing,-ed.**
to collect for oneself; to collect into a mass
Synonyms: collect, accumulate, hoard, stockpile

ENTREAT (ehn treet) *v.* **-ing,-ed.**
to plead, beg
Synonyms: beseech, implore, importune, request

my power to **derive** its most important benefits from such a conviction, that I perceived the necessity of becoming acquainted with more languages than that of my native country. Now I am twenty-eight, and am in reality more illiterate than many school-boys of fifteen. It is true that I have thought more, and that my day dreams are more extended and magnificent; but they want (as the painters call it) *keeping*; and I greatly need a friend who would have sense enough not to despise me as romantic, and affection enough for me to endeavour to regulate my mind.

Well, these are useless complaints; I shall certainly find no friend on the wide ocean, nor even here in Archangel, among merchants and seamen. Yet some feelings, unallied to the **dross** of human nature, beat even in these rugged bosoms. My lieutenant, for instance, is a man of wonderful courage and enterprise; he is madly desirous of glory. He is an Englishman, and in the midst of national and professional prejudices, unsoftened by cultivation, **retains** some of the noblest **endowments** of humanity. I first became acquainted with him on board a whale vessel. Finding that he was unemployed in this city, I easily engaged him to assist in my enterprise.

The master is a person of an excellent disposition, and is remarkable in the ship for his gentleness, and the mildness of his discipline. He is, indeed, of so **amiable** a nature, that he will not hunt (a favourite, and almost the only amusement here), because he cannot endure to spill blood. He is, moreover, heroically generous. Some years ago he loved a young Russian lady, of moderate fortune; and having **amassed** a considerable sum in prize-money, the father of the girl consented to the match. He saw his mistress once before the destined ceremony; but she was bathed in tears, and, throwing herself at his feet, **entreated** him to spare her, confessing at the same time that she loved another, but that he was poor, and that her father would never consent to the union. My generous

SUPPLIANT (suh plee ehnt) *n.*
one who asks humbly and earnestly
Synonyms: petitioner, appellant, applicant, suitor, supplicant

BESTOW (bih stoh) *v.* **-ing,-ed.**
to give as a gift
Synonyms: award, endow, donate, confer, present

SOLICIT (suh lih siht) *v.* **-ing,-ed.**
to petition persistently
Synonyms: entice, tempt, request, entreat

INEXORABLE (ihn ehk suhr uh buhl) *adj.*
inflexible, unyielding
Synonyms: adamant, obdurate, relentless

INCLINATION (ihn cluh nay shuhn) *n.*
tendency toward
Synonyms: leaning, trend, preference, disposition, propensity

CONSOLATION (kahn suh lay shuhn) *n.*
something providing comfort or solace for a loss or hardship
Synonyms: condolence, solace

RESOLUTION (reh suh loo shuhn) *n.*
a firm decision
Synonyms: determination, will, explanation

PRUDENCE (proo dehnts) *n.*
carefulness, caution
Synonyms: circumspection, deliberation, thoughtfulness

TRAVERSE (truh vuhrs) (traa vuhrs) *v.* **-ing,-ed.**
to travel or travel across; to turn or move laterally
Synonyms: cross, travel, intersect, pass through

friend reassured the **suppliant**, and on being informed of the name of her lover instantly abandoned his pursuit. He had already bought a farm with his money, on which he had designed to pass the remainder of his life; but he **bestowed** the whole on his rival, together with the remains of his prize-money to purchase stock, and then himself **solicited** the young woman's father to consent to her marriage with her lover. But the old man decidedly refused, thinking himself bound in honour to my friend; who, when he found the father **inexorable**, quitted his country, nor returned until he heard that his former mistress was married according to her **inclinations**. "What a noble fellow!" you will exclaim. He is so; but then he has passed all his life on board a vessel, and has scarcely an idea beyond the rope and the shroud.

But do not suppose that, because I complain a little, or because I can conceive a **consolation** for my toils which I may never know, that I am wavering in my **resolutions**. Those are as fixed as fate; and my voyage is only now delayed until the weather shall permit my embarkation. The winter has been dreadfully severe; but the spring promises well, and it is considered as a remarkably early season; so that, perhaps, I may sail sooner than I expected. I shall do nothing rashly; you know me sufficiently to confide in my **prudence** and considerateness whenever the safety of others is committed to my care.

I cannot describe to you my sensations on the near prospect of my undertaking. It is impossible to communicate to you a conception of the trembling sensation, half pleasurable and half fearful, with which I am preparing to depart. I am going to unexplored regions, to "the land of mist and snow" but I shall kill no albatross, therefore do not be alarmed for my safety.

Shall I meet you again, after having **traversed** immense seas, and returned by the most southern cape of Africa or America? I dare not expect such success, yet I cannot bear to look on the reverse of the picture. Continue to

ARDENTLY (ahr dihnt lee) *adv.*
passionately, enthusiastically, fervently
Synonyms: intensely, vehemently

RENOVATE (reh nuh vayt) *v.* **-ing,-ed.**
to renew, modernize
Synonyms: restore, revive, refurbish

write to me by every opportunity. I may receive your letters (though the chance is very doubtful) on some occasions when I need them most to support my spirits. I love you very tenderly. Remember me with affection, should you never hear from me again.

Your affectionate brother,
Robert Walton.

LETTER III

To Mrs. Saville, England.

July 7th, 17—.

My dear Sister,

I write a few lines in haste, to say that I am safe, and well advanced on my voyage. This letter will reach England by a merchant-man now on its homeward voyage from Archangel; more fortunate than I, who may not see my native land, perhaps, for many years. I am, however, in good spirits. My men are bold, and apparently firm of purpose; nor do the floating sheets of ice that continually pass us, indicating the dangers of the region towards which we are advancing, appear to dismay them. We have already reached a very high latitude; but it is the height of summer, and although not so warm as in England, the southern gales, which blow us speedily towards those shores which I so **ardently** desire to attain, breathe a degree of **renovating** warmth which I had not expected.

No incidents have hitherto befallen us, that would make a figure in a letter. One or two stiff gales, and the breaking of a mast, are accidents which experienced navigators scarcely remember to record; and I shall be well content, if nothing worse happens to us during our voyage.

PRUDENT (proo dehnt) *adj.*
careful, cautious
Synonyms: circumspect, politic, pragmatic, judicious, sensible

FORBEAR (fohr bayr) *v.* **-ing,-bore.**
to refrain or resist
Synonyms: avoid

SOLICITUDE (suh lih sih tood) *n.*
concern, attentiveness; eagerness
Synonyms: thoughtfulness, consideration, uneasiness

Adieu, my dear Margaret. Be assured, that for my own sake, as well as yours, I will not rashly encounter danger. I will be cool, persevering, and **prudent**.

Remember me to all my English friends.

Most affectionately yours,
R. W.

LETTER IV

To Mrs. Saville, England.

August 5th, 17—.

So strange an accident has happened to us, that I cannot **forbear** recording it, although it is very probable that you will see me before these papers can come into your possession.

Last Monday (July 31st), we were nearly surrounded by ice, which closed in the ship on all sides, scarcely leaving her the sea room in which she floated. Our situation was somewhat dangerous, especially as we were compassed round by a very thick fog. We accordingly lay to, hoping that some change would take place in the atmosphere and weather.

About two o'clock the mist cleared away, and we beheld, stretched out in every direction, vast and irregular plains of ice, which seemed to have no end. Some of my comrades groaned, and my own mind began to grow watchful with anxious thoughts, when a strange sight suddenly attracted our attention, and diverted our **solicitude** from our own situation. We perceived a low carriage, fixed on a sledge and drawn by dogs, pass on towards the north, at the distance of half a mile. A being which had the shape of a man, but apparently of gigantic stature, sat in the sledge, and guided the dogs. We watched

APPARITION (aa puh rih shuhn) *n.*
an unexpected or unusual sight; a ghostly figure
Synonyms: ghost, illusion, spirit, specter

DENOTE (dih noht) (dee noht) *v.* **-ing,-ed.**
to indicate; to make known; to stand for
Synonyms: show, signify, imply, symbolize, typify

the rapid progress of the traveller with our telescopes, until he was lost among the distant inequalities of the ice.

This appearance excited our unqualified wonder. We were, as we believed, many hundred miles from any land; but this **apparition** seemed to **denote** that it was not, in reality, so distant as we had supposed. Shut in, however, by ice, it was impossible to follow his track, which we had observed with the greatest attention.

About two hours after this occurrence, we heard the ground sea; and before night the ice broke, and freed our ship. We, however, lay to until the morning, fearing to encounter in the dark those large loose masses which float about after the breaking up of the ice. I profited of this time to rest for a few hours.

In the morning, however, as soon as it was light, I went upon deck, and found all the sailors busy on one side of the vessel, apparently talking to some one in the sea. It was, in fact, a sledge, like that we had seen before, which had drifted towards us in the night, on a large fragment of ice. Only one dog remained alive; but there was a human being within it, whom the sailors were persuading to enter the vessel. He was not, as the other traveller seemed to be, a savage inhabitant of some undiscovered island, but an European. When I appeared on deck, the master said, "Here is our captain, and he will not allow you to perish on the open sea."

On perceiving me, the stranger addressed me in English, although with a foreign accent. "Before I come on board your vessel," said he, "will you have the kindness to inform me whither you are bound?"

You may conceive my astonishment on hearing such a question addressed to me from a man on the brink of destruction, and to whom I should have supposed that my vessel would have been a resource which he would not have exchanged for the most precious wealth the earth can afford. I replied, however, that we were on a voyage of discovery towards the northern pole.

CAPITULATE (kuh pih choo layt) *v.* **-ing,-ed.**
to submit completely, surrender
Synonyms: yield, succumb, acquiesce

EMACIATED (ih may shee ay tihd) *adj.*
very thin due to hunger or disease, feeble
Synonyms: bony, gaunt, haggard, skeletal

ANIMATION (aa nih may shuhn) *n.*
the quality or condition of being alive, spirited, active or vigorous
Synonyms: life, vitality, invigoration, liveliness

TRIFLING (trie fling) *adj.*
of slight worth, trivial, insignificant
Synonyms: paltry, petty, picayune, frivolous, idle

COUNTENANCE (kown tuh nuhns) *n.*
appearance, facial expression
Synonyms: face, features, visage

BENEVOLENCE (buh neh vuh luhnts) *n.*
kindness, compassion
Synonyms: charity, altruism, generosity

MELANCHOLY (mehl uhn kahl ee) *adj.*
sad, gloomy
Synonyms: depressed, despondent, woeful, sorrowful

REPOSE (rih pohz) *v.* **-ing,-ed.**
1. to relax or rest; to lie dead
   Synonyms: sleep, slumber
2. to place (trust) or to count on
   Synonyms: entrust, invest, place

Upon hearing this he appeared satisfied, and consented to come on board. Good God! Margaret, if you had seen the man who thus **capitulated** for his safety, your surprise would have been boundless. His limbs were nearly frozen, and his body dreadfully **emaciated** by fatigue and suffering. I never saw a man in so wretched a condition. We attempted to carry him into the cabin; but as soon as he had quitted the fresh air, he fainted. We accordingly brought him back to the deck, and restored him to **animation** by rubbing him with brandy, and forcing him to swallow a small quantity. As soon as he showed signs of life, we wrapped him up in blankets, and placed him near the chimney of the kitchen-stove. By slow degrees he recovered, and ate a little soup, which restored him wonderfully.

Two days passed in this manner before he was able to speak; and I often feared that his sufferings had deprived him of understanding. When he had in some measure recovered, I removed him to my own cabin, and attended on him as much as my duty would permit. I never saw a more interesting creature—his eyes have generally an expression of wildness, and even madness; but there are moments when, if any one performs an act of kindness towards him, or does him any of the most **trifling** service, his whole **countenance** is lighted up, as it were, with a beam of **benevolence** and sweetness that I never saw equalled. But he is generally **melancholy** and despairing; and sometimes he gnashes his teeth, as if impatient of the weight of woes that oppresses him.

When my guest was a little recovered, I had great trouble to keep off the men, who wished to ask him a thousand questions; but I would not allow him to be tormented by their idle curiosity, in a state of body and mind whose restoration evidently depended upon entire **repose**. Once, however, the lieutenant asked, Why he had come so far upon the ice in so strange a vehicle?

His **countenance** instantly assumed an aspect of the

MULTITUDE (muhl tuh tood) *n.*
the state of being many; a great number
Synonyms: mass, myriad, slew, crowd

IMPERTINENT (ihm puhr tuh nuhnt) *adj.*
rude
Synonyms: improper, bold, impolite, discourteous

PERILOUS (pehr uh luhs) *adj.*
full of danger
Synonyms: dangerous, risky, hazardous, unsafe

BENEVOLENTLY (buh neh vuh lunt lee) *adv.*
compassionately, with kindness
Synonyms: charitably, altruistically, generously

SUSTAIN (suh stayn) *v.* **-ing,-ed.**
to support, uphold; endure, undergo
Synonyms: maintain, prop, encourage, withstand, confirm

CONCILIATING (kuhn sih lee ayt ing) *adj.*
becoming agreeable, appeasing
Synonyms: diplomatic, friendly, generous

deepest gloom; and he replied, "To seek one who fled from me."

"And did the man whom you pursued travel in the same fashion?"

"Yes."

"Then I fancy we have seen him; for, the day before we picked you up, we saw some dogs drawing a sledge, with a man in it, across the ice."

This aroused the stranger's attention; and he asked a **multitude** of questions concerning the route which the daemon, as he called him, had pursued. Soon after, when he was alone with me, he said, "I have, doubtless, excited your curiosity, as well as that of these good people; but you are too considerate to make inquiries."

"Certainly; it would indeed be very **impertinent** and inhuman of me to trouble you with any inquisitiveness of mine."

"And yet you rescued me from a strange and **perilous** situation; you have **benevolently** restored me to life."

Soon after this he inquired, if I thought that the breaking up of the ice had destroyed the other sledge? I replied, that I could not answer with any degree of certainty; for the ice had not broken until near midnight, and the traveller might have arrived at a place of safety before that time; but of this I could not judge.

From this time the stranger seemed very eager to be upon deck, to watch for the sledge which had before appeared; but I have persuaded him to remain in the cabin, for he is far too weak to **sustain** the rawness of the atmosphere. But I have promised that some one should watch for him, and give him instant notice if any new object should appear in sight.

Such is my journal of what relates to this strange occurrence up to the present day. The stranger has gradually improved in health, but is very silent, and appears uneasy when any one except myself enters his cabin. Yet his manners are so **conciliating** and gentle, that the sailors

AMIABLE (ay mee uh buhl) *adj.*
friendly, pleasant, likable
Synonyms: affable, convivial, amicable, agreeable, genial

POIGNANT (poy nyaant) *adj.*
emotionally moving
Synonyms: stirring, touching, pathetic, piquant

CULL (kuhl) *v.* **-ing,-ed.**
to select, weed out
Synonyms: glean, pick, extract, harvest, garner

ELOQUENCE (eh luh kwuhns) *n.*
fluent and effective speech
Synonyms: persuasiveness, expressiveness, fluency

PEDANTRY (peh daan tree) *n.*
the habit of paying attention to academic details or rules, a vain display of learning
Synonyms: bookishness, ostentation

are all interested in him, although they have had very little communication with him. For my own part, I begin to love him as a brother; and his constant and deep grief fills me with sympathy and compassion. He must have been a noble creature in his better days, being even now in wreck so attractive and **amiable**.

I said in one of my letters, my dear Margaret, that I should find no friend on the wide ocean; yet I have found a man who, before his spirit had been broken by misery, I should have been happy to have possessed as the brother of my heart.

I shall continue my journal concerning the stranger at intervals, should I have any fresh incidents to record.

August 13th, 17—.

My affection for my guest increases every day. He excites at once my admiration and my pity to an astonishing degree. How can I see so noble a creature destroyed by misery without feeling the most **poignant** grief? He is so gentle, yet so wise; his mind is so cultivated; and when he speaks, although his words are **culled** with the choicest art, yet they flow with rapidity and unparalleled **eloquence**.

He is now much recovered from his illness, and is continually on the deck, apparently watching for the sledge that preceded his own. Yet, although unhappy, he is not so utterly occupied by his own misery, but that he interests himself deeply in the employments of others. He has asked me many questions concerning my design; and I have related my little history frankly to him. He appeared pleased with the confidence, and suggested several alterations in my plan, which I shall find exceedingly useful. There is no **pedantry** in his manner; but all he does appears to spring solely from the interest he instinctively takes in the welfare of those who surround him. He is often overcome by gloom, and then he sits by himself,

SULLEN (suh luhn) *adj.*
brooding, gloomy
Synonyms: morose, sulky, somber, glum

DEJECTION (dih jehk shuhn) *n.*
a state of depression or melancholy
Synonyms: grief, sadness, low spirits

COUNTENANCE (kown tuh nuhns) *n.*
appearance, facial expression
Synonyms: face, features, visage

and tries to overcome all that is **sullen** or unsocial in his humour. These paroxysms pass from him like a cloud from before the sun, though his **dejection** never leaves him. I have endeavoured to win his confidence; and I trust that I have succeeded. One day I mentioned to him the desire I had always felt of finding a friend who might sympathize with me, and direct me by his counsel. I said I did not belong to that class of men who are offended by advice. "I am self-educated, and perhaps I hardly rely sufficiently upon my own powers. I wish therefore that my companion should be wiser and more experienced than myself, to confirm and support me; nor have I believed it impossible to find a true friend."

"I agree with you," replied the stranger, "in believing that friendship is not only a desirable, but a possible acquisition. I once had a friend, the most noble of human creatures, and am entitled, therefore, to judge respecting friendship. You have hope, and the world before you, and have no cause for despair. But I—I have lost everything, and cannot begin life anew."

As he said this, his **countenance** became expressive of a calm settled grief, that touched me to the heart. But he was silent, and presently retired to his cabin.

Even broken in spirit as he is, no one can feel more deeply than he does the beauties of nature. The starry sky, the sea, and every sight afforded by these wonderful regions, seems still to have the power of elevating his soul from earth. Such a man has a double existence. He may suffer misery and be overwhelmed by disappointments; yet when he has retired into himself, he will be like a celestial spirit, that has a halo around him, within whose circle no grief or folly ventures.

Will you laugh at the enthusiasm I express concerning this divine wanderer? If you do, you must have certainly lost that simplicity which was once your characteristic charm. Yet, if you will, smile at the warmth of my expressions, while I find every day new causes for repeating them.

ARDENTLY (ahr dihnt lee) *adv.*
passionately, enthusiastically, fervently
Synonyms: intensely, vehemently, fervidly

FACULTY (faa kuhl tee) *n.*
the ability to act or do
Synonyms: aptitude, capability, sense, skill

AMELIORATE (uh meel yuhr ayt) *v.* **-ing,-ed.**
to make better, improve
Synonyms: amend, better, reform

REPOSE (rih pohz) *v.* **-ing,-ed.**
1. to relax or rest; to lie dead
Synonyms: sleep, slumber
2. to place (trust) or to count on
Synonyms: entrust, invest, place

IRREVOCABLY (ih rehv oh kuh blee) *adv.*
conclusively, irreversibly
Synonyms: permanently, indelibly, irreparably

RESOLVE (rih sahlv) *v.* **-ing,-ed.**
to determine or to make a firm decision about
Synonyms: solve, decide

August 19th, 17—.

Yesterday the stranger said to me, "You may easily perceive, Captain Walton, that I have suffered great and unparalleled misfortunes. I had determined, once, that the memory of these evils should die with me; but you have won me to alter my determination. You seek for knowledge and wisdom, as I once did; and I **ardently** hope that the gratification of your wishes may not be a serpent to sting you, as mine has been. I do not know that the relation of my misfortunes will be useful to you, yet, if you are inclined, listen to my tale. I believe that the strange incidents connected with it will afford a view of nature, which may enlarge your **faculties** and understanding. You will hear of powers and occurrences, such as you have been accustomed to believe impossible, but I do not doubt that my tale conveys in its series internal evidence of the truth of the events of which it is composed."

You may easily conceive that I was much gratified by the offered communication; yet I could not endure that he should renew his grief by a recital of his misfortunes. I felt the greatest eagerness to hear the promised narrative, partly from curiosity, and partly from a strong desire to **ameliorate** his fate, if it were in my power. I expressed these feelings in my answer.

"I thank you," he replied, "for your sympathy, but it is useless; my fate is nearly fulfilled. I wait but for one event, and then I shall **repose** in peace. I understand your feeling," continued he, perceiving that I wished to interrupt him; "but you are mistaken, my friend, if thus you will allow me to name you; nothing can alter my destiny; listen to my history, and you will perceive how **irrevocably** it is determined."

He then told me, that he would commence his narrative the next day when I should be at leisure. This promise drew from me the warmest thanks. I have **resolved** every night, when I am not engaged, to record,

INDEFATIGABLE (ihn dih faat ih guh buhl) *adj.*
never tired
Synonyms: unflagging, weariless, inexhaustible

PERPETUALLY (puhr peht chyoo uh lee) *adv.*
endlessly, always
Synonyms: continuously, constantly, eternally, perennially

BESTOW (bih stoh) *v.* **-ing,-ed.**
to give as a gift
Synonyms: award, endow, donate, confer, present

OBLIVION (oh blih vee ihn) *n.*
the state of being completely forgotten
Synonyms: limbo, nonexistence

as nearly as possible in his own words, what he has related during the day. If I should be engaged, I will at least make notes. This manuscript will doubtless afford you the greatest pleasure; but to me, who know him, and who hear it from his own lips, with what interest and sympathy shall I read it in some future day!

CHAPTER I

I am by birth a Genevese; and my family is one of the most distinguished of that republic. My ancestors had been for many years counsellors and syndics; and my father had filled several public situations with honour and reputation. He was respected by all who knew him for his integrity and **indefatigable** attention to public business. He passed his younger days **perpetually** occupied by the affairs of his country; and it was not until the decline of life that he thought of marrying, and **bestowing** on the state sons who might carry his virtues and his name down to posterity.

As the circumstances of his marriage illustrate his character, I cannot refrain from relating them. One of his most intimate friends was a merchant, who, from a flourishing state, fell, through numerous mischances, into poverty. This man, whose name was Beaufort, was of a proud and unbending disposition, and could not bear to live in poverty and **oblivion** in the same country where he had formerly been distinguished for his rank and magnificence. Having paid his debts, therefore, in the most honourable manner, he retreated with his daughter to the town of Lucerne, where he lived unknown and in wretchedness. My father loved Beaufort with the truest friendship, and was deeply grieved by his retreat in these unfortunate circumstances. He grieved also for the loss of

RESOLVE (rih <u>sahlv</u>) *v.* **-ing,-ed.**
to determine or to make a firm decision about
Synonyms: solve, decide

SUSTENANCE (<u>suh</u> steh nehns) *n.*
means of living, source of nourishment
Synonyms: food, provisions, necessities

PROCURE (proh <u>kyoor</u>) *v.* **-ing,-ed.**
to obtain
Synonyms: acquire, secure, get, gain

ADVERSITY (aad <u>vuhr</u> sih tee) *n.*
hardship
Synonyms: suffering, distress, tribulation

CONTRIVE (kuhn <u>triev</u>) *v.* **-ing,-ed.**
to devise, plan, or manage; to form in an artistic manner
Synonyms: concoct, create, scheme, design

PITTANCE (<u>pih</u> tehnts) *n.*
a small portion, amount, or wage
Synonyms: ration, trace, bit, insufficiency

SUBSISTENCE (suhb <u>sihs</u> tehnts) *n.*
means for existence; the necessities of life
Synonyms: nourishment, livelihood, sustenance

INTERMENT (ihn <u>tuhr</u> mehnt) *n.*
burial
Synonyms: entombment, inhumation

his society, and **resolved** to seek him out and endeavour to persuade him to begin the world again through his credit and assistance.

Beaufort had taken effectual measures to conceal himself; and it was ten months before my father discovered his abode. Overjoyed at this discovery, he hastened to the house, which was situated in a mean street, near the Reuss. But when he entered, misery and despair alone welcomed him. Beaufort had saved but a very small sum of money from the wreck of his fortunes; but it was sufficient to provide him with **sustenance** for some months, and in the mean time he hoped to **procure** some respectable employment in a merchant's house. The interval was consequently spent in inaction; his grief only became more deep and rankling, when he had leisure for reflection; and at length it took so fast hold of his mind, that at the end of three months he lay on a bed of sickness, incapable of any exertion.

His daughter attended him with the greatest tenderness; but she saw with despair that their little fund was rapidly decreasing, and that there was no other prospect of support. But Caroline Beaufort possessed a mind of an uncommon mould; and her courage rose to support her in her **adversity**. She **procured** plain work; she plaited straw; and by various means **contrived** to earn a **pittance** scarcely sufficient to support life.

Several months passed in this manner. Her father grew worse; her time was more entirely occupied in attending him; her means of **subsistence** decreased; and in the tenth month her father died in her arms, leaving her an orphan and a beggar. This last blow overcame her; and she knelt by Beaufort's coffin, weeping bitterly, when my father entered the chamber. He came like a protecting spirit to the poor girl, who committed herself to his care, and after the **interment** of his friend he conducted her to Geneva, and placed her under the protection of a relation. Two years after this event Caroline became his wife.

RELINQUISH (rih lihn kwihsh) *v.* **-ing,-ed.**
to renounce or surrender something
Synonyms: yield, resign, abandon, cede, waive

UTILITY (yoo tih lih tee) *n.*
usefulness, efficiency, functionality
Synonyms: practicality, pragmatism

REPENT (rih pehnt) *v.* **-ing,-ed.**
to regret a past action
Synonyms: rue, atone, apologize

When my father became a husband and a parent, he found his time so occupied by the duties of his new situation, that he **relinquished** many of his public employments, and devoted himself to the education of his children. Of these I was the eldest, and the destined successor to all his labours and **utility**. No creature could have more tender parents than mine. My improvement and health were their constant care, especially as I remained for several years their only child. But before I continue my narrative, I must record an incident which took place when I was four years of age.

My father had a sister, whom he tenderly loved, and who had married early in life an Italian gentleman. Soon after her marriage, she had accompanied her husband into his native country, and for some years my father had very little communication with her. About the time I mentioned she died; and a few months afterwards he received a letter from her husband, acquainting him with his intention of marrying an Italian lady, and requesting my father to take charge of the infant Elizabeth, the only child of his deceased sister. "It is my wish," he said, "that you should consider her as your own daughter, and educate her thus. Her mother's fortune is secured to her, the documents of which I will commit to your keeping. Reflect upon this proposition; and decide whether you would prefer educating your niece yourself to her being brought up by a stepmother."

My father did not hesitate, and immediately went to Italy, that he might accompany the little Elizabeth to her future home. I have often heard my mother say, that she was at that time the most beautiful child she had ever seen, and showed signs even then of a gentle and affectionate disposition. These indications, and a desire to bind as closely as possible the ties of domestic love, determined my mother to consider Elizabeth as my future wife; a design which she never found reason to **repent**.

DOCILE (dah suhl) (dah siel) *adj.*
tame, willing to be taught
Synonyms: domesticated, mild, tractable, obedient

ANIMATED (aa nih may tihd) *adj.*
1. lively, excited; filled with spirit
Synonyms: elated, vivacious, spirited, inspired
2. having life, alive
Synonyms: vital, moving, alert, functioning

CONSTRAINT (kuhn straynt) *n.*
something that forces or compels; something that restrains or confines
Synonyms: restriction, curb, control

CAPRICE (kuh prees) *n.*
an impulsive change of mind, fickleness
Synonym: whim

LUXURIANT (luhg zhoor ee ehnt) *adj.*
elegant, lavish
Synonyms: rich, abundant, profuse

PRETENSION (prih tehn shuhn) *n.*
1. the quality of being arrogant, snobbishness
Synonyms: ostentation, conceit, phoniness
2. a false claim; an allegation of doubtful value
Synonyms: allegation, assumption, falsity

INTERCESSION (ihn tuhr seh shuhn) *n.*
the act of intervening between feuding parties to help achieve an agreement
Synonyms: intervention, mediation, influence

DISSIMILITUDE (dih sih mih luh tood) *n.*
lack of resemblance or similarity
Synonyms: disparity, unlikeness, variance, diversity

AERIAL (ayr ee uhl) *adj.*
celestial, imaginary
Synonyms: dreamy, lofty, airy

COMPENSATE (kahm pehn sayt) *v.* **-ing,-ed.**
to repay or reimburse
Synonyms: indemnify, recompense, balance

From this time Elizabeth Lavenza became my playfellow, and, as we grew older, my friend. She was **docile** and good tempered, yet gay and playful as a summer insect. Although she was lively and **animated**, her feelings were strong and deep, and her disposition uncommonly affectionate. No one could better enjoy liberty, yet no one could submit with more grace than she did to **constraint** and **caprice**. Her imagination was **luxuriant**, yet her capability of application was great. Her person was the image of her mind; her hazel eyes, although as lively as a bird's, possessed an attractive softness. Her figure was light and airy; and, though capable of enduring great fatigue, she appeared the most fragile creature in the world. While I admired her understanding and fancy, I loved to tend on her, as I should on a favourite animal; and I never saw so much grace both of person and mind united to so little **pretension**.

Every one adored Elizabeth. If the servants had any request to make, it was always through her **intercession**. We were strangers to any species of disunion and dispute; for although there was a great **dissimilitude** in our characters, there was an harmony in that very **dissimilitude**. I was more calm and philosophical than my companion; yet my temper was not so yielding. My application was of longer endurance; but it was not so severe whilst it endured. I delighted in investigating the facts relative to the actual world; she busied herself in following the **aerial** creations of the poets. The world was to me a secret, which I desired to discover; to her it was a vacancy, which she sought to people with imaginations of her own.

My brothers were considerably younger than myself; but I had a friend in one of my schoolfellows, who **compensated** for this deficiency. Henry Clerval was the son of a merchant of Geneva, an intimate friend of my father. He was a boy of singular talent and fancy. I remember, when he was nine years old, he wrote a fairy tale, which

CHIVALRY (shih vuhl ree) *n.*
the qualities of an ideal knight: honor, courtesy, and generosity
Synonyms: valor, courtesy, gallantry

INDULGENT (ihn duhl jehnt) *adj.*
lenient, tolerant
Synonyms: gratifying, pleasing

AMIABLE (ay mee uh buhl) *adj.*
friendly, pleasant, likable
Synonyms: affable, convivial, amicable, agreeable, genial

ARDOUR or ARDOR (ahr duhr) *n.*
passion, enthusiasm
Synonyms: intensity, vehemence

EMULATION (ehm yuh lay shuhn) *n.*
jealous rivalry, ambition to excel
Synonyms: imitation, envy

INCITE (ihn siet) *v.* **-ing,-ed.**
to move to action; to urge on
Synonyms: encourage, instigate, motivate, prompt

ODIOUS (oh dee uhs) *adj.*
hateful, contemptible
Synonyms: detestable, obnoxious, offensive, repellent, loathsome

DESTITUTE (dehs tih toot) (dehs tih tyoot) *adj.*
very poor, poverty-stricken, lacking
Synonyms: insolvent, impecunious, penurious, needy, broke

TAINT (taynt) *v.* **-ing,-ed.**
to spoil or infect; to stain honor
Synonyms: contaminate, befoul, poison, pollute, besmirch

was the delight and amazement of all his companions. His favourite study consisted in books of **chivalry** and romance; and when very young, I can remember, that we used to act plays composed by him out of these favourite books, the principal characters of which were Orlando, Robin Hood, Amadis, and St. George.

No youth could have passed more happily than mine. My parents were **indulgent**, and my companions **amiable**. Our studies were never forced; and by some means we always had an end placed in view, which excited us to **ardour** in the prosecution of them. It was by this method, and not by **emulation**, that we were urged to application. Elizabeth was not **incited** to apply herself to drawing, that her companions might not outstrip her; but through the desire of pleasing her aunt, by the representation of some favourite scene done by her own hand. We learned Latin and English, that we might read the writings in those languages; and so far from study being made **odious** to us through punishment, we loved application, and our amusements would have been the labours of other children. Perhaps we did not read so many books, or learn languages so quickly, as those who are disciplined according to the ordinary methods; but what we learned was impressed the more deeply on our memories.

In this description of our domestic circle I include Henry Clerval; for he was constantly with us. He went to school with me, and generally passed the afternoon at our house; for being an only child, and **destitute** of companions at home, his father was well pleased that he should find associates at our house; and we were never completely happy when Clerval was absent.

I feel pleasure in dwelling on the recollections of childhood, before misfortune had **tainted** my mind, and changed its bright visions of extensive usefulness into gloomy and narrow reflections upon self. But, in drawing the picture of my early days, I must not omit to record those events which led, by insensible steps to my after

IGNOBLE (ihg noh buhl) *adj.*
dishonorable, not noble in character
Synonyms: mean, low, base, disreputable, sordid

TORRENT (tawr rehnt) *n.*
a turbulent, fast-flowing stream
Synonyms: outpouring, deluge, flood

PREDILECTION (preh dih lehk shuhn) *n.*
preference, liking
Synonyms: bias, leaning, partiality, penchant, proclivity

INCLEMENCY (ihn kleh muhn see) *n.*
storminess; unmercifulness, lack of lenience
Synonyms: intolerance, severity

APATHY (aa pah thee) *n.*
lack of feeling or emotion
Synonyms: indifference, insouciance, disregard, unconcern

NEGLECT (neh glehkt) *v.* **-ing,-ed.**
to ignore or disregard, to be negligent
Synonyms: overlook, skimp

CHIMERICAL (kie mehr ih kuhl) (kie meer ih kuhl) (kih mehr ih kuhl) *adj.*
fanciful, imaginary, visionary
Synonyms: illusory, unreal, impossible

CURSORY (kuhr suh ree) *adj.*
hastily done, superficial
Synonyms: shallow, careless

tale of misery. For when I would account to myself for the birth of that passion, which afterwards ruled my destiny, I find it arises, like a mountain river, from **ignoble** and almost forgotten sources; but, swelling as it proceeded, it became the **torrent** which, in its course, has swept away all my hopes and joys.

Natural philosophy is the genius that has regulated my fate; I desire therefore, in this narration, to state those facts which led to my **predilection** for that science. When I was thirteen years of age, we all went on a party of pleasure to the baths near Thonon. The **inclemency** of the weather obliged us to remain a day confined to the inn. In this house I chanced to find a volume of the works of Cornelius Agrippa. I opened it with **apathy**; the theory which he attempts to demonstrate, and the wonderful facts which he relates, soon changed this feeling into enthusiasm. A new light seemed to dawn upon my mind; and, bounding with joy, I communicated my discovery to my father. I cannot help remarking here the many opportunities instructors possess of directing the attention of their pupils to useful knowledge, which they utterly **neglect**. My father looked carelessly at the title page of my book, and said, "Ah! Cornelius Agrippa! My dear Victor, do not waste your time upon this; it is sad trash."

If, instead of this remark, my father had taken the pains to explain to me, that the principles of Agrippa had been entirely exploded, and that a modern system of science had been introduced, which possessed much greater powers than the ancient, because the powers of the latter were **chimerical**, while those of the former were real and practical; under such circumstances, I should certainly have thrown Agrippa aside, and, with my imagination warmed as it was, should probably have applied myself to the more rational theory of chemistry which has resulted from modern discoveries. It is even possible, that the train of my ideas would never have received the fatal impulse that led to my ruin. But the **cursory** glance my

AVIDITY (uh vihd ih tee) *n.*
keen eagerness; consuming greed
Synonyms: ardor, desire, enthusiasm

PROCURE (proh kyoor) *v.* **-ing,-ed.**
to obtain
Synonyms: acquire, secure, get, gain

CENSURE (sehn shuhr) *n.*
an expression of disapproval or criticism
Synonyms: denouncement, condemnation

DISCLOSE (dihs klohs) *v.* **-ing,-ed.**
to open up, divulge
Synonyms: confide, reveal, impart

DILIGENCE (dihl uh juhns) *n.*
steady and earnest application of effort
Synonyms: doggedness, persistence, assiduity

ELIXIR (ih lihk suhr) *n.*
a substance capable of sustaining life indefinitely; a medicinal concoction
Synonyms: solution, medication, remedy

BANISH (baan ish) *v.* **-ing,-ed.**
to force to leave, exile
Synonyms: expel, deport

INVULNERABLE (ihn vuhl nuhr uh buhl) *adj.*
impossible to harm, protected
Synonyms: impregnable, immune, strong

FIDELITY (fih dehl ih tee) (fie dehl ih tee) *n.*
loyalty
Synonyms: allegiance, fealty, faithfulness

DISTILLATION (dihs tih lay shuhn) *n.*
the evaporation and collection of a liquid by condensing as a means of purifying
Synonyms: purification, condensation, precipitation

father had taken of my volume by no means assured me that he was acquainted with its contents; and I continued to read with the greatest **avidity**.

When I returned home, my first care was to **procure** the whole works of this author, and afterwards of Paracelsus and Albertus Magnus. I read and studied the wild fancies of these writers with delight; they appeared to me treasures known to few beside myself; and although I often wished to communicate these secret stores of knowledge to my father, yet his indefinite **censure** of my favourite Agrippa always withheld me. I **disclosed** my discoveries to Elizabeth, therefore, under a promise of strict secrecy; but she did not interest herself in the subject, and I was left by her to pursue my studies alone.

It may appear very strange, that a disciple of Albertus Magnus should arise in the eighteenth century; but our family was not scientifical, and I had not attended any of the lectures given at the schools of Geneva. My dreams were therefore undisturbed by reality; and I entered with the greatest **diligence** into the search of the philosopher's stone and the **elixir** of life. But the latter obtained my most undivided attention—wealth was an inferior object; but what glory would attend the discovery, if I could **banish** disease from the human frame, and render man **invulnerable** to any but a violent death!

Nor were these my only visions. The raising of ghosts or devils was a promise liberally accorded by my favourite authors, the fulfilment of which I most eagerly sought; and if my incantations were always unsuccessful, I attributed the failure rather to my own inexperience and mistake, than to a want of skill or **fidelity** in my instructors.

The natural phaenomena that take place every day before our eyes did not escape my examinations. **Distillation**, and the wonderful effects of steam, processes of which my favourite authors were utterly ignorant, excited my astonishment; but my utmost wonder was engaged by some experiments on an air-pump,

DISINCLINATION (dihs ihn cluh nay shuhn) *n.*
aversion, reluctance
Synonyms: dislike, unwillingness, repugnance

which I saw employed by a gentleman whom we were in the habit of visiting.

The ignorance of the early philosophers on these and several other points served to decrease their credit with me, but I could not entirely throw them aside before some other system should occupy their place in my mind.

When I was about fifteen years old, we had retired to our house near Belrive, when we witnessed a most violent and terrible thunder-storm. It advanced from behind the mountains of Jura; and the thunder burst at once with frightful loudness from various quarters of the heavens. I remained, while the storm lasted, watching its progress with curiosity and delight. As I stood at the door, on a sudden I beheld a stream of fire issue from an old and beautiful oak, which stood about twenty yards from our house; and so soon as the dazzling light vanished, the oak had disappeared, and nothing remained but a blasted stump. When we visited it the next morning, we found the tree shattered in a singular manner. It was not splintered by the shock, but entirely reduced to thin ribbands of wood. I never beheld any thing so utterly destroyed.

The catastrophe of this tree excited my extreme astonishment; and I eagerly inquired of my father the nature and origin of thunder and lightning. He replied, "Electricity;" describing at the same time the various effects of that power. He constructed a small electrical machine, and exhibited a few experiments; he made also a kite, with a wire and string, which drew down that fluid from the clouds.

This last stroke completed the overthrow of Cornelius Agrippa, Albertus Magnus, and Paracelsus, who had so long reigned the lords of my imagination. But by some fatality I did not feel inclined to commence the study of any modern system; and this **disinclination** was influenced by the following circumstance.

My father expressed a wish that I should attend a course of lectures upon natural philosophy, to which I

DISCOURSE (dihs kohrs) *v.* **-ing,-ed.**
to talk or converse
Synonyms: speak, discuss, lecture

UTILITY (yoo tih lih tee) *n.*
usefulness, efficiency, functionality
Synonyms: practicality, pragmatism

LEXICON (lehk suh kahn) *n.*
a dictionary; the vocabulary of a language
Synonyms: reference book; vocabulary

DEVOLVE (dih vahlv) (dee vahlv) *v.* **-ing,-ed.**
to pass on; to degenerate gradually
Synonyms: transfer, deliver, delegate

AFFLICT (uh flihkt) *v.* **-ing,-ed.**
to distress severely so as to cause persistent anguish
Synonyms: harass, trouble, torment, wound

BANISH (baan ish) *v.* **-ing,-ed.**
to force to leave, exile
Synonyms: expel, deport

PRE-EMINENCE or PREEMINENCE
(pree ehm uh nuhns) *n.*
superiority, sense of being outstanding
Synonyms: notability, prominence, importance

COMPLY (kuhm plie) *v.* **-ing,-ed.**
to yield or agree, to go along with
Synonyms: accord, submit, acquiesce, obey, respect

cheerfully consented. Some accident prevented my attending these lectures until the course was nearly finished. The lecture, being therefore one of the last, was entirely incomprehensible to me. The professor **discoursed** with the greatest fluency of potassium and boron, of sulphates and oxyds, terms to which I could affix no idea; and I became disgusted with the science of natural philosophy, although I still read Pliny and Buffon with delight, authors, in my estimation, of nearly equal interest and **utility**.

My occupations at this age were principally the mathematics, and most of the branches of study appertaining to that science. I was busily employed in learning languages; Latin was already familiar to me, and I began to read some of the easiest Greek authors without the help of a **lexicon**. I also perfectly understood English and German. This is the list of my accomplishments at the age of seventeen; and you may conceive that my hours were fully employed in acquiring and maintaining a knowledge of this various literature.

Another task also **devolved** upon me, when I became the instructor of my brothers. Ernest was six years younger than myself, and was my principal pupil. He had been **afflicted** with ill health from his infancy, through which Elizabeth and I had been his constant nurses. His disposition was gentle, but he was incapable of any severe application. William, the youngest of our family, was yet an infant, and the most beautiful little fellow in the world; his lively blue eyes, dimpled cheeks, and endearing manners, inspired the tenderest affection.

Such was our domestic circle, from which care and pain seemed for ever **banished**. My father directed our studies, and my mother partook of our enjoyments. Neither of us possessed the slightest **pre-eminence** over the other; the voice of command was never heard amongst us; but mutual affection engaged us all to **comply** with and obey the slightest desire of each other.

RESOLVE (rih sahlv) *v.* **-ing,-ed.**
to determine or to make a firm decision about
Synonyms: solve, decide

ENTREATY (ehn tree tee) *n.*
a plea or request
Synonyms: imploration, prayer, petition

IMPRUDENCE (ihm proo dehnts) *n.*
carelessness, lack of caution
Synonyms: indiscretion, thoughtlessness

MALIGNANT (muh lihg nehnt) *adj.*
evil in influence of effect; aggressively malicious; tending to produce death
Synonyms: deadly, destructive, poisonous

PROGNOSTICATE (prahg nahs tih kayt) *v.* **-ing,-ed.**
to indicate in advance; to forecast
Synonyms: predict, foreshadow, portend

FORTITUDE (fohr tih tood) (fohr tih tyood) *n.*
strength, stamina
Synonyms: endurance, hardiness, toughness, courage

BENIGNITY (bih nihg nih tee) *n.*
kindness, gentleness, charity
Synonyms: innocuity, mildness

CONSOLATION (kahn suh lay shuhn) *n.*
something providing comfort or solace for a loss or hardship
Synonyms: condolence, solace

CHAPTER II

When I had attained the age of seventeen, my parents **resolved** that I should become a student at the university of Ingolstadt. I had hitherto attended the schools of Geneva; but my father thought it necessary, for the completion of my education, that I should be made acquainted with other customs than those of my native country. My departure was therefore fixed at an early date; but, before the day **resolved** upon could arrive, the first misfortune of my life occurred—an omen, as it were, of my future misery.

Elizabeth had caught the scarlet fever; but her illness was not severe, and she quickly recovered. During her confinement, many arguments had been urged to persuade my mother to refrain from attending upon her. She had, at first, yielded to our **entreaties**; but when she heard that her favourite was recovering, she could no longer debar herself from her society, and entered her chamber long before the danger of infection was past. The consequences of this **imprudence** were fatal. On the third day my mother sickened; her fever was very **malignant**, and the looks of her attendants **prognosticated** the worst event. On her death-bed the **fortitude** and **benignity** of this admirable woman did not desert her. She joined the hands of Elizabeth and myself: "My children," she said, "my firmest hopes of future happiness were placed on the prospect of your union. This expectation will now be the **consolation** of your father. Elizabeth, my love, you must supply my place to your younger cousins. Alas! I regret that I am taken from you; and, happy and beloved as I have been, is it not hard to quit you all? But these are not thoughts befitting me; I will endeavour to resign myself

INDULGE (ihn duhlj) *v.* **-ing,-ed.**
to give in to a craving or desire
Synonyms: humor, gratify, allow, pamper

COUNTENANCE (kown tuh nuhns) *n.*
appearance, facial expression
Synonyms: face, features, visage

IRREPARABLE (ih reh puhr uh buhl) *adj.*
unable to be repaired
Synonyms: ruined, hopeless, incurable, irreplaceable

INDULGENCE (ihn duhl jehns) *n.*
lenience, the act of giving into desires
Synonyms: gratification, tolerance, pampering

SACRILEGE (saak ruh lihj) *n.*
a technical violation of something, someone, or someplace sacred
Synonyms: irreverence, crime, mockery, violation

BANISH (baan ish) *v.* **-ing,-ed.**
to force to leave, exile
Synonyms: expel, deport

DEFER (dih fuhr) *v.* **-ing,-ed.**
to delay; to delegate to another
Synonyms: extend, impede, postpone, stall

RESPITE (reh spiht) *n.*
interval of relief
Synonyms: rest, pause, intermission, recess, suspension

IMPERIOUS (ihm pihr ee uhs) *adj.*
arrogantly self-assured, domineering, overbearing
Synonyms: authoritarian, despotic

DEVOLVE (dih vahlv) (dee vahlv) *v.* **-ing,-ed.**
to pass on; to degenerate gradually
Synonyms: transfer, deliver, delegate

CONSOLE (kuhn sohl) *v.* **-ing,-ed.**
to alleviate grief and raise the spirits of, provide solace
Synonyms: relieve, comfort, soothe

cheerfully to death, and will **indulge** a hope of meeting you in another world."

She died calmly; and her **countenance** expressed affection even in death. I need not describe the feelings of those whose dearest ties are rent by that most **irreparable** evil, the void that presents itself to the soul, and the despair that is exhibited on the **countenance**. It is so long before the mind can persuade itself that she, whom we saw every day, and whose very existence appeared a part of our own, can have departed for ever—that the brightness of a beloved eye can have been extinguished, and the sound of a voice so familiar, and dear to the ear, can be hushed, never more to be heard. These are the reflections of the first days; but when the lapse of time proves the reality of the evil, then the actual bitterness of grief commences. Yet from whom has not that rude hand rent away some dear connexion; and why should I describe a sorrow which all have felt, and must feel? The time at length arrives, when grief is rather an **indulgence** than a necessity; and the smile that plays upon the lips, although it may be deemed a **sacrilege**, is not **banished**. My mother was dead, but we had still duties which we ought to perform; we must continue our course with the rest, and learn to think ourselves fortunate, whilst one remains whom the spoiler has not seized.

My journey to Ingolstadt, which had been **deferred** by these events, was now again determined upon. I obtained from my father a **respite** of some weeks. This period was spent sadly; my mother's death, and my speedy departure, depressed our spirits; but Elizabeth endeavoured to renew the spirit of cheerfulness in our little society. Since the death of her aunt, her mind had acquired new firmness and vigour. She determined to fulfil her duties with the greatest exactness; and she felt that that most **imperious** duty, of rendering her uncle and cousins happy, had **devolved** upon her. She **consoled** me, amused her uncle, instructed my brothers; and I never beheld her so enchanting as at this time, when she was continually

LAMENT (luh mehnt) *v.* **-ing,-ed.**
to deplore, grieve
Synonyms: mourn, sorrow, regret, bewail

COMPLIANCE (kuhm plie uhns) *n.*
Concession, submission, obedience
Synonyms: complacency, acquiescence

SUPERFLUOUS (soo puhr floo uhs) *adj.*
extra, more than necessary
Synonyms: excess, spare, supernumerary, surplus

INDULGE (ihn duhlj) *v.* **-ing,-ed.**
to give in to a craving or desire
Synonyms: humor, gratify, allow, pamper

MELANCHOLY (mehl uhn kahl ee) *adj.*
sad, depressing
Synonyms: dejected, despondent, woeful, sorrowful

AMIABLE (ay mee uh buhl) *adj.*
friendly, pleasant, likable
Synonyms: affable, convivial, amicable, agreeable, genial

BESTOW (bih stoh) *v.* **-ing,-ed.**
to give as a gift
Synonyms: award, endow, donate, confer, present

INVINCIBLE (ihn vihn suh buhl) *adj.*
invulnerable, unbeatable
Synonyms: unconquerable, insuperable

REPUGNANCE (rih puhg nehnts) *n.*
strong dislike, distaste, or antagonism; an instance of contradiction or inconsistency
Synonyms: repulsion, hatred, aversion

COUNTENANCE (kown tuh nuhns) *n.*
appearance, facial expression
Synonyms: face, features, visage

ARDENTLY (ahr dihnt lee) *adv.*
passionately, enthusiastically, fervently
Synonyms: intensely, vehemently, fervidly

endeavouring to contribute to the happiness of others, entirely forgetful of herself.

The day of my departure at length arrived. I had taken leave of all my friends, excepting Clerval, who spent the last evening with us. He bitterly **lamented** that he was unable to accompany me; but his father could not be persuaded to part with him, intending that he should become a partner with him in business, in **compliance** with his favourite theory, that learning was **superfluous** in the commerce of ordinary life. Henry had a refined mind; he had no desire to be idle, and was well pleased to become his father's partner, but he believed that a man might be a very good trader, and yet possess a cultivated understanding.

We sat late, listening to his complaints, and making many little arrangements for the future. The next morning early I departed. Tears gushed from the eyes of Elizabeth; they proceeded partly from sorrow at my departure, and partly because she reflected that the same journey was to have taken place three months before, when a mother's blessing would have accompanied me.

I threw myself into the chaise that was to convey me away, and **indulged** in the most **melancholy** reflections. I, who had ever been surrounded by **amiable** companions, continually engaged in endeavouring to **bestow** mutual pleasure, I was now alone. In the university, whither I was going, I must form my own friends, and be my own protector. My life had hitherto been remarkably secluded and domestic; and this had given me **invincible repugnance** to new **countenances**. I loved my brothers, Elizabeth, and Clerval; these were "old familiar faces;" but I believed myself totally unfitted for the company of strangers. Such were my reflections as I commenced my journey; but as I proceeded, my spirits and hopes rose. I **ardently** desired the acquisition of knowledge. I had often, when at home, thought it hard to remain during my youth cooped up in one place, and had longed to

COMPLY (kuhm plie) *v.* **-ing,-ed.**
to yield or agree, to go along with
Synonyms: accord, submit, acquiesce, obey, respect

REPENT (rih pehnt) *v.* **-ing,-ed.**
to regret a past action
Synonyms: rue, atone, apologize

AFFIRMATIVE (uh fuhrm ih tihv) *n.*
a statement of agreement; a valid confirmation
Synonyms: assent, nod, yes

PROCURE (proh kyoor) *v.* **-ing,-ed.**
to obtain
Synonyms: acquire, secure, get, gain

enter the world, and take my station among other human beings. Now my desires were **complied** with, and it would, indeed, have been folly to **repent**.

I had sufficient leisure for these and many other reflections during my journey to Ingolstadt, which was long and fatiguing. At length the high white steeple of the town met my eyes. I alighted, and was conducted to my solitary apartment, to spend the evening as I pleased.

The next morning I delivered my letters of introduction, and paid a visit to some of the principal professors, and among others to M. Krempe, professor of natural philosophy. He received me with politeness, and asked me several questions concerning my progress in the different branches of science appertaining to natural philosophy. I mentioned, it is true, with fear and trembling, the only authors I had ever read upon those subjects. The professor stared: "Have you," he said, "really spent your time in studying such nonsense?"

I replied in the **affirmative**. "Every minute," continued M. Krempe with warmth, "every instant that you have wasted on those books is utterly and entirely lost. You have burdened your memory with exploded systems, and useless names. Good God! In what desert land have you lived, where no one was kind enough to inform you that these fancies, which you have so greedily imbibed, are a thousand years old, and as musty as they are ancient? I little expected in this enlightened and scientific age to find a disciple of Albertus Magnus and Paracelsus. My dear Sir, you must begin your studies entirely anew."

So saying, he stept aside, and wrote down a list of several books treating of natural philosophy, which he desired me to **procure**, and dismissed me, after mentioning that in the beginning of the following week he intended to commence a course of lectures upon natural philosophy in its general relations, and that M. Waldman, a fellow-professor, would lecture upon chemistry the alternate days that he missed.

REPROBATE (reh pruh bayt) *v.* **-ing,-ed.**
to disapprove of, condemn
Synonyms: reject, censure, reprehend

PROCURE (proh kyoor) *v.* **-ing,-ed.**
to obtain
Synonyms: acquire, secure, get, gain

REPULSIVE (rih puhl sihv) *adj.*
offensive, disgusting, sickening
Synonyms: repugnant, nauseating, detestable

COUNTENANCE (kown tuh nuhns) *n.*
appearance, facial expression
Synonyms: face, features, visage

DOCTRINE (dahk truhn) *n.*
instruction, teaching, a body of theories or principles
Synonyms: dogma, tenet

CONTEMPT (kuhn tehmpt) *n.*
disrespect, scorn
Synonyms: derision, disdain

FUTILE (fyoo tuhl) (fyoo tiel) *adj.*
serving no useful purpose; hopeless
Synonyms: worthless, unproductive, useless

CHIMERA (kie mehr uh) (kie meer uh) (kih mehr uh) *adj.*
a fanciful mental illusion
Synonyms: fabrication, dream, vision, impossiblity

BENEVOLENCE (buh neh vuh luhns) *n.*
kindness, compassion, charity, goodness
Synonyms: altruism, beneficence, generosity

RECAPITULATION (ree kuh piht yuoo lay shun) *n.*
a brief summary
Synonyms: synopsis, digest, encapsulation, abstract

FERVOUR or FERVOR (fuhr vuhr) *n.*
passion, intensity, zeal
Synonyms: vehemence, eagerness, enthusiasm

CURSORY (kuhr suh ree) *adj.*
hastily done, superficial
Synonyms: shallow, careless

I returned home, not disappointed, for I had long considered those authors useless whom the professor had so strongly **reprobated**; but I did not feel much inclined to study the books which I **procured** at his recommendation. M. Krempe was a little squat man, with a gruff voice and **repulsive countenance**; the teacher, therefore, did not prepossess me in favour of his **doctrine**. Besides, I had a **contempt** for the uses of modern natural philosophy. It was very different, when the masters of the science sought immortality and power; such views, although **futile**, were grand, but now the scene was changed. The ambition of the inquirer seemed to limit itself to the annihilation of those visions on which my interest in science was chiefly founded. I was required to exchange **chimeras** of boundless grandeur for realities of little worth.

Such were my reflections during the first two or three days spent almost in solitude. But as the ensuing week commenced, I thought of the information which M. Krempe had given me concerning the lectures. And although I could not consent to go and hear that little conceited fellow deliver sentences out of a pulpit, I recollected what he had said of M. Waldman, whom I had never seen, as he had hitherto been out of town.

Partly from curiosity, and partly from idleness, I went into the lecturing room, which M. Waldman entered shortly after. This professor was very unlike his colleague. He appeared about fifty years of age, but with an aspect expressive of the greatest **benevolence**; a few gray hairs covered his temples, but those at the back of his head were nearly black. His person was short, but remarkably erect; and his voice the sweetest I had ever heard. He began his lecture by a **recapitulation** of the history of chemistry and the various improvements made by different men of learning, pronouncing with **fervour** the names of the most distinguished discoverers. He then took a **cursory** view of the present state of the science, and explained many of its elementary terms. After

PANEGYRIC (paan uh geer ihk) *n.*
elaborate praise; formal hymn of praise
Synonyms: eulogy, compliment, laudation, homage

TRANSMUTE (traans myoot) *v.* **-ing,-ed.**
to change in appearance or shape
Synonyms: transform, convert, metamorphose

ELIXIR (ih lihk suhr) *n.* ***See page 44.***

CHIMERA (kie mehr uh) (kie meer uh) (kih mehr uh) *adj.*
See page 58.

ASCEND (uh sehnd) *v.* **-ing,-ed.**
to rise to another level or climb; move upward
Synonyms: elevate, escalate, hoist, lift, mount

MIMIC (mih mihk) *v.* **-ing,-ed.**
to imitate or copy
Synonyms: ape, simulate, impersonate

MIEN (meen) *n.*
characteristics expressive of attitude or personality
Synonyms: manner, demeanor, expression, style

AFFABILITY (aa fuh bih lih tee) *n.*
friendliness, courteousness
Synonyms: sociability, geniality, amiability

CONTEMPT (kuhn tehmpt) *n.*
disrespect, scorn
Synonyms: derision, disdain

INDEFATIGABLE (ihn dih faat ih guh buhl) *adj.*
See page 32.

ZEAL (zeel) *n.*
passion or devotion for a cause
Synonyms: fanaticism, enthusiasm, ardor

ERRONEOUSLY (eh roh nee uhs lee) *adv.*
with errors; mistakenly
Synonyms: wrongly, improperly, incorrectly

PRESUMPTION (pree suhmp shuhn) *n.*
rudeness, improper boldness
Synonyms: brashness, sass, impertinence

AFFECTATION (uh fehk tay shun) *n.*
fakeness, phoniness, artificiality, false display
Synonyms: insincerity, pose, pretension

having made a few preparatory experiments, he concluded with a **panegyric** upon modern chemistry, the terms of which I shall never forget:

"The ancient teachers of this science," said he, "promised impossibilities, and performed nothing. The modern masters promise very little; they know that metals cannot be **transmuted**, and that the **elixir** of life is a **chimera**. But these philosophers, whose hands seem only made to dabble in dirt, and their eyes to pour over the microscope or crucible, have indeed performed miracles. They penetrate into the recesses of nature, and show how she works in her hiding places. They **ascend** into the heavens; they have discovered how the blood circulates, and the nature of the air we breathe. They have acquired new and almost unlimited powers; they can command the thunders of heaven, **mimic** the earthquake, and even mock the invisible world with its own shadows."

I departed highly pleased with the professor and his lecture, and paid him a visit the same evening. His manners in private were even more mild and attractive than in public; for there was a certain dignity in his **mien** during his lecture, which in his own house was replaced by the greatest **affability** and kindness. He heard with attention my little narration concerning my studies, and smiled at the names of Cornelius Agrippa, and Paracelsus, but without the **contempt** that M. Krempe had exhibited. He said, that "these were men to whose **indefatigable zeal** modern philosophers were indebted for most of the foundations of their knowledge. They had left to us, as an easier task, to give new names, and arrange in connected classifications, the facts which they in a great degree had been the instruments of bringing to light. The labours of men of genius, however **erroneously** directed, scarcely ever fail in ultimately turning to the solid advantage of mankind." I listened to his statement, which was delivered without any **presumption** or **affectation**; and then added that his lecture had removed my prejudices

PROCURE (proh kyoor) *v.* **-ing,-ed.**
to obtain
Synonyms: acquire, secure, get, gain

NEGLECT (neh glehkt) *v.* **-ing,-ed.**
to ignore or disregard, to be negligent
Synonyms: overlook, remiss, skimp

DERANGE (dih raynj) *v.* **-ing,-ed.**
to disturb the functions of; to make insane
Synonyms: disarrange, madden, mess, confound

ARDOUR or ARDOR (ahr duhr) *n.*
passion, enthusiasm
Synonyms: intensity, vehemence

against modern chemists; and I, at the same time, requested his advice concerning the books I ought to **procure**.

"I am happy," said M. Waldman, "to have gained a disciple; and if your application equals your ability, I have no doubt of your success. Chemistry is that branch of natural philosophy in which the greatest improvements have been and may be made; it is on that account that I have made it my peculiar study; but at the same time I have not **neglected** the other branches of science. A man would make but a very sorry chemist, if he attended to that department of human knowledge alone. If your wish is to become really a man of science, and not merely a petty experimentalist, I should advise you to apply to every branch of natural philosophy, including mathematics."

He then took me into his laboratory, and explained to me the uses of his various machines; instructing me as to what I ought to **procure**, and promising me the use of his own, when I should have advanced far enough in the science not to **derange** their mechanism. He also gave me the list of books which I had requested, and I took my leave.

Thus ended a day memorable to me—it decided my future destiny.

CHAPTER III

From this day natural philosophy, and particularly chemistry, in the most comprehensive sense of the term, became nearly my sole occupation. I read with **ardour** those works, so full of genius and discrimination, which modern inquirers have written on these subjects. I attended the lectures, and cultivated the acquaintance, of the men of science of the university; and I found even in

REPULSIVE (rih puhl sihv) *adj.*
offensive, disgusting, sickening
Synonyms: repugnant, nauseating, detestable

TINGE (tihnj) *v.* **-ing,-ed.**
to affect or modify in character; to color with a slight shade, stain, odor, or taste
Synonyms: infuse, tint

DOGMATISM (dahg mah tihz uhm) *n.*
a stubborn assertion of an opinion
Synonyms: inflexibility, stubbornness, obstinacy

BANISH (baan ish) *v.* **-ing,-ed.**
to force to leave, exile
Synonyms: expel, deport

PEDANTRY (peh daan tree) *n.*
the habit of paying attention to academic details or rules, a vain display of learning
Synonyms: bookishness, ostentation

AMIABLE (ay mee uh buhl) *adj.* ***See page 54.***

INTRINSIC (ihn trihn zihk) (ihn trihn sihk) *adj.*
inherent, internal
Synonyms: fundamental, essential, innate

RESOLUTION (reh suh loo shun) *n.*
firm determination; a formal decision
Synonyms: firmness, intention, resolve

ARDENT (ahr dihnt) *adj.*
passionate, enthusiastic, fervent
Synonyms: intense, vehement, fervid

ARDOUR or ARDOR (ahr duhr) *n.* ***See page 62.***

PROFICIENCY (proh fih shehn see) *n.*
expertise, skillfulness in a certain subject
Synonyms: deftness, experience, competence

EXULTATION (ihg suhl tay shuhn) *n.*
the act of being extremely joyful
Synonyms: celebration, delight, jubilation

INFALLIBLY (ihn faal ih blee) *adv.*
unfailingly, unerringly
Synonym: certainly

M. Krempe a great deal of sound sense and real information, combined, it is true, with a **repulsive** physiognomy and manners, but not on that account the less valuable. In M. Waldman I found a true friend. His gentleness was never **tinged** by **dogmatism**; and his instructions were given with an air of frankness and good nature, that **banished** every idea of **pedantry**. It was, perhaps, the **amiable** character of this man that inclined me more to that branch of natural philosophy which he professed, than an **intrinsic** love for the science itself. But this state of mind had place only in the first steps towards knowledge. The more fully I entered into the science, the more exclusively I pursued it for its own sake. That application, which at first had been a matter of duty and **resolution**, now became so **ardent** and eager, that the stars often disappeared in the light of morning whilst I was yet engaged in my laboratory.

As I applied so closely, it may be easily conceived that I improved rapidly. My **ardour** was indeed the astonishment of the students; and my **proficiency**, that of the masters. Professor Krempe often asked me, with a sly smile, how Cornelius Agrippa went on whilst M. Waldman expressed the most heartfelt **exultation** in my progress. Two years passed in this manner, during which I paid no visit to Geneva, but was engaged, heart and soul, in the pursuit of some discoveries, which I hoped to make. None but those who have experienced them can conceive of the enticements of science. In other studies you go as far as others have gone before you, and there is nothing more to know; but in a scientific pursuit there is continual food for discovery and wonder. A mind of moderate capacity, which closely pursues one study, must **infallibly** arrive at great proficiency in that study; and I, who continually sought the attainment of one object of pursuit, and was solely wrapt up in this, improved so rapidly, that, at the end of two years, I made some discoveries in the improvement of some chemical

PROCURE (proh kyoor) *v.* **-ing,-ed.**
to obtain
Synonyms: acquire, secure, get, gain

CONDUCIVE (kuhn doo sihv) *adj.*
tending to lead to a particular outcome; favorable
Synonyms: contributive, helpful, promotive

PROTRACT (proh traakt) *v.* **-ing,-ed.**
to prolong, draw out, extend
Synonyms: lengthen, elongate, stretch

RESTRAIN (rih strayn) *v.* **-ing,-ed.**
control, repress, restrict
Synonyms: hamper, bridle, curb, check

ANIMATE (aa nih mayt) *v.* **-ing,-ed.**
1. to make lively, excited; to fill with spirit
Synonyms: elate, inspire, stimulate
2. to give life to or make alive
Synonyms: activate, enliven, vitalize

APPARITION (aa puh rih shuhn) *n.*
an unexpected or unusual sight; a ghostly figure
Synonyms: ghost, illusion, spirit, specter

instruments, which **procured** me great esteem and admiration at the university. When I had arrived at this point, and had become as well acquainted with the theory and practice of natural philosophy as depended on the lessons of any of the professors at Ingolstadt, my residence there being no longer **conducive** to my improvements, I thought of returning to my friends and my native town, when an incident happened that **protracted** my stay.

One of the phaenomena which had peculiarly attracted my attention was the structure of the human frame, and, indeed, any animal endued with life. Whence, I often asked myself, did the principle of life proceed? It was a bold question, and one which has ever been considered as a mystery; yet with how many things are we upon the brink of becoming acquainted, if cowardice or carelessness did not **restrain** our inquiries. I revolved these circumstances in my mind, and determined thenceforth to apply myself more particularly to those branches of natural philosophy which relate to physiology. Unless I had been **animated** by an almost supernatural enthusiasm, my application to this study would have been irksome, and almost intolerable. To examine the causes of life, we must first have recourse to death. I became acquainted with the science of anatomy, but this was not sufficient; I must also observe the natural decay and corruption of the human body. In my education my father had taken the greatest precautions that my mind should be impressed with no supernatural horrors. I do not ever remember to have trembled at a tale of superstition, or to have feared the **apparition** of a spirit. Darkness had no effect upon my fancy; and a churchyard was to me merely the receptacle of bodies deprived of life, which, from being the scat of beauty and strength, had become food for the worm. Now I was led to examine the cause and progress of this decay, and forced to spend days and nights in vaults and charnel houses. My attention was fixed upon every object the most insup-

DEGRADE (dih grayd) (dee grayd) *v.* **-ing,-ed.**
to lower in rank or status; to drag down in moral or intellectual character
Synonyms: shame, demean, dishonor, weaken

EXEMPLIFY (ihg zehm plih fie) *v.* **-ing,-ed.**
to act as an especially good example of something
Synonyms: represent, illustrate

AFFIRM (uh fihrm) *v.* **-ing,-ed.**
to state positively; to assert as valid or confirmed
Synonyms: declare, avow, maintain, guarantee

BESTOW (bih stoh) *v.* **-ing,-ed.**
to give as a gift
Synonyms: award, endow, donate, confer, present

ANIMATION (aa nih may shuhn) *n.*
the quality or condition of being alive, spirited, active or vigorous
Synonyms: life, vitality, invigoration, liveliness

RAPTURE (raap chuhr) *n.*
deep absorption; ecstasy or extreme joy
Synonyms: exaltation, immersion

CONSUMMATION (kahn suh may shun) (kahn soo may shun) *n.*
fulfillment; ultimate goal or accomplishment
Synonym: completion

portable to the delicacy of the human feelings. I saw how the fine form of man was **degraded** and wasted; I beheld the corruption of death succeed to the blooming cheek of life; I saw how the worm inherited the wonders of the eye and brain. I paused, examining and analysing all the minutiae of causation, as **exemplified** in the change from life to death, and death to life, until from the midst of this darkness a sudden light broke in upon me—a light so brilliant and wondrous, yet so simple, that while I became dizzy with the immensity of the prospect which it illustrated, I was surprised that among so many men of genius, who had directed their inquiries towards the same science, that I alone should be reserved to discover so astonishing a secret.

Remember, I am not recording the vision of a madman. The sun does not more certainly shine in the heavens, than that which I now **affirm** is true. Some miracle might have produced it, yet the stages of the discovery were distinct and probable. After days and nights of incredible labour and fatigue, I succeeded in discovering the cause of generation and life; nay, more, I became myself capable of **bestowing animation** upon lifeless matter.

The astonishment which I had at first experienced on this discovery soon gave place to delight and **rapture**. After so much time spent in painful labour, to arrive at once at the summit of my desires, was the most gratifying **consummation** of my toils. But this discovery was so great and overwhelming, that all the steps by which I had been progressively led to it were obliterated, and I beheld only the result. What had been the study and desire of the wisest men since the creation of the world, was now within my grasp. Not that, like a magic scene, it all opened upon me at once. The information I had obtained was of a nature rather to direct my endeavours so soon as I should point them towards the object of my search, than to exhibit that object already accomplished. I was like the

ARDENT (ahr dihnt) *adj.*
passionate, enthusiastic, fervent
Synonyms: intense, vehement, fervid

INFALLIBLE (ihn faal uh buhl) *adj.*
incapable of making a mistake
Synonyms: certain, guaranteed

PRECEPT (pree sehpt) *n.*
a command or principle intended as a general rule
Synonyms: law, axiom, guideline, tenet, rule

ASPIRE (uh spier) *v.* **-ing,-ed.**
to have great hopes; to aim at a goal
Synonyms: intend, strive, purpose, resolve, expect

BESTOW (bih stoh) *v.* **-ing,-ed.**
to give as a gift
Synonyms: award, endow, donate, confer, present

ANIMATION (aa nih may shuhn) *n.*
the quality or condition of being alive, spirited, active, or vigorous
Synonyms: life, vitality, invigoration, liveliness

EXALT (ek sahlt) *v.* **-ing,-ed.**
to raise in rank, power, or character; to elevate through praise; to enhance the activity of
Synonyms: praise, commend, glorify

ARDUOUS (ahr jyoo uhs) (aar dyoo uhs) *adj.*
extremely difficult, laborious
Synonyms: burdensome, onerous, hard, toilsome

MULTITUDE (muhl tuh tood) *n.*
the state of being many; a great number
Synonyms: mass, myriad, slew, crowd

INCESSANTLY (ihn sehs uhnt lee) *adv.*
continuously, endlessly
Synonyms: constantly, relentlessly, unremittingly

IMPRACTICABILITY (ihm praak tihk uh bihl ih tee) *n.*
impossibility; the state of being impassable
Synonyms: insanity, imprudence, absurdity

Arabian who had been buried with the dead, and found a passage to life aided only by one glimmering, and seemingly ineffectual light.

I see by your eagerness, and the wonder and hope which your eyes express, my friend, that you expect to be informed of the secret with which I am acquainted. That cannot be—listen patiently until the end of my story, and you will easily perceive why I am reserved upon that subject. I will not lead you on, unguarded and **ardent** as I then was, to your destruction and **infallible** misery. Learn from me, if not by my **precepts**, at least by my example, how dangerous is the acquirement of knowledge, and how much happier that man is who believes his native town to be the world, than he who **aspires** to become greater than his nature will allow.

When I found so astonishing a power placed within my hands, I hesitated a long time concerning the manner in which I should employ it. Although I possessed the capacity of **bestowing animation**, yet to prepare a frame for the reception of it, with all its intricacies of fibres, muscles, and veins, still remained a work of inconceivable difficulty and labour. I doubted at first whether I should attempt the creation of a being like myself or one of simpler organization; but my imagination was too much **exalted** by my first success to permit me to doubt of my ability to give life to an animal as complex and wonderful as man. The materials at present within my command hardly appeared adequate to so **arduous** an undertaking; but I doubted not that I should ultimately succeed. I prepared myself for a **multitude** of reverses; my operations might be **incessantly** baffled, and at last my work be imperfect. Yet, when I considered the improvement which every day takes place in science and mechanics, I was encouraged to hope my present attempts would at least lay the foundations of future success. Nor could I consider the magnitude and complexity of my plan as any argument of its **impracticability**. It was with these

HINDRANCE (hihn drehnts) *n.*
the act or state of being delayed; an impediment
Synonyms: obstacle, difficulty, obstruction

RESOLVE (rih sahlv) *v.* **-ing,-ed.**
to determine or to make a firm decision about
Synonyms: solve, decide

TORRENT (tawr rehnt) *n.*
a turbulent, fast-flowing stream
Synonyms: outpouring, deluge, flood

BESTOW (bih stoh) *v.* **-ing,-ed.**
to give as a gift
Synonyms: award, endow, donate, confer, present

ANIMATION (aa nih may shuhn) *n.*
the quality or condition of being alive, spirited, active, or vigorous
Synonyms: life, vitality, invigoration, liveliness

UNREMITTING (uhn rih mih ting) *adj.*
never lessening, persistent
Synonyms: incessant, continued, persevering

ARDOUR or ARDOR (ahr duhr) *n.*
passion, enthusiasm
Synonyms: intensity, vehemence

EMACIATED (ih may shee ay tihd) *adj.*
very thin due to hunger or disease, feeble
Synonyms: bony, gaunt, haggard, skeletal

UNHALLOWED (uhn haa lohd) *adj.*
unholy; desecrated
Synonyms: profane, wicked

ANIMATE (aa nih mayt) *v.* **-ing,-ed.**
1. to make lively, excited; to fill with spirit
Synonyms: elate, inspire, stimulate
2. to give life to or make alive
Synonyms: activate, enliven, vitalize

feelings that I began the creation of a human being. As the minuteness of the parts formed a great **hindrance** to my speed, I **resolved**, contrary to my first intention, to make the being of a gigantic stature; that is to say, about eight feet in height, and proportionably large. After having formed this determination, and having spent some months in successfully collecting and arranging my materials, I began.

No one can conceive the variety of feelings which bore me onwards, like a hurricane, in the first enthusiasm of success. Life and death appeared to me ideal bounds, which I should first break through, and pour a **torrent** of light into our dark world. A new species would bless me as its creator and source; many happy and excellent natures would owe their being to me. No father could claim the gratitude of his child so completely as I should deserve theirs. Pursuing these reflections, I thought, that if I could **bestow animation** upon lifeless matter, I might in process of time (although I now found it impossible) renew life where death had apparently devoted the body to corruption.

These thoughts supported my spirits, while I pursued my undertaking with **unremitting ardour**. My cheek had grown pale with study, and my person had become **emaciated** with confinement. Sometimes, on the very brink of certainty, I failed; yet still I clung to the hope which the next day or the next hour might realize. One secret which I alone possessed was the hope to which I had dedicated myself; and the moon gazed on my midnight labours, while, with unrelaxed and breathless eagerness, I pursued nature to her hiding places. Who shall conceive the horrors of my secret toil, as I dabbled among the **unhallowed** damps of the grave, or tortured the living animal to **animate** the lifeless clay? My limbs now tremble, and my eyes swim with the remembrance; but then a resistless, and almost frantic impulse, urged me forward; I seemed to have lost all soul or sensation

ACUTENESS (uh kyoot nehs) *n.*
sharpness, pointedness, severity
Synonyms: intensity, acuity, keenness

PROFANE (proh fayn) *adj.*
impure; contrary to religion; sacrilegious
Synonyms: secular, uninitiated; vulgar, coarse, blasphemous

LOATHING (lohth ing) *n.*
hatred or great dislike
Synonyms: detestation, abhorrence

PERPETUALLY (puhr peht chyoo uh lee) *adv.*
endlessly, always
Synonyms: continuously, constantly, eternally, perennially

BESTOW (bih stoh) *v.* **-ing,-ed.**
to give as a gift
Synonyms: award, endow, donate, confer, present

LUXURIANT (luhg zhoor ee ihnt) (luhk shoor ee ihnt) *adj.*
elegant, lavish
Synonyms: rich, abundant, profuse

NEGLECT (neh glehkt) *v.* **-ing,-ed.**
to ignore or disregard, to be negligent
Synonyms: overlook, skimp

DISQUIET (dihs kwie eht) *v.* **-ing,-ed.**
to take away the peace or tranquility of
Synonyms: disturb, agitate, distract, perturb

LOATHSOME (lohth suhm) *adj.*
abhorrent, hateful
Synonyms: offensive, disgusting

PROCRASTINATE (proh craa stuhn ayt) *v.* **-ing,-ed.**
to postpone continually and unjustifiably
Synonyms: delay, stall, postpone

but for this one pursuit. It was indeed but a passing trance, that only made me feel with renewed **acuteness** so soon as, the unnatural stimulus ceasing to operate, I had returned to my old habits. I collected bones from charnel houses; and disturbed, with **profane** fingers, the tremendous secrets of the human frame. In a solitary chamber, or rather cell, at the top of the house, and separated from all the other apartments by a gallery and staircase, I kept my workshop of filthy creation; my eyeballs were starting from their sockets in attending to the details of my employment. The dissecting room and the slaughter-house furnished many of my materials; and often did my human nature turn with **loathing** from my occupation, whilst, still urged on by an eagerness which **perpetually** increased, I brought my work near to a conclusion.

The summer months passed while I was thus engaged, heart and soul, in one pursuit. It was a most beautiful season; never did the fields **bestow** a more plentiful harvest, or the vines yield a more **luxuriant** vintage—but my eyes were insensible to the charms of nature. And the same feelings which made me **neglect** the scenes around me caused me also to forget those friends who were so many miles absent, and whom I had not seen for so long a time. I knew my silence **disquieted** them; and I well remembered the words of my father: "I know that while you are pleased with yourself, you will think of us with affection, and we shall hear regularly from you. You must pardon me, if I regard any interruption in your correspondence as a proof that your other duties are equally **neglected**."

I knew well therefore what would be my father's feelings; but I could not tear my thoughts from my employment, **loathsome** in itself, but which had taken an irresistible hold of my imagination. I wished, as it were, to **procrastinate** all that related to my feelings of affection until the great object, which swallowed up every habit of my nature, should be completed.

ASCRIBE (uh skrieb) *v.* **-ing,-ed.**
to attribute to, assign
Synonyms: accredit, impute, refer

NEGLECT (neh glehkt) *n.*
ignorance or disregard; negligence
Synonyms: carelessness, oversight, disrespect

TRANSITORY (traan sih tohr ee) *adj.*
short-lived, existing only briefly
Synonyms: transient, ephemeral, fleeting, fugitive, momentary

REPROACH (rih prohch) *n.*
discredit; expressed disappointment or displeasure
Synonyms: blame, disgrace

I then thought that my father would be unjust if he **ascribed** my **neglect** to vice, or faultiness on my part; but I am now convinced that he was justified in conceiving that I should not be altogether free from blame. A human being in perfection ought always to preserve a calm and peaceful mind, and never to allow passion or a **transitory** desire to disturb his tranquillity. I do not think that the pursuit of knowledge is an exception to this rule. If the study to which you apply yourself has a tendency to weaken your affections, and to destroy your taste for those simple pleasures in which no alloy can possibly mix, then that study is certainly unlawful, that is to say, not befitting the human mind. If this rule were always observed; if no man allowed any pursuit whatsoever to interfere with the tranquillity of his domestic affections, Greece had not been enslaved; Caesar would have spared his country; America would have been discovered more gradually; and the empires of Mexico and Peru had not been destroyed.

But I forget that I am moralizing in the most interesting part of my tale; and your looks remind me to proceed.

My father made no **reproach** in his letters; and only took notice of my silence by inquiring into my occupations more particularly than before. Winter, spring, and summer, passed away during my labours; but I did not watch the blossom or the expanding leaves—sights which before always yielded me supreme delight, so deeply was I engrossed in my occupation. The leaves of that year had withered before my work drew near to a close; and now every day showed me more plainly how well I had succeeded. But my enthusiasm was checked by my anxiety, and I appeared rather like one doomed by slavery to toil in the mines, or any other unwholesome trade, than an artist occupied by his favourite employment. Every night I was oppressed by a slow fever, and I became nervous to a most painful degree; a disease that I regretted the more

INFUSE (ihn fyooz) *v.* **-ing,-ed.**
to inspire or animate; to cause to be permeated with something that alters for the better
Synonyms: instill, flavor, introduce, pervade, inject

AGITATE (aa gih tayt) *v.* **-ing,-ed.**
to upset or excite; to make uneasy
Synonyms: disturb, fluster, bother

DELINEATE (dih lihn ee ayt) *v.* **-ing,-ed.**
to depict; represent
Synonyms: portray, illustrate

LUXURIANCE (luhg zhoor ee uhns) *n.*
elegance, lavishness
Synonyms: richness, abundance, profusion

INANIMATE (ihn aan ih miht) *adj.*
not alive, lacking energy
Synonyms: dead, lifeless, dull, inactive, soulless

ARDOUR or ARDOR (ahr duhr) *n.*
passion, enthusiasm
Synonyms: intensity, vehemence

because I had hitherto enjoyed most excellent health, and had always boasted of the firmness of my nerves. But I believed that exercise and amusement would soon drive away such symptoms; and I promised myself both of these, when my creation should be complete.

CHAPTER IV

It was on a dreary night of November, that I beheld the accomplishment of my toils. With an anxiety that almost amounted to agony, I collected the instruments of life around me, that I might **infuse** a spark of being into the lifeless thing that lay at my feet. It was already one in the morning; the rain pattered dismally against the panes, and my candle was nearly burnt out, when, by the glimmer of the half-extinguished light, I saw the dull yellow eye of the creature open; it breathed hard, and a convulsive motion **agitated** its limbs.

How can I describe my emotions at this catastrophe, or how **delineate** the wretch whom with such infinite pains and care I had endeavoured to form? His limbs were in proportion, and I had selected his features as beautiful. Beautiful!—Great God! His yellow skin scarcely covered the work of muscles and arteries beneath; his hair was of a lustrous black, and flowing; his teeth of a pearly whiteness; but these **luxuriances** only formed a more horrid contrast with his watery eyes, that seemed almost of the same colour as the dun white sockets in which they were set, his shrivelled complexion, and straight black lips.

The different accidents of life are not so changeable as the feelings of human nature. I had worked hard for nearly two years, for the sole purpose of **infusing** life into an **inanimate** body. For this I had deprived myself of rest and health. I had desired it with an **ardour** that far

TRAVERSE (truh vuhrs) (traa vuhrs) *v.* **-ing,-ed.**
to travel or travel across; to turn or move laterally
Synonyms: cross, travel, intersect, pass through

LASSITUDE (laas ih tood) *n.*
lethargy, sluggishness
Synonyms: weariness, listlessness, torpor, stupor

TUMULT (tuh muhlt) *n.*
state of confusion; agitation
Synonyms: disturbance, turmoil, din, commotion, chaos

LIVID (lih vihd) *adj.*
discolored from a bruise; pale; reddened with anger
Synonyms: furious, ashen, pallid, black-and-blue

INARTICULATE (ihn ahr tih kyoo liht) *adj.*
unable to speak clearly, incomprehensible
Synonym: unintelligible

DETAIN (dih tayn) (dee tayn) *v.* **-ing,-ed.**
to hold as if in custody; to restrain from continuing on
Synonyms: arrest, confine, nab, hinder

AGITATION (aa gih tay shuhn) *n.*
commotion, excitement; uneasiness
Synonyms: disturbance, restlessness, anxiety, fluster, disquiet

COUNTENANCE (kown tuh nuhns) *n.*
appearance, facial expression
Synonyms: face, features, visage

ANIMATION (aa nih may shuhn) *n.*
the quality or condition of being alive, spirited, active, or vigorous
Synonyms: life, vitality, invigoration, liveliness

exceeded moderation; but now that I had finished, the beauty of the dream vanished, and breathless horror and disgust filled my heart. Unable to endure the aspect of the being I had created, I rushed out of the room, and continued a long time **traversing** my bed-chamber, unable to compose my mind to sleep. At length **lassitude** succeeded to the **tumult** I had before endured; and I threw myself on the bed in my clothes, endeavouring to seek a few moments of forgetfulness. But it was in vain—I slept indeed, but I was disturbed by the wildest dreams. I thought I saw Elizabeth, in the bloom of health, walking in the streets of Ingolstadt. Delighted and surprised, I embraced her; but as I imprinted the first kiss on her lips, they became **livid** with the hue of death; her features appeared to change, and I thought that I held the corpse of my dead mother in my arms; a shroud enveloped her form, and I saw the grave-worms crawling in the folds of the flannel. I started from my sleep with horror; a cold dew covered my forehead, my teeth chattered, and every limb became convulsed; when, by the dim and yellow light of the moon, as it forced its way through the window-shutters, I beheld the wretch—the miserable monster whom I had created. He held up the curtain of the bed; and his eyes, if eyes they may be called, were fixed on me. His jaws opened, and he muttered some **inarticulate** sounds, while a grin wrinkled his cheeks. He might have spoken, but I did not hear; one hand was stretched out, seemingly to **detain** me, but I escaped, and rushed down stairs. I took refuge in the court-yard belonging to the house which I inhabited; where I remained during the rest of the night, walking up and down in the greatest **agitation**, listening attentively, catching and fearing each sound as if it were to announce the approach of the demoniacal corpse to which I had so miserably given life.

Oh! No mortal could support the horror of that **countenance**. A mummy again endued with **animation** could not be so hideous as that wretch. I had gazed on

PALPITATION (paal pih tay shuhn) *n.*
rapid and strong beating
Synonyms: fluttering, pounding, throbbing

LANGUOR (laang guhr) (laang uhr) *n.*
lack of energy, indifference, slowness
Synonyms: weakness, listlessness, sluggishness

ASYLUM (uh sie luhm) *n.*
refuge, sanctuary
Synonyms: haven, shelter

IMPEL (ihm pehl) *v.* **-ing,-ed.**
to urge forward as if driven by a strong moral pressure
Synonyms: push, prompt, drive, incite, instigate

TRAVERSE (truh vuhrs) (traa vuhrs) *v.* **-ing,-ed.**
to travel or travel across; to turn or move laterally
Synonyms: cross, travel, intersect, pass through

PALPITATE (paal pih tayt) *v.* **-ing,-ed.**
to beat rapidly and strongly
Synonyms: flutter, pound, pulsate, throb

him while unfinished; he was ugly then; but when those muscles and joints were rendered capable of motion, it became a thing such as even Dante could not have conceived.

I passed the night wretchedly. Sometimes my pulse beat so quickly and hardly, that I felt the **palpitation** of every artery; at others, I nearly sank to the ground through **languor** and extreme weakness. Mingled with this horror, I felt the bitterness of disappointment. Dreams that had been my food and pleasant rest for so long a space, were now become a hell to me; and the change was so rapid, the overthrow so complete!

Morning, dismal and wet, at length dawned, and discovered to my sleepless and aching eyes the church of Ingolstadt, its white steeple and clock, which indicated the sixth hour. The porter opened the gates of the court, which had that night been my **asylum**, and I issued into the streets, pacing them with quick steps, as if I sought to avoid the wretch whom I feared every turning of the street would present to my view. I did not dare return to the apartment which I inhabited, but felt **impelled** to hurry on, although wetted by the rain, which poured from a black and comfortless sky.

I continued walking in this manner for some time, endeavouring, by bodily exercise, to ease the load that weighed upon my mind. I **traversed** the streets, without any clear conception of where I was, or what I was doing. My heart **palpitated** in the sickness of fear; and I hurried on with irregular steps, not daring to look about me:

Like one who, on a lonely road,
Doth walk in fear and dread,
And, having once turn'd round, walks on,
And turns no more his head;
Because he knows a frightful fiend
Doth close behind him tread.

DILIGENCE (dihl uh juhns) *n.*

1. a horse-drawn vehicle
   Synonym: stagecoach
2. steady, earnest application of effort
   Synonyms: perseverance, attentiveness

INCREDULOUS (ihn krehj uh luhs) *adj.*

skeptical, doubtful

Synonyms: disbelieving, suspicious

ENTREATY (ehn tree tee) *n.*

a plea or request

Synonyms: solicitation, imploration, petition, importunity

Continuing thus, I came at length opposite to the inn at which the various **diligences** and carriages usually stopped. Here I paused, I knew not why; but I remained some minutes with my eyes fixed on a coach that was coming towards me from the other end of the street. As it drew nearer, I observed that it was the Swiss **diligence**. It stopped just where I was standing; and, on the door being opened, I perceived Henry Clerval, who, on seeing me, instantly sprung out. "My dear Frankenstein," exclaimed he, "How glad I am to see you! How fortunate that you should be here at the very moment of my alighting!"

Nothing could equal my delight on seeing Clerval; his presence brought back to my thoughts my father, Elizabeth, and all those scenes of home so dear to my recollection. I grasped his hand, and in a moment forgot my horror and misfortune; I felt suddenly, and for the first time during many months, calm and serene joy. I welcomed my friend, therefore, in the most cordial manner, and we walked towards my college. Clerval continued talking for some time about our mutual friends, and his own good fortune in being permitted to come to Ingolstadt. "You may easily believe," said he, "how great was the difficulty to persuade my father that it was not absolutely necessary for a merchant not to understand any thing except book-keeping; and, indeed, I believe I left him **incredulous** to the last, for his constant answer to my unwearied **entreaties** was the same as that of the Dutch school-master in the *Vicar of Wakefield*: 'I have ten thousand florins a year without Greek, I eat heartily without Greek.' But his affection for me at length overcame his dislike of learning, and he has permitted me to undertake a voyage of discovery to the land of knowledge."

"It gives me the greatest delight to see you; but tell me how you left my fathers, brothers, and Elizabeth."

"Very well, and very happy, only a little uneasy that

ALLUDE (uh lood) *v.* **-ing,-ed.**
to make an indirect reference
Synonyms: intimate, suggest, refer, indicate, hint

ENTREAT (ehn treet) *v.* **-ing,-ed.**
to plead, beg
Synonyms: beseech, implore, importune, request, petition

ASCEND (uh sehnd) *v.* **-ing,-ed.**
to rise to another level or climb; move upward
Synonyms: elevate, escalate, hoist, lift, mount

they hear from you so seldom. By the bye, I mean to lecture you a little upon their account myself.—But, my dear Frankenstein," continued he, stopping short, and gazing full in my face, "I did not before remark how very ill you appear; so thin and pale; you look as if you had been watching for several nights."

"You have guessed right; I have lately been so deeply engaged in one occupation, that I have not allowed myself sufficient rest, as you see. But I hope, I sincerely hope, that all these employments are now at an end, and that I am at length free."

I trembled excessively; I could not endure to think of, and far less to **allude** to the occurrences of the preceding night. I walked with a quick pace, and we soon arrived at my college. I then reflected, and the thought made me shiver, that the creature whom I had left in my apartment might still be there, alive, and walking about. I dreaded to behold this monster; but I feared still more that Henry should see him. **Entreating** him therefore to remain a few minutes at the bottom of the stairs, I darted up towards my own room. My hand was already on the lock of the door before I recollected myself. I then paused; and a cold shivering came over me. I threw the door forcibly open, as children are accustomed to do when they expect a spectre to stand in waiting for them on the other side; but nothing appeared. I stepped fearfully in—the apartment was empty; and my bed-room was also freed from its hideous guest. I could hardly believe that so great a good-fortune could have befallen me; but when I became assured that my enemy had indeed fled, I clapped my hands for joy, and ran down to Clerval.

We **ascended** into my room, and the servant presently brought breakfast; but I was unable to contain myself. It was not joy only that possessed me; I felt my flesh tingle with excess of sensitiveness, and my pulse beat rapidly. I was unable to remain for a single instant in the same place; I jumped over the chairs, clapped my hands, and

UNRESTRAINED (uhn rih straynd) *adj.*
uncontrolled, unrepressed, unrestricted
Synonyms: unbridled, unchecked

UNREMITTING (uhn rih mih tihng) *adj.*
never lessening, persistent
Synonyms: incessant, continued, persevering

BESTOW (bih stoh) *v.* **-ing,-ed.**
to give as a gift
Synonyms: award, endow, donate, confer, present

INCESSANTLY (ihn sehs uhnt lee) *adj.*
continuous, never ceasing
Synonyms: constant, interminable, relentless, unending, unremitting

PERTINACITY (pur tihn aas ih tee) *n.*
persistant determination
Synonyms: obstinacy, perseverence, doggedness, tenacity

laughed aloud. Clerval at first attributed my unusual spirits to joy on his arrival; but when he observed me more attentively, he saw a wildness in my eyes for which he could not account; and my loud, **unrestrained**, heartless laughter, frightened and astonished him.

"My dear Victor," cried he, "what, for God's sake, is the matter? Do not laugh in that manner. How ill you are! What is the cause of all this?"

"Do not ask me," cried I, putting my hands before my eyes, for I thought I saw the dreaded spectre glide into the room; "*he* can tell.—Oh, save me! Save me!" I imagined that the monster seized me; I struggled furiously, and fell down in a fit.

Poor Clerval! What must have been his feelings? A meeting, which he anticipated with such joy, so strangely turned to bitterness. But I was not the witness of his grief; for I was lifeless, and did not recover my senses for a long, long time.

This was the commencement of a nervous fever, which confined me for several months. During all that time Henry was my only nurse. I afterwards learned that, knowing my father's advanced age, and unfitness for so long a journey, and how wretched my sickness would make Elizabeth, he spared them this grief by concealing the extent of my disorder. He knew that I could not have a more kind and attentive nurse than himself; and, firm in the hope he felt of my recovery, he did not doubt that, instead of doing harm, he performed the kindest action that he could towards them.

But I was in reality very ill; and surely nothing but the unbounded and **unremitting** attentions of my friend could have restored me to life. The form of the monster on whom I had **bestowed** existence was for ever before my eyes, and I raved **incessantly** concerning him. Doubtless my words surprised Henry. He at first believed them to be the wanderings of my disturbed imagination, but the **pertinacity** with which I continually recurred to the same

CONVALESCENCE (kahn vuhl ehs uhns) *n.*
a gradual recovery after an illness
Synonyms: healing, recuperation

REMORSE (rih mohrs) *n.*
a gnawing distress arising from a sense of guilt
Synonyms: anguish, ruefulness, shame, penitence

DISCOMPOSE (dihs kuhm pohz) *v.* **-ing,-ed.**
to destroy the composure of; to disturb the order of
Synonyms: perplex, unsettle, disconcert, provoke

ALLUDE (uh lood) *v.* **-ing,-ed.**
to make an indirect reference
Synonyms: intimate, suggest, refer, indicate, hint

AGITATE (aa gih tayt) *v.* **-ing,-ed.**
to upset or excite; to make uneasy
Synonyms: disturb, fluster, bother

subject persuaded him that my disorder indeed owed its origin to some uncommon and terrible event.

By very slow degrees, and with frequent relapses, that alarmed and grieved my friend, I recovered. I remember the first time I became capable of observing outward objects with any kind of pleasure, I perceived that the fallen leaves had disappeared, and that the young buds were shooting forth from the trees that shaded my window. It was a divine spring; and the season contributed greatly to my **convalescence**. I felt also sentiments of joy and affection revive in my bosom; my gloom disappeared, and in a short time I became as cheerful as before I was attacked by the fatal passion.

"Dearest Clerval," exclaimed I, "how kind, how very good you are to me. This whole winter, instead of being spent in study, as you promised yourself, has been consumed in my sick room. How shall I ever repay you? I feel the greatest **remorse** for the disappointment of which I have been the occasion; but you will forgive me."

"You will repay me entirely, if you do not **discompose** yourself, but get well as fast as you can; and since you appear in such good spirits, I may speak to you on one subject, may I not?"

I trembled. One subject! What could it be? Could he **allude** to an object on whom I dared not even think?

"Compose yourself," said Clerval, who observed my change of colour, "I will not mention it, if it **agitates** you; but your father and cousin would be very happy if they received a letter from you in your own handwriting. They hardly know how ill you have been, and are uneasy at your long silence."

"Is that all, my dear Henry? How could you suppose that my first thought would not fly towards those dear, dear friends whom I love, and who are so deserving of my love."

"If this is your present temper, my friend, you will

RESTRAIN (rih <u>strayn</u>) *v.* **-ing,-ed.**
to controll, repress, restrict
Synonyms: hamper, bridle, curb, check

ROBUST (roh <u>buhst</u>) *adj.*
strong and healthy; hardy
Synonyms: vigorous, sturdy, sound, well, hale

perhaps be glad to see a letter that has been lying here some days for you. It is from your cousin, I believe."

CHAPTER V

Clerval then put the following letter into my hands.

"*To V. Frankenstein.*

"My dear Cousin,

"I cannot describe to you the uneasiness we have all felt concerning your health. We cannot help imagining that your friend Clerval conceals the extent of your disorder. For it is now several months since we have seen your hand-writing, and all this time you have been obliged to dictate your letters to Henry. Surely, Victor, you must have been exceedingly ill; and this makes us all very wretched, as much so nearly as after the death of your dear mother. My uncle was almost persuaded that you were indeed dangerously ill, and could hardly be **restrained** from undertaking a journey to Ingolstadt. Clerval always writes that you are getting better; I eagerly hope that you will confirm this intelligence soon in your own hand-writing; for indeed, indeed, Victor, we are all very miserable on this account. Relieve us from this fear, and we shall be the happiest creatures in the world. Your father's health is now so vigorous, that he appears ten years younger since last winter. Ernest also is so much improved, that you would hardly know him. He is now nearly sixteen, and has lost that sickly appearance which he had some years ago; he is grown quite **robust** and active.

"My uncle and I conversed a long time last night about what profession Ernest should follow. His constant illness when young has deprived him of the habits of application; and now that he enjoys good health, he is

ADVOCATE (aad vuh kiht) *n.*
a lawyer; one who urges or recommends
Synonyms: supporter, defender

SUSTENANCE (suh steh nehns) *n.*
means of living, source of nourishment
Synonyms: food, provisions, necessities

PROSPEROUS (prah spuhr uhs) *adj.*
wealthy or successful
Synonyms: affluent, abundant, opulent

PERVERSITY (puhr vuhr sih tee) *n.*
deliberate unruliness; immorality
Synonyms: corruption, debauchery, depravity

continually in the open air, climbing the hills, or rowing on the lake. I therefore proposed that he should be a farmer; which you know, Cousin, is a favourite scheme of mine. A farmer's is a very healthy happy life; and the least hurtful, or rather the most beneficial profession of any. My uncle had an idea of his being educated as an **advocate**, that through his interest he might become a judge. But, besides that he is not at all fitted for such an occupation, it is certainly more creditable to cultivate the earth for the **sustenance** of man, than to be the confidant, and sometimes the accomplice, of his vices; which is the profession of a lawyer. I said, that the employments of a **prosperous** farmer, if they were not a more honourable, they were at least a happier species of occupation than that of a judge, whose misfortune it was always to meddle with the dark side of human nature. My uncle smiled, and said that I ought to be an **advocate** myself, which put an end to the conversation on that subject.

"And now I must tell you a little story that will please, and perhaps amuse you. Do you not remember Justine Moritz? Probably you do not; I will relate her history, therefore, in a few words. Madame Moritz, her mother, was a widow with four children, of whom Justine was the third. This girl had always been the favourite of her father; but, through a strange **perversity**, her mother could not endure her, and, after the death of M. Moritz, treated her very ill. My aunt observed this; and, when Justine was twelve years of age, prevailed on her mother to allow her to live at her house. The republican institutions of our country have produced simpler and happier manners than those which prevail in the great monarchies that surround it. Hence there is less distinction between the several classes of its inhabitants; and the lower orders being neither so poor nor so despised, their manners are more refined and moral. A servant in Geneva does not mean the same thing as a servant in France and England. Justine, thus received in our family,

DISSIPATE (dihs uh payt) *v.* **-ing,-ed.**
to scatter; to pursue pleasure to excess
Synonyms: carouse, squander, consume; disperse, dissolve

INDUCE (ihn doos) (ihn dyoos) *v.* **-ing,-ed.**
to persuade; bring about
Synonyms: prevail, convince, lead, effect, occasion

NEGLECTED (neh glehk tihd) *adj.*
ignored or disregarded
Synonyms: overlooked, forgotten, rejected

CHASTISE (chaa stiez) *v.* **-ing,-ed.**
to punish, discipline, scold
Synonyms: castigate, penalize

REPENTANT (rih pehnt ehnt) *adj.*
apologetic, guilty, remorseful
Synonyms: contrite, regretful, penitent, sorry

learned the duties of a servant; a condition which, in our fortunate country, does not include the idea of ignorance, and a sacrifice of the dignity of a human being.

"After what I have said, I dare say you well remember the heroine of my little tale, for Justine was a great favourite of yours; and I recollect you once remarked, that if you were in an ill humour, one glance from Justine could **dissipate** it, for the same reason that Ariosto gives concerning the beauty of Angelica—she looked so frank-hearted and happy. My aunt conceived a great attachment for her, by which she was **induced** to give her an education superior to that which she had at first intended. This benefit was fully repaid; Justine was the most grateful little creature in the world. I do not mean that she made any professions, I never heard one pass her lips; but you could see by her eyes that she almost adored her protectress. Although her disposition was gay, and in many respects inconsiderate, yet she paid the greatest attention to every gesture of my aunt. She thought her the model of all excellence, and endeavoured to imitate her phraseology and manners, so that even now she often reminds me of her.

"When my dearest aunt died, every one was too much occupied in their own grief to notice poor Justine, who had attended her during her illness with the most anxious affection. Poor Justine was very ill; but other trials were reserved for her.

"One by one, her brothers and sister died; and her mother, with the exception of her **neglected** daughter, was left childless. The conscience of the woman was troubled; she began to think that the deaths of her favourites was a judgment from heaven to **chastise** her partiality. She was a Roman Catholic; and I believe her confessor confirmed the idea which she had conceived. Accordingly, a few months after your departure for Ingolstadt, Justine was called home by her **repentant** mother. Poor girl! She wept when she quitted our

VIVACITY (vih vahs ih tee) *n.*
liveliness, spiritedness
Synonyms: vibrance, zest

VACILLATING (vaa sihl ay tihng) *adj.*
wavering, showing indecision
Synonyms: swaying, oscillating, hesitant, faltering

REPENTANCE (rih pehnt ehnts) *n.*
guilt, remorse for one's past conduct
Synonyms: contrition, regret, penitence

PERPETUAL (puhr peht chyoo uhl) *adj.*
endless, lasting
Synonyms: continuous, constant, ceaseless, eternal, perennial

MIEN (meen) *n.*
characteristics expressive of attitude or personality
Synonyms: manner, demeanor, expression, style

INDULGE (ihn duhlj) *v.* **-ing,-ed.**
to give in to a craving or desire
Synonyms: humor, gratify, allow, pamper

house—she was much altered since the death of my aunt; grief had given softness and a winning mildness to her manners, which had before been remarkable for **vivacity**. Nor was her residence at her mother's house of a nature to restore her gaiety. The poor woman was very **vacillating** in her **repentance**. She sometimes begged Justine to forgive her unkindness, but much oftener accused her of having caused the deaths of her brothers and sister. **Perpetual** fretting at length threw Madame Moritz into a decline, which at first increased her irritability, but she is now at peace for ever. She died on the first approach of cold weather, at the beginning of this last winter. Justine has returned to us; and I assure you I love her tenderly. She is very clever and gentle, and extremely pretty; as I mentioned before, her **mien** and her expressions continually remind me of my dear aunt.

"I must say also a few words to you, my dear cousin, of little darling William. I wish you could see him; he is very tall of his age, with sweet laughing blue eyes, dark eyelashes, and curling hair. When he smiles, two little dimples appear on each cheek, which are rosy with health. He has already had one or two little *wives*, but Louisa Biron is his favourite, a pretty little girl of five years of age.

"Now, dear Victor, I dare say you wish to be **indulged** in a little gossip concerning the good people of Geneva. The pretty Miss Mansfield has already received the congratulatory visits on her approaching marriage with a young Englishman, John Melbourne, Esq. Her ugly sister, Manon, married M. Duvillard, the rich banker, last autumn. Your favourite schoolfellow, Louis Manoir, has suffered several misfortunes since the departure of Clerval from Geneva. But he has already recovered his spirits, and is reported to be on the point of marrying a very lively pretty Frenchwoman, Madame Tavernier. She is a widow, and much older than Manoir; but she is very much admired, and a favourite with everybody.

CONVALESCENCE (kahn vuhl ehs uhns) *n.*
a gradual recovery after an illness
Synonyms: healing, recuperation

SUSTAIN (suh stayn) *v.* **-ing,-ed.**
to support, uphold; endure, undergo
Synonyms: maintain, prop, encourage, withstand, confirm

ANTIPATHY (aan tihp uh thee) *n.*
dislike, hostility; extreme opposition or aversion
Synonyms: enmity, malice, antagonism

AVAIL (uh vayl) *n.*
use or advantage
Synonyms: benefit, service, usefulness

"I have written myself into good spirits, dear cousin; yet I cannot conclude without again anxiously inquiring concerning your health. Dear Victor, if you are not very ill, write yourself, and make your father and all of us happy; or—I cannot bear to think of the other side of the question; my tears already flow. Adieu, my dearest cousin.

"Elizabeth Lavenza.
"Geneva, March 18th, 17—"

"Dear, dear Elizabeth!" I exclaimed when I had read her letter, "I will write instantly, and relieve them from the anxiety they must feel." I wrote, and this exertion greatly fatigued me; but my **convalescence** had commenced, and proceeded regularly. In another fortnight I was able to leave my chamber.

One of my first duties on my recovery was to introduce Clerval to the several professors of the university. In doing this, I underwent a kind of rough usage, ill befitting the wounds that my mind had **sustained**. Ever since the fatal night, the end of my labours, and the beginning of my misfortunes, I had conceived a violent **antipathy** even to the name of natural philosophy. When I was otherwise quite restored to health, the sight of a chemical instrument would renew all the agony of my nervous symptoms. Henry saw this, and had removed all my apparatus from my view. He had also changed my apartment; for he perceived that I had acquired a dislike for the room which had previously been my laboratory. But these cares of Clerval were made of no **avail** when I visited the professors. M. Waldman inflicted torture when he praised, with kindness and warmth, the astonishing progress I had made in the sciences. He soon perceived that I disliked the subject; but, not guessing the real cause, he attributed my feelings to modesty, and changed the subject from my improvement to the science itself, with a desire, as I evidently saw, of drawing me out. What

DISCERN (dihs uhrn) *v.* **-ing,-ed.**
to perceive something obscure
Synonyms: descry, observe, recognize, glimpse, distinguish

REVERENCE (rehv uhr ehnts) *n.*
a feeling of great awe and respect
Synonyms: veneration, adoration, idolization, admiration

DOCILE (dah suhl) (dah siel) *adj.*
tame, willing to be taught
Synonyms: domesticated, mild, tractable, obedient

BENEVOLENT (buh neh vuh luhnt) *adj.*
kind, compassionate
Synonyms: charitable, altruistic, beneficent, generous, good

APPROBATION (aa pruh bay shuhn) *n.*
praise; official approval
Synonyms: acclaim, accolade, encomium, applause, homage

COUNTENANCE (kown tuh nuhns) *n.*
appearance, facial expression
Synonyms: face, features, visage

DIFFIDENT (dih fih duhnt) (dih fih dehnt) *adj.*
shy, lacking confidence
Synonyms: timid, reticent, modest

EULOGY (yoo luh jee) *n.*
high praise, often in a public speech
Synonyms: tribute, commendation, encomium, panegyric, salute

could I do? He meant to please, and he tormented me. I felt as if he had placed carefully, one by one, in my view those instruments which were to be afterwards used in putting me to a slow and cruel death. I writhed under his words, yet dared not exhibit the pain I felt. Clerval, whose eyes and feelings were always quick in **discerning** the sensations of others, declined the subject, alleging, in excuse, his total ignorance; and the conversation took a more general turn. I thanked my friend from my heart, but I did not speak. I saw plainly that he was surprised, but he never attempted to draw my secret from me; and although I loved him with a mixture of affection and **reverence** that knew no bounds, yet I could never persuade myself to confide to him that event which was so often present to my recollection, but which I feared the detail to another would only impress more deeply.

M. Krempe was not equally **docile**; and in my condition at that time, of almost insupportable sensitiveness, his harsh blunt encomiums gave me even more pain than the **benevolent approbation** of M. Waldman. "D--n the fellow!" cried he; "Why, M. Clerval, I assure you he has outstript us all. Aye, stare if you please; but it is nevertheless true. A youngster who, but a few years ago, believed Cornelius Agrippa as firmly as the gospel, has now set himself at the head of the university; and if he is not soon pulled down, we shall all be out of **countenance**.—Aye, aye," continued he, observing my face expressive of suffering, "M. Frankenstein is modest; an excellent quality in a young man. Young men should be **diffident** of themselves, you know, M. Clerval; I was myself when young, but that wears out in a very short time."

M. Krempe had now commenced an **eulogy** on himself, which happily turned the conversation from a subject that was so annoying to me.

Clerval was no natural philosopher. His imagination was too vivid for the minutiae of science. Languages were his principal study; and he sought, by acquiring

CONSOLATION (kahn suh lay shuhn) *n.*
something providing comfort or solace for a loss or hardship
Synonyms: condolence, solace

MELANCHOLY (mehl uhn kahl ee) *n.*
sadness, depression
Synonyms: dejection, despondency, woe, sorrow

COMPENSATE (kahm pehn sayt) *v.* **-ing,-ed.**
to repay or reimburse
Synonyms: indemnify, recompense, balance

DILATORINESS (dihl uh tohr ee nehs) *n.*
lateness, tendency to delay
Synonyms: sluggishness, tardiness, slowness

ACCEDE (aak seed) *v.* **-ing,-ed.**
to express approval; agree to
Synonyms: assent, acquiesce, consent, concur

their elements, to open a field for self-instruction on his return to Geneva. Persian, Arabic, and Hebrew, gained his attention, after he had made himself perfectly master of Greek and Latin. For my own part, idleness had ever been <u>irksome</u> to me; and now that I wished to fly from reflection, and hated my former studies, I felt great relief in being the fellow-pupil with my friend, and found not only instruction but **consolation** in the works of the orientalists. Their **melancholy** is soothing, and their joy elevating to a degree I never experienced in studying the authors of any other country. When you read their writings, life appears to consist in a warm sun and garden of roses—in the smiles and frowns of a fair enemy, and the fire that consumes your own heart. How different from the manly and heroical poetry of Greece and Rome.

Summer passed away in these occupations, and my return to Geneva was fixed for the latter end of autumn; but being delayed by several accidents, winter and snow arrived, the roads were deemed impassable, and my journey was retarded until the ensuing spring. I felt this delay very bitterly; for I longed to see my native town, and my beloved friends. My return had only been delayed so long from an unwillingness to leave Clerval in a strange place, before he had become acquainted with any of its inhabitants. The winter, however, was spent cheerfully; and although the spring was uncommonly late, when it came, its beauty **compensated** for its **dilatoriness**.

The month of May had already commenced, and I expected the letter daily which was to fix the date of my departure, when Henry proposed a pedestrian tour in the environs of Ingolstadt that I might bid a personal farewell to the country I had so long inhabited. I **acceded** with pleasure to this proposition. I was fond of exercise, and Clerval had always been my favourite companion in the <u>rambles</u> of this nature that I had taken among the scenes of my native country.

SALUBRIOUS (suh <u>loo</u> bree uhs) *adj.*
healthful
Synonyms: curative, medicinal, tonic, therapeutic, bracing

INANIMATE (ihn <u>aan</u> ih miht) *adj.*
not alive, lacking energy
Synonyms: dead, lifeless, dull, inactive, soulless

BESTOW (bih <u>stoh</u>) *v.* **-ing,-ed.**
to give as a gift
Synonyms: award, endow, donate, confer, present

SERENE (suh <u>reen</u>) *adj.*
calm, peaceful
Synonyms: tranquil, composed, content

VERDANT (<u>vuhr</u> dnt) *adj.*
green with vegetation; inexperienced
Synonyms: grassy, leafy, wooded

INVINCIBLE (ihn <u>vihn</u> suh buhl) *adj.*
invulnerable, unbeatable
Synonyms: unconquerable, insuperable

INGENUITY (ihn jeh <u>noo</u> ih tee) *n.*
cleverness, inventive skill or imagination
Synonyms: inventiveness, cunning, genius

We passed a fortnight in these perambulations; my health and spirits had long been restored, and they gained additional strength from the **salubrious** air I breathed, the natural incidents of our progress, and the conversation of my friend. Study had before secluded me from the intercourse of my fellow-creatures, and rendered me unsocial; but Clerval called forth the better feelings of my heart; he again taught me to love the aspect of nature, and the cheerful faces of children. Excellent friend! How sincerely did you love me, and endeavour to elevate my mind, until it was on a level with your own. A selfish pursuit had cramped and narrowed me, until your gentleness and affection warmed and opened my senses; I became the same happy creature who, a few years ago, loving and beloved by all, had no sorrow or care. When happy, **inanimate** nature had the power of **bestowing** on me the most delightful sensations. A **serene** sky and **verdant** fields filled me with ecstacy. The present season was indeed divine; the flowers of spring bloomed in the hedges, while those of summer were already in bud. I was undisturbed by thoughts which during the preceding year had pressed upon me, notwithstanding my endeavours to throw them off, with an **invincible** burden.

Henry rejoiced in my gaiety, and sincerely sympathized in my feelings. He exerted himself to amuse me, while he expressed the sensations that filled his soul. The resources of his mind on this occasion were truly astonishing. His conversation was full of imagination; and very often, in imitation of the Persian and Arabic writers, he invented tales of wonderful fancy and passion. At other times he repeated my favourite poems, or drew me out into arguments, which he supported with great **ingenuity**.

We returned to our college on a Sunday afternoon—the peasants were dancing, and every one we met appeared gay and happy. My own spirits were high, and I bounded along with feelings of unbridled joy and hilarity.

CALLOUS (kaa luhs) *adj.*
thick-skinned, insensitive
Synonyms: impervious, indifferent, stony, unmoved, unfeeling

CONSOLE (kuhn sohl) *v.* **-ing,-ed.**
to alleviate grief and raise the spirits of, provide solace
Synonyms: relieve, comfort, soothe

SERENE (suh reen) *adj.*
calm, peaceful
Synonyms: tranquil, composed, content

CHAPTER VI

On my return, I found the following letter from my father:

"*To V. Frankenstein.*

"My dear Victor,

"You have probably waited impatiently for a letter to fix the date of your return to us; and I was at first tempted to write only a few lines, merely mentioning the day on which I should expect you. But that would be a cruel kindness, and I dare not do it. What would be your surprise, my son, when you expected a happy and gay welcome, to behold, on the contrary, tears and wretchedness? And how, Victor, can I relate our misfortune? Absence cannot have rendered you **callous** to our joys and griefs; and how shall I inflict pain on an absent child? I wish to prepare you for the woeful news, but I know it is impossible; even now your eye skims over the page, to seek the words which are to convey to you the horrible tidings.

"William is dead! That sweet child, whose smiles delighted and warmed my heart, who was so gentle, yet so gay! Victor, he is murdered!

"I will not attempt to **console** you; but will simply relate the circumstances of the transaction.

"Last Thursday (May 7th) I, my niece, and your two brothers, went to walk in Plainpalais. The evening was warm and **serene**, and we prolonged our walk farther than usual. It was already dusk before we thought of returning; and then we discovered that William and Ernest, who had gone on before, were not to be found. We accordingly rested on a seat until they should return.

CONJECTURE (kuhn jehk shuhr) *v.* **-ing,-ed.**
to infer, predict, guess
Synonyms: postulate, hypothesize, suppose, surmise

LIVID (lih vihd) *adj.*
discolored from a bruise; pale; reddened with anger
Synonyms: furious, ashen, pallid, black-and-blue

COUNTENANCE (kown tuh nuhns) *n.*
appearance, facial expression
Synonyms: face, features, visage

UNREMITTED (uhn rih mih tihd) *adj.*
never lessening, persistent
Synonyms: incessant, continued, persevering

CONSOLE (kuhn sohl) *v.* **-ing,-ed.**
to alleviate grief and raise the spirits of, provide solace
Synonyms: relieve, comfort, soothe

Presently Ernest came, and inquired if we had seen his brother. He said that they had been playing together, that William had run away to hide himself, and that he vainly sought for him, and afterwards waited for him a long time, but that he did not return.

"This account rather alarmed us, and we continued to search for him until night fell, when Elizabeth **conjectured** that he might have returned to the house. He was not there. We returned again, with torches; for I could not rest, when I thought that my sweet boy had lost himself, and was exposed to all the damps and dews of night. Elizabeth also suffered extreme anguish. About five in the morning I discovered my lovely boy, whom the night before I had seen blooming and active in health, stretched on the grass **livid** and motionless; the print of the murderer's finger was on his neck.

"He was conveyed home, and the anguish that was visible in my **countenance** betrayed the secret to Elizabeth. She was very earnest to see the corpse. At first I attempted to prevent her; but she persisted, and entering the room where it lay, hastily examined the neck of the victim, and clasping her hands exclaimed, 'Oh God! I have murdered my darling infant!'

"She fainted, and was restored with extreme difficulty. When she again lived, it was only to weep and sigh. She told me, that that same evening William had teased her to let him wear a very valuable miniature that she possessed of your mother. This picture is gone, and was doubtless the temptation which urged the murderer to the deed. We have no trace of him at present, although our exertions to discover him are **unremitted**; but they will not restore my beloved William.

"Come, dearest Victor; you alone can **console** Elizabeth. She weeps continually, and accuses herself unjustly as the cause of his death; her words pierce my heart. We are all unhappy; but will not that be an additional motive for you, my son, to return and be our

BROODING (brood ihng) *adj.*
persistently or morbidly thoughtful
Synonyms: worried, comtemplative, pensive

VENGEANCE (vehn juhns) *n.*
punishment inflicted in retaliation; vehemence
Synonyms: revenge, repayment, wrath

FESTER (fehs tuhr) *v.* **-ing,-ed.**
to generate puss; to rot; to cause increasing poisoning, irritation, or bitterness
Synonyms: aggravate, inflame, rankle, smolder

AFFLICTED (uh flihk tihd) *adj.*
severely distressed, anguished
Synonyms: troubled, tormented, wounded

COUNTENANCE (kown tuh nuhns) *n.*
appearance, facial expression
Synonyms: face, features, visage

AGITATION (aa gih tay shuhn) *n.*
commotion, excitement; uneasiness
Synonyms: disturbance, restlessness, anxiety

CONSOLATION (kahn suh lay shuhn) *n.*
something providing comfort or solace for a loss or hardship
Synonyms: condolence, solace

IRREPARABLE (ih reh puhr uh buhl) *adj.*
unable to be repaired
Synonyms: ruined, hopeless, incurable, irreplaceable

comforter? Your dear mother! Alas, Victor! I now say, Thank God she did not live to witness the cruel, miserable death of her youngest darling!

"Come, Victor; not **brooding** thoughts of **vengeance** against the assassin, but with feelings of peace and gentleness, that will heal, instead of **festering** the wounds of our minds. Enter the house of mourning, my friend, but with kindness and affection for those who love you, and not with hatred for your enemies.

"Your affectionate and **afflicted** father,
"Alphonse Frankenstein.
"Geneva, May 12th, 17—."

Clerval, who had watched my **countenance** as I read this letter, was surprised to observe the despair that succeeded to the joy I at first expressed on receiving news from my friends. I threw the letter on the table, and covered my face with my hands.

"My dear Frankenstein," exclaimed Henry, when he perceived me weep with bitterness, "are you always to be unhappy? My dear friend, what has happened?"

I motioned to him to take up the letter, while I walked up and down the room in the extremest **agitation**. Tears also gushed from the eyes of Clerval, as he read the account of my misfortune.

"I can offer you no **consolation**, my friend," said he; "your disaster is **irreparable**. What do you intend to do?"

"To go instantly to Geneva. Come with me, Henry, to order the horses."

During our walk, Clerval endeavoured to raise my spirits. He did not do this by common topics of **consolation**, but by exhibiting the truest sympathy. "Poor William!" said he, "that dear child; he now sleeps with his angel mother. His friends mourn and weep, but he is at rest; he does not now feel the murderer's grasp; a sod covers his gentle form, and he knows no pain. He can no longer be a fit subject for pity; the survivors are the

CONSOLATION (kahn suh lay shuhn) *n.*
something providing comfort or solace for a loss or hardship
Synonyms: condolence, solace

MELANCHOLY (mehl uhn kahl ee) *adj.*
sad, depressing
Synonyms: dejected, despondent, woeful, sorrowful

CONSOLE (kuhn sohl) *v.* **-ing,-ed.**
to alleviate grief and raise the spirits of, provide solace
Synonyms: relieve, comfort, soothe

SUSTAIN (suh stayn) *v.* **-ing,-ed.**
to support, uphold; endure, undergo
Synonyms: maintain, prop, encourage, withstand, confirm

MULTITUDE (muhl tuh tood) *n.*
the state of being many; a great number
Synonyms: mass, myriad, slew, crowd

DESOLATING (deh suh layt ihng) *adj.*
devastating and wasteful; wretched
Synonyms: destroying, desecrating, pillaging

greatest sufferers, and for them time is the only **consolation**. Those maxims of the Stoics, that death was no evil, and that the mind of man ought to be superior to despair on the eternal absence of a beloved object, ought not to be urged. Even Cato wept over the dead body of his brother."

Clerval spoke thus as we hurried through the streets; the words impressed themselves on my mind, and I remembered them afterwards in solitude. But now, as soon as the horses arrived, I hurried into a cabriolet, and bade farewell to my friend.

My journey was very **melancholy**. At first I wished to hurry on, for I longed to **console** and sympathize with my loved and sorrowing friends; but when I drew near my native town, I slackened my progress. I could hardly **sustain** the **multitude** of feelings that crowded into my mind. I passed through scenes familiar to my youth, but which I had not seen for nearly six years. How altered every thing might be during that time? One sudden and **desolating** change had taken place; but a thousand little circumstances might have by degrees worked other alterations which, although they were done more tranquilly, might not be the less decisive. Fear overcame me; I dared not advance, dreading a thousand nameless evils that made me tremble, although I was unable to define them.

I remained two days at Lausanne, in this painful state of mind. I contemplated the lake—the waters were placid; all around was calm, and the snowy mountains, "the palaces of nature," were not changed. By degrees the calm and heavenly scene restored me, and I continued my journey towards Geneva.

The road ran by the side of the lake, which became narrower as I approached my native town. I discovered more distinctly the black sides of Jura, and the bright summit of Mont Blanc; I wept like a child: "Dear mountains! My own beautiful lake! How do you welcome your

PLACID (plaa sihd) *adj.*
calm
Synonyms: tranquil, serene, peaceful, complacent

PROGNOSTICATE (prahg nahs tih kayt) *v.* **-ing,-ed.**
to indicate in advance; to forecast
Synonyms: predict, foreshadow, portend

TEDIOUS (tee dee uhs) *adj.*
tiresome because of length or dullness
Synonyms: dull, fatiguing, unexciting, wearisome

OBSCURELY (uhb skyoor lee) *adv.*
dimly, unclearly
Synonyms: faintly, remotely

SERENE (suh reen) *adj.*
calm, peaceful
Synonyms: tranquil, composed, content

RESOLVE (rih sahlv) *v.* **-ing,-ed.**
to determine or to make a firm decision about
Synonyms: solve, decide

ASCEND (uh sehnd) *v.* **-ing,-ed.**
to rise to another level or climb; move upward
Synonyms: elevate, escalate, hoist, lift, mount

wanderer? Your summits are clear; the sky and lake are blue and **placid**. Is this to **prognosticate** peace, or to mock at my unhappiness?"

I fear, my friend, that I shall render myself **tedious** by dwelling on these preliminary circumstances; but they were days of comparative happiness, and I think of them with pleasure. My country, my beloved country! Who but a native can tell the delight I took in again beholding thy streams, thy mountains, and, more than all, thy lovely lake.

Yet, as I drew nearer home, grief and fear again overcame me. Night also closed around; and when I could hardly see the dark mountains, I felt still more gloomily. The picture appeared a vast and dim scene of evil, and I foresaw **obscurely** that I was destined to become the most wretched of human beings. Alas! I prophesied truly, and failed only in one single circumstance, that in all the misery I imagined and dreaded, I did not conceive the hundredth part of the anguish I was destined to endure.

It was completely dark when I arrived in the environs of Geneva; the gates of the town were already shut; and I was obliged to pass the night at Secheron, a village half a league to the east of the city. The sky was **serene**; and, as I was unable to rest, I **resolved** to visit the spot where my poor William had been murdered. As I could not pass through the town, I was obliged to cross the lake in a boat to arrive at Plainpalais. During this short voyage I saw the lightnings playing on the summit of Mont Blanc in the most beautiful figures. The storm appeared to approach rapidly; and, on landing, I **ascended** a low hill, that I might observe its progress. It advanced; the heavens were clouded, and I soon felt the rain coming slowly in large drops, but its violence quickly increased.

I quitted my seat, and walked on, although the darkness and storm increased every minute, and the thunder burst with a terrific crash over my head. It was echoed from Saleve, the Juras, and the Alps of Savoy; vivid

DISCLOSE (dihs klohs) *v.* **-ing,-ed.**
to open up, divulge
Synonyms: confide, reveal, impart

DIRGE (duhrj) *n.*
funeral hymn
Synonyms: elegy, threnody, lament

DEFORMITY (dih fohr mih tee) *n.*
disfigurement, the state of being misshapen
Synonyms: contortion, malformation, disproportion

ASCENT (uh sehnt) *n.*
upward slope; a climb or rising to another level; movement upward

flashes of lightning dazzled my eyes, illuminating the lake, making it appear like a vast sheet of fire; then for an instant every thing seemed of a pitchy darkness, until the eye recovered itself from the preceding flash. The storm, as is often the case in Switzerland, appeared at once in various parts of the heavens. The most violent storm hung exactly north of the town, over that part of the lake which lies between the promontory of Belrive and the village of Copet. Another storm enlightened Jura with faint flashes; and another darkened and sometimes **disclosed** the Mole, a peaked mountain to the east of the lake.

While I watched the storm, so beautiful yet terrific, I wandered on with a hasty step. This noble war in the sky elevated my spirits; I clasped my hands, and exclaimed aloud, "William, dear angel! This is thy funeral, this thy **dirge**!" As I said these words, I perceived in the gloom a figure which stole from behind a clump of trees near me; I stood fixed, gazing intently; I could not be mistaken. A flash of lightning illuminated the object, and discovered its shape plainly to me; its gigantic stature, and the **deformity** of its aspect, more hideous than belongs to humanity, instantly informed me that it was the wretch, the filthy daemon to whom I had given life. What did he there? Could he be (I shuddered at the conception) the murderer of my brother? No sooner did that idea cross my imagination, than I became convinced of its truth; my teeth chattered, and I was forced to lean against a tree for support. The figure passed me quickly, and I lost it in the gloom. Nothing in human shape could have destroyed that fair child. *He* was the murderer! I could not doubt it. The mere presence of the idea was an irresistible proof of the fact. I thought of pursuing the devil; but it would have been in vain, for another flash discovered him to me hanging among the rocks of the nearly perpendicular **ascent** of Mont Saleve, a hill that bounds Plainpalais on the south. He soon reached the summit, and disappeared.

Synonyms: elevation, incline, mounting

DEPRAVED (dih prayvd) *adj.*
sinful, morally corrupted
Synonyms: wicked, evil

ENDOW (ehn dow) *v.* **-ing,-ed.**
to furnish with an income or grant; to provide with something naturally or freely
Synonyms: bestow, donate, empower, grant, support

PRECIPICE (prehs ih pihs) *n.*
edge, steep overhang
Synonyms: crag, cliff, brink

ELUDE (ih lood) *v.* **-ing,-ed.**
escape, avoid
Synonyms: evade, dodge

I remained motionless. The thunder ceased; but the rain still continued, and the scene was enveloped in an impenetrable darkness. I revolved in my mind the events which I had until now sought to forget—the whole train of my progress towards the creation; the appearance of the work of my own hands alive at my bed side; its departure. Two years had now nearly elapsed since the night on which he first received life; and was this his first crime? Alas! I had turned loose into the world a **depraved** wretch, whose delight was in carnage and misery; had he not murdered my brother?

No one can conceive the anguish I suffered during the remainder of the night, which I spent, cold and wet, in the open air. But I did not feel the inconvenience of the weather; my imagination was busy in scenes of evil and despair. I considered the being whom I had cast among mankind, and **endowed** with the will and power to effect purposes of horror, such as the deed which he had now done, nearly in the light of my own vampire, my own spirit let loose from the grave, and forced to destroy all that was dear to me.

Day dawned; and I directed my steps toward the town. The gates were open; and I hastened to my father's house. My first thought was to discover what I knew of the murderer, and cause instant pursuit to be made. But I paused when I reflected on the story that I had to tell. A being whom I myself had formed, and endued with life, had met me at midnight among the **precipices** of an inaccessible mountain. I remembered also the nervous fever with which I had been seized just at the time that I dated my creation, and which would give an air of delirium to a tale otherwise so utterly improbable. I well knew that if any other had communicated such a relation to me, I should have looked upon it as the ravings of insanity. Besides, the strange nature of the animal would **elude** all pursuit, even if I were so far credited as to persuade my relatives to commence it. Besides, of what use would be

RESOLVE (rih sahlv) *v.* **-ing,-ed.**
to determine or to make a firm decision about
Synonyms: solve, decide

INDELIBLE (ihn dehl uh buhl) *adj.*
permanent, not erasable
Synonyms: ineffaceable, inexpugnible, permanent

RUSTIC (ruh stihk) *adj.*
rural
Synonyms: bucolic, pastoral

INCONSOLABLE (ihn kuhn sohl uh buhl) *adj.*
unable to be comforted
Synonyms: despondent, disconsolate

CONSOLATION (kahn suh lay shuhn) *n.*
something providing comfort or solace for a loss or hardship
Synonyms: condolence, solace

pursuit? Who could arrest a creature capable of scaling the overhanging sides of Mont Saleve? These reflections determined me, and I **resolved** to remain silent.

It was about five in the morning when I entered my father's house. I told the servants not to disturb the family, and went into the library to attend their usual hour of rising.

Six years had elapsed, passed as a dream but for one **indelible** trace, and I stood in the same place where I had last embraced my father before my departure for Ingolstadt. Beloved and respectable parent he still remained to me. I gazed on the picture of my mother, which stood over the mantlepiece. It was an historical subject, painted at my father's desire, and represented Caroline Beaufort in an agony of despair, kneeling by the coffin of her dead father. Her garb was **rustic**, and her cheek pale; but there was an air of dignity and beauty, that hardly permitted the sentiment of pity. Below this picture was a miniature of William; and my tears flowed when I looked upon it. While I was thus engaged, Ernest entered. He had heard me arrive, and hastened to welcome me. He expressed a sorrowful delight to see me: "Welcome, my dearest Victor," said he. "Ah! I wish you had come three months ago, and then you would have found us all joyous and delighted. But we are now unhappy; and, I am afraid, tears instead of smiles will be your welcome. Our father looks so sorrowful—this dreadful event seems to have revived in his mind his grief on the death of Mamma. Poor Elizabeth also is quite **inconsolable**." Ernest began to weep as he said these words.

"Do not," said I, "welcome me thus; try to be more calm, that I may not be absolutely miserable the moment I enter my father's house after so long an absence. But, tell me, how does my father support his misfortunes? And how is my poor Elizabeth?"

"She indeed requires **consolation**; she accused herself of having caused the death of my brother, and that made

AMIABLE (ay mee uh buhl) *adj.*
friendly, pleasant, likable
Synonyms: affable, convivial, amicable, agreeable, genial

MAGISTRATE (maa juh strayt) *n.*
an official who can administrate laws
Synonyms: judge, arbiter, authority, marshal

DEPOSITION (deh puh zih shun) *n.*
a testimony under oath that has been written down
Synonyms: affidavit, attestation

her very wretched. But since the murderer has been discovered—"

"The murderer discovered! Good God! How can that be? Who could attempt to pursue him? It is impossible; one might as well try to overtake the winds, or confine a mountain-stream with a straw."

"I do not know what you mean; but we were all very unhappy when she was discovered. No one would believe it at first; and even now Elizabeth will not be convinced; notwithstanding all the evidence. Indeed, who would credit that Justine Moritz, who was so **amiable**, and fond of all the family, could all at once become so extremely wicked?"

"Justine Moritz! Poor, poor girl, is she the accused? But it is wrongfully; every one knows that; no one believes it, surely, Ernest?"

"No one did at first; but several circumstances came out, that have almost forced conviction upon us. And her own behaviour has been so confused, as to add to the evidence of facts a weight that, I fear, leaves no hope for doubt. But she will be tried to-day, and you will then hear all."

He related that, the morning on which the murder of poor William had been discovered, Justine had been taken ill, and confined to her bed; and, after several days, one of the servants, happening to examine the apparel she had worn on the night of the murder, had discovered in her pocket the picture of my mother, which had been judged to be the temptation of the murderer. The servant instantly showed it to one of the others, who, without saying a word to any of the family, went to a **magistrate**; and, upon their **deposition**, Justine was apprehended. On being charged with the fact, the poor girl confirmed the suspicion in a great measure by her extreme confusion of manner.

This was a strange tale, but it did not shake my faith; and I replied earnestly, "You are all mistaken; I know the murderer. Justine, poor, good Justine, is innocent."

COUNTENANCE (kown tuh nuhns) *n.*
appearance, facial expression
Synonyms: face, features, visage

DEPRAVITY (dih praav ih tee) *n.*
sinfulness, moral corruption
Synonyms: decadence, debauchery, corruption, degradation

PROGNOSTICATE (prahg nahs tih kayt) *v.* **-ing,-ed.**
to indicate in advance; to forecast
Synonyms: predict, foreshadow, portend

CAPACIOUS (kuh pay shuhs) *adj.*
large, roomy; extensive
Synonyms: ample, commodious

AFFLICTION (uh flihk shuhn) *n.*
severe distress; persistent anguish
Synonyms: hurt, adversity, hardship, plight, suffering

At that instant my father entered. I saw unhappiness deeply impressed on his **countenance**, but he endeavoured to welcome me cheerfully; and, after we had exchanged our mournful greeting, would have introduced some other topic than that of our disaster, had not Ernest exclaimed, "Good God, Papa! Victor says that he knows who was the murderer of poor William."

"We do also, unfortunately," replied my father, "for indeed I had rather have been forever ignorant than have discovered so much **depravity** and ingratitude in one I valued so highly."

"My dear father, you are mistaken; Justine is innocent."

"If she is, God forbid that she should suffer as guilty. She is to be tried to-day, and I hope, I sincerely hope, that she will be acquitted."

This speech calmed me. I was firmly convinced in my own mind that Justine, and indeed every human being, was guiltless of this murder. I had no fear, therefore, that any circumstantial evidence could be brought forward strong enough to convict her; and, in this assurance, I calmed myself, expecting the trial with eagerness, but without **prognosticating** an evil result.

We were soon joined by Elizabeth. Time had made great alterations in her form since I had last beheld her. Six years before she had been a pretty, good-humoured girl, whom every one loved and caressed. She was now a woman in stature and expression of **countenance**, which was uncommonly lovely. An open and **capacious** forehead gave indications of a good understanding, joined to great frankness of disposition. Her eyes were hazel, and expressive of mildness, now through recent **affliction** allied to sadness. Her hair was of a rich dark auburn, her complexion fair, and her figure slight and graceful. She welcomed me with the greatest affection. "Your arrival, my dear cousin," said she, "fills me with hope. You perhaps will find some means to justify my poor guiltless

INFAMY (ihn fuh mee) *n.*
reputation for bad deeds.
Synonyms: disgrace, dishonor, shame, ignominy

MERIT (mehr iht) *n.*
high quality or excellence
Synonyms: virtue, credit

Justine. Alas! Who is safe, if she be convicted of crime? I rely on her innocence as certainly as I do upon my own. Our misfortune is doubly hard to us; we have not only lost that lovely darling boy, but this poor girl, whom I sincerely love, is to be torn away by even a worse fate. If she is condemned, I never shall know joy more. But she will not, I am sure she will not; and then I shall be happy again, even after the sad death of my little William."

"She is innocent, my Elizabeth," said I, "and that shall be proved; fear nothing, but let your spirits be cheered by the assurance of her acquittal."

"How kind you are! Every one else believes in her guilt, and that made me wretched; for I knew that it was impossible. To see every one else prejudiced in so deadly a manner, rendered me hopeless and despairing." She wept.

"Sweet niece," said my father, "dry your tears. If she is, as you believe, innocent, rely on the justice of our judges, and the activity with which I shall prevent the slightest shadow of partiality."

CHAPTER VII

We passed a few sad hours, until eleven o'clock, when the trial was to commence. My father and the rest of the family being obliged to attend as witnesses, I accompanied them to the court. During the whole of this wretched mockery of justice, I suffered living torture. It was to be decided, whether the result of my curiosity and lawless devices would cause the death of two of my fellow-beings— onc a smiling babe, full of innocence and joy; the other far more dreadfully murdered, with every aggravation of **infamy** that could make the murder memorable in horror. Justine also was a girl of **merit**, and possessed qualities which promised to render her life

IGNOMINIOUS (ihg nuh mih nee uhs) *adj.*
disgraceful and dishonorable
Synonyms: despicable, degrading, debasing

EXCULPATE (ehk skuhl payt) (ihk skuhl payt) *v.* **-ing.-ed.**
to clear of blame or fault, vindicate
Synonyms: exonerate, acquit

COUNTENANCE (kown tuh nuhns) *n.*
appearance, facial expression
Synonyms: face, features, visage

SOLEMNITY (suh lehm nih tee) *n.*
dignified seriousness
Synonyms: ceremoniousness, formality, observance

EXECRATE (ehk sih krayt) *v.* **-ing,-ed.**
to curse, to declare to be evil
Synonyms: hate, abhor, loathe

CONSTRAIN (kuhn strayn) *v.* **-ing,-ed.**
to restrain or confine; to hold back
Synonyms: restrict, control, inhibit

ADDUCE (uh doos) (uh dyoos) *v.* **-ing,-ed.**
to lead to; to cite as proof
Synonyms: allege, further, propose, urge, promote

ATTEST (uh tehst) *v.* **-ing,-ed.**
to testify, stand as proof of, bear witness
Synonyms: corroborate, confirm, substantiate

ADVOCATE (aad vuh kiht) *n.*
a lawyer; one who urges or recommends
Synonyms: supporter, defender

happy; now all was to be obliterated in an **ignominious** grave; and I the cause! A thousand times rather would I have confessed myself guilty of the crime ascribed to Justine; but I was absent when it was committed, and such a declaration would have been considered as the ravings of a madman, and would not have **exculpated** her who suffered through me.

The appearance of Justine was calm. She was dressed in mourning; and her **countenance**, always engaging, was rendered, by the **solemnity** of her feelings, exquisitely beautiful. Yet she appeared confident in innocence, and did not tremble, although gazed on and **execrated** by thousands; for all the kindness which her beauty might otherwise have excited, was obliterated in the minds of the spectators by the imagination of the enormity she was supposed to have committed. She was tranquil, yet her tranquillity was evidently **constrained**; and as her confusion had before been **adduced** as a proof of her guilt, she worked up her mind to an appearance of courage. When she entered the court, she threw her eyes round it, and quickly discovered where we were seated. A tear seemed to dim her eye when she saw us; but she quickly recovered herself, and a look of sorrowful affection seemed to **attest** her utter guiltlessness.

The trial began; and after the **advocate** against her had stated the charge, several witnesses were called. Several strange facts combined against her, which might have staggered any one who had not such proof of her innocence as I had. She had been out the whole of the night on which the murder had been committed, and towards morning had been perceived by a market-woman not far from the spot where the body of the murdered child had been afterwards found. The woman asked her what she did there; but she looked very strangely, and only returned a confused and unintelligible answer. She returned to the house about eight o'clock; and when one inquired where she had passed the night, she replied, that

INDIGNATION (ihn dihg nay shun) *n.*
anger caused by something mean or unjust
Synonyms: fury, ire, wrath

COUNTENANCE (kown tuh nuhns) *n.*
appearance, facial expression
Synonyms: face, features, visage

AUDIBLE (aw dih buhl) *adj.*
capable of being heard
Synonyms: detectable, perceptible

ADDUCE (uh doos) (uh dyoos) *v.* **-ing,-ed.**
to lead to; to cite as proof
Synonyms: allege, further, propose, urge, promote

ASYLUM (uh sie luhm) *n.*
refuge, sanctuary
Synonyms: haven, shelter

she had been looking for the child, and demanded earnestly, if any thing had been heard concerning him. When shown the body, she fell into violent hysterics, and kept her bed for several days. The picture was then produced, which the servant had found in her pocket; and when Elizabeth, in a faltering voice, proved that it was the same which, an hour before the child had been missed, she had placed round his neck, a murmur of horror and **indignation** filled the court.

Justine was called on for her defence. As the trial had proceeded, her **countenance** had altered. Surprise, horror, and misery, were strongly expressed. Sometimes she struggled with her tears; but when she was desired to plead, she collected her powers, and spoke in an **audible** although variable voice:

"God knows," she said, "how entirely I am innocent. But I do not pretend that my protestations should acquit me. I rest my innocence on a plain and simple explanation of the facts which have been **adduced** against me; and I hope the character I have always borne will incline my judges to a favourable interpretation, where any circumstance appears doubtful or suspicious."

She then related that, by the permission of Elizabeth, she had passed the evening of the night on which the murder had been committed, at the house of an aunt at Chene, a village situated at about a league from Geneva. On her return, at about nine o'clock, she met a man, who asked her if she had seen any thing of the child who was lost. She was alarmed by this account, and passed several hours in looking for him, when the gates of Geneva were shut, and she was forced to remain several hours of the night in a barn belonging to a cottage, being unwilling to call up the inhabitants, to whom she was well known. Unable to rest or sleep, she quitted her **asylum** early, that she might again endeavour to find my brother. If she had gone near the spot where his body lay, it was without her knowledge. That she had been bewildered when

CONJECTURE (kuhn jehk shuhr) *v.* **-ing,-ed.**
infer, predict, guess
Synonyms: postulate, hypothesize, suppose, surmise

WANTONLY (wahn tuhn lee) *adv.*
without discipline, without restraint, recklessly
Synonyms: capriciously, lewdly, licentiously

TIMOROUS (tih muhr uhs) *adj.*
timid, shy, full of apprehension
Synonyms: fearful, anxious, frightened

IRREPROACHABLE (ih rih prohch uh buhl) *adj.*
faultless and exemplary; perfect
Synonyms: innocent, virtuous, good, impeccable

AGITATED (aa gih tay tihd) *adj.*
upset or uneasy
Synonyms: disturbed, flustered, bothered

questioned by the market-woman, was not surprising, since she had passed a sleepless night, and the fate of poor William was yet uncertain. Concerning the picture she could give no account.

"I know," continued the unhappy victim, "how heavily and fatally this one circumstance weighs against me, but I have no power of explaining it; and when I have expressed my utter ignorance, I am only left to **conjecture** concerning the probabilities by which it might have been placed in my pocket. But here also I am checked. I believe that I have no enemy on earth, and none surely would have been so wicked as to destroy me **wantonly**. Did the murderer place it there? I know of no opportunity afforded him for so doing; or if I had, why should he have stolen the jewel, to part with it again so soon?

"I commit my cause to the justice of my judges, yet I see no room for hope. I beg permission to have a few witnesses examined concerning my character; and if their testimony shall not overweigh my supposed guilt, I must be condemned, although I would pledge my salvation on my innocence."

Several witnesses were called, who had known her for many years, and they spoke well of her; but fear, and hatred of the crime of which they supposed her guilty, rendered them **timorous**, and unwilling to come forward. Elizabeth saw even this last resource, her excellent dispositions and **irreproachable** conduct, about to fail the accused, when, although violently **agitated**, she desired permission to address the court.

"I am," said she, "the cousin of the unhappy child who was murdered, or rather his sister, for I was educated by and have lived with his parents ever since and even long before his birth. It may therefore be judged indecent in me to come forward on this occasion; but when I see a fellow-creature about to perish through the cowardice of her pretended friends, I wish to be allowed to speak, that I may say what I know of her character. I am well

AMIABLE (ay mee uh buhl) *adj.*
friendly, pleasant, likable
Synonyms: affable, convivial, amicable, agreeable

BENEVOLENT (buh neh vuh luhnt) *adj.*
kind, compassionate
Synonyms: charitable, altruistic, beneficent, generous, good

TEDIOUS (tee dee uhs) *adj.*
tiresome because of length or dullness
Synonyms: dull, fatiguing, unexciting, wearisome

APPROBATION (aa pruh bay shuhn) *n.*
praise; official approval
Synonyms: acclaim, accolade, encomium, applause

INDIGNATION (ihn dihg nay shun) *n.*
anger caused by something mean or unjust
Synonyms: fury, ire, wrath

AGITATION (aa gih tay shuhn) *n.*
commotion, excitement; uneasiness
Synonyms: disturbance, restlessness, anxiety

IGNOMINY (ihg nuh mih nee) *n.*
disgrace, dishonor
Synonyms: reproach, shame, debasement

SUSTAIN (suh stayn) *v.* **-ing,-ed.**
to support, uphold; endure, undergo
Synonyms: maintain, prop, encourage, withstand, confirm

COUNTENANCE (kown tuh nuhns) *n.*
appearance, facial expression
Synonyms: face, features, visage

REMORSE (rih mohrs) *n.*
a gnawing distress arising from a sense of guilt
Synonyms: anguish, ruefulness, shame, penitence

acquainted with the accused. I have lived in the same house with her, at one time for five, and at another for nearly two years. During all that period she appeared to me the most **amiable** and **benevolent** of human creatures. She nursed Madame Frankenstein, my aunt, in her last illness with the greatest affection and care; and afterwards attended her own mother during a **tedious** illness, in a manner that excited the admiration of all who knew her. After which she again lived in my uncle's house, where she was beloved by all the family. She was warmly attached to the child who is now dead, and acted towards him like a most affectionate mother. For my own part, I do not hesitate to say, that, notwithstanding all the evidence produced against her, I believe and rely on her perfect innocence. She had no temptation for such an action. As to the bauble on which the chief proof rests, if she had earnestly desired it, I should have willingly given it to her; so much do I esteem and value her."

Excellent Elizabeth! A murmur of **approbation** was heard; but it was excited by her generous interference, and not in favour of poor Justine, on whom the public **indignation** was turned with renewed violence, charging her with the blackest ingratitude. She herself wept as Elizabeth spoke, but she did not answer. My own **agitation** and anguish was extreme during the whole trial. I believed in her innocence; I knew it. Could the daemon, who had (I did not for a minute doubt) murdered my brother, also in his hellish sport have betrayed the innocent to death and **ignominy**. I could not **sustain** the horror of my situation; and when I perceived that the popular voice, and the **countenances** of the judges, had already condemned my unhappy victim, I rushed out of the court in agony. The tortures of the accused did not equal mine; she was **sustained** by innocence, but the fangs of **remorse** tore my bosom, and would not forego their hold.

I passed a night of unmingled wretchedness. In the morning I went to the court; my lips and throat were

PARCHED (pahrchd) *adj.*
extremely thirsty; shriveled
Synonyms: dehydrated, desiccated, scorched

BESTOW (bih stoh) *v.* **-ing,-ed.**
to give as a gift
Synonyms: award, endow, donate, confer, present

BENEVOLENCE (buh neh vuh luhns) *n.*
kindness, compassion
Synonyms: charity, altruism, beneficence, generosity, goodness

parched. I dared not ask the fatal question; but I was known, and the officer guessed the cause of my visit. The ballots had been thrown; they were all black, and Justine was condemned.

I cannot pretend to describe what I then felt. I had before experienced sensations of horror; and I have endeavoured to **bestow** upon them adequate expressions, but words cannot convey an idea of the heart-sickening despair that I then endured. The person to whom I addressed myself added, that Justine had already confessed her guilt. "That evidence," he observed, "was hardly required in so glaring a case, but I am glad of it; and, indeed, none of our judges like to condemn a criminal upon circumstantial evidence, be it ever so decisive."

When I returned home, Elizabeth eagerly demanded the result.

"My cousin," replied I, "it is decided as you may have expected; all judges had rather that ten innocent should suffer, than that one guilty should escape. But she has confessed."

This was a dire blow to poor Elizabeth, who had relied with firmness upon Justine's innocence. "Alas!" said she, "how shall I ever again believe in human **benevolence**? Justine, whom I loved and esteemed as my sister, how could she put on those smiles of innocence only to betray; her mild eyes seemed incapable of any severity or ill-humour, and yet she has committed a murder."

Soon after we heard that the poor victim had expressed a wish to see my cousin. My father wished her not to go; but said, that he left it to her own judgment and feelings to decide. "Yes," said Elizabeth, "I will go, although she is guilty; and you, Victor, shall accompany me. I cannot go alone." The idea of this visit was torture to me, yet I could not refuse.

We entered the gloomy prison-chamber, and beheld Justine sitting on some straw at the further end; her

CONSOLATION (kahn suh lay shuhn) *n.*
something providing comfort or solace for a loss or hardship
Synonyms: condolence, solace

ABSOLUTION (aab suh loo shun) *n.*
forgiveness, redemption
Synonyms: acquittal, exculpation, exoneration

BESIEGE (bih seej) *v.* **-ing,-ed.**
to surround with armed forces; to press with requests; to cause worry or distress
Synonyms: attack, hound, trouble, bother

EXCOMMUNICATION (ehks kuh myoo nih kay shun) *n.*
to bar from membership in the church
Synonyms: exclusion, expulsion, censure

OBDURATE (ahb duhr uht) *adj.*
stubborn
Synonyms: inflexible, inexorable, adamant, impenitent, intractable

IGNOMINY (ihg nuh mih nee) *n.*
disgrace, dishonor
Synonyms: reproach, shame, debasement

PERDITION (puhr dih shuhn) *n.*
eternal damnation
Synonyms: suffering, anguish, wretchedness, hell

PERPETRATE (puhr peh trayt) *v.* **-ing,-ed.**
to bring about; to carry out
Synonyms: commit, act, do, perform

hands were manacled, and her head rested on her knees. She rose on seeing us enter; and when we were left alone with her, she threw herself at the feet of Elizabeth, weeping bitterly. My cousin wept also.

"Oh, Justine!" said she, "why did you rob me of my last **consolation**? I relied on your innocence; and although I was then very wretched, I was not so miserable as I am now."

"And do you also believe that I am so very, very wicked? Do you also join with my enemies to crush me?" Her voice was suffocated with sobs.

"Rise, my poor girl," said Elizabeth, "why do you kneel, if you are innocent? I am not one of your enemies; I believed you guiltless, notwithstanding every evidence, until I heard that you had yourself declared your guilt. That report, you say, is false; and be assured, dear Justine, that nothing can shake my confidence in you for a moment, but your own confession."

"I did confess; but I confessed a lie. I confessed, that I might obtain **absolution**; but now that falsehood lies heavier at my heart than all my other sins. The God of heaven forgive me! Ever since I was condemned, my confessor has **besieged** me; he threatened and menaced, until I almost began to think that I was the monster that he said I was. He threatened **excommunication** and hell fire in my last moments, if I continued **obdurate**. Dear lady, I had none to support me; all looked on me as a wretch doomed to **ignominy** and **perdition**. What could I do? In an evil hour I subscribed to a lie; and now only am I truly miserable."

She paused, weeping, and then continued—"I thought with horror, my sweet lady, that you should believe your Justine, whom your blessed aunt had so highly honoured, and whom you loved, was a creature capable of a crime which none but the devil himself could have **perpetrated**. Dear William! Dearest blessed child! I soon shall see you again in heaven, where we shall all be happy; and that

CONSOLE (kuhn sohl) *v.* **-ing,-ed.**
to alleviate grief and raise the spirits of, provide solace
Synonyms: relieve, comfort, soothe

IGNOMINY (ihg nuh mih nee) *n.*
disgrace, dishonor
Synonyms: reproach, shame, debasement

POIGNANT (poy nyaant) *adj.*
emotionally moving
Synonyms: stirring, touching, pathetic, affecting

CONSOLATION (kahn suh lay shuhn) *n.*
something providing comfort or solace for a loss or hardship
Synonyms: condolence, solace

EXECUTIONER (ek sih cyoo shuh nuhr) *n.*
a person who puts a condemned person to death
Synonyms: murderer, assassin, killer

SATIATE (say shee ayt) *v.* **-ing,-ed.**
to satisfy
Synonyms: sate, cloy, glut, gorge, surfeit

VISAGE (vih sihj) *n.*
the appearance of a person or place
Synonyms: expression, look, style, manner

ABHOR (uhb hohr) *v.* **-ing,-ed.**
to loathe, detest
Synonyms: hate, condemn, abominate, execrate, despise

LANGUIDLY (laang gwihd lee) *adv.*
without energy, indifferently, slowly
Synonyms: weakly, listlessly, lackadaisically, sluggishly

consoles me, going as I am to suffer **ignominy** and death."

"Oh, Justine! Forgive me for having for one moment distrusted you. Why did you confess? But do not mourn, my dear girl; I will every where proclaim your innocence, and force belief. Yet you must die; you, my playfellow, my companion, my more than sister. I never can survive so horrible a misfortune."

"Dear, sweet Elizabeth, do not weep. You ought to raise me with thoughts of a better life, and elevate me from the petty cares of this world of injustice and strife. Do not you, excellent friend, drive me to despair."

"I will try to comfort you; but this, I fear, is an evil too deep and **poignant** to admit of **consolation**, for there is no hope. Yet heaven bless thee, my dearest Justine, with resignation, and a confidence elevated beyond this world. Oh! How I hate its shows and mockeries! When one creature is murdered, another is immediately deprived of life in a slow torturing manner; then the **executioners**, their hands yet reeking with the blood of innocence, believe that they have done a great deed. They call this *retribution*. Hateful name! When that word is pronounced, I know greater and more horrid punishments are going to be inflicted than the gloomiest tyrant has ever invented to **satiate** his utmost revenge. Yet this is not **consolation** for you, my Justine, unless indeed that you may glory in escaping from so miserable a den. Alas! I would I were in peace with my aunt and my lovely William, escaped from a world which is hateful to me, and the **visages** of men which I **abhor**."

Justine smiled **languidly**. "This, dear lady, is despair, and not resignation. I must not learn the lesson that you would teach me. Talk of something else, something that will bring peace, and not increase of misery."

During this conversation I had retired to a corner of the prison-room, where I could conceal the horrid anguish that possessed me. Despair! Who dared talk of that? The poor victim, who on the morrow was to pass

CONSOLATION (kahn suh lay shuhn) *n.*
something providing comfort or solace for a loss or hardship
Synonyms: condolence, solace

TARNISH (tahr nihsh) *v.* **-ing,-ed.**
to corrode, discolor; discredit, disgrace
Synonyms: taint, sully, mar, soil, blacken

SUPPRESSED (suh prehsd) *adj.*
held back, restrained
Synonyms: subdued, stifled, muffled, quelled, curbed

the dreary boundary between life and death, felt not as I did, such deep and bitter agony. I gnashed my teeth, and ground them together, uttering a groan that came from my inmost soul. Justine started. When she saw who it was, she approached me, and said, "Dear Sir, you are very kind to visit me; you, I hope, do not believe that I am guilty."

I could not answer. "No, Justine," said Elizabeth, "he is more convinced of your innocence than I was; for even when he heard that you had confessed, he did not credit it."

"I truly thank him. In these last moments I feel the sincerest gratitude towards those who think of me with kindness. How sweet is the affection of others to such a wretch as I am! It removes more than half my misfortune; and I feel as if I could die in peace, now that my innocence is acknowledged by you, dear lady, and your cousin."

Thus the poor sufferer tried to comfort others and herself. She indeed gained the resignation she desired. But I, the true murderer, felt the never-dying worm alive in my bosom, which allowed of no hope or **consolation**. Elizabeth also wept, and was unhappy; but hers also was the misery of innocence, which, like a cloud that passes over the fair moon, for a while hides, but cannot **tarnish** its brightness. Anguish and despair had penetrated into the core of my heart; I bore a hell within me, which nothing could extinguish. We stayed several hours with Justine; and it was with great difficulty that Elizabeth could tear herself away. "I wish," cried she, "that I were to die with you; I cannot live in this world of misery."

Justine assumed an air of cheerfulness, while she with difficulty repressed her bitter tears. She embraced Elizabeth, and said, in a voice of half-**suppressed** emotion, "Farewell, sweet lady, dearest Elizabeth, my beloved and only friend; may heaven in its bounty bless and preserve you; may this be the last misfortune that you will

SUSTAIN (suh stayn) *v.* **-ing,-ed.**
to support, uphold; endure, undergo
Synonyms: maintain, prop, encourage, withstand, confirm

AMIABLE (ay mee uh buhl) *adj.*
friendly, pleasant, likable
Synonyms: affable, convivial, amicable, agreeable, genial

REPOSE (rih pohz) *v.* **-ing,-ed.**
1. to place (trust) or to count on
Synonyms: entrust, invest, place
2. to relax or rest; to lie dead
Synonyms: sleep, slumber

CONSOLE (kuhn sohl) *v.* **-ing,-ed.**
to alleviate grief and raise the spirits of, provide solace
Synonyms: relieve, comfort, soothe

ever suffer. Live, and be happy, and make others so."

As we returned, Elizabeth said, "You know not, my dear Victor, how much I am relieved, now that I trust in the innocence of this unfortunate girl. I never could again have known peace, if I had been deceived in my reliance on her. For the moment that I did believe her guilty, I felt an anguish that I could not have long **sustained**. Now my heart is lightened. The innocent suffers; but she whom I thought **amiable** and good has not betrayed the trust I **reposed** in her, and I am **consoled**."

Amiable cousin! Such were your thoughts, mild and gentle as your own dear eyes and voice. But I—I was a wretch, and none ever conceived of the misery that I then endured.

Volume II

REMORSE (rih mohrs) *n.*
a gnawing distress arising from a sense of guilt
Synonyms: anguish, ruefulness, shame, penitence

BENEVOLENT (buh neh vuh luhnt) *adj.*
kind, compassionate
Synonyms: charitable, altruistic, beneficent, generous, good

SERENITY (suh reh nih tee) *n.*
calmness, peace
Synonyms: tranquility, composure, contentment

SUSTAIN (suh stayn) *v.* **-ing,-ed.**
to support, uphold; endure, undergo
Synonyms: maintain, prop, encourage, withstand, confirm

COMPLACENCY (kuhm play sihn see) *n.*
self-satisfaction
Synonyms: contentment, peace of mind, serenity

CONSOLATION (kahn suh lay shuhn) *n.*
something providing comfort or solace for a loss or hardship
Synonyms: condolence, solace

CHAPTER I

Nothing is more painful to the human mind than, after the feelings have been worked up by a quick succession of events, the dead calmness of inaction and certainty which follows, and deprives the soul both of hope and fear. Justine died; she rested; and I was alive. The blood flowed freely in my veins, but a weight of despair and **remorse** pressed on my heart, which nothing could remove. Sleep fled from my eyes; I wandered like an evil spirit, for I had committed deeds of mischief beyond description horrible, and more, much more (I persuaded myself) was yet behind. Yet my heart overflowed with kindness and the love of virtue. I had begun life with **benevolent** intentions, and thirsted for the moment when I should put them in practice, and make myself useful to my fellow-beings. Now all was blasted; instead of that **serenity** of conscience, which allowed me to look back upon the past with self-satisfaction, and from thence to gather promise of new hopes, I was seized by **remorse** and the sense of guilt, which hurried me away to a hell of intense tortures, such as no language can describe.

This state of mind preyed upon my health, which had entirely recovered from the first shock it had **sustained**. I shunned the face of man; all sound of joy or **complacency** was torture to me; solitude was my only **consolation**—deep, dark, death-like solitude.

My father observed with pain the alteration perceptible in my disposition and habits, and endeavoured to reason with me on the folly of giving way to immoderate grief. "Do you think, Victor," said he, "that I do not suffer also? No one could love a child more than I loved

AUGMENT (awg <u>mehnt</u>) *v.* **-ing,-ed.**
to expand, extend
Synonyms: enhance, compound, increase, enlarge, inflate

CONSOLE (kuhn <u>sohl</u>) *v.* **-ing,-ed.**
to alleviate grief and raise the spirits of, provide solace
Synonyms: relieve, comfort, soothe

REMORSE (rih <u>mohrs</u>) *n.*
a gnawing distress arising from a sense of guilt
Synonyms: anguish, ruefulness, shame, penitence

RESTRAIN (rih <u>strayn</u>) *v.* **-ing,-ed.**
to controll, repress, restrict
Synonyms: hamper, bridle, curb, check

BASE (bays) *adj.*
lacking qualities of higher mind or spirit
Synonyms: vulgar, corrupt, immoral, menial

MALICE (<u>maal</u> ihs) *n.*
animosity, spite, hatred
Synonyms: malevolence, cruelty, enmity, rancor, hostility

your brother," (tears came into his eyes as he spoke) "but is it not a duty to the survivors, that we should refrain from **augmenting** their unhappiness by an appearance of immoderate grief? It is also a duty owed to yourself; for excessive sorrow prevents improvement or enjoyment, or even the discharge of daily usefulness, without which no man is fit for society."

This advice, although good, was totally inapplicable to my case; I should have been the first to hide my grief, and **console** my friends, if **remorse** had not mingled its bitterness with my other sensations. Now I could only answer my father with a look of despair, and endeavour to hide myself from his view.

About this time we retired to our house at Belrive. This change was particularly agreeable to me. The shutting of the gates regularly at ten o'clock, and the impossibility of remaining on the lake after that hour, had rendered our residence within the walls of Geneva very irksome to me. I was now free. Often, after the rest of the family had retired for the night, I took the boat, and passed many hours upon the water. Sometimes, with my sails set, I was carried by the wind; and sometimes, after rowing into the middle of the lake, I left the boat to pursue its own course, and gave way to my own miserable reflections. I was often tempted, when all was at peace around me, and I the only unquiet thing that wandered restless in a scene so beautiful and heavenly, if I except some bat, or the frogs, whose harsh and interrupted croaking was heard only when I approached the shore—often, I say, I was tempted to plunge into the silent lake, that the waters might close over me and my calamities for ever. But I was **restrained**, when I thought of the heroic and suffering Elizabeth, whom I tenderly loved, and whose existence was bound up in mine. I thought also of my father, and surviving brother. Should I by my **base** desertion leave them exposed and unprotected to the **malice** of the fiend whom I had let loose among them?

CONSOLATION (kahn suh lay shuhn) *n.*
something providing comfort or solace for a loss or hardship
Synonyms: condolence, solace

REMORSE (rih mohrs) *n.*
a gnawing distress arising from a sense of guilt
Synonyms: anguish, ruefulness, shame, penitence

PERPETRATE (puhr peh trayt) *v.* **-ing,-ed.**
to bring about; to carry out
Synonyms: commit, act, do, perform

OBSCURE (uhb skyoor) *adj.*
dim, unclear; not well known
Synonyms: dark, faint, remote, dim, minor

EFFACE (ih fays) (eh fays) *v.* **-ing,-ed.**
to erase or make indistinct
Synonyms: expunge, obliterate

ABHORRENCE (uhb hohr ehnts) *n.*
loathing, detestation
Synonyms: hatred, condemnation, abomination

ARDENTLY (ahr dihnt lee) *adv.*
passionately, enthusiastically, fervently
Synonyms: intensely, vehemently

BESTOW (bih stoh) *v.* **-ing,-ed.**
to give as a gift
Synonyms: award, endow, donate, confer, present

MALICE (maal ihs) *n.*
animosity, spite, hatred
Synonyms: malevolence, cruelty, enmity, rancor

PRECIPITATE (preh sih puh tayt) *v.* **-ing,-ed.**
to throw, usually from a great height
Synonyms: hurl, fall, rush

DESPONDING (dih spahn dihng) *adj.*
feeling discouraged and dejected
Synonyms: sad, depressed, desolate, dejected, forlorn

SACRILEGE (saak ruh lihj) *n.*
a technical violation of something, someone, or some place sacred
Synonyms: irreverence, crime, mockery, violation

At these moments I wept bitterly, and wished that peace would revisit my mind only that I might afford them **consolation** and happiness. But that could not be. **Remorse** extinguished every hope. I had been the author of unalterable evils, and I lived in daily fear, lest the monster whom I had created should **perpetrate** some new wickedness. I had an **obscure** feeling that all was not over, and that he would still commit some signal crime, which by its enormity should almost **efface** the recollection of the past. There was always scope for fear, so long as any thing I loved remained behind. My **abhorrence** of this fiend cannot be conceived. When I thought of him, I gnashed my teeth, my eyes became inflamed, and I **ardently** wished to extinguish that life which I had so thoughtlessly **bestowed**. When I reflected on his crimes and **malice**, my hatred and revenge burst all bounds of moderation. I would have made a pilgrimage to the highest peak of the Andes, could I, when there, have **precipitated** him to their base. I wished to see him again, that I might wreak the utmost extent of anger on his head, and avenge the deaths of William and Justine.

Our house was the house of mourning. My father's health was deeply shaken by the horror of the recent events. Elizabeth was sad and **desponding**; she no longer took delight in her ordinary occupations; all pleasure seemed to her **sacrilege** towards the dead; eternal woe and tears she then thought was the just tribute she should pay to innocence so blasted and destroyed. She was no longer that happy creature, who in earlier youth wandered with me on the banks of the lake, and talked with ecstacy of our future prospects. She had become grave, and often conversed of the inconstancy of fortune, and the instability of human life.

"When I reflect, my dear cousin," said she, "on the miserable death of Justine Moritz, I no longer see the world and its works as they before appeared to me. Before, I looked upon the accounts of vice and injustice,

DEPRAVED (dih prayvd) *adj.*
sinful, morally corrupt
Synonyms: decadent, hateful, evil

BENEFACTOR (behn uh faak tohr) *n.*
someone giving aid or money
Synonyms: contributor, backer, donor, patron

PRECIPICE (prehs ih pihs) *n.*
edge, steep overhang
Synonyms: crag, cliff, brink

DISCOURSE (dihs kohrs) *n.*
the verbal interchange of ideas; a formal, orderly, and extended expression of thought
Synonyms: dialogue, communication, oration

COUNTENANCE (kown tuh nuhns) *n.*
appearance, facial expression
Synonyms: face, features, visage

AFFECT (uh fekt) *v.* **-ing,-ed.**
1. to touch emotionally
Synonyms: move, inspire, stir, upset
2. to influence or cause a change in
Synonyms: change, alter, transform

that I read in books or heard from others, as tales of ancient days, or imaginary evils; at least they were remote, and more familiar to reason than to the imagination; but now misery has come home, and men appear to me as monsters thirsting for each other's blood. Yet I am certainly unjust. Every body believed that poor girl to be guilty; and if she could have committed the crime for which she suffered, assuredly she would have been the most **depraved** of human creatures. For the sake of a few jewels, to have murdered the son of her **benefactor** and friend, a child whom she had nursed from its birth, and appeared to love as if it had been her own! I could not consent to the death of any human being; but certainly I should have thought such a creature unfit to remain in the society of men. Yet she was innocent. I know, I feel she was innocent; you are of the same opinion, and that confirms me. Alas! Victor, when falsehood can look so like the truth, who can assure themselves of certain happiness? I feel as if I were walking on the edge of a **precipice**, towards which thousands are crowding, and endeavouring to plunge me into the abyss. William and Justine were assassinated, and the murderer escapes; he walks about the world free, and perhaps respected. But even if I were condemned to suffer on the scaffold for the same crimes, I would not change places with such a wretch."

I listened to this **discourse** with the extremest agony. I, not in deed, but in effect, was the true murderer. Elizabeth read my anguish in my **countenance**, and kindly taking my hand said, "My dearest cousin, you must calm yourself. These events have **affected** me, God knows how deeply; but I am not so wretched as you are. There is an expression of despair, and sometimes of revenge, in your **countenance**, that makes me tremble. Be calm, my dear Victor; I would sacrifice my life to your peace. We surely shall be happy—quiet in our native country, and not mingling in the world, what can disturb our tranquillity?"

SOLACE (sah lihs) *n.*
comfort in distress; consolation
Synonyms: succor, balm, cheer, condolence, assuagement

SERENITY (suh reh nuh tee) *n.*
calm, peacefulness
Synonyms: tranquility, equanimity, composure, sangfroid, contentment

INDUCE (ihn doos) (ihn dyoos) *v.* **-ing,-ed.**
to persuade; bring about
Synonyms: prevail, convince, lead, effect, occasion

SUBLIME (suh bliem) *adj.*
awe-inspiring; of high spiritual or moral value
Synonyms: noble, majestic, supreme, ideal

PRECIPICE (prehs ih pihs) *n.*
edge, steep overhang
Synonyms: crag, cliff, brink

ASCEND (uh sehnd) *v.* **-ing,-ed.**
to rise to another level or climb; move upward
Synonyms: elevate, escalate, hoist, lift, mount

IMPETUOUS (ihm peh choo uhs) (ihm pehch wuhs) *adj.*
quick to act without thinking
Synonyms: impulsive, passionate

She shed tears as she said this, distrusting the very **solace** that she gave; but at the same time she smiled, that she might chase away the fiend that lurked in my heart. My father, who saw in the unhappiness that was painted in my face only an exaggeration of that sorrow which I might naturally feel, thought that an amusement suited to my taste would be the best means of restoring to me my wonted **serenity**. It was from this cause that he had removed to the country; and, **induced** by the same motive, he now proposed that we should all make an excursion to the valley of Chamounix. I had been there before, but Elizabeth and Ernest never had; and both had often expressed an earnest desire to see the scenery of this place, which had been described to them as so wonderful and **sublime**. Accordingly we departed from Geneva on this tour about the middle of the month of August, nearly two months after the death of Justine.

The weather was uncommonly fine; and if mine had been a sorrow to be chased away by any fleeting circumstance, this excursion would certainly have had the effect intended by my father. As it was, I was somewhat interested in the scene; it sometimes lulled, although it could not extinguish my grief. During the first day we travelled in a carriage. In the morning we had seen the mountains at a distance, towards which we gradually advanced. We perceived that the valley through which we wound, and which was formed by the river Arve, whose course we followed, closed in upon us by degrees; and when the sun had set, we beheld immense mountains and **precipices** overhanging us on every side, and heard the sound of the river raging among rocks, and the dashing of waterfalls around.

The next day we pursued our journey upon mules; and as we **ascended** still higher, the valley assumed a more magnificent and astonishing character. Ruined castles hanging on the **precipices** of piny mountains; the **impetuous** Arve, and cottages every here and there peeping forth from among the trees, formed a scene of

AUGMENT (awg mehnt) *v.* **-ing,-ed.**
to expand, extend
Synonyms: enhance, compound, increase, enlarge, inflate

SUBLIME (suh bliem) *adj.*
awe-inspiring; of high spiritual or moral value
Synonyms: noble, majestic, supreme, ideal

ASCEND (uh sehnd) *v.* **-ing,-ed.**
to rise to another level or climb; move upward
Synonyms: elevate, escalate, hoist, lift, mount

INDULGE (ihn duhlj) *v.* **-ing,-ed.**
to give in to a craving or desire
Synonyms: humor, gratify, allow, pamper

PALLID (paa lihd) *adj.*
lacking color or liveliness
Synonyms: pale, wan, ashen, blanched, ghostly

singular beauty. But it was **augmented** and rendered **sublime** by the mighty Alps, whose white and shining pyramids and domes towered above all, as belonging to another earth, the habitations of another race of beings.

We passed the bridge of Pelissier, where the ravine, which the river forms, opened before us, and we began to **ascend** the mountain that overhangs it. Soon after we entered the valley of Chamounix. This valley is more wonderful and **sublime**, but not so beautiful and picturesque as that of Servox, through which we had just passed. The high and snowy mountains were its immediate boundaries; but we saw no more ruined castles and fertile fields. Immense glaciers approached the road; we heard the rumbling thunder of the falling avalanche, and marked the smoke of its passage. Mont Blanc, the supreme and magnificent Mont Blanc, raised itself from the surrounding aiguilles, and its tremendous dome overlooked the valley.

During this journey, I sometimes joined Elizabeth, and exerted myself to point out to her the various beauties of the scene. I often suffered my mule to lag behind, and **indulged** in the misery of reflection. At other times I spurred on the animal before my companions, that I might forget them, the world, and, more than all, myself. When at a distance, I alighted, and threw myself on the grass, weighed down by horror and despair. At eight in the evening I arrived at Chamounix. My father and Elizabeth were very much fatigued; Ernest, who accompanied us, was delighted, and in high spirits. The only circumstance that detracted from his pleasure was the south wind, and the rain it seemed to promise for the next day.

We retired early to our apartments, but not to sleep; at least I did not. I remained many hours at the window, watching the **pallid** lightning that played above Mont Blanc, and listening to the rushing of the Arve, which ran below my window.

PROGNOSTICATION (prahg nahs tih kay shuhn) *n.*
an indication in advance; the act of forecasting
Synonyms: omen, prophecy, forewarning

SUBLIME (suh bliem) *adj.*
awe-inspiring; of high spiritual or moral value
Synonyms: noble, majestic, supreme, ideal

CONSOLATION (kahn suh lay shuhn) *n.*
something providing comfort or solace for a loss or hardship
Synonyms: condolence, solace

DIVERT (die vuhrt) *v.* **-ing,-ed.**
to distract, to move in different directions from a particular point
Synonyms: deviate, separate

BROOD (brood) *v.* **-ing,-ed.**
to think gloomily about
Synonyms: incubate, cover, ponder, worry, obsess

DIFFUSE (dih fyooz) *v.* **-ing,-ed.**
to spread out widely
Synonyms: scatter, disperse

TORRENT (tawr rehnt) *n.*
a turbulent, fast-flowing stream
Synonyms: outpouring, deluge, flood

MELANCHOLY (mehl uhn kahl ee) *adj.*
sad, depressing
Synonyms: dejected, despondent, woeful, sorrowful

INURE (ihn yoor) *v.* **-ing,-ed.**
to harden; accustom; become used to
Synonyms: habituate, familiarize, condition

RESOLVE (rih sahlv) *v.* **-ing,-ed.**
to determine or to make a firm decision about
Synonyms: solve, decide

OBSCURE (uhb skyoor) *adj.*
dim, unclear; not well known
Synonyms: dark, faint, remote, dim, minor

SOLEMNIZE (sah luhm niez) *v.* **-ing,-ed.**
to perform with pomp or ceremony; to make solemn
Synonyms: commemorate, ceremonialize, extol

CHAPTER II

The next day, contrary to the **prognostications** of our guides, was fine, although clouded. We visited the source of the Arveiron, and rode about the valley until evening. These **sublime** and magnificent scenes afforded me the greatest **consolation** that I was capable of receiving. They elevated me from all littleness of feeling; and although they did not remove my grief, they subdued and tranquillized it. In some degree, also, they **diverted** my mind from the thoughts over which it had **brooded** for the last month. I returned in the evening, fatigued, but less unhappy, and conversed with my family with more cheerfulness than had been my custom for some time. My father was pleased, and Elizabeth overjoyed. "My dear cousin," said she, "you see what happiness you **diffuse** when you are happy; do not relapse again!"

The following morning the rain poured down in **torrents**, and thick mists hid the summits of the mountains. I rose early, but felt unusually **melancholy**. The rain depressed me; my old feelings recurred, and I was miserable. I knew how disappointed my father would be at this sudden change, and I wished to avoid him until I had recovered myself so far as to be enabled to conceal those feelings that overpowered me. I knew that they would remain that day at the inn; and as I had ever **inured** myself to rain, moisture, and cold, I **resolved** to go alone to the summit of Montanvert. I remembered the effect that the view of the tremendous and ever-moving glacier had produced upon my mind when I first saw it. It had then filled me with a **sublime** ecstacy that gave wings to the soul, and allowed it to soar from the **obscure** world to light and joy. The sight of the awful and majestic in nature had indeed always the effect of **solemnizing** my

ASCENT (uh sehnt) *n.*
upward slope; a climb or rising to another level; movement upward
Synonyms: elevation, incline, mounting

PRECIPITOUS (pree sih puh tuhs) *adj.*
extremely steep
Synonyms: inclined, headlong, reckless, abrupt

SURMOUNT (suhr mownt) *v.* **-ing,-ed.**
to conquer, overcome
Synonyms: clear, hurdle, leap, surpass, exceed

DESOLATE (deh soh liht) *adj.*
showing the effects of abandonment or neglect; devoid of warmth or comfort
Synonyms: barren, bleak, forsaken, vacant

ASCEND (uh sehnd) *v.* **-ing,-ed.**
to rise to another level or climb; move upward
Synonyms: elevate, escalate, hoist, lift, mount

LUXURIANT (luhg zhoor ee ehnt) *adj.*
elegant, lavish
Synonyms: rich, abundant, profuse

SOMBRE or **SOMBER** (sahm buhr) *adj.*
dark and gloomy; melancholy, dismal
Synonyms: serious, grave, mournful, lugubrious, funereal

MELANCHOLY (mehl uhn kahl ee) *adj.*
sad, depressing
Synonyms: dejected, despondent, woeful, sorrowful

mind, and causing me to forget the passing cares of life. I determined to go alone, for I was well acquainted with the path, and the presence of another would destroy the solitary grandeur of the scene.

The **ascent** is **precipitous**, but the path is cut into continual and short windings, which enable you to **surmount** the perpendicularity of the mountain. It is a scene terrifically **desolate**. In a thousand spots the traces of the winter avalanche may be perceived, where trees lie broken and strewed on the ground; some entirely destroyed, others bent, leaning upon the jutting rocks of the mountain, or transversely upon other trees. The path, as you **ascend** higher, is intersected by ravines of snow, down which stones continually roll from above; one of them is particularly dangerous, as the slightest sound, such as even speaking in a loud voice, produces a concussion of air sufficient to draw destruction upon the head of the speaker. The pines are not tall or **luxuriant**, but they are **sombre**, and add an air of severity to the scene. I looked on the valley beneath; vast mists were rising from the rivers which ran through it, and curling in thick wreaths around the opposite mountains, whose summits were hid in the uniform clouds, while rain poured from the dark sky, and added to the **melancholy** impression I received from the objects around me. Alas! Why does man boast of sensibilities superior to those apparent in the brute; it only renders them more necessary beings. If our impulses were confined to hunger, thirst, and desire, we might be nearly free; but now we are moved by every wind that blows, and a chance word or scene that that word may convey to us.

We rest; a dream has power to poison sleep.
We rise; one wand'ring thought pollutes the day.
We feel, conceive, or reason; laugh, or weep,
Embrace fond woe, or cast our cares away;
It is the same: for, be it joy or sorrow,

MUTABILITY (myoo tuh bihl uh tee) *n.*
changeability, inconsistency
Synonyms: inconstancy, impermanence

ASCENT (uh sehnt) *n.*
upward slope; a climb or rising to another level; movement upward
Synonyms: elevation, incline, mounting

DISSIPATE (dihs uh payt) *v.* **-ing,-ed.**
to scatter; to pursue pleasure to excess
Synonyms: carouse, squander, consume; disperse, dissolve

INTERSPERSE (ihn tuhr spuhrs) *v.* **-ing,-ed.**
to distribute among, mix with
Synonyms: commingle, intermix

AERIAL (ayr ee uhl) *adj.*
celestial, imaginary
Synonyms: dreamy, lofty, airy

ABHORRED (uhb hohr ehd) *adj.*
loathed, detested
Synonyms: hated, condemned, abominated, execrated, despised

The path of its departure still is free.
Man's yesterday may ne'er be like his morrow;
Nought may endure but ***mutability****!*

It was nearly noon when I arrived at the top of the **ascent**. For some time I sat upon the rock that overlooks the sea of ice. A mist covered both that and the surrounding mountains. Presently a breeze **dissipated** the cloud, and I descended upon the glacier. The surface is very uneven, rising like the waves of a troubled sea, descending low, and **interspersed** by rifts that sink deep. The field of ice is almost a league in width, but I spent nearly two hours in crossing it. The opposite mountain is a bare perpendicular rock. From the side where I now stood Montanvert was exactly opposite, at the distance of a league; and above it rose Mont Blanc, in awful majesty. I remained in a recess of the rock, gazing on this wonderful and stupendous scene. The sea, or rather the vast river of ice, wound among its dependent mountains, whose **aerial** summits hung over its recesses. Their icy and glittering peaks shone in the sunlight over the clouds. My heart, which was before sorrowful, now swelled with something like joy; I exclaimed, "Wandering spirits, if indeed ye wander, and do not rest in your narrow beds, allow me this faint happiness, or take me, as your companion, away from the joys of life."

As I said this, I suddenly beheld the figure of a man, at some distance, advancing towards me with superhuman speed. He bounded over the crevices in the ice, among which I had walked with caution; his stature also, as he approached, seemed to exceed that of man. I was troubled—a mist came over my eyes, and I felt a faintness seize me; but I was quickly restored by the cold gale of the mountains. I perceived, as the shape came nearer, (sight tremendous and **abhorred**!) that it was the wretch whom I had created. I trembled with rage and horror, resolving to wait his approach, and then close with him

COUNTENANCE (kown tuh nuhns) *n.* ***See page 156.***
DISDAIN (dihs dayn) *n.*
scorn and contempt
Synonyms: disrespect, disparagement
MALIGNITY (muh lihg nih tee) *n.*
evil or aggressive malice; something that produces death
Synonyms: malevolence, bitterness, resentment
DETESTATION (dee tehs tay shuhn) *n.*
intense and violent hatred
Synonyms: hate, disgust, loathing, abhorrence
CONTEMPT (kuhn tehmpt) *n.* ***See page 60.***
VENGEANCE (vehn juhns) *n.* ***See page 112.***
EXTINCTION (ihk stingk shuhn) *n.*
end of a living thing or species
Synonyms: extermination, eradication, annihilation
DIABOLICALLY (die uh bahl ih kuh lee) *adv.*
in the characteristic of the devil, devilishly
Synonyms: cruelly, heartlessly, ruthlessly, brutally
DETEST(dee tehst) (dih tehst) *v.* **-ing,-ed.**
to feel intense and violent hatred toward
Synonyms: hate, dislike, loathe
SPURN (spuhrn) *v.* **-ing,-ed.**
to reject or refuse contemptuously; scorn
Synonyms: disdain, snub, ostracize, ignore, cut
DISSOLUBLE (dih sahl yuh buhl) *adj.*
capable of being dissolved or disintegrated
Synonyms: dissolvable
COMPLY (kuhm plie) *v.* **-ing,-ed.** ***See page 56.***
GLUT (gluht) *v.* **-ing,-ed.**
eat and drink to excess
Synonyms: stuff, cram, gormandize
SATIATE (say shee ayt) *v.* **-ing,-ed.** ***See page 142.***
ABHORRED (uhb hohr ehd) *adj.* ***See page 166.***
REPROACH (rih prohch) *v.* **-ing,-ed.** ***See page 76.***
NEGLIGENTLY (nehg lih jehnt lee) *adv.*
carelessly, inattentively
Synonyms: indifferently, casually, offhandedly
BESTOW (bih stoh) *v.* **-ing,-ed.** ***See page 154.***
IMPEL (ihm pehl) *v.* **-ing,-ed.** ***See page 82.***
ELUDE (ih lood) *v.* **-ing,-ed.** ***See page 120.***
ENTREAT (ehn treet) *v.* **-ing,-ed.** ***See page 86.***

in mortal combat. He approached; his **countenance** bespoke bitter anguish, combined with **disdain** and **malignity**, while its unearthly ugliness rendered it almost too horrible for human eyes. But I scarcely observed this; anger and hatred had at first deprived me of utterance, and I recovered only to overwhelm him with words expressive of furious **detestation** and **contempt**.

"Devil!" I exclaimed. "Do you dare approach me? And do not you fear the fierce **vengeance** of my arm wreaked on your miserable head? Begone, vile insect! Or rather stay, that I may trample you to dust! And, oh, that I could, with the **extinction** of your miserable existence, restore those victims whom you have so **diabolically** murdered!"

"I expected this reception," said the daemon. "All men hate the wretched; how then must I be hated, who am miserable beyond all living things! Yet you, my creator, **detest** and **spurn** me, thy creature, to whom thou art bound by ties only **dissoluble** by the annihilation of one of us. You purpose to kill me. How dare you sport thus with life? Do your duty towards me, and I will do mine towards you and the rest of mankind. If you will **comply** with my conditions, I will leave them and you at peace; but if you refuse, I will **glut** the maw of death, until it be **satiated** with the blood of your remaining friends."

"**Abhorred** monster! Fiend that thou art! The tortures of hell are too mild a **vengeance** for thy crimes. Wretched devil! You **reproach** me with your creation; come on then, that I may extinguish the spark which I so **negligently bestowed**."

My rage was without bounds; I sprang on him, **impelled** by all the feelings which can arm one being against the existence of another.

He casily **eluded** me and said, "Be calm! I **entreat** you to hear me, before you give vent to your hatred on my devoted head. Have I not suffered enough, that you seek to increase my misery? Life, although it may only be an

SUPPLE (suh puhl) *adj.*
flexible, pliant
Synonyms: limber, elastic, lithe

DOCILE (dah suhl) (dah siel) *adj.*
tame, willing to be taught
Synonyms: domesticated, mild, tractable, obedient

EQUITABLE (eh kwih tuh buhl) *adj.*
exhibiting the quality of dealing fairly with everyone
Synonyms: impartial, fair, honest, unprejudiced

CLEMENCY (kleh muhn see) *n.*
merciful leniency
Synonyms: indulgence, pardon

IRREVOCABLY (ih rehv oh kuh blee) *adv.*
conclusively, irreversibly
Synonyms: permanently, indelibly, irreparably

BENEVOLENT (buh neh vuh luhnt) *adj.*
kind, compassionate
Synonyms: charitable, altruistic, beneficent, good

VIRTUOUS (vuhr choo ihs) *adj.*
good, worthy, moral
Synonyms: exemplary, admirable, dutiful, righteous

ENTREATY (ehn tree tee) *n.*
a plea or request
Synonyms: imploration, prayer, petition

IMPLORE (ihm plohr) *v.* **-ing,-ed.**
to call upon in supplication, beg
Synonyms: plead, entreat, solicit

ABHOR (uhb hohr) *v.* **-ing,-ed.**
to loathe, detest
Synonyms: hate, condemn, abominate, despise

SPURN (spuhrn) *v.* **-ing,-ed.**
to reject or refuse contemptuously; scorn
Synonyms: disdain, snub, ostracize, ignore, cut

MULTITUDE (muhl tuh tood) *n.* ***See page 114.***

RECOMPENSE (reh kuhm pehns) *v.* **-ing,-ed.**
to give something to as a means of compensation; to return in kind
Synonyms: compensate, repay, reimburse, return

accumulation of anguish, is dear to me, and I will defend it. Remember, thou hast made me more powerful than thyself; my height is superior to thine; my joints more **supple**. But I will not be tempted to set myself in opposition to thee. I am thy creature, and I will be even mild and **docile** to my natural lord and king, if thou wilt also perform thy part, that which thou owest me. Oh, Frankenstein, be not **equitable** to every other, and trample upon me alone, to whom thy justice, and even thy **clemency** and affection, is most due. Remember, that I am thy creature. I ought to be thy Adam; but I am rather the fallen angel, whom thou drivest from joy for no misdeed. Every where I see bliss, from which I alone am **irrevocably** excluded. I was **benevolent** and good; misery made me a fiend. Make me happy, and I shall again be **virtuous**."

"Begone! I will not hear you. There can be no community between you and me; we are enemies. Begone, or let us try our strength in a fight, in which one must fall."

"How can I move thee? Will no **entreaties** cause thee to turn a favourable eye upon thy creature, who **implores** thy goodness and compassion. Believe me, Frankenstein, I was **benevolent**. My soul glowed with love and humanity, but am I not alone, miserably alone? You, my creator, **abhor** me; what hope can I gather from your fellow-creatures, who owe me nothing? They **spurn** and hate me. The desert mountains and dreary glaciers are my refuge. I have wandered here many days; the caves of ice, which I only do not fear, are a dwelling to me, and the only one which man does not grudge. These bleak skies I hail, for they are kinder to me than your fellow-beings. If the **multitude** of mankind knew of my existence, they would do as you do, and arm themselves for my destruction. Shall I not then hate them who **abhor** me? I will keep no terms with my enemies. I am miserable, and they shall share my wretchedness. Yet it is in your power to **recompense** me, and deliver them from an evil which it

DISDAIN (dihs dayn) *v.* **-ing,-ed.**
to scorn; to reject as inferior
Synonyms: disrespect, disparage, despise, condemn

ABHORRED (uhb hohr ehd) *adj.*
loathed, detested
Synonyms: hated, condemned, abominated, despised

DETESTED (dee tehst ehd) (dih tehst ehd) *adj.*
intensely and violently hated
Synonyms: hated, disliked, loathed

ABHOR (uhb hohr) *v.* **-ing,-ed.**
to loathe, detest
Synonyms: hate, contemn, abominate, execrate, despise

PRECIPICE (prehs ih pihs) *n.*
edge, steep overhang
Synonyms: crag, cliff, brink

only remains for you to make so great, that not only you and your family, but thousands of others, shall be swallowed up in the whirlwinds of its rage. Let your compassion be moved, and do not **disdain** me. Listen to my tale; when you have heard that, abandon or commiserate me, as you shall judge that I deserve. But hear me. The guilty are allowed, by human laws, bloody as they may be, to speak in their own defence before they are condemned. Listen to me, Frankenstein. You accuse me of murder; and yet you would, with a satisfied conscience, destroy your own creature. Oh, praise the eternal justice of man! Yet I ask you not to spare me. Listen to me; and then, if you can, and if you will, destroy the work of your hands."

"Why do you call to my remembrance circumstances of which I shudder to reflect, that I have been the miserable origin and author? Cursed be the day, **abhorred** devil, in which you first saw light! Cursed (although I curse myself) be the hands that formed you! You have made me wretched beyond expression. You have left me no power to consider whether I am just to you, or not. Begone! Relieve me from the sight of your **detested** form."

"Thus I relieve thee, my creator," he said, and placed his hated hands before my eyes, which I flung from me with violence. "Thus I take from thee a sight which you **abhor**. Still thou canst listen to me, and grant me thy compassion. By the virtues that I once possessed, I demand this from you. Hear my tale; it is long and strange, and the temperature of this place is not fitting to your fine sensations; come to the hut upon the mountain. The sun is yet high in the heavens; before it descends to hide itself behind yon snowy **precipices**, and illuminate another world, you will have heard my story and can decide. On you it rests, whether I quit for ever the neighbourhood of man, and lead a harmless life, or become the scourge of your fellow-creatures and the author of your own speedy ruin."

RESOLUTION (reh suh <u>loo</u> shuhn) *n.*
a firm decision
Synonyms: determination, will, explanation

COMPLY (kuhm <u>plie</u>) *v.* **-ing,-ed.**
to yield or agree, to go along with
Synonyms: accord, submit, acquiesce, obey, respect

ASCEND (uh <u>sehnd</u>) *v.* **-ing,-ed.**
to rise to another level or climb; move upward
Synonyms: elevate, escalate, hoist, lift, mount

EXULTATION (ihg suhl <u>tay</u> shuhn) *n.*
the act of being extremely joyful
Synonyms: celebration, delight, jubilation

ODIOUS (<u>oh</u> dee uhs) *adj.*
hateful, contemptible
Synonyms: detestable, obnoxious, offensive, repellent, loathsome

MULTIPLICITY (muhl tuh <u>plih</u> suh tee) *n.*
the state of being various; a great number
Synonyms: variance, multitude, diversity

OPAQUE (oh <u>payk</u>) *adj.*
impervious to light; difficult to understand
Synonyms: impenetrable, obscure, dense

IMPERVIOUS (ihm <u>puhr</u> vee uhs) *adj.*
impossible to penetrate; incapable of being affected
Synonyms: immune, callous

As he said this, he led the way across the ice; I followed. My heart was full, and I did not answer him; but, as I proceeded, I weighed the various arguments that he had used, and determined at least to listen to his tale. I was partly urged by curiosity, and compassion confirmed my **resolution**. I had hitherto supposed him to be the murderer of my brother, and I eagerly sought a confirmation or denial of this opinion. For the first time, also, I felt what the duties of a creator towards his creature were, and that I ought to render him happy before I complained of his wickedness. These motives urged me to **comply** with his demand. We crossed the ice, therefore, and **ascended** the opposite rock. The air was cold, and the rain again began to descend. We entered the hut, the fiend with an air of **exultation**, I with a heavy heart, and depressed spirits. But I consented to listen; and, seating myself by the fire which my **odious** companion had lighted, he thus began his tale.

CHAPTER III

"It is with considerable difficulty that I remember the original era of my being; all the events of that period appear confused and indistinct. A strange **multiplicity** of sensations seized me, and I saw, felt, heard, and smelt, at the same time; and it was, indeed, a long time before I learned to distinguish between the operations of my various senses. By degrees, I remember, a stronger light pressed upon my nerves, so that I was obliged to shut my eyes. Darkness then came over me, and troubled me; but hardly had I felt this, when, by opening my eyes, as I now suppose, the light poured in upon me again. I walked, and, I believe, descended; but I presently found a great alteration in my sensations. Before, dark and **opaque** bodies had surrounded me, **impervious** to my touch or

SURMOUNT (suhr mownt) *v.* **-ing,-ed.**
to conquer, overcome
Synonyms: clear, hurdle, leap, surpass, exceed

DORMANT (dohr muhnt) *adj.*
at rest, inactive, in suspended animation
Synonyms: quiescent, potential, latent

DESOLATE (deh soh liht) *adj.*
showing the effects of abandonment or neglect; devoid of warmth or comfort
Synonyms: barren, bleak, forsaken, vacant

INNUMERABLE (ih noo muhr uh buhl) (ih nyoo muhr uh buhl) *adj.*
too many to be counted
Synonyms: incalculable, immeasurable, infinite, inestimable

sight; but I now found that I could wander on at liberty, with no obstacles, which I could not either **surmount** or avoid. The light became more and more oppressive to me; and, the heat wearying me as I walked, I sought a place where I could receive shade. This was the forest near Ingolstadt; and here I lay by the side of a brook resting from my fatigue, until I felt tormented by hunger and thirst. This roused me from my nearly **dormant** state, and I ate some berries which I found hanging on the trees or lying on the ground. I slaked my thirst at the brook, and then lying down, was overcome by sleep.

"It was dark when I awoke; I felt cold also, and half-frightened as it were instinctively, finding myself so **desolate**. Before I had quitted your apartment, on a sensation of cold, I had covered myself with some clothes; but these were insufficient to secure me from the dews of night. I was a poor, helpless, miserable wretch; I knew, and could distinguish, nothing; but, feeling pain invade me on all sides, I sat down and wept.

"Soon a gentle light stole over the heavens, and gave me a sensation of pleasure. I started up, and beheld a radiant form rise from among the trees. I gazed with a kind of wonder. It moved slowly, but it enlightened my path; and I again went out in search of berries. I was still cold, when under one of the trees I found a huge cloak, with which I covered myself, and sat down upon the ground. No distinct ideas occupied my mind; all was confused. I felt light, and hunger, and thirst, and darkness; **innumerable** sounds rung in my ears, and on all sides various scents saluted me. The only object that I could distinguish was the bright moon, and I fixed my eyes on that with pleasure.

"Several changes of day and night passed, and the orb of night had greatly lessened when I began to distinguish my sensations from each other. I gradually saw plainly the clear stream that supplied me with drink and the trees that shaded me with their foliage. I was delighted when I

UNCOUTH (uhn kooth) *adj.*
lacking in refinement; awkward and uncultivated in appearance or manner
Synonyms: clumsy, ungraceful, crude, unrefined

INARTICULATE (ihn ahr tih kyoo liht) *adj.*
unable to speak clearly, incomprehensible
Synonym: unintelligible

first discovered that a pleasant sound, which often saluted my ears, proceeded from the throats of the little winged animals who had often intercepted the light from my eyes. I began also to observe, with greater accuracy, the forms that surrounded me, and to perceive the boundaries of the radiant roof of light which canopied me. Sometimes I tried to imitate the pleasant songs of the birds, but was unable. Sometimes I wished to express my sensations in my own mode, but the **uncouth** and **inarticulate** sounds which broke from me frightened me into silence again.

"The moon had disappeared from the night, and again, with a lessened form, showed itself, while I still remained in the forest. My sensations had, by this time, become distinct, and my mind received every day additional ideas. My eyes became accustomed to the light, and perceived objects in their right forms; I distinguished the insect from the herb, and, by degrees, one herb from another. I found that the sparrow uttered none but harsh notes, whilst those of the blackbird and thrush were sweet and enticing.

"One day, when I was oppressed by cold, I found a fire which had been left by some wandering beggars, and was overcome with delight at the warmth I experienced from it. In my joy I thrust my hand into the live embers, but quickly drew it out again with a cry of pain. How strange, I thought, that the same cause should produce such opposite effects! I examined the materials of the fire, and to my joy found it to be composed of wood. I quickly collected some branches, but they were wet and would not burn. I was pained at this, and sat still watching the operation of the fire. The wet wood which I had placed near the heat dried, and itself became inflamed. I reflected on this; and, by touching the various branches, I discovered the cause, and busied myself in collecting a great quantity of wood, that I might dry it, and have a plentiful supply of fire. When night came on, and

CONTRIVE (kuhn triev) *v.* **-ing,-ed.**
to devise, plan, or manage; to form in an artistic manner
Synonyms: concoct, create, scheme, design

SAVOURY or SAVORY (say vuhr ee) *adj.*
agreeable in taste or smell
Synonyms: appetizing, pungent, piquant, delectable, succulent

ASSUAGE (uh swayj) (uh swayzh) (uh swahzh) *v.* **-ing,-ed.**
to make less severe; to ease, relieve
Synonyms: mitigate, alleviate, ease, appease, mollify

RESOLVE (rih sahlv) *v.* **-ing,-ed.**
to determine or to make a firm decision about
Synonyms: solve, decide

LAMENT (luh mehnt) *v.* **-ing,-ed.**
to deplore, grieve
Synonyms: mourn, sorrow, regret, bewail

RELINQUISH (rih lihn kwihsh) *v.* **-ing,-ed.**
to renounce or surrender something
Synonyms: yield, resign, abandon, cede, waive

DISCONSOLATE (dihs kahn soh liht) *adj.*
hopelessly sad, forlorn
Synonyms: dismal, inconsolable, comfortless

brought sleep with it, I was in the greatest fear lest my fire should be extinguished. I covered it carefully with dry wood and leaves, and placed wet branches upon it; and then, spreading my cloak, I lay on the ground, and sunk into sleep.

"It was morning when I awoke, and my first care was to visit the fire. I uncovered it, and a gentle breeze quickly fanned it into a flame. I observed this also, and **contrived** a fan of branches, which roused the embers when they were nearly extinguished. When night came again, I found, with pleasure, that the fire gave light as well as heat, and that the discovery of this element was useful to me in my food; for I found some of the offals that the travellers had left had been roasted, and tasted much more **savoury** than the berries I gathered from the trees. I tried, therefore, to dress my food in the same manner, placing it on the live embers. I found that the berries were spoiled by this operation, and the nuts and roots much improved.

"Food, however, became scarce, and I often spent the whole day searching in vain for a few acorns to **assuage** the pangs of hunger. When I found this, I **resolved** to quit the place that I had hitherto inhabited, to seek for one where the few wants I experienced would be more easily satisfied. In this emigration, I exceedingly **lamented** the loss of the fire which I had obtained through accident, and knew not how to re-produce it. I gave several hours to the serious consideration of this difficulty; but I was obliged to **relinquish** all attempts to supply it; and, wrapping myself up in my cloak, I struck across the wood towards the setting sun. I passed three days in these rambles, and at length discovered the open country. A great fall of snow had taken place the night before, and the fields were of one uniform white; the appearance was **disconsolate**, and I found my feet chilled by the cold damp substance that covered the ground.

"It was about seven in the morning, and I longed to

DEBILITATED (dih bih lih tay tihd) *adj.*
weakened, feeble
Synonyms: devitalized, enervated, exhausted, drained

ALLURE (uh lohr) *v.* **-ing,-ed.**
to entice by charm; attract
Synonyms: lure, entice, draw, captivate

obtain food and shelter; at length I perceived a small hut, on a rising ground, which had doubtless been built for the convenience of some shepherd. This was a new sight to me; and I examined the structure with great curiosity. Finding the door open, I entered. An old man sat in it, near a fire, over which he was preparing his breakfast. He turned on hearing a noise, and perceiving me, shrieked loudly and, quitting the hut, ran across the fields with a speed of which his **debilitated** form hardly appeared capable. His appearance, different from any I had ever before seen, and his flight, somewhat surprised me. But I was enchanted by the appearance of the hut. Here the snow and rain could not penetrate; the ground was dry; and it presented to me then as exquisite and divine a retreat as Pandaemonium appeared to the daemons of hell after their sufferings in the lake of fire. I greedily devoured the remnants of the shepherd's breakfast, which consisted of bread, cheese, milk, and wine; the latter, however, I did not like. Then overcome by fatigue, I lay down among some straw and fell asleep.

"It was noon when I awoke; and, **allured** by the warmth of the sun, which shone brightly on the white ground, I determined to recommence my travels; and, depositing the remains of the peasant's breakfast in a wallet I found, I proceeded across the fields for several hours, until at sunset I arrived at a village. How miraculous did this appear! The huts, the neater cottages, and stately houses, engaged my admiration by turns. The vegetables in the gardens, the milk and cheese that I saw placed at the windows of some of the cottages, **allured** my appetite. One of the best of these I entered; but I had hardly placed my foot within the door, before the children shrieked, and one of the women fainted. The whole village was roused; some fled, some attacked me, until, grievously bruised by stones and many other kinds of missile weapons, I escaped to the open country, and fearfully took refuge in a low hovel, quite bare, and making a

ASYLUM (uh sie luhm) *n.*
refuge, sanctuary
Synonyms: haven, shelter

INCLEMENCY (ihn kleh muhn see) *n.*
storminess; unmercifulness, lack of lenience
Synonyms: intolerance, severity

BARBARITY (bahr baa rih tee) *n.*
lack of culture or refinement; merciless cruelty
Synonyms: savagery, vulgarity, inhumanity

ADJACENT (uh jay suhnt) *adj.*
next to, close
Synonyms: neighboring, adjoining, abutting, bordering

SUSTENANCE (suh steh nehns) *n.*
means of living, souce of nourishment
Synonyms: food, provisions, necessities

PURLOIN (puhr loyn) *v.* **-ing,-ed.**
to steal
Synonyms: filch, pilfer, embezzle, misappropriate, pirate

RESOLVE (rih sahlv) *v.* **-ing,-ed.**
to determine or to make a firm decision about
Synonyms: solve, decide

wretched appearance after the palaces I had beheld in the village. This hovel, however, joined a cottage of a neat and pleasant appearance; but, after my late dearly-bought experience, I dared not enter it. My place of refuge was constructed of wood, but so low, that I could with difficulty sit upright in it. No wood, however, was placed on the earth, which formed the floor, but it was dry; and although the wind entered it by innumerable chinks, I found it an agreeable **asylum** from the snow and rain.

"Here then I retreated, and lay down, happy to have found a shelter, however miserable, from the **inclemency** of the season, and still more from the **barbarity** of man.

"As soon as morning dawned, I crept from my kennel, that I might view the **adjacent** cottage and discover if I could remain in the habitation I had found. It was situated against the back of the cottage, and surrounded on the sides, which were exposed by a pig-stye and a clear pool of water. One part was open, and by that I had crept in; but now I covered every crevice by which I might be perceived with stones and wood, yet in such a manner that I might move them on occasion to pass out. All the light I enjoyed came through the stye, and that was sufficient for me.

"Having thus arranged my dwelling, and carpeted it with clean straw, I retired; for I saw the figure of a man at a distance, and I remembered too well my treatment the night before, to trust myself in his power. I had first, however, provided for my **sustenance** for that day with a loaf of coarse bread, which I **purloined**, and a cup with which I could drink, more conveniently than from my hand, of the pure water which flowed by my retreat. The floor was a little raised, so that it was kept perfectly dry, and by its vicinity to the chimney of the cottage it was tolerably warm.

"Being thus provided, I **resolved** to reside in this hovel, until something should occur which might alter my

PROCURE (proh kyoor) *v.* **-ing,-ed.**
to obtain
Synonyms: acquire, secure, get, gain

COUNTENANCE (kown tuh nuhns) *n.*
appearance, facial expression
Synonyms: face, features, visage

DESPONDENCE (dih spahn duhnts) *n.*
discouragement and dejection
Synonyms: sadness, depression, desolation, forlornness

MELANCHOLY (mehl uhn kahl ee) *n.*
sadness, gloom
Synonyms: depression, despondence, woe, sorrow

DISCONSOLATE (dihs kahn soh liht) *adj.*
hopelessly sad, forlorn
Synonyms: dismal, inconsolable, comfortless

determination. It was indeed a paradise, compared to the bleak forest, my former residence, the raindropping branches, and dank earth. I ate my breakfast with pleasure, and was about to remove a plank to **procure** myself a little water, when I heard a step, and, looking through a small chink, I beheld a young creature, with a pail on her head, passing before my hovel. The girl was young and of gentle demeanour, unlike what I have since found cottagers and farm-house servants to be. Yet she was meanly dressed, a coarse blue petticoat and a linen jacket being her only garb; her fair hair was plaited, but not adorned; she looked patient, yet sad. I lost sight of her; and in about a quarter of an hour she returned, bearing the pail, which was now partly filled with milk. As she walked along, seemingly incommoded by the burden, a young man met her, whose **countenance** expressed a deeper **despondence**. Uttering a few sounds with an air of **melancholy**, he took the pail from her head, and bore it to the cottage himself. She followed, and they disappeared. Presently I saw the young man again, with some tools in his hand, cross the field behind the cottage; and the girl was also busied, sometimes in the house, and sometimes in the yard.

"On examining my dwelling, I found that one of the windows of the cottage had formerly occupied a part of it, but the panes had been filled up with wood. In one of these was a small and almost imperceptible chink, through which the eye could just penetrate. Through this crevice, a small room was visible, white-washed and clean, but very bare of furniture. In one corner, near a small fire, sat an old man, leaning his head on his hands in a **disconsolate** attitude. The young girl was occupied in arranging the cottage; but presently she took something out of a drawer, which employed her hands, and she sat down beside the old man, who, taking up an instrument, began to play, and to produce sounds sweeter than the voice of the thrush or the nightingale. It was a lovely

BENEVOLENT (buh neh vuh luhnt) *adj.*
kind, compassionate
Synonyms: charitable, altruistic, beneficent, generous, good

COUNTENANCE (kown tuh nuhns) *n.*
appearance, facial expression
Synonyms: face, features, visage

REVERENCE (rehv uhr ehnts) *n.*
a feeling of great awe and respect
Synonyms: veneration, adoration, idolization, admiration

AMIABLE (ay mee uh buhl) *adj.*
friendly, pleasant, likable
Synonyms: affable, convivial, amicable, agreeable, genial

PENSIVE (pehn sihv) *adj.*
thoughtful
Synonyms: contemplative, reflective, meditative

sight, even to me, poor wretch, who had never beheld aught beautiful before. The silver hair and **benevolent countenance** of the aged cottager won my **reverence**; while the gentle manners of the girl enticed my love. He played a sweet mournful air, which I perceived drew tears from the eyes of his **amiable** companion, of which the old man took no notice, until she sobbed audibly; he then pronounced a few sounds, and the fair creature, leaving her work, knelt at his feet. He raised her, and smiled with such kindness and affection, that I felt sensations of a peculiar and overpowering nature; they were a mixture of pain and pleasure, such as I had never before experienced, either from hunger or cold, warmth or food; and I withdrew from the window, unable to bear these emotions.

"Soon after this the young man returned, bearing on his shoulders a load of wood. The girl met him at the door, helped to relieve him of his burden, and, taking some of the fuel into the cottage, placed it on the fire; then she and the youth went apart into a nook of the cottage, and he showed her a large loaf and a piece of cheese. She seemed pleased and went into the garden for some roots and plants, which she placed in water, and then upon the fire. She afterwards continued her work, whilst the young man went into the garden, and appeared busily employed in digging and pulling up roots. After he had been employed thus about an hour, the young woman joined him, and they entered the cottage together.

"The old man had, in the mean time, been **pensive**; but, on the appearance of his companions, he assumed a more cheerful air, and they sat down to eat. The meal was quickly dispatched. The young woman was again occupied in arranging the cottage; the old man walked before the cottage in the sun for a few minutes, leaning on the arm of the youth. Nothing could exceed in beauty the contrast between these two excellent creatures. One was

COUNTENANCE (kown tuh nuhns) *n.*
appearance, facial expression
Synonyms: face, features, visage

BENEVOLENCE (buh neh vuh luhnts) *n.*
kindness, compassion
Synonyms: charity, altruism, generosity

DESPONDENCY (dih spahn duhn see) *n.*
discouragement and dejection
Synonyms: sadness, depression, desolation, forlornness

MONOTONOUS (muh nah tuh nihs) *adj.*
repetitive, unvaried
Synonyms: recurrent, tedious, boring, dull

CONJECTURE (kuhn jehk shuhr) *v.* **-ing,-ed.**
to infer, predict, guess
Synonyms: postulate, hypothesize, suppose, surmise

BARBAROUS (baar buh ruhs) *adj.*
lacking culture or refinement; mercilessly cruel
Synonyms: savage, vulgar, inhumane

RESOLVE (rih sahlv) *v.* **-ing,-ed.**
to determine or to make a firm decision about
Synonyms: solve, decide

old, with silver hairs and a **countenance** beaming with **benevolence** and love; the younger was slight and graceful in his figure, and his features were moulded with the finest symmetry; yet his eyes and attitude expressed the utmost sadness and **despondency**. The old man returned to the cottage; and the youth, with tools different from those he had used in the morning, directed his steps across the fields.

"Night quickly shut in; but, to my extreme wonder, I found that the cottagers had a means of prolonging light, by the use of tapers, and was delighted to find that the setting of the sun did not put an end to the pleasure I experienced in watching my human neighbours. In the evening, the young girl and her companion were employed in various occupations which I did not understand; and the old man again took up the instrument, which produced the divine sounds that had enchanted me in the morning. So soon as he had finished, the youth began, not to play, but to utter sounds that were **monotonous**, and neither resembling the harmony of the old man's instrument or the songs of the birds; I since found that he read aloud, but at that time I knew nothing of the science of words or letters.

"The family, after having been thus occupied for a short time, extinguished their lights, and retired, as I **conjectured**, to rest.

CHAPTER IV

"I lay on my straw, but I could not sleep. I thought of the occurrences of the day. What chiefly struck me was the gentle manners of these people; and I longed to join them, but dared not. I remembered too well the treatment I had suffered the night before from the **barbarous** villagers, and **resolved**, whatever course of conduct I

VENERABLE (veh nehr uh buhl) *adj.*
respected because of age
Synonyms: respectable, distinguished, elderly

BENEVOLENT (buh neh vuh luhnt) *adj.*
kind, compassionate.
Synonyms: charitable, altruistic, beneficent, generous, good

AFFECT (uh fekt) *v.* **-ing,-ed.**
1. to touch emotionally
Synonyms: move, inspire, stir, upset
2. to influence or cause a change in
Synonyms: change, alter, transform

PERPETUAL (puhr peht chyoo uhl) *adj.*
endless, lasting
Synonyms: continuous, constant, ceaseless, eternal, perennial

ENIGMATIC (eh nihg mah tihk) *adj.*
puzzling, inexplicable
Synonyms: mysterious, cryptic, baffling

AMIABLE (ay mee uh buhl) *adj.*
friendly, pleasant, likable
Synonyms: affable, convivial, amicable, agreeable, genial

might hereafter think it right to pursue, that for the present I would remain quietly in my hovel, watching, and endeavouring to discover the motives which influenced their actions.

"The cottagers arose the next morning before the sun. The young woman arranged the cottage, and prepared the food; and the youth departed after the first meal.

"This day was passed in the same routine as that which preceded it. The young man was constantly employed out of doors, and the girl in various laborious occupations within. The old man, whom I soon perceived to be blind, employed his leisure hours on his instrument, or in contemplation. Nothing could exceed the love and respect which the younger cottagers exhibited towards their **venerable** companion. They performed towards him every little office of affection and duty with gentleness; and he rewarded them with his **benevolent** smiles.

"They were not entirely happy. The young man and his companion often went apart, and appeared to weep. I saw no cause for their unhappiness; but I was deeply **affected** by it. If such lovely creatures were miserable, it was less strange that I, an imperfect and solitary being, should be wretched. Yet why were these gentle beings unhappy? They possessed a delightful house (for such it was in my eyes), and every luxury; they had a fire to warm them when chill, and delicious viands when hungry; they were dressed in excellent clothes; and, still more, they enjoyed one another's company and speech, interchanging each day looks of affection and kindness. What did their tears imply? Did they really express pain? I was at first unable to solve these questions; but **perpetual** attention, and time, explained to me many appearances which were at first **enigmatic**.

"A considerable period elapsed before I discovered one of the causes of the uneasiness of this **amiable** family; it was poverty; and they suffered that evil in a very distressing degree. Their nourishment consisted entirely of the

PROCURE (proh kyoor) *v.* **-ing,-ed.**
to obtain
Synonyms: acquire, secure, get, gain

POIGNANTLY (poy nyaant lee) *adv.*
intensely
Synonyms: profoundly, deeply, sharply, keenly

ABSTAIN (uhb stayn) *v.* **-ing,-ed.**
not partaking in some activity or action
Synonyms: forbear, refrain

ARTICULATE (ahr tih kyoo liht) *adj.*
well spoken, expressing oneself clearly
Synonyms: eloquent, persuasive

COUNTENANCE (kown tuh nuhns) *n.*
appearance, facial expression
Synonyms: face, features, visage

ARDENTLY (ahr dihnt lee) *adv.*
passionately, enthusiastically, fervently
Synonyms: intensely, vehemently

vegetables of their garden, and the milk of one cow, who gave very little during the winter, when its masters could scarcely **procure** food to support it. They often, I believe, suffered the pangs of hunger very **poignantly**, especially the two younger cottagers; for several times they placed food before the old man, when they reserved none for themselves.

"This trait of kindness moved me sensibly. I had been accustomed, during the night, to steal a part of their store for my own consumption; but when I found that in doing this I inflicted pain on the cottagers, I **abstained**, and satisfied myself with berries, nuts, and roots, which I gathered from a neighbouring wood.

"I discovered also another means through which I was enabled to assist their labours. I found that the youth spent a great part of each day in collecting wood for the family fire; and, during the night, I often took his tools, the use of which I quickly discovered, and brought home firing sufficient for the consumption of several days.

"I remember, the first time that I did this, the young woman, when she opened the door in the morning, appeared greatly astonished on seeing a great pile of wood on the outside. She uttered some words in a loud voice, and the youth joined her, who also expressed surprise. I observed, with pleasure, that he did not go to the forest that day, but spent it in repairing the cottage, and cultivating the garden.

"By degrees I made a discovery of still greater moment. I found that these people possessed a method of communicating their experience and feelings to one another by **articulate** sounds. I perceived that the words they spoke sometimes produced pleasure or pain, smiles or sadness, in the minds and **countenances** of the hearers. This was indeed a godlike science, and I **ardently** desired to become acquainted with it. But I was baffled in every attempt I made for this purpose. Their pronunciation was quick; and the words they uttered, not having any

DISCOURSE (dihs kohrs) *n.*
the verbal interchange of ideas; a formal, orderly, and extended expression of thought
Synonyms: dialogue, communication, oration

APPROPRIATE (uh proh pree ayt) *v.* **-ing,-ed.**
to set aside or assign for a particular purpose; to take possession of
Synonyms: usurp, arrogate, commandeer

ENHANCE (ehn haans) *v.* **-ing,-ed.**
to improve, bring to a greater level of intensity
Synonyms: heighten, intensify, amplify, improve

MELANCHOLY (mehl uhn kahl ee) *n.*
sadness, gloom
Synonyms: depression, despondence, woe, sorrow

BESTOW (bih stoh) *v.* **-ing,-ed.**
to give as a gift
Synonyms: award, endow, donate, confer, present

COUNTENANCE (kown tuh nuhns) *n.*
appearance, facial expression
Synonyms: face, features, visage

EXHORTATION (ihg zohr tay shun) *n.*
urging or incitement by strong appeals
Synonyms: persuasion, proposal, provocation, inspiration

apparent connection with visible objects, I was unable to discover any clue by which I could unravel the mystery of their reference. By great application, however, and after having remained during the space of several revolutions of the moon in my hovel, I discovered the names that were given to some of the most familiar objects of **discourse**; I learned and applied the words *fire, milk, bread*, and *wood.* I learned also the names of the cottagers themselves. The youth and his companion had each of them several names, but the old man had only one, which was *father*. The girl was called *sister*, or *Agatha*; and the youth *Felix, brother*, or *son*. I cannot describe the delight I felt when I learned the ideas **appropriated** to each of these sounds, and was able to pronounce them. I distinguished several other words, without being able as yet to understand or apply them; such as *good, dearest, unhappy*.

"I spent the winter in this manner. The gentle manners and beauty of the cottagers greatly endeared them to me; when they were unhappy, I felt depressed; when they rejoiced, I sympathized in their joys. I saw few human beings beside them; and if any other happened to enter the cottage, their harsh manners and rude gait only **enhanced** to me the superior accomplishments of my friends. The old man, I could perceive, often endeavoured to encourage his children, as sometimes I found that he called them, to cast off their **melancholy**. He would talk in a cheerful accent, with an expression of goodness that **bestowed** pleasure even upon me. Agatha listened with respect, her eyes sometimes filled with tears, which she endeavoured to wipe away unperceived; but I generally found that her **countenance** and tone were more cheerful after having listened to the **exhortations** of her father. It was not thus with Felix. He was always the saddest of the group; and, even to my unpractised senses, he appeared to have suffered more deeply than his friends. But if his **countenance** was more sorrowful, his voice was more

INNUMERABLE (ih noo muhr uh buhl)
(ih nyoo muhr uh buhl) *adj.*
too many to be counted
Synonyms: incalculable, immeasurable, infinite, inestimable

AMIABLE (ay mee uh buhl) *adj.*
friendly, pleasant, likable
Synonyms: affable, convivial, amicable, agreeable, genial

PERPETUAL (puhr peht chyoo uhl) *adj.*
endless, lasting
Synonyms: continuous, constant, ceaseless, eternal, perennial

CONJECTURE (kuhn jehk shuhr) *v.* **-ing,-ed.**
to infer, predict, guess
Synonyms: postulate, hypothesize, suppose, surmise

ARDENTLY (ahr dihnt lee) *adv.*
passionately, enthusiastically, fervently
Synonyms: intensely, vehemently

DEFORMITY (dih fohr mih tee) *n.*
disfigurement, the state of being misshapen
Synonyms: contortion, malformation, disproportion

PERPETUALLY (puhr peht chyoo uh lee) *adv.*
endlessly, always
Synonyms: continuously, constantly, eternally, perennially

cheerful than that of his sister, especially when he addressed the old man.

"I could mention **innumerable** instances, which, although slight, marked the dispositions of these **amiable** cottagers. In the midst of poverty and want, Felix carried with pleasure to his sister the first little white flower that peeped out from beneath the snowy ground. Early in the morning before she had risen, he cleared away the snow that obstructed her path to the milk-house, drew water from the well, and brought the wood from the outhouse, where, to his **perpetual** astonishment, he found his store always replenished by an invisible hand. In the day, I believe, he worked sometimes for a neighbouring farmer, because he often went forth, and did not return until dinner, yet brought no wood with him. At other times he worked in the garden; but, as there was little to do in the frosty season, he read to the old man and Agatha.

"This reading had puzzled me extremely at first; but, by degrees, I discovered that he uttered many of the same sounds when he read as when he talked. I **conjectured**, therefore, that he found on the paper signs for speech which he understood, and I **ardently** longed to comprehend these also; but how was that possible, when I did not even understand the sounds for which they stood as signs? I improved, however, sensibly in this science, but not sufficiently to follow up any kind of conversation, although I applied my whole mind to the endeavour. For I easily perceived that, although I eagerly longed to discover myself to the cottagers, I ought not to make the attempt until I had first become master of their language; which knowledge might enable me to make them overlook the **deformity** of my figure; for with this also the contrast **perpetually** presented to my eyes had made me acquainted.

"I had admired the perfect forms of my cottagers—their grace, beauty, and delicate complexions, but how was I terrified, when I viewed myself in a transparent

DESPONDENCE (dih spahn duhnts) *n.*
discouragement and dejection
Synonyms: sadness, depression, desolation, forlornness

DEFORMITY (dih fohr mih tee) *n.*
disfigurement, the state of being misshapen
Synonyms: contortion, malformation, disproportion

IMPENDING (ihm pehn dihng) *adj.*
hovering threateningly; about to occur, approaching
Synonyms: looming, ominous, forthcoming

PROCURE (proh kyoor) *v.* **-ing,-ed.**
to obtain
Synonyms: acquire, secure, get, gain

UNIFORM (yoo nuh fohrm) *adj.*
consistent and unchanging; identical
Synonyms: unvarying, steady, even, homogeneous, constant

pool! At first I started back, unable to believe that it was indeed I who was reflected in the mirror; and when I became fully convinced that I was in reality the monster that I am, I was filled with the bitterest sensations of **despondence** and mortification. Alas! I did not yet entirely know the fatal effects of this miserable **deformity**.

"As the sun became warmer, and the light of day longer, the snow vanished, and I beheld the bare trees and the black earth. From this time Felix was more employed; and the heart-moving indications of **impending** famine disappeared. Their food, as I afterwards found, was coarse, but it was wholesome; and they **procured** a sufficiency of it. Several new kinds of plants sprung up in the garden, which they dressed; and these signs of comfort increased daily as the season advanced.

"The old man, leaning on his son, walked each day at noon, when it did not rain, as I found it was called when the heavens poured forth its waters. This frequently took place; but a high wind quickly dried the earth, and the season became far more pleasant than it had been.

"My mode of life in my hovel was **uniform**. During the morning I attended the motions of the cottagers, and when they were dispersed in various occupations, I slept. The remainder of the day was spent in observing my friends. When they had retired to rest, if there was any moon, or the night was star-light, I went into the woods, and collected my own food and fuel for the cottage. When I returned, as often as it was necessary, I cleared their path from the snow, and performed those offices that I had seen done by Felix. I afterwards found that these labours, performed by an invisible hand, greatly astonished them; and once or twice I heard them, on these occasions, utter the words *good spirit* and *wonderful*; but I did not then understand the signification of these terms.

"My thoughts now became more active, and I longed to discover the motives and feelings of these lovely

VENERABLE (veh nehr uh buhl) *adj.*
respected because of age
Synonyms: respectable, distinguished, elderly

ARBITER (ahr bih tihr) *n.*
one who decides or holds the power
Synonyms: judge, mediator

CONCILIATING (kuhn sih lee ayt ing) *adj.*
becoming agreeable, appeasing
Synonyms: diplomatic, friendly, generous

EXHILARATE (ihg zihl uh rayt) *v.* **-ing,-ed.**
to fill with happiness; to invigorate
Synonyms: elate, delight, energize, gladden

ARDOUR or ARDOR (ahr duhr) *n.*
passion, enthusiasm
Synonyms: intensity, vehemence

SUPPLE (suh puhl) *adj.*
flexible, pliant
Synonyms: limber, elastic, lithe

EXECRATION (ehk sih kray shun) *n.*
utter detestation; the act of cursing
Synonyms: hatred, denouncement, loathing, abhorence

GENIAL (jeen yuhl) (jee nee uhl) *adj.*
favorable to growth or comfort; displaying or characterized by genius
Synonyms: good-natured, favorable, cordial, warm

DISPERSE (dihs puhrs) *v.* **-ing,-ed.**
to break up, scatter
Synonyms: dissipate, disintegrate, dispel

creatures; I was inquisitive to know why Felix appeared so miserable, and Agatha so sad. I thought (foolish wretch!) that it might be in my power to restore happiness to these deserving people. When I slept, or was absent, the forms of the **venerable** blind father, the gentle Agatha, and the excellent Felix, flitted before me. I looked upon them as superior beings, who would be the **arbiters** of my future destiny. I formed in my imagination a thousand pictures of presenting myself to them, and their reception of me. I imagined that they would be disgusted, until, by my gentle demeanour and **conciliating** words, I should first win their favour, and afterwards their love.

"These thoughts **exhilarated** me, and led me to apply with fresh **ardour** to acquiring the art of language. My organs were indeed harsh, but **supple**; and although my voice was very unlike the soft music of their tones, yet I pronounced such words as I understood with tolerable ease. It was as the ass and the lap-dog; yet surely the gentle ass, whose intentions were affectionate, although his manners were rude, deserved better treatment than blows and **execration**.

"The pleasant showers and **genial** warmth of spring greatly altered the aspect of the earth. Men, who before this change seemed to have been hid in caves, **dispersed** themselves, and were employed in various arts of cultivation. The birds sang in more cheerful notes, and the leaves began to bud forth on the trees. Happy, happy earth! Fit habitation for gods, which, so short a time before, was bleak, damp, and unwholesome. My spirits were elevated by the enchanting appearance of nature; the past was blotted from my memory, the present was tranquil, and the future gilded by bright rays of hope, and anticipations of joy.

VERDURE (vuhr juhr) *n.*
lush vegetation
Synonyms: grass, greenery, growth

COUNTENANCE (kown tuh nuhns) *n.*
appearance, facial expression
Synonyms: face, features, visage

MELANCHOLY (mehl uhn kahl ee) *adj.*
sad, depressed
Synonyms: dejected, despondent, woeful, sorrowful

CONJECTURE (kuhn jehk shuhr) *v.* **-ing,-ed.**
to infer, predict, guess
Synonyms: postulate, hypothesize, suppose, surmise

ANIMATED (aa nih may tihd) *adj.*
1. lively, excited; filled with spirit
Synonyms: elated, vivacious, spirited, inspired
2. having life, alive
Synonyms: vital, moving, alert, functioning

TINGE (tihnj) *v.* **-ing,-ed.**
to affect or modify in character; to color with a slight shade, stain, odor, or taste
Synonyms: infuse, tint

RAVISH (raa vihsh) *v.* **-ing,-ed.**
to overcome with emotion; to seize and take away through violence
Synonyms: enchant, captivate, enthrall; assault

CHAPTER V

"I now hasten to the more moving part of my story. I shall relate events that impressed me with feelings which, from what I was, have made me what I am.

"Spring advanced rapidly; the weather became fine, and the skies cloudless. It surprised me, that what before was desert and gloomy should now bloom with the most beautiful flowers and **verdure**. My senses were gratified and refreshed by a thousand scents of delight, and a thousand sights of beauty.

"It was on one of these days, when my cottagers periodically rested from labour—the old man played on his guitar, and the children listened to him—I observed that the **countenance** of Felix was **melancholy** beyond expression; he sighed frequently; and once his father paused in his music, and I **conjectured** by his manner that he inquired the cause of his son's sorrow. Felix replied in a cheerful accent, and the old man was recommencing his music, when some one tapped at the door.

"It was a lady on horseback, accompanied by a countryman as a guide. The lady was dressed in a dark suit, and covered with a thick black veil. Agatha asked a question; to which the stranger only replied by pronouncing, in a sweet accent, the name of Felix. Her voice was musical, but unlike that of either of my friends. On hearing this word, Felix came up hastily to the lady; who, when she saw him, threw up her veil, and I beheld a **countenance** of angelic beauty and expression. Her hair of a shining raven black, and curiously braided; her eyes were dark, but gentle, although **animated**; her features of a regular proportion, and her complexion wondrously fair, each cheek **tinged** with a lovely pink.

"Felix seemed **ravished** with delight when he saw her,

ECSTATIC (ehk staa tihk) (ihk staa tihk) *adj.*
joyful
Synonyms: blissful, rapturous, delighted, exultant, jubilant

AFFECT (uh fekt) *v.* **-ing,-ed.**
1. to touch emotionally
Synonyms: move, inspire, stir, upset
2. to influence or cause a change in
Synonyms: change, alter, transform

RAPTUROUSLY (raap chuhr uhs lee) *adv.*
with extreme joy or ecstasy
Synonyms: blissfully, delightfully

ARTICULATE (ahr tih kyoo liht) *adj.*
well spoken, expressing oneself clearly
Synonyms: eloquent, persuasive

DIFFUSE (dih fyooz) *v.* **-ing,-ed.**
to spread out widely
Synonyms: scatter, disperse

DISPEL (dihs pehl) *v.* **-ing,-ed.**
to drive out or scatter
Synonyms: disband, disperse

DISSIPATE (dihs uh payt) *v.* **-ing,-ed.**
to scatter; to pursue pleasure to excess
Synonyms: carouse, squander, consume; disperse, dissolve

COUNTENANCE (kown tuh nuhns) *n.*
appearance, facial expression
Synonyms: face, features, visage

every trait of sorrow vanished from his face, and it instantly expressed a degree of **ecstatic** joy, of which I could hardly have believed it capable; his eyes sparkled, as his cheek flushed with pleasure; and at that moment I thought him as beautiful as the stranger. She appeared **affected** by different feelings; wiping a few tears from her lovely eyes, she held out her hand to Felix, who kissed it **rapturously**, and called her, as well as I could distinguish, his sweet Arabian. She did not appear to understand him, but smiled. He assisted her to dismount, and, dismissing her guide, conducted her into the cottage. Some conversation took place between him and his father; and the young stranger knelt at the old man's feet, and would have kissed his hand, but he raised her, and embraced her affectionately.

"I soon perceived, that although the stranger uttered **articulate** sounds, and appeared to have a language of her own, she was neither understood by, or herself understood, the cottagers. They made many signs which I did not comprehend; but I saw that her presence **diffused** gladness through the cottage, **dispelling** their sorrow as the sun **dissipates** the morning mists. Felix seemed peculiarly happy, and with smiles of delight welcomed his Arabian. Agatha, the ever-gentle Agatha, kissed the hands of the lovely stranger; and, pointing to her brother, made signs which appeared to me to mean that he had been sorrowful until she came. Some hours passed thus, while they, by their **countenance**s, expressed joy, the cause of which I did not comprehend. Presently I found, by the frequent recurrence of one sound which the stranger repeated after them, that she was endeavouring to learn their language; and the idea instantly occurred to me, that I should make use of the same instructions to the same end. The stranger learned about twenty words at the first lesson, most of them indeed were those which I had before understood, but I profited by the others.

"As night came on, Agatha and the Arabian retired

CONJECTURE (kuhn <u>jehk</u> shuhr) *v.* **-ing,-ed.**
to infer, predict, guess
Synonyms: postulate, hypothesize, suppose, surmise

ARDENTLY (<u>ahr</u> dihnt lee) *adv.*
passionately, enthusiastically, fervently
Synonyms: intensely, vehemently

FACULTY (<u>faa</u> kuhl tee) *n.*
the ability to act or do
Synonyms: aptitude, capability, sense, skill

ENRAPTURED (ehn <u>raap</u> chuhrd) *adj.*
captivated, enchanted, enslaved
Synonyms: bewitched, fascinated, enthralled, transfixed, mesmerized

BESTOW (bih <u>stoh</u>) *v.* **-ing,-ed.**
to give as a gift
Synonyms: award, endow, donate, confer, present

COUNTENANCE (<u>kown</u> tuh nuhns) *n.*
appearance, facial expression
Synonyms: face, features, visage

INTERSPERSE (ihn tuhr <u>spuhrs</u>) *v.* **-ing,-ed.**
to distribute among, mix with
Synonyms: commingle, intermix

INNUMERABLE (ih <u>noo</u> muhr uh buhl) (ih <u>nyoo</u> muhr uh buhl) *adj.*
too many to be counted
Synonyms: incalculable, immeasurable, infinite

BALMY (<u>bah</u> mee) *adj.*
mild and pleasant; soothing
Synonyms: temperate, refreshing, warm

NOCTURNAL (nok <u>tuhr</u> nuhl) *adj.*
pertaining to night; active at night
Synonyms: nightly, night-time

early. When they separated, Felix kissed the hand of the stranger, and said, 'Good night, sweet Safie.' He sat up much longer, conversing with his father; and, by the frequent repetition of her name, I **conjectured** that their lovely guest was the subject of their conversation. I **ardently** desired to understand them, and bent every **faculty** towards that purpose, but found it utterly impossible.

"The next morning Felix went out to his work; and, after the usual occupations of Agatha were finished, the Arabian sat at the feet of the old man, and, taking his guitar, played some airs so entrancingly beautiful, that they at once drew tears of sorrow and delight from my eyes. She sang, and her voice flowed in a rich cadence, swelling or dying away, like a nightingale of the woods.

"When she had finished, she gave the guitar to Agatha, who at first declined it. She played a simple air, and her voice accompanied it in sweet accents, but unlike the wondrous strain of the stranger. The old man appeared **enraptured**, and said some words, which Agatha endeavoured to explain to Safie, and by which he appeared to wish to express that she **bestowed** on him the greatest delight by her music.

"The days now passed as peaceably as before, with the sole alteration, that joy had taken place of sadness in the **countenances** of my friends. Safie was always gay and happy; she and I improved rapidly in the knowledge of language, so that in two months I began to comprehend most of the words uttered by my protectors.

"In the meanwhile the black ground was covered with herbage, and the green banks **interspersed** with **innumerable** flowers, sweet to the scent and the eyes, stars of pale radiance among the moonlight woods; the sun became warmer, the nights clear and **balmy**; and my **nocturnal** rambles were an extreme pleasure to me, although they were considerably shortened by the late setting and early rising of the sun; for I never ventured

PURPORT (puhr pohrt) *n.*
intention or purpose
Synonyms: importance, meaning

DECLAMATORY (dih klaa muh tohr ee) *adj.*
pretentiously rhetorical
Synonyms: pompous, verbose, ostentatious

CURSORY (kuhr suh ree) *adj.*
hastily done, superficial
Synonyms: shallow, careless

SLOTHFUL (slawth fuhl) *adj.*
sluggish, lazy
Synonyms: indolent, idle

DEGENERATION (dih jeh nuh ray shuhn) *n.*
intellectual, moral, or artistic decline; a progressive deterioration of physical condition
Synonyms: disintegration, downfall

CHIVALRY (shih vuhl ree) *n.*
the qualities of an ideal knight: honor, courtesy, and generosity
Synonyms: valor, courtesy, gallantry

BASE (bays) *adj.*
lacking qualities of higher mind or spirit
Synonyms: vulgar, corrupt, immoral, menial

abroad during day-light, fearful of meeting with the same treatment as I had formerly endured in the first village which I entered.

"My days were spent in close attention, that I might more speedily master the language; and I may boast that I improved more rapidly than the Arabian, who understood very little, and conversed in broken accents, whilst I comprehended and could imitate almost every word that was spoken.

"While I improved in speech, I also learned the science of letters, as it was taught to the stranger; and this opened before me a wide field for wonder and delight.

"The book from which Felix instructed Safie was Volney's *Ruins of Empires*. I should not have understood the **purport** of this book, had not Felix, in reading it, given very minute explanations. He had chosen this work, he said, because the **declamatory** style was framed in imitation of the eastern authors. Through this work I obtained a **cursory** knowledge of history, and a view of the several empires at present existing in the world; it gave me an insight into the manners, governments, and religions of the different nations of the earth. I heard of the **slothful** Asiatics; of the stupendous genius and mental activity of the Grecians; of the wars and wonderful virtue of the early Romans—of their subsequent **degeneration**—of the decline of that mighty empire; of **chivalry**, Christianity, and kings. I heard of the discovery of the American hemisphere, and wept with Safie over the hapless fate of its original inhabitants.

"These wonderful narrations inspired me with strange feelings. Was man, indeed, at once so powerful, so virtuous, and magnificent, yet so vicious and **base**? He appeared at one time a mere scion of the evil principle, and at another as all that can be conceived of noble and godlike. To be a great and virtuous man appeared the highest honour that can befall a sensitive being; to be **base** and vicious, as many on record have been, appeared

DEGRADATION (day greh day shuhn) *n.*
the act of falling in rank or status; the act of losing moral or intellectual character
Synonyms: abasement, demotion, disgrace, shame

ABJECT (aab jehkt) *adj.*
miserable, pitiful
Synonyms: pathetic, lamentable, sorry

LOATHING (lohth ing) *n.*
hatred or great dislike
Synonyms: detestation, abhorrence

BESTOW (bih stoh) *v.* **-ing,-ed.** ***See page 208.***

SQUALID (skwa lihd) *adj.*
filthy; morally repulsive
Synonyms: dirty, foul, nasty, wretched, sordid

INDUCE (ihn doos) (ihn dyoos) *v.* **-ing,-ed.**
to persuade; bring about
Synonyms: prevail, convince, lead, effect, occasion

UNSULLIED (uhn suh leed) *adj.*
unsoiled, unstained
Synonyms: clean, untarnished, untainted

VAGABOND (vaa guh bahnd) *n.*
one who moves from place to place with no fixed home
Synonyms: wanderer, floater, vagrant, nomad

ENDOW (ehn dow) *v.* **-ing,-ed.** ***See page 120.***

DEFORMED (dih fohrmd) *adj.*
disfigured, spoiled
Synonyms: contorted, twisted, marred, misshapen

LOATHSOME (lohth suhm) *adj.*
abhorrent, hateful
Synonyms: offensive, disgusting

AGILE (aa giel) *adj.*
well coordinated, nimble
Synonyms: spry, limber, lithe

SUBSIST (suhb sihst) *v.* **-ing,-ed.**
to have existence; to nourish and take care of oneself
Synonyms: live, manage, survive, sustain

DISPEL (dihs pehl) *v.* **-ing,-ed.**
to drive out or scatter
Synonyms: disband, disperse

the lowest **degradation**, a condition more **abject** than that of the blind mole or harmless worm. For a long time I could not conceive how one man could go forth to murder his fellow, or even why there were laws and governments; but when I heard details of vice and bloodshed, my wonder ceased, and I turned away with disgust and **loathing**.

"Every conversation of the cottagers now opened new wonders to me. While I listened to the instructions which Felix **bestowed** upon the Arabian, the strange system of human society was explained to me. I heard of the division of property, of immense wealth and **squalid** poverty; of rank, descent, and noble blood.

"The words **induced** me to turn towards myself. I learned that the possessions most esteemed by your fellow-creatures were high and **unsullied** descent united with riches. A man might be respected with only one of these acquisitions; but without either he was considered, except in very rare instances, as a **vagabond** and a slave, doomed to waste his powers for the profit of the chosen few. And what was I? Of my creation and creator I was absolutely ignorant; but I knew that I possessed no money, no friends, no kind of property. I was, besides, **endowed** with a figure hideously **deformed** and **loathsome**; I was not even of the same nature as man. I was more **agile** than they, and could **subsist** upon coarser diet; I bore the extremes of heat and cold with less injury to my frame; my stature far exceeded theirs. When I looked around, I saw and heard of none like me. Was I then a monster, a blot upon the earth, from which all men fled, and whom all men disowned?

"I cannot describe to you the agony that these reflections inflicted upon me; I tried to **dispel** them, but sorrow only increased with knowledge. Oh, that I had for ever remained in my native wood, nor known or felt beyond the sensations of hunger, thirst, and heat!

"Of what a strange nature is knowledge! It clings to

AMIABLE (ay mee uh buhl) *adj.*
friendly, pleasant, likable
Synonyms: affable, convivial, amicable, agreeable, genial

ANIMATED (aa nih may tihd) *adj.*
1. lively, excited; filled with spirit
Synonyms: elated, vivacious, spirited, inspired
2. having life, alive
Synonyms: vital, moving, alert, functioning

EXHORTATION (ihg zohr tay shun) *n.*
urging or incitement by strong appeals
Synonyms: pressing, prodding, provocation, inspiration

DOTE (doht) *v.* **-ing,-ed.**
to lavish attention, love to excess
Synonyms: adore, cherish, spoil

INDIGNATION (ihn dihg nay shun) *n.*
anger caused by something mean or unjust
Synonyms: fury, ire, wrath

the mind, when it has once seized on it, like a lichen on the rock. I wished sometimes to shake off all thought and feeling; but I learned that there was but one means to overcome the sensation of pain, and that was death—a state which I feared yet did not understand. I admired virtue and good feelings, and loved the gentle manners and **amiable** qualities of my cottagers; but I was shut out from intercourse with them, except through means which I obtained by stealth, when I was unseen and unknown, and which rather increased than satisfied the desire I had of becoming one among my fellows. The gentle words of Agatha, and the **animated** smiles of the charming Arabian, were not for me. The mild **exhortations** of the old man, and the lively conversation of the loved Felix, were not for me. Miserable, unhappy wretch!

"Other lessons were impressed upon me even more deeply. I heard of the difference of sexes; of the birth and growth of children; how the father **doted** on the smiles of the infant, and the lively sallies of the older child; how all the life and cares of the mother were wrapt up in the precious charge; how the mind of youth expanded and gained knowledge; of brother, sister, and all the various relationships which bind one human being to another in mutual bonds.

"But where were my friends and relations? No father had watched my infant days, no mother had blessed me with smiles and caresses; or if they had, all my past life was now a blot, a blind vacancy in which I distinguished nothing. From my earliest remembrance I had been as I then was in height and proportion. I had never yet seen a being resembling me, or who claimed any intercourse with me. What was I? The question again recurred, to be answered only with groans.

"I will soon explain to what these feelings tended; but allow me now to return to the cottagers, whose story excited in me such various feelings of **indignation**, delight, and wonder, but which all terminated in additional love

REVERENCE (rehv uhr ehnts) *n.*
a feeling of great awe and respect
Synonyms: veneration, adoration, idolization, admiration

AFFLUENCE (aa floo uhnts) (uh floo uhnts) *n.*
riches, abundance
Synonyms: wealth, prosperity

LUXURIOUS (luhg zhoor ee uhs) (luhk shoor ee uhs) *adj.*
elegant, lavish
Synonyms: rich, abundant, profuse

FLAGRANT (flay gruhnt) *adj.*
outrageous, conspicuous
Synonyms: glaring, egregious, blatant, gross, rank

INDIGNANT (ihn dihg nuhnt) *adj.*
angry, incensed, offended
Synonyms: furious, irate, mad, wrathful, ireful

INDIGNATION (ihn dihg nay shun) *n.*
anger caused by something mean or unjust
Synonyms: fury, ire, wrath

SOLEMN (sah luhm) *adj.*
deeply serious; somberly impressive
Synonyms: dignified, earnest, ceremonial

and **reverence** for my protectors (for so I loved, in an innocent, half painful self-deceit, to call them).

CHAPTER VI

"Some time elapsed before I learned the history of my friends. It was one which could not fail to impress itself deeply on my mind, unfolding as it did a number of circumstances each interesting and wonderful to one so utterly inexperienced as I was.

"The name of the old man was De Lacey. He was descended from a good family in France, where he had lived for many years in **affluence**, respected by his superiors, and beloved by his equals. His son was bred in the service of his country; and Agatha had ranked with ladies of the highest distinction. A few months before my arrival, they had lived in a large and **luxurious** city, called Paris, surrounded by friends, and possessed of every enjoyment which virtue, refinement of intellect, or taste, accompanied by a moderate fortune, could afford.

"The father of Safie had been the cause of their ruin. He was a Turkish merchant, and had inhabited Paris for many years, when, for some reason which I could not learn, he became obnoxious to the government. He was seized and cast into prison the very day that Safie arrived from Constantinople to join him. He was tried, and condemned to death. The injustice of his sentence was very **flagrant**; all Paris was **indignant**; and it was judged that his religion and wealth, rather than the crime alleged against him, had been the cause of his condemnation.

"Felix had been present at the trial; his horror and **indignation** were uncontrollable when he heard the decision of the court. He made, at that moment, a **solemn** vow to deliver him, and then looked around for the means. After many fruitless attempts to gain admittance

EXECUTION (ehk sih kyoo shuhn) *n.*
1. the act of performing or carrying out a task
   Synonyms: accomplishment, achievement
2. the act of putting to death
   Synonyms: killing, capital punishment, murder

BARBAROUS (baar buh ruhs) *adj.*
lacking culture or refinement; mercilessly cruel
Synonyms: savage, vulgar, inhumane

KINDLE (kihn duhl) *v.* **-ing,-ed.**
to set fire to or ignite; excite or inspire
Synonyms: light, spark, arouse, awaken

ZEAL (zeel) *n.*
passion or devotion to a cause
Synonyms: fanaticism, enthusiasm

CONTEMPT (kuhn tehmpt) *n.*
disrespect, scorn
Synonyms: derision, disdain

CONSUMMATION (kahn suh may shun) (kahn soo may shun) *n.*
fulfillment; ultimate goal or accomplishment
Synonyms: completion

ARDENT (ahr dihnt) *adj.*
passionate, enthusiastic, fervent
Synonyms: intense, vehement, fervid

DEPLORE (dih plohr) *v.* **-ing,-ed.**
to express or feel grief of; regret strongly
Synonyms: bemoan, lament, complain

PROCURE (proh kyoor) *v.* **-ing,-ed.**
to obtain
Synonyms: acquire, secure, get, gain

to the prison, he found a strongly grated window in an unguarded part of the building, which lighted the dungeon of the unfortunate Mahometan; who, loaded with chains, waited in despair the **execution** of the **barbarous** sentence. Felix visited the grate at night, and made known to the prisoner his intentions in his favour. The Turk, amazed and delighted, endeavoured to **kindle** the **zeal** of his deliverer by promises of reward and wealth. Felix rejected his offers with **contempt**; yet when he saw the lovely Safie, who was allowed to visit her father, and who, by her gestures, expressed her lively gratitude, the youth could not help owning to his own mind, that the captive possessed a treasure which would fully reward his toil and hazard.

"The Turk quickly perceived the impression that his daughter had made on the heart of Felix, and endeavoured to secure him more entirely in his interests by the promise of her hand in marriage, so soon as he should be conveyed to a place of safety. Felix was too delicate to accept this offer; yet he looked forward to the probability of that event as to the **consummation** of his happiness.

"During the ensuing days, while the preparations were going forward for the escape of the merchant, the **zeal** of Felix was warmed by several letters that he received from this lovely girl, who found means to express her thoughts in the language of her lover by the aid of an old man, a servant of her father's who understood French. She thanked him in the most **ardent** terms for his intended services towards her father; and at the same time she gently **deplored** her own fate.

"I have copies of these letters; for I found means, during my residence in the hovel, to **procure** the implements of writing; and the letters were often in the hands of Felix or Agatha. Before I depart, I will give them to you, they will prove the truth of my tale; but at present, as the sun is already far declined, I shall only have time to repeat the substance of them to you.

SPURN (spuhrn) *v.* **-ing,-ed.**
to reject or refuse contemptuously; scorn
Synonyms: disdain, snub, ostracize, ignore, cut

TENET (teh niht) *n.*
belief, doctrine
Synonyms: principle, dogma, creed

ASPIRE (uh spier) *v.* **-ing,-ed.**
to have great hopes; to aim at a goal
Synonyms: intend, strive, purpose, resolve, expect

INDELIBLY (ihn dehl uh blee) *adv.*
permanently, lastingly
Synonyms: ineffaceably, immovably, eternally

IMMURE (ih myoor) *v.* **-ing,-ed.**
to enclose within; to build into a wall
Synonyms: confine, restrain, envelop

PUERILE (pyoo ruhl) *adj.*
childish, immature, silly
Synonyms: juvenile, infantile, jejune

EMULATION (ehm yuh lay shuhn) *n.*
jealous rivalry, ambition to excel
Synonyms: imitation, envy

EXECUTION (ehk sih kyoo shuhn) *n.*
1. the act of performing or carrying out a task
Synonyms: accomplishment, achievement
2. the act of putting to death
Synonyms: killing, capital punishment, murder

PROCURE (proh kyoor) *v.* **-ing,-ed.**
to obtain
Synonyms: acquire, secure, get, gain

OBSCURE (uhb skyoor) *adj.*
dim, unclear; not well known
Synonyms: dark, faint, remote, dim, minor

RESOLVE (rih sahlv) *v.* **-ing,-ed.**
to determine or to make a firm decision about
Synonyms: solve, decide

"Safie related that her mother was a Christian Arab, seized and made a slave by the Turks; recommended by her beauty, she had won the heart of the father of Safie, who married her. The young girl spoke in high and enthusiastic terms of her mother, who, born in freedom **spurned** the bondage to which she was now reduced. She instructed her daughter in the **tenets** of her religion, and taught her to **aspire** to higher powers of intellect, and an independence of spirit, forbidden to the female followers of Mahomet. This lady died; but her lessons were **indelibly** impressed on the mind of Safie, who sickened at the prospect of again returning to Asia, and the being **immured** within the walls of a harem, allowed only to occupy herself with **puerile** amusements, ill suited to the temper of her soul, now accustomed to grand ideas and a noble **emulation** for virtue. The prospect of marrying a Christian, and remaining in a country where women were allowed to take a rank in society, was enchanting to her.

"The day for the **execution** of the Turk was fixed; but, on the night previous to it, he had quitted prison, and before morning was distant many leagues from Paris. Felix had **procured** passports in the name of his father, sister, and himself. He had previously communicated his plan to the former, who aided the deceit by quitting his house, under the pretence of a journey, and concealed himself, with his daughter, in an **obscure** part of Paris.

"Felix conducted the fugitives through France to Lyons, and across Mont Cenis to Leghorn, where the merchant had decided to wait a favourable opportunity of passing into some part of the Turkish dominions.

"Safie **resolved** to remain with her father until the moment of his departure, before which time the Turk renewed his promise that she should be united to his deliverer; and Felix remained with them in expectation of that event; and in the mean time he enjoyed the society of the Arabian, who exhibited towards him the simplest and tenderest affection. They conversed with one another

LOATHE (lohth) *v.* **-ing,-ed.**
to abhor, despise, hate
Synonyms: abominate, execrate, detest, condemn

FACILITATE (fuh <u>sihl</u> ih tayt) *v.* **-ing,-ed.**
to aid, assist
Synonyms: expedite, ease, simplify

NOISOME (<u>noy</u> suhm) *adj.*
stinking, putrid
Synonyms: foul, disgusting, malodorous

VENGEANCE (<u>vehn</u> juhns) *n.*
punishment inflicted in retaliation; vehemence
Synonyms: revenge, repayment, wrath

PERPETUAL (puhr <u>peht</u> chyoo uhl) *adj.*
endless, lasting
Synonyms: continuous, constant, ceaseless, eternal, perennial

EXILE (<u>ehg</u> ziel) (<u>ehk</u> siel) *n.*
1. the state or period of time where one is forced or volunteers to live outside of their country of origin
Synonyms: banishment, displacement, ostracism
2. one who lives outside of his native country
Synonyms: fugitive, deportee, outcast, refugee

ASYLUM (uh <u>sie</u> luhm) *n.*
refuge, sanctuary
Synonyms: haven, shelter

TREACHEROUS (<u>treh</u> chuhr uhs) *adj.*
untrustworthy, deceitful
Synonyms: perfidious, treasonous, disloyal, false

through the means of an interpreter, and sometimes with the interpretation of looks; and Safie sang to him the divine airs of her native country.

"The Turk allowed this intimacy to take place, and encouraged the hopes of the youthful lovers, while in his heart he had formed far other plans. He **loathed** the idea that his daughter should be united to a Christian; but he feared the resentment of Felix if he should appear lukewarm; for he knew that he was still in the power of his deliverer, if he should choose to betray him to the Italian state which they inhabited. He revolved a thousand plans by which he should be enabled to prolong the deceit until it might be no longer necessary, and secretly to take his daughter with him when he departed. His plans were greatly **facilitated** by the news which arrived from Paris.

"The government of France were greatly enraged at the escape of their victim, and spared no pains to detect and punish his deliverer. The plot of Felix was quickly discovered, and De Lacey and Agatha were thrown into prison. The news reached Felix, and roused him from his dream of pleasure. His blind and aged father, and his gentle sister, lay in a **noisome** dungeon, while he enjoyed the free air, and the society of her whom he loved. This idea was torture to him. He quickly arranged with the Turk that if the latter should find a favourable opportunity for escape before Felix could return to Italy, Safie should remain as a boarder at a convent at Leghorn; and then, quitting the lovely Arabian, he hastened to Paris, and delivered himself up to the **vengeance** of the law, hoping to free De Lacey and Agatha by this proceeding.

"He did not succeed. They remained confined for five months before the trial took place; the result of which deprived them of their fortune, and condemned them to a **perpetual exile** from their native country.

"They found a miserable **asylum** in the cottage in Germany, where I discovered them. Felix soon learned that the **treacherous** Turk, for whom he and his family

PITTANCE (pih tehnts) *n.*
a small portion, amount, or wage
Synonyms: ration, trace, bit, insufficiency

IRREPARABLE (ih reh puhr uh buhl) *adj.*
unable to be repaired
Synonyms: ruined, hopeless, incurable, irreplaceable

INFUSE (ihn fyooz) *v.* **-ing,-ed.**
to inspire or animate; to cause to be permeated with something that alters for the better
Synonyms: instill, flavor, introduce, pervade, inject

EXPOSTULATE (ihk spahs chuh layt) *v.* **-ing,-ed.**
to discuss or examine; to reason earnestly with another
Synonyms: argue, protest, dissuade

REITERATE (ree ih tuhr ayt) *v.* **-ing,-ed.**
to say or do again, repeat
Synonyms: echo, iterate, rehash, restate, retell

MANDATE (maan date) *n.*
a command or order
Synonyms: edict, statute, instruction

RESOLVE (rih sahlv) *v.* **-ing,-ed.**
to determine or to make a firm decision about
Synonyms: solve, decide

ABHORRENT (uhb hohr ehnt) *adj.*
loathsome, disgusting
Synonyms: hateful, condemnable, repellant

ADVERSE (aad vuhrs) (aad vuhrs) *adj.*
against, opposed
Synonyms: antagonistic, hostile, unsupportive

EXILE (ehg ziel) (ehk siel) *n.*
1. the state or period of time where one is forced or volunteers to live outside of their country of origin
Synonyms: banishment, displacement, ostracism
2. one who lives outside of his native country
Synonyms: fugitive, deportee, outcast, refugee

endured such unheard-of oppression, on discovering that his deliverer was thus reduced to poverty and impotence, became a traitor to good feeling and honour, and had quitted Italy with his daughter, insultingly sending Felix a **pittance** of money to aid him, as he said, in some plan of future maintenance.

"Such were the events that preyed on the heart of Felix, and rendered him, when I first saw him, the most miserable of his family. He could have endured poverty, and when this distress had been the meed of his virtue, he would have gloried in it, but thc ingratitude of the Turk and the loss of his beloved Safie were misfortunes more bitter and **irreparable**. The arrival of the Arabian now **infused** new life into his soul.

"When the news reached Leghorn, that Felix was deprived of his wealth and rank, the merchant commanded his daughter to think no more of her lover, but to prepare to return with him to her native country. The generous nature of Safie was outraged by this command; she attempted to **expostulate** with her father, but he left her angrily, **reiterating** his tyrannical **mandate**.

"A few days after, the Turk entered his daughter's apartment, and told her hastily that he had reason to believe that his residence at Leghorn had been divulged, and that he should speedily be delivered up to the French government; he had, consequently, hired a vessel to convey him to Constantinople, for which city he should sail in a few hours. He intended to leave his daughter under the care of a confidential servant, to follow at her leisure with the greater part of his property, which had not yet arrived at Leghorn.

"When alone, Safie **resolved** in her own mind the plan of conduct that it would becomc her to pursue in this emergency. A residence in Turkey was **abhorrent** to her; her religion and feelings were alike **adverse** to it. By some papers of her father's, which fell into her hands, she heard of the **exile** of her lover, and learnt the name of the

DEPRECATE (dehp rih kayt) *v.* **-ing,-ed.**
to belittle, disparage
Synonyms: minimize, denigrate, discount

BENEVOLENCE (buh neh vuh luhnts) *n.*
kindness, compassion
Synonyms: charity, altruism, generosity

INCITE (ihn siet) *v.* **-ing,-ed.**
to move to action; to urge on
Synonyms: encourage, instigate, motivate, prompt

spot where he then resided. She hesitated some time, but at length she formed her determination. Taking with her some jewels that belonged to her and a small sum of money, she quitted Italy, with an attendant, a native of Leghorn, but who understood the common language of Turkey, and departed for Germany.

"She arrived in safety at a town about twenty leagues from the cottage of De Lacey, when her attendant fell dangerously ill. Safie nursed her with the most devoted affection; but the poor girl died, and the Arabian was left alone, unacquainted with the language of the country, and utterly ignorant of the customs of the world. She fell, however, into good hands. The Italian had mentioned the name of the spot for which they were bound; and, after her death, the woman of the house in which they had lived took care that Safie should arrive in safety at the cottage of her lover.

CHAPTER VII

"Such was the history of my beloved cottagers. It impressed me deeply. I learned, from the views of social life which it developed, to admire their virtues, and to **deprecate** the vices of mankind.

"As yet I looked upon crime as a distant evil; **benevolence** and generosity were ever present before me, **inciting** within me a desire to become an actor in the busy scene where so many admirable qualities were called forth and displayed. But, in giving an account of the progress of my intellect, I must not omit a circumstance which occurred in the beginning of the month of August of the same year.

"One night, during my accustomed visit to the neighbouring wood, where I collected my own food, and brought home firing for my protectors, I found on the

DEJECTION (dih jehk shuhn) *n.*
a state of depression or melancholy
Synonyms: grief, sadness, low spirits

AFFECTING (uh fehk tihng) *adj.*
1. emotionally touching
Synonyms: moving, inspiring, stirring, upsetting
2. able to influence or cause a change in
Synonyms: changing, altering, transforming

OBSCURE (uhb skyoor) *adj.*
dim, unclear; not well known
Synonyms: dark, faint, remote, dim, minor

PRETENSION (prih tehn shuhn) *n.*
1. the quality of being arrogant, snobbishness
Synonyms: ostentation, conceit, phoniness
2. a false claim; an allegation of doubtful value
Synonyms: allegation, assumption, falsity

DISQUISITION (dihs kwuh zih shuhn) *n.*
a formal inquiry or discussion
Synonyms: dialogue, dissertation, speech

MERIT (mehr iht) *n.*
high quality or excellence
Synonyms: virtue, credit

EXTINCTION (ihk stingk shuhn) *n.*
end of a living thing or species
Synonyms: extermination, eradication, annihilation, elimination, destruction

ground a leathern portmanteau, containing several articles of dress and some books. I eagerly seized the prize, and returned it to my hovel. Fortunately the books were written in the language the elements of which I had acquired at the cottage; they consisted of *Paradise Lost*, a volume of *Plutarch's Lives*, and the *Sorrows of Werter*. The possession of these treasures gave me extreme delight; I now continually studied and exercised my mind upon these histories, whilst my friends were employed in their ordinary occupations.

"I can hardly describe to you the effect of these books. They produced in me an infinity of new images and feelings, that sometimes raised me to ecstacy, but more frequently sunk me into the lowest **dejection**. In the *Sorrows of Werter*, besides the interest of its simple and **affecting** story, so many opinions are canvassed, and so many lights thrown upon what had hitherto been to me **obscure** subjects, that I found in it a never-ending source of speculation and astonishment. The gentle and domestic manners it described, combined with lofty sentiments and feelings, which had for their object something out of self, accorded well with my experience among my protectors, and with the wants which were for ever alive in my own bosom. But I thought Werter himself a more divine being than I had ever beheld or imagined; his character contained no **pretension**, but it sunk deep. The **disquisitions** upon death and suicide were calculated to fill me with wonder. I did not pretend to enter into the **merits** of the case, yet I inclined towards the opinions of the hero, whose **extinction** I wept, without precisely understanding it.

"As I read, however, I applied much personally to my own feelings and condition. I found myself similar, yet at the same time strangely unlike the beings concerning whom I read, and to whose conversation I was a listener. I sympathized with, and partly understood them, but I was unformed in mind; I was dependent on none, and related to none. 'The path of my departure was free,' and

LAMENT (luh mehnt) *v.* **-ing,-ed.**
to deplore, grieve
Synonyms: mourn, sorrow, regret, bewail

DESPONDENCY (dih spahn duhn see) *n.*
discouragement and dejection
Synonyms: sadness, depression, desolation, forlornness

SURPASS (suhr paas) *v.* **-ing,-ed.**
to do better than, be superior to
Synonyms: transcend, exceed, excel, outdo

ARDOUR or ARDOR (ahr duhr) *n.*
passion, enthusiasm
Synonyms: intensity, vehemence

ABHORRENCE (uhb hohr ehnts) *n.*
loathing, detestation
Synonyms: hatred, condemnation, abomination, execration

INDUCE (ihn doos) (ihn dyoos) *v.* **-ing,-ed.**
to persuade; bring about
Synonyms: prevail, convince, lead, effect, occasion

IMBUE (ihm byoo) *v.* **-ing,-ed.**
to infuse; dye, wet, moisten
Synonyms: charge, freight, impregnate, permeate, pervade

OMNIPOTENT (ahm nihp uh tuhnt) *adj.*
having unlimited or universal power, authority, or force; all-powerful
Synonyms: divine, godlike, supreme, almighty

there was none to **lament** my annihilation. My person was hideous, and my stature gigantic. What did this mean? Who was I? What was I? Whence did I come? What was my destination? These questions continually recurred, but I was unable to answer them.

"The volume of *Plutarch's Lives* which I possessed, contained the histories of the first founders of the ancient republics. This book had a far different effect upon me from the *Sorrows of Werter*. I learned from Werter's imaginations **despondency** and gloom. But Plutarch taught me high thoughts; he elevated me above the wretched sphere of my own reflections, to admire and love the heroes of past ages. Many things I read **surpassed** my understanding and experience. I had a very confused knowledge of kingdoms, wide extents of country, mighty rivers, and boundless seas. But I was perfectly unacquainted with towns, and large assemblages of men. The cottage of my protectors had been the only school in which I had studied human nature; but this book developed new and mightier scenes of action. I read of men concerned in public affairs governing or massacring their species. I felt the greatest **ardour** for virtue rise within me, and **abhorrence** for vice, as far as I understood the signification of those terms, relative as they were, as I applied them, to pleasure and pain alone. **Induced** by these feelings, I was of course led to admire peaceable law-givers, Numa, Solon, and Lycurgus, in preference to Romulus and Theseus. The patriarchal lives of my protectors caused these impressions to take a firm hold on my mind; perhaps, if my first introduction to humanity had been made by a young soldier, burning for glory and slaughter, I should have been **imbued** with different sensations.

"But *Paradise Lost* excited different and far deeper emotions. I read it, as I had read the other volumes which had fallen into my hands, as a true history. It moved every feeling of wonder and awe, that the picture of an **omnipotent** God warring with his creatures was capable

PROSPEROUS (prah spuhr uhs) *adj.*
wealthy or successful
Synonyms: affluent, abundant, opulent

GALL (gahl) *n.*
bitterness; careless nerve
Synonyms: temerity, audacity, effrontery, rancor

NEGLECT (neh glehkt) *v.* **-ing,-ed.**
to ignore or disregard, to be negligent
Synonyms: overlook, skimp

DILIGENCE (dihl uh juhns) *n.*
1. steady, earnest application of effort
Synonyms: perseverance, attentiveness
2. a horse-drawn vehicle
Synonym: stagecoach

ODIOUS (oh dee uhs) *adj.*
hateful, contemptible
Synonyms: detestable, obnoxious, offensive, repellent, loathsome

LOATHSOME (lohth suhm) *adj.*
abhorrent, hateful
Synonyms: offensive, disgusting

INEFFACEABLE (ihn eh fays uh buhl) *adj.*
unable to be erased or unable to be made indistinct
Synonyms: inexpungeable, indestructable

ALLURING (uh lohr ing) *adj.*
charming; attractive
Synonyms: enticing, captivating

DETESTED (dee tehst ehd) (dih tehst ehd) *adj.*
intensely and violently hated
Synonyms: hated, disliked, loathed

of exciting. I often referred the several situations, as their similarity struck me, to my own. Like Adam, I was created apparently united by no link to any other being in existence; but his state was far different from mine in every other respect. He had come forth from the hands of God a perfect creature, happy and **prosperous**, guarded by the especial care of his Creator; he was allowed to converse with, and acquire knowledge from, beings of a superior nature. But I was wretched, helpless, and alone. Many times I considered Satan as the fitter emblem of my condition; for often, like him, when I viewed the bliss of my protectors, the bitter **gall** of envy rose within me.

"Another circumstance strengthened and confirmed these feelings. Soon after my arrival in the hovel, I discovered some papers in the pocket of the dress which I had taken from your laboratory. At first I had **neglected** them; but now that I was able to decipher the characters in which they were written, I began to study them with **diligence**. It was your journal of the four months that preceded my creation. You minutely described in these papers every step you took in the progress of your work; this history was mingled with accounts of domestic occurrences. You, doubtless, recollect these papers. Here they are. Every thing is related in them which bears reference to my accursed origin; the whole detail of that series of disgusting circumstances which produced it is set in view; the minutest description of my **odious** and **loathsome** person is given, in language which painted your own horrors, and rendered mine **ineffaceable**. I sickened as I read. 'Hateful day when I received life!' I exclaimed in agony. 'Cursed creator! Why did you form a monster so hideous that even you turned from me in disgust? God in pity made man beautiful and **alluring**, after his own image; but my form is a filthy type of yours, more horrid from its very resemblance. Satan had his companions, fellow-devils, to admire and encourage him; but I am solitary and **detested**.'

DESPONDENCY (dih spahn duhn see) *n.*
discouragement and dejection
Synonyms: sadness, depression, desolation

AMIABLE (ay mee uh buhl) *adj.*
friendly, pleasant, likable
Synonyms: affable, convivial, amicable, agreeable

BENEVOLENT (buh neh vuh luhnt) *adj.*
kind, compassionate.
Synonyms: charitable, altruistic, generous, good

DEFORMITY (dih fohr mih tee) *n.*
disfigurement, the state of being misshapen
Synonyms: contortion, malformation, disproportion

SOLICIT (suh lih siht) *v.* **-ing,-ed.**
to petition persistently
Synonyms: entice, tempt, request, entreat

RESOLVE (rih sahlv) *v.* **-ing,-ed.**
to determine or to make a firm decision about
Synonyms: solve, decide

DIFFUSE (dih fyooz) *v.* **-ing,-ed.**
to spread out widely
Synonyms: scatter, disperse

SERENE (suh reen) *adj.*
calm, peaceful
Synonyms: tranquil, composed, content

TUMULTUOUS (tuh muhlt choo uhs) *adj.*
confused; agitated
Synonyms: disturbed, chaotic

FORTIFY (fohr tih fie) *v.* **-ing,-ed.**
to make stronger
Synonyms: strengthen, invigorate, encourage

COUNTENANCE (kown tuh nuhns) *n.*
appearance, facial expression
Synonyms: face, features, visage

CONSOLATION (kahn suh lay shuhn) *n.*
something providing comfort for a loss or hardship
Synonyms: condolence, solace

"These were the reflections of my hours of **despondency** and solitude; but when I contemplated the virtues of the cottagers, their **amiable** and **benevolent** dispositions, I persuaded myself that when they should become acquainted with my admiration of their virtues, they would compassionate me, and overlook my personal **deformity**. Could they turn from their door one, however monstrous, who **solicited** their compassion and friendship? I **resolved**, at least, not to despair, but in every way to fit myself for an interview with them which would decide my fate. I postponed this attempt for some months longer; for the importance attached to its success inspired me with a dread lest I should fail. Besides, I found that my understanding improved so much with every day's experience, that I was unwilling to commence this undertaking until a few more months should have added to my wisdom.

"Several changes, in the mean time, took place in the cottage. The presence of Safie **diffused** happiness among its inhabitants; and I also found that a greater degree of plenty reigned there. Felix and Agatha spent more time in amusement and conversation, and were assisted in their labours by servants. They did not appear rich, but they were contented and happy; their feelings were **serene** and peaceful, while mine became every day more **tumultuous**. Increase of knowledge only discovered to me more clearly what a wretched outcast I was. I cherished hope, it is true; but it vanished, when I beheld my person reflected in water, or my shadow in the moon-shine, even as that frail image and that inconstant shade.

"I endeavoured to crush these fears, and to **fortify** myself for the trial which in a few months I **resolved** to undergo; and sometimes I allowed my thoughts, unchecked by reason, to ramble in the fields of Paradise, and dared to fancy **amiable** and lovely creatures sympathizing with my feelings and cheering my gloom; their angelic **countenances** breathed smiles of **consolation**. But

SUPPLICATION (suh plih kay shun) *n.*
a humble and earnest request
Synonyms: petition, appellation, application

CONFORMATION (kahn fohr may shun) *n.*
1. the arrangment or structure of the parts of a thing
   Synonyms: formation, shape, anatomy, configuration
2. compliance with accepted rules and customs
   Synonyms: abidance, conformity, agreement

AMIABLE (ay mee uh buhl) *adj.*
friendly, pleasant, likable
Synonyms: affable, convivial, amicable, agreeable, genial

DISDAIN (dihs dayn) *n.*
scorn and contempt
Synonyms: disrespect, disparagement

SAGACITY (suh gaa sih tee) *n.*
shrewdness
Synonyms: wisdom, knowledge

it was all a dream—no Eve soothed my sorrows or shared my thoughts; I was alone. I remembered Adam's **supplication** to his Creator; but where was mine? He had abandoned me, and, in the bitterness of my heart, I cursed him.

"Autumn passed thus. I saw, with surprise and grief, the leaves decay and fall, and nature again assume the barren and bleak appearance it had worn when I first beheld the woods and the lovely moon. Yet I did not heed the bleakness of the weather; I was better fitted by my **conformation** for the endurance of cold than heat. But my chief delights were the sight of the flowers, the birds, and all the gay apparel of summer; when those deserted me, I turned with more attention towards the cottagers. Their happiness was not decreased by the absence of summer. They loved, and sympathized with one another; and their joys, depending on each other, were not interrupted by the casualties that took place around them. The more I saw of them, the greater became my desire to claim their protection and kindness; my heart yearned to be known and loved by these **amiable** creatures; to see their sweet looks turned towards me with affection, was the utmost limit of my ambition. I dared not think that they would turn them from me with **disdain** and horror. The poor that stopped at their door were never driven away. I asked, it is true, for greater treasures than a little food or rest; I required kindness and sympathy; but I did not believe myself utterly unworthy of it.

"The winter advanced, and an entire revolution of the seasons had taken place since I awoke into life. My attention, at this time, was solely directed towards my plan of introducing myself into the cottage of my protectors. I revolved many projects; but that on which I finally fixed was to enter the dwelling when the blind old man should be alone. I had **sagacity** enough to discover that the unnatural hideousness of my person was the chief object of horror with those who had formerly beheld me. My

MEDIATION (mee dee ay shuhn) *n.*
the act of being a middle-man in communication
Synonyms: intervention, arbitration, intercession

DIFFUSE (dih fyooz) *v.* **-ing,-ed.**
to spread out widely
Synonyms: scatter, disperse

COUNTENANCE (kown tuh nuhns) *n.*
appearance, facial expression
Synonyms: face, features, visage

EXECUTE (ehk sih kyoot) *v.* **-ing,-ed.**
1. to carry out fully; to make or produce
   Synonyms: accomplish, achieve, perform
2. to put to death by penalty of crime
   Synonyms: kill, punish, murder

PROCURE (proh kyoor) *v.* **-ing,-ed.**
to obtain
Synonyms: acquire, secure, get, gain

voice, although harsh, had nothing terrible in it; I thought, therefore, that if, in the absence of his children, I could gain the good-will and **mediation** of the old De Lacey, I might, by his means, be tolerated by my younger protectors.

"One day, when the sun shone on the red leaves that strewed the ground, and **diffused** cheerfulness, although it denied warmth, Safie, Agatha, and Felix, departed on a long country walk, and the old man, at his own desire, was left alone in the cottage. When his children had departed, he took up his guitar, and played several mournful, but sweet airs, more sweet and mournful than I had ever heard him play before. At first his **countenance** was illuminated with pleasure, but, as he continued, thoughtfulness and sadness succeeded; at length, laying aside the instrument, he sat absorbed in reflection.

"My heart beat quick; this was the hour and moment of trial, which would decide my hopes or realize my fears. The servants were gone to a neighbouring fair. All was silent in and around the cottage. It was an excellent opportunity; yet, when I proceeded to **execute** my plan, my limbs failed me, and I sunk to the ground. Again I rose; and, exerting all the firmness of which I was master, removed the planks which I had placed before my hovel to conceal my retreat. The fresh air revived me, and, with renewed determination, I approached the door of their cottage.

"I knocked. 'Who is there?' said the old man. 'Come in.'

"I entered. 'Pardon this intrusion,' said I, 'I am a traveller in want of a little rest; you would greatly oblige me, if you would allow me to remain a few minutes before the fire.'

"'Enter,' said De Lacey, 'and I will try in what manner I can relieve your wants; but, unfortunately, my children are from home, and, as I am blind, I am afraid I shall find it difficult to **procure** food for you.'

IRRESOLUTE (ih reh suh loot) *adj.*
undecided, uncertain
Synonyms: wavering, indecisive, hesitant

AMIABLE (ay mee uh buhl) *adj.*
friendly, pleasant, likable
Synonyms: affable, convivial, amicable, agreeable, genial

DETESTABLE (dee tehst uh buhl) *adj.*
deserving of intense and violent hated
Synonyms: disgusting, despicable, loathsome

"'Do not trouble yourself, my kind host, I have food; it is warmth and rest only that I need.'

"I sat down, and a silence ensued. I knew that every minute was precious to me, yet I remained **irresolute** in what manner to commence the interview; when the old man addressed me—

"'By your language, stranger, I suppose you are my countryman—are you French?'

"'No, but I was educated by a French family, and understand that language only. I am now going to claim the protection of some friends, whom I sincerely love, and of whose favour I have some hopes.'

"'Are these Germans?'

"'No, they are French. But let us change the subject. I am an unfortunate and deserted creature; I look around, and I have no relation or friend upon earth. These **amiable** people to whom I go have never seen me, and know little of me. I am full of fears; for if I fail there, I am an outcast in the world for ever.'

"'Do not despair. To be friendless is indeed to be unfortunate; but the hearts of men, when unprejudiced by any obvious self-interest, are full of brotherly love and charity. Rely, therefore, on your hopes; and if these friends are good and **amiable**, do not despair.'

"'They are kind—they are the most excellent creatures in the world; but, unfortunately, they are prejudiced against me. I have good dispositions; my life has been hitherto harmless, and, in some degree, beneficial; but a fatal prejudice clouds their eyes, and where they ought to see a feeling and kind friend, they behold only a **detestable** monster.'

"'That is indeed unfortunate; but if you are really blameless, cannot you undeceive them?'

"'I am about to undertake that task; and it is on that account that I feel so many overwhelming terrors. I tenderly love these friends; I have, unknown to them, been for many months in the habits of daily kindness towards

COUNTENANCE (kown tuh nuhns) *n.*
appearance, facial expression
Synonyms: face, features, visage

EXILE (ehg ziel) (ehk siel) *n.*
1. one who lives outside of his native country
Synonyms: fugitive, deportee, outcast, refugee
2. the state or period of time where one is forced or volunteers to live outside of their country of origin
Synonyms: banishment, displacement, ostracism

INSTIGATE (ihn stih gayt) *v.* **-ing,-ed.**
to incite, urge, agitate
Synonyms: foment, goad, spark

BENEFACTOR (behn uh faak torh) *n.*
someone giving aid or money
Synonyms: contributor, backer, donor, patron

BESTOW (bih stoh) *v.* **-ing,-ed.**
to give as a gift
Synonyms: award, endow, donate, confer, present

them; but they believe that I wish to injure them, and it is that prejudice which I wish to overcome.'

"'Where do these friends reside?'

"'Near this spot.'

"The old man paused, and then continued, 'If you will unreservedly confide to me the particulars of your tale, I perhaps may be of use in undeceiving them. I am blind, and cannot judge of your **countenance**, but there is something in your words which persuades me that you are sincere. I am poor, and an **exile**; but it will afford me true pleasure to be in any way serviceable to a human creature.'

"'Excellent man! I thank you, and accept your generous offer. You raise me from the dust by this kindness; and I trust that, by your aid, I shall not be driven from the society and sympathy of your fellow-creatures.'

"'Heaven forbid! Even if you were really criminal; for that can only drive you to desperation, and not **instigate** you to virtue. I also am unfortunate; I and my family have been condemned, although innocent; judge, therefore, if I do not feel for your misfortunes.'

"'How can I thank you, my best and only **benefactor**? From your lips first have I heard the voice of kindness directed towards me; I shall be for ever grateful; and your present humanity assures me of success with those friends whom I am on the point of meeting.'

"'May I know the names and residence of those friends?'

"I paused. This, I thought, was the moment of decision, which was to rob me of, or **bestow** happiness on me for ever. I struggled vainly for firmness sufficient to answer him, but the effort destroyed all my remaining strength; I sank on the chair, and sobbed aloud. At that moment I heard the steps of my younger protectors. I had not a moment to lose; but, seizing the hand of the old man, I cried, 'Now is the time!—save and protect me! You and your family are the friends whom I seek. Do not you desert me in the hour of trial!'

CONSTERNATION (kahn stuhr nay shuhn) *n.*
amazement or distress that leads to confusion
Synonyms: alarm, bewilderment, perplexity

TUMULT (tuh muhlt) *n.*
state of confusion; agitation
Synonyms: disturbance, turmoil, din, commotion, chaos

WANTONLY (wahn tuhn lee) *adv.*
without discipline, without restraint, recklessly
Synonyms: capriciously, lewdly, licentiously

BESTOW (bih stoh) *v.* **-ing,-ed.**
to give as a gift
Synonyms: award, endow, donate, confer, present

GLUT (gluht) *v.* **-ing,-ed.**
eat and drink to excess
Synonyms: stuff, cram, gormandize

RESTRAINED (rih straynd) *adj.*
controlled, repressed, restricted
Synonyms: hampered, bridled, curbed, checked

"'Great God!' exclaimed the old man. 'Who are you?'

"At that instant the cottage door was opened, and Felix, Safie, and Agatha entered. Who can describe their horror and **consternation** on beholding me? Agatha fainted; and Safie, unable to attend to her friend, rushed out of the cottage. Felix darted forward, and with supernatural force tore me from his father, to whose knees I clung. In a transport of fury, he dashed me to the ground and struck me violently with a stick. I could have torn him limb from limb, as the lion rends the antelope. But my heart sunk within me as with bitter sickness, and I refrained. I saw him on the point of repeating his blow, when, overcome by pain and anguish, I quitted the cottage, and in the general **tumult** escaped unperceived to my hovel.

CHAPTER VIII

"Cursed, cursed creator! Why did I live? Why, in that instant, did I not extinguish the spark of existence which you had so **wantonly bestowed**? I know not; despair had not yet taken possession of me; my feelings were those of rage and revenge. I could with pleasure have destroyed the cottage and its inhabitants, and have **glutted** myself with their shrieks and misery.

"When night came, I quitted my retreat, and wandered in the wood; and now, no longer **restrained** by the fear of discovery, I gave vent to my anguish in fearful howlings. I was like a wild beast that had broken the toils; destroying the objects that obstructed me, and ranging through the wood with a stag-like swiftness. Oh! What a miserable night I passed! The cold stars shone in mockery, and the bare trees waved their branches above me. Now and then the sweet voice of a bird burst forth amidst the universal stillness. All, save I, were at rest or in enjoyment. I, like

MYRIAD (<u>mihr</u> ee uhd) *n.*
immense number, multitude
Synonyms: crowd, army, legion, mass

IMPRUDENTLY (ihm <u>proo</u> dehnt lee) *adv.*
indiscreetly, carelessly
Synonyms: unwisely, foolishly

RESOLVE (<u>rih</u> sahlv) *v.* **-ing,-ed.**
to determine or to make a firm decision about
Synonyms: solve, decide

PROFOUND (pruh <u>fownd</u>) (proh <u>fownd</u>) *adj.*
having intellectual depth; difficult to understand; extending far below the surface; all encompassing
Synonyms: deep, intellectual, shrewd, thoughtful

the arch fiend, bore a hell within me; and, finding myself unsympathized with, wished to tear up the trees, spread havoc and destruction around me, and then to have sat down and enjoyed the ruin.

"But this was a luxury of sensation that could not endure; I became fatigued with excess of bodily exertion, and sank on the damp grass in the sick impotence of despair. There was none among the **myriads** of men that existed who would pity or assist me; and should I feel kindness towards my enemies? No—from that moment I declared everlasting war against the species, and, more than all, against him who had formed me, and sent me forth to this insupportable misery.

"The sun rose; I heard the voices of men, and knew that it was impossible to return to my retreat during that day. Accordingly I hid myself in some thick underwood, determining to devote the ensuing hours to reflection on my situation.

"The pleasant sunshine, and the pure air of day, restored me to some degree of tranquillity; and when I considered what had passed at the cottage, I could not help believing that I had been too hasty in my conclusions. I had certainly acted **imprudently**. It was apparent that my conversation had interested the father in my behalf, and I was a fool in having exposed my person to the horror of his children. I ought to have familiarized the old De Lacey to me, and by degrees have discovered myself to the rest of his family, when they should have been prepared for my approach. But I did not believe my errors to be irretrievable; and, after much consideration, **I resolved** to return to the cottage, seek the old man, and by my representations win him to my party.

"These thoughts calmed me, and in the afternoon I sank into a **profound** sleep; but the fever of my blood did not allow me to be visited by peaceful dreams. The horrible scene of the preceding day was for ever acting before my eyes; the females were flying, and the enraged

APPEASE (uh pees) *v.* **-ing,-ed.**
to satisfy, placate, calm, pacify
Synonyms: assuage, mollify, propitiate, soothe

GESTICULATION (jeh stih kyuh lay shuhn) *n.*
the act of making gestures; an expressive gesture
Synonyms: expression, body language, signal

DISCOURSE (dihs kohrs) *n.*
the verbal interchange of ideas; a formal, orderly, and extended expression of thought
Synonyms: dialogue, communication, oration

ENTREAT (ehn treet) *v.* **-ing,-ed.**
to plead, beg
Synonyms: beseech, implore, importune, request

TENEMENT (teh nuh muhnt) *n.*
a house used as a dwelling; any form of property held by one person leasing it from another
Synonyms: lodging, residence

Felix tearing me from his father's feet. I awoke exhausted; and, finding that it was already night, I crept forth from my hiding place, and went in search of food.

"When my hunger was **appeased**, I directed my steps towards the well-known path that conducted to the cottage. All there was at peace. I crept into my hovel, and remained in silent expectation of the accustomed hour when the family arose. That hour past, the sun mounted high in the heavens, but the cottagers did not appear. I trembled violently, apprehending some dreadful misfortune. The inside of the cottage was dark, and I heard no motion; I cannot describe the agony of this suspence.

"Presently two countrymen passed by; but, pausing near the cottage, they entered into conversation, using violent **gesticulations**; but I did not understand what they said, as they spoke the language of the country, which differed from that of my protectors. Soon after, however, Felix approached with another man; I was surprised, as I knew that he had not quitted the cottage that morning, and waited anxiously to discover, from his **discourse**, the meaning of these unusual appearances.

"'Do you consider,' said his companion to him, 'that you will be obliged to pay three months' rent, and to lose the produce of your garden? I do not wish to take any unfair advantage, and I beg therefore that you will take some days to consider your determination.'

"'It is utterly useless,' replied Felix. 'We can never again inhabit your cottage. The life of my father is in the greatest danger, owing to the dreadful circumstance that I have related. My wife and my sister will never recover from their horror. I **entreat** you not to reason with me any more. Take possession of your **tenement**, and let me fly from this place.'

"Felix trembled violently as he said this. He and his companion entered the cottage, in which they remained for a few minutes, and then departed. I never saw any of the family of De Lacey again.

SPURN (spuhrn) *v.* **-ing,-ed.**
to reject or refuse contemptuously; scorn
Synonyms: disdain, snub, ostracize, ignore, cut

INANIMATE (ihn aan ih miht) *adj.*
not alive, lacking energy
Synonyms: dead, lifeless, dull, inactive, soulless

VESTIGE (veh stihj) n.
trace, remnant
Synonyms: relic, remains, token, sign, spoor

DISPERSE (dihs puhrs) *v.* **-ing,-ed.**
to break up, scatter
Synonyms: dissipate, disintegrate, dispel

LOITER (loy tuhr) *v.* **-ing,-ed.**
to stand around idly
Synonyms: linger, delay, dawdle

RESOLVE (rih sahlv) *v.* **-ing,-ed.**
to determine or to make a firm decision about
Synonyms: solve, decide

"I continued for the remainder of the day in my hovel in a state of utter and stupid despair. My protectors had departed, and had broken the only link that held me to the world. For the first time the feelings of revenge and hatred filled my bosom, and I did not strive to control them; but, allowing myself to be borne away by the stream, I bent my mind towards injury and death. When I thought of my friends, of the mild voice of De Lacey, the gentle eyes of Agatha, and the exquisite beauty of the Arabian, these thoughts vanished, and a gush of tears somewhat soothed me. But again, when I reflected that they had **spurned** and deserted me, anger returned, a rage of anger; and, unable to injure any thing human, I turned my fury towards **inanimate** objects. As night advanced, I placed a variety of combustibles around the cottage; and, after having destroyed every **vestige** of cultivation in the garden, I waited with forced impatience until the moon had sunk to commence my operations.

"As the night advanced, a fierce wind arose from the woods, and quickly **dispersed** the clouds that had **loitered** in the heavens. The blast tore along like a mighty avalanche, and produced a kind of insanity in my spirits, that burst all bounds of reason and reflection. I lighted the dry branch of a tree, and danced with fury around the devoted cottage, my eyes still fixed on the western horizon, the edge of which the moon nearly touched. A part of its orb was at length hid, and I waved my brand; it sunk, and, with a loud scream, I fired the straw, and heath, and bushes, which I had collected. The wind fanned the fire, and the cottage was quickly enveloped by the flames, which clung to it, and licked it with their forked and destroying tongues.

"As soon as I was convinced that no assistance could save any part of the habitation, I quitted the scene, and sought for refuge in the woods.

"And now, with the world before me, whither should I bend my steps? I **resolved** to fly far from the scene of my

BESTOW (bih stoh) *v.* **-ing,-ed.**
to give as a gift
Synonyms: award, endow, donate, confer, present

RESOLVE (rih sahlv) *v.* **-ing,-ed.**
to determine or to make a firm decision about
Synonyms: solve, decide

SUCCOUR or SUCCOR (suh kuhr) *n.*
relief; a thing that furnishes relief
Synonyms: aid, help, support

ENDOW (ehn dow) *v.* **-ing,-ed.**
to furnish with an income or grant; to provide with something naturally or freely
Synonyms: bestow, donate, empower, grant, support

REDRESS (rih drehs) *n.*
relief from wrong or injury
Synonyms: reparation, amends, restitution, indemnity, quittance

VISAGE (vih sihj) *n.*
the appearance of a person or place
Synonyms: expression, look, style, manner

IMPRECATE (ihm prih kayt) *v.* **-ing,-ed.**
curse, vilify, threaten
Synonyms: execrate, damn, scold

GALL (gahl) *n.*
bitterness; careless nerve
Synonyms: temerity, audacity, effrontery, rancor

misfortunes; but to me, hated and despised, every country must be equally horrible. At length the thought of you crossed my mind. I learned from your papers that you were my father, my creator; and to whom could I apply with more fitness than to him who had given me life? Among the lessons that Felix had **bestowed** upon Safie, geography had not been omitted; I had learned from these the relative situations of the different countries of the earth. You had mentioned Geneva as the name of your native town; and towards this place I **resolved** to proceed.

"But how was I to direct myself? I knew that I must travel in a southwesterly direction to reach my destination; but the sun was my only guide. I did not know the names of the towns that I was to pass through, nor could I ask information from a single human being; but I did not despair. From you only could I hope for **succour**, although towards you I felt no sentiment but that of hatred. Unfeeling, heartless creator! You had **endowed** me with perceptions and passions, and then cast me abroad an object for the scorn and horror of mankind. But on you only had I any claim for pity and **redress**, and from you I determined to seek that justice which I vainly attempted to gain from any other being that wore the human form.

"My travels were long, and the sufferings I endured intense. It was late in autumn when I quitted the district where I had so long resided. I travelled only at night, fearful of encountering the **visage** of a human being. Nature decayed around me, and the sun became heatless; rain and snow poured around me; mighty rivers were frozen; the surface of the earth was hard, and chill, and bare, and I found no shelter. Oh, earth! How often did I **imprecate** curses on the cause of my being! The mildness of my nature had fled, and all within me was turned to **gall** and bitterness. The nearer I approached to your habitation, the more deeply did I feel the spirit of revenge

ENKINDLE (ehn kihn duhl) *v.* **-ing,-ed.**
to set fire to or ignite; excite or inspire
Synonyms: light, spark, arouse, awaken

RESPITE (reh spiht) *n.*
interval of relief
Synonyms: rest, pause, intermission, recess, suspension

BALMINESS (bah mee nehs) *n.*
mildness; soothing
Synonyms: temperateness, freshness, warmth

DEFORMITY (dih fohr mih tee) *n.*
disfigurement, the state of being misshapen
Synonyms: contortion, malformation, disproportion

BESTOW (bih stoh) *v.* **-ing,-ed.**
to give as a gift
Synonyms: award, endow, donate, confer, present

INDUCE (ihn doos) (ihn dyoos) *v.* **-ing,-ed.**
to persuade; bring about
Synonyms: prevail, convince, lead, effect, occasion

PRECIPITOUS (pree sih puh tuhs) *adj.*
extremely steep
Synonyms: inclined, headlong, reckless, abrupt

enkindled in my heart. Snow fell, and the waters were hardened, but I rested not. A few incidents now and then directed me, and I possessed a map of the country; but I often wandered wide from my path. The agony of my feelings allowed me no **respite**—no incident occurred from which my rage and misery could not extract its food; but a circumstance that happened when I arrived on the confines of Switzerland, when the sun had recovered its warmth, and the earth again began to look green, confirmed in an especial manner the bitterness and horror of my feelings.

"I generally rested during the day, and travelled only when I was secured by night from the view of man. One morning, however, finding that my path lay through a deep wood, I ventured to continue my journey after the sun had risen; the day, which was one of the first of spring, cheered even me by the loveliness of its sunshine and the **balminess** of the air. I felt emotions of gentleness and pleasure, that had long appeared dead, revive within me. Half surprised by the novelty of these sensations, I allowed myself to be borne away by them; and, forgetting my solitude and **deformity**, dared to be happy. Soft tears again bedewed my cheeks, and I even raised my humid eyes with thankfulness towards the blessed sun which **bestowed** such joy upon me.

"I continued to wind among the paths of the wood, until I came to its boundary, which was skirted by a deep and rapid river, into which many of the trees bent their branches, now budding with the fresh spring. Here I paused, not exactly knowing what path to pursue, when I heard the sound of voices, that **induced** me to conceal myself under the shade of a cypress. I was scarcely hid, when a young girl came running toward the spot where I was concealed, laughing as if she ran from some one in sport. She continued her course along the **precipitous** sides of the river, when suddenly her foot slipt, and she fell into the rapid stream. I rushed from my hiding place,

ANIMATION (aa nih may shuhn) *n.*
the quality or condition of being alive, spirited, active, or vigorous
Synonyms: life, vitality, invigoration, liveliness

BENEVOLENCE (buh neh vuh luhnts) *n.*
kindness, compassion
Synonyms: charity, altruism, generosity

RECOMPENSE (reh kuhm pehns) *n.*
something given as a means of compensation or returned in kind
Synonyms: compensation, repayment, reimbursement

VENGEANCE (vehn juhns) *n.*
punishment inflicted in retaliation; vehemence
Synonyms: revenge, repayment, wrath

AUGMENT (awg mehnt) *v.* **-ing,-ed.**
to expand, extend
Synonyms: enhance, compound, increase, enlarge, inflate

COMPENSATE (kahm pehn sayt) *v.* **-ing,-ed.**
to repay or reimburse
Synonyms: indemnify, recompense, balance

ALLEVIATE (uh lee vee ayt) *v.* **-ing,-ed.**
to relieve, improve partially
Synonyms: allay, assuage, palliate, mitigate, quell

DESOLATE (deh soh liht) *adj.*
showing the effects of abandonment or neglect; devoid of warmth or comfort
Synonyms: barren, bleak, forsaken, vacant

and, with extreme labour from the force of the current, saved her, and dragged her to shore. She was senseless; and I endeavoured, by every means in my power, to restore **animation**, when I was suddenly interrupted by the approach of a rustic, who was probably the person from whom she had playfully fled. On seeing me, he darted towards me, and, tearing the girl from my arms, hastened towards the deeper parts of the wood. I followed speedily, I hardly knew why; but when the man saw me draw near, he aimed a gun, which he carried, at my body, and fired. I sunk to the ground, and my injurer, with increased swiftness, escaped into the wood.

"This was then the reward of my **benevolence**! I had saved a human being from destruction, and, as a **recompense**, I now writhed under the miserable pain of a wound, which shattered the flesh and bone. The feelings of kindness and gentleness, which I had entertained but a few moments before, gave place to hellish rage and gnashing of teeth. Inflamed by pain, I vowed eternal hatred and **vengeance** to all mankind. But the agony of my wound overcame me; my pulses paused, and I fainted.

"For some weeks I led a miserable life in the woods, endeavouring to cure the wound which I had received. The ball had entered my shoulder, and I knew not whether it had remained there or passed through; at any rate I had no means of extracting it. My sufferings were **augmented** also by the oppressive sense of the injustice and ingratitude of their infliction. My daily vows rose for revenge—a deep and deadly revenge, such as would alone **compensate** for the outrages and anguish I had endured.

"After some weeks my wound healed, and I continued my journey. The labours I endured were no longer to be **alleviated** by the bright sun or gentle breezes of spring; all joy was but a mockery, which insulted my **desolate** state, and made me feel more painfully that I was not made for the enjoyment of pleasure.

SPORTIVENESS (spohr tihv nehs) *n.*
playfulness
Synonyms: friskiness, merriness, liveliness

DEFORMITY (dih fohr mih tee) *n.*
disfigurement, the state of being misshapen
Synonyms: contortion, malformation, disproportion

DESOLATE (deh soh liht) *adj.*
showing the effects of abandonment or neglect; devoid of warmth or comfort
Synonyms: barren, bleak, forsaken, vacant

EPITHET (eh puh theht) *n.*
an abusive word or phrase; a descriptive term or phrase substituted for a real name
Synonyms: nickname, motto, catchphrase, invective

"But my toils now drew near a close; and, two months from this time, I reached the environs of Geneva.

"It was evening when I arrived, and I retired to a hiding place among the fields that surround it, to meditate in what manner I should apply to you. I was oppressed by fatigue and hunger, and far too unhappy to enjoy the gentle breezes of evening, or the prospect of the sun setting behind the stupendous mountains of Jura.

"At this time a slight sleep relieved me from the pain of reflection, which was disturbed by the approach of a beautiful child, who came running into the recess I had chosen with all the **sportiveness** of infancy. Suddenly, as I gazed on him, an idea seized me, that this little creature was unprejudiced, and had lived too short a time to have imbibed a horror of **deformity**. If, therefore, I could seize him, and educate him as my companion and friend, I should not be so **desolate** in this peopled earth.

"Urged by this impulse, I seized on the boy as he passed, and drew him towards me. As soon as he beheld my form, he placed his hands before his eyes, and uttered a shrill scream. I drew his hand forcibly from his face, and said, 'Child, what is the meaning of this? I do not intend to hurt you; listen to me.'

"He struggled violently. 'Let me go,' he cried. 'Monster! Ugly wretch! You wish to eat me, and tear me to pieces—you are an ogre—let me go, or I will tell my papa.'

"'Boy, you will never see your father again; you must come with me.'

"'Hideous monster! Let me go; My papa is a syndic—he is M. Frankenstein—he would punish you. You dare not keep me.'

"'Frankenstein! You belong then to my enemy—to him toward whom I have sworn eternal revenge; you shall be my first victim.'

"The child still struggled, and loaded me with **epithets** which carried despair to my heart. I grasped his throat to silence him, and in a moment he lay dead at my feet.

EXULTATION (ihg suhl tay shuhn) *n.*
the act of being extremely joyful
Synonyms: celebration, delight, jubilation

DESOLATION (deh suh lay shuhn) *n.*
barren wasteland; sadness, loneliness
Synonyms: bleakness, devastation, ruin; despair

IMPREGNABLE (ihm prehg nuh buhl) *adj.*
totally safe from attack, able to resist defeat
Synonyms: unassailable, invincible, secure, inviolable, invulnerable

MALIGNITY (muh lihg nih tee) *n.*
evil or aggressive malice; something that produces death
Synonyms: malevolence, bitterness, resentment

BESTOW (bih stoh) *v.* **-ing,-ed.**
to give as a gift
Synonyms: award, endow, donate, confer, present

BENIGNITY (bih nihg nih tee) *n.*
kindness, gentleness, charity
Synonyms: innocuity, mildness

SANGUINARY (saan gwuh naa ree) *adj.*
cruel, bloodthirsty
Synonyms: savage, murderous, gory

RESOLVE (rih sahlv) *v.* **-ing,-ed.**
to determine or to make a firm decision about
Synonyms: solve, decide

"I gazed on my victim, and my heart swelled with **exultation** and hellish triumph. Clapping my hands, I exclaimed, 'I, too, can create **desolation**; my enemy is not **impregnable**; this death will carry despair to him, and a thousand other miseries shall torment and destroy him.'

"As I fixed my eyes on the child, I saw something glittering on his breast. I took it; it was a portrait of a most lovely woman. In spite of my **malignity**, it softened and attracted me. For a few moments I gazed with delight on her dark eyes, fringed by deep lashes, and her lovely lips; but presently my rage returned. I remembered that I was for ever deprived of the delights that such beautiful creatures could **bestow**; and that she whose resemblance I contemplated would, in regarding me, have changed that air of divine **benignity** to one expressive of disgust and affright.

"Can you wonder that such thoughts transported me with rage? I only wonder that at that moment, instead of venting my sensations in exclamations and agony, I did not rush among mankind, and perish in the attempt to destroy them.

"While I was overcome by these feelings, I left the spot where I had committed the murder, and was seeking a more secluded hiding place, when I perceived a woman passing near me. She was young, not indeed so beautiful as her whose portrait I held, but of an agreeable aspect, and blooming in the loveliness of youth and health. Here, I thought, is one of those whose smiles are **bestowed** on all but me; she shall not escape; thanks to the lessons of Felix, and the **sanguinary** laws of man, I have learned how to work mischief. I approached her unperceived, and placed the portrait securely in one of the folds of her dress.

"For some days I haunted the spot where these scenes had taken place; sometimes wishing to see you, sometimes **resolved** to quit the world and its miseries for ever. At length I wandered towards these mountains, and have

COMPLY (kuhm plie) *v.* **-ing,-ed.**
to yield or agree, to go along with
Synonyms: accord, submit, acquiesce, obey, respect

DEFORMED (dih fohrmd) *adj.*
disfigured, spoiled
Synonyms: contorted, twisted, marred, misshapen

KINDLE (kihn duhl) *v.* **-ing,-ed.**
to set fire to or ignite; excite or inspire
Synonyms: light, spark, arouse, awaken

SUPPRESS (suh prehs) *v.* **-ing,-ed.**
to hold back, restrain
Synonyms: subdue, stifle, muffle, quell, curb

EXTORT (ihk stohrt) *v.* **-ing,-ed.**
to obtain something by threats or force
Synonyms: wring, coerce, blackmail, bludgeon, bully

BASE (bays) *adj.*
lacking qualities of higher mind or spirit
Synonyms: vulgar, corrupt, immoral, menial

DESOLATE (deh suh layt) *v.* **-ing,-ed.**
to lay waste or make wretched; to deprive of inhabitants
Synonyms: destroy, devastate, pillage, plunder

MALICIOUS (muh lihsh uhs) *adj.*
spiteful, hateful
Synonyms: malevolent, cruel, rancorous, hostile

ranged through their immense recesses, consumed by a burning passion which you alone can gratify. We may not part until you have promised to **comply** with my requisition. I am alone, and miserable; man will not associate with me; but one as **deformed** and horrible as myself would not deny herself to me. My companion must be of the same species, and have the same defects. This being you must create."

CHAPTER IX

The being finished speaking, and fixed his looks upon me in expectation of a reply. But I was bewildered, perplexed, and unable to arrange my ideas sufficiently to understand the full extent of his proposition. He continued—

"You must create a female for me, with whom I can live in the interchange of those sympathies necessary for my being. This you alone can do; and I demand it of you as a right which you must not refuse."

The latter part of his tale had **kindled** anew in me the anger that had died away while he narrated his peaceful life among the cottagers, and, as he said this, I could no longer **suppress** the rage that burned within me.

"I do refuse it," I replied, "and no torture shall ever **extort** a consent from me. You may render me the most miserable of men, but you shall never make me **base** in my own eyes. Shall I create another like yourself, whose joint wickedness might **desolate** the world. Begone! I have answered you; you may torture me, but I will never consent."

"You are in the wrong," replied the fiend, "and, instead of threatening, I am content to reason with you. I am **malicious** because I am miserable; am I not shunned and hated by all mankind? You, my creator, would tear

PRECIPITATE (preh sih puh tayt) *v.* **-ing,-ed.**
1. to throw, usually from a great height
   Synonyms: hurl, fall, rush
2. to bring about abruptly
   Synonyms: speed, launch, accelerate, quicken

BESTOW (bih stoh) *v.* **-ing,-ed.**
to give as a gift
Synonyms: award, endow, donate, confer, present

INSURMOUNTABLE (ihn suhr mownt uh buhl) *adj.*
impossible, unable to be overcome
Synonyms: unachievable, insuperable, unattainable

ABJECT (aab jehkt) *adj.*
miserable, pitiful
Synonyms: pathetic, lamentable, sorry

DESOLATE (deh suh layt) *v.* **-ing,-ed.**
to lay waste or make wretched; to deprive of inhabitants
Synonyms: destroy, devastate, pillage, plunder

ANIMATE (aa nih mayt) *v.* **-ing,-ed.**
1. to make lively, excited; to fill with spirit
   Synonyms: elate, inspire, stimulate
2. to give life to or make alive
   Synonyms: activate, enliven, vitalize

DETRIMENTAL (deht ruh mehn tuhl) *adj.*
causing harm or injury
Synonyms: adverse, deleterious, inimical, destructive, hurtful

BENEVOLENCE (buh neh vuh luhns) *n.*
kindness, compassion, charity, goodness
Synonyms: altruism, beneficence, generosity

INDULGE (ihn duhlj) *v.* **-ing,-ed.**
to give in to a craving or desire
Synonyms: humor, gratify, allow, pamper

me to pieces, and triumph; remember that, and tell me why I should pity man more than he pities me? You would not call it murder, if you could **precipitate** me into one of those ice-rifts, and destroy my frame, the work of your own hands. Shall I respect man, when he condemns me? Let him live with me in the interchange of kindness, and, instead of injury, I would **bestow** every benefit upon him with tears of gratitude at his acceptance. But that cannot be; the human senses are **insurmountable** barriers to our union. Yet mine shall not be the submission of **abject** slavery. I will revenge my injuries. If I cannot inspire love, I will cause fear; and chiefly towards you my arch-enemy, my creator, do I swear inextinguishable hatred. Have a care, I will work at your destruction, nor finish until I **desolate** your heart, so that you curse the hour of your birth."

A fiendish rage **animated** him as he said this; his face was wrinkled into contortions too horrible for human eyes to behold; but presently he calmed himself, and proceeded—

"I intended to reason. This passion is **detrimental** to me; for you do not reflect that you are the cause of its excess. If any being felt emotions of **benevolence** towards me, I should return them a hundred and a hundred fold; for that one creature's sake, I would make peace with the whole kind! But I now **indulge** in dreams of bliss that cannot be realized. What I ask of you is reasonable and moderate; I demand a creature of another sex, but as hideous as myself. The gratification is small, but it is all that I can receive, and it shall content me. It is true, we shall be monsters, cut off from all the world; but on that account we shall be more attached to one another. Our lives will not be happy, but they will be harmless, and free from the misery I now feel. Oh! My creator, make me happy; let me feel gratitude towards you for one benefit! Let me see that I excite the sympathy of some existing thing; do not deny me my request!"

BESTOW (bih stoh) *v.* **-ing,-ed.**
to give as a gift
Synonyms: award, endow, donate, confer, present

GLUT (gluht) *v.* **-ing,-ed.**
to eat and drink to excess
Synonyms: stuff, cram, gormandize

WANTONNESS (wahn tuhn nehs) *n.*
lack of discipline, looseness, recklessness
Synonyms: immorality, lewdness

ARDENTLY (ahr dihnt lee) *adv.*
passionately, enthusiastically, fervently
Synonyms: intensely, vehemently

PERSEVERE (pehr suh veer) *v.* **-ing,-ed.**
to continue with determination, remain steadfast
Synonyms: persist, remain, endure, plod

EXILE (ehg ziel) (ehk siel) *n.*
1. the state or period of time where one is forced or volunteers to live outside of their country of origin
Synonyms: banishment, displacement, ostracism
2. one who lives outside of his native country
Synonyms: fugitive, deportee, outcast, refugee

DETESTATION (dee tehs tay shuhn) *n.*
intense and violent hatred
Synonyms: hate, disgust, loathing, abhorrence

I was moved. I shuddered when I thought of the possible consequences of my consent; but I felt that there was some justice in his argument. His tale, and the feelings he now expressed, proved him to be a creature of fine sensations; and did I not, as his maker, owe him all the portion of happiness that it was in my power to **bestow**? He saw my change of feeling, and continued—

"If you consent, neither you nor any other human being shall ever see us again; I will go to the vast wilds of South America. My food is not that of man; I do not destroy the lamb and the kid, to **glut** my appetite; acorns and berries afford me sufficient nourishment. My companion will be of the same nature as myself, and will be content with the same fare. We shall make our bed of dried leaves; the sun will shine on us as on man, and will ripen our food. The picture I present to you is peaceful and human, and you must feel that you could deny it only in the **wantonness** of power and cruelty. Pitiless as you have been towards me, I now see compassion in your eyes; let me seize the favourable moment, and persuade you to promise what I so **ardently** desire."

"You propose," replied I, "to fly from the habitations of man, to dwell in those wilds where the beasts of the field will be your only companions. How can you, who long for the love and sympathy of man, **persevere** in this **exile**? You will return, and again seek their kindness, and you will meet with their **detestation**; your evil passions will be renewed, and you will then have a companion to aid you in the task of destruction. This may not be; cease to argue the point, for I cannot consent."

"How inconstant are your feelings! But a moment ago you were moved by my representations, and why do you again harden yourself to my complaints? I swear to you, by the earth which I inhabit, and by you that made me, that, with the companion you **bestow**, I will quit the neighbourhood of man, and dwell, as it may chance, in the most savage of places. My evil passions will have fled,

CONSOLE (kuhn sohl) *v.* **-ing,-ed.**
to alleviate grief and raise the spirits of, provide solace
Synonyms: relieve, comfort, soothe

STIFLE (stie fuhl) *v.* **-ing,-ed.**
to smother or suffocate; suppress
Synonyms: repress, strangle, throttle

BESTOW (bih stoh) *v.* **-ing,-ed.**
to give as a gift
Synonyms: award, endow, donate, confer, present

MALICE (maal ihs) *n.*
animosity, spite, hatred
Synonyms: malevolence, cruelty, enmity, rancor, hostility

FEINT (faynt) *n.*
a trick; a fake or false impression
Synonyms: evasion, diversion, pretense, simulation

ABHOR (uhb hohr) *v.* **-ing,-ed.**
to loathe, detest
Synonyms: hate, contemn, abominate, execrate, despise

BLIGHT (bliet) *n.*
affliction, destruction, ruin
Synonyms: damage, plague

LOATHING (lohth ing) *n.*
hatred or great dislike
Synonyms: detestation, abhorrence

MANIFEST (maan uh fehst) *v.* **-ing,-ed.**
to make evident or certain by display
Synonyms: exhibit, display, showcase, expose

for I shall meet with sympathy; my life will flow quietly away, and, in my dying moments, I shall not curse my maker."

His words had a strange effect upon me. I compassionated him, and sometimes felt a wish to **console** him; but when I looked upon him, when I saw the filthy mass that moved and talked, my heart sickened, and my feelings were altered to those of horror and hatred. I tried to **stifle** these sensations; I thought, that as I could not sympathize with him, I had no right to withhold from him the small portion of happiness which was yet in my power to **bestow**.

"You swear," I said, "to be harmless; but have you not already shown a degree of **malice** that should reasonably make me distrust you? May not even this be a **feint** that will increase your triumph by affording a wider scope for your revenge?"

"How is this? I thought I had moved your compassion, and yet you still refuse to **bestow** on me the only benefit that can soften my heart, and render me harmless. If I have no ties and no affections, hatred and vice must be my portion; the love of another will destroy the cause of my crimes, and I shall become a thing, of whose existence every one will be ignorant. My vices are the children of a forced solitude that I **abhor**; and my virtues will necessarily arise when I live in communion with an equal. I shall feel the affections of a sensitive being, and become linked to the chain of existence and events, from which I am now excluded."

I paused some time to reflect on all he had related, and the various arguments which he had employed. I thought of the promise of virtues which he had displayed on the opening of his existence, and the subsequent **blight** of all kindly feeling by the **loathing** and scorn which his protectors had **manifested** towards him. His power and threats were not omitted in my calculations—a creature who could exist in the ice caves of the glaciers, and hide

PRECIPICE (prehs ih pihs) *n.*
edge, steep overhang
Synonyms: crag, cliff, brink

FACULTY (faa kuhl tee) *n.*
the ability to act or do
Synonyms: aptitude, capability, sense, skill

COMPLY (kuhm plie) *v.* **-ing,-ed.**
to yield or agree, to go along with
Synonyms: accord, submit, acquiesce, obey, respect

SOLEMN (sah luhm) *adj.*
deeply serious; somberly impressive
Synonyms: dignified, earnest, ceremonial

EXILE (ehg ziel) (ehk siel) *n.*
1. the state or period of time where one is forced or volunteers to live outside of their country of origin
Synonyms: banishment, displacement, ostracism
2. one who lives outside of his native country
Synonyms: fugitive, deportee, outcast, refugee

UNDULATION (uhn dyoo lay shun) *n.*
a wavy motion
Synonyms: oscillation, fluctuation, surge, pulse

ENCOMPASS (ehn kuhm puhs) *v.* **-ing,-ed**.
to include, cover, take in
Synonyms: surround, enclose, envelop, constitute, include

SOLEMNITY (suh lehm nih tee) *n.*
dignified seriousness
Synonyms: ceremoniousness, formality, observance

himself from pursuit among the ridges of inaccessible **precipices**, was a being possessing **faculties** it would be vain to cope with. After a long pause of reflection, I concluded that the justice due both to him and my fellow creatures demanded of me that I should **comply** with his request. Turning to him, therefore, I said—

"I consent to your demand, on your **solemn** oath to quit Europe for ever, and every other place in the neighbourhood of man, as soon as I shall deliver into your hands a female who will accompany you in your **exile**."

"I swear," he cried, "by thc sun, and by the blue sky of heaven, that if you grant my prayer, while they exist you shall never behold me again. Depart to your home, and commence your labours. I shall watch their progress with unutterable anxiety, and fear not but that when you are ready I shall appear."

Saying this, he suddenly quitted me, fearful, perhaps, of any change in my sentiments. I saw him descend the mountain with greater speed than the flight of an eagle, and quickly lost him among the **undulations** of the sea of ice.

His tale had occupied the whole day; and the sun was upon the verge of the horizon when he departed. I knew that I ought to hasten my descent towards the valley, as I should soon be **encompassed** in darkness; but my heart was heavy, and my steps slow. The labour of winding among the little paths of the mountains, and fixing my feet firmly as I advanced, perplexed me, occupied as I was by the emotions which the occurrences of the day had produced. Night was far advanced, when I came to the half-way resting place, and seated myself beside the fountain. The stars shone at intervals, as the clouds passed from over them; the dark pines rose before me, and every here and there a broken tree lay on the ground. It was a scene of wonderful **solemnity**, and stirred strange thoughts within me. I wept bitterly; and, clasping my hands in agony, I exclaimed, "Oh! Stars, and clouds, and winds, ye are all about to mock me. If ye really pity

MONOTONY (muh <u>naht</u> nee) *n.*
tedium, dull sameness
Synonyms: sameness, repetitiousness, boredom, ennui

ALLEVIATE (uh <u>lee</u> vee ayt) *v.* **-ing,-ed.**
to relieve, improve partially
Synonyms: allay, assuage, palliate, mitigate, quell

HYPOCRITE (<u>hih</u> puh kriht) *n.*
person claiming beliefs or virtues he or she doesn't really possess
Synonyms: fraud, liar, sham, fake, phony

MULTITUDE (<u>muhl</u> tuh tood) *n.*
the state of being many; a great number
Synonyms: mass, myriad, slew, crowd

INCESSANT (ihn <u>sehs</u> uhnt) *adj.*
continuous, never ceasing
Synonyms: constant, interminable, relentless, unending, unremitting

EXTORT (ihk <u>stohrt</u>) *v.* **-ing,-ed.**
to obtain something by threats or force
Synonyms: wring, coerce, blackmail, bludgeon, bully

me, crush sensation and memory; let me become as nought; but if not, depart, depart and leave me in darkness."

These were wild and miserable thoughts; but I cannot describe to you how the eternal twinkling of the stars weighed upon me, and how I listened to every blast of wind, as if it were a dull ugly siroc on its way to consume me.

Morning dawned before I arrived at the village of Chamounix; but my presence, so haggard and strange, hardly calmed the fears of my family, who had waited the whole night in anxious expectation of my return.

The following day we returned to Geneva. The intention of my father in coming had been to divert my mind, and to restore me to my lost tranquillity; but the medicine had been fatal. And, unable to account for the excess of misery I appeared to suffer, he hastened to return home, hoping the quiet and **monotony** of a domestic life would by degrees **alleviate** my sufferings from whatsoever cause they might spring.

For myself, I was passive in all their arrangements; and the gentle affection of my beloved Elizabeth was inadequate to draw me from the depth of my despair. The promise I had made to the daemon weighed upon my mind, like Dante's iron cowl on the heads of the hellish **hypocrites**. All pleasures of earth and sky passed before me like a dream, and that thought only had to me the reality of life. Can you wonder that sometimes a kind of insanity possessed me, or that I saw continually about me a **multitude** of filthy animals inflicting on me **incessant** torture, that often **extorted** screams and bitter groans?

By degrees, however, these feelings became calmed. I entered again into the every-day scene of life, if not with interest, at least with some degree of tranquillity.

Volume III

VENGEANCE (vehn juhns) *n.*
punishment inflicted in retaliation; vehemence
Synonyms: revenge, repayment, wrath

REPUGNANCE (rih puhg nehnts) *n.*
strong dislike, distaste, or antagonism; an instance of contradiction or inconsistency
Synonyms: repulsion, hatred, aversion

ENJOIN (ehn joyn) *v.* **-ing,-ed.**
to urge, order, command; forbid or prohibit, as by judicial order
Synonyms: direct, instruct, charge; prohibit, proscribe

PROFOUND (pruh fownd) (proh fownd) *adj.*
having intellectual depth; difficult to understand; extending far below the surface; all encompassing
Synonyms: deep, intellectual, shrewd, thoughtful

DISQUISITION (dihs kwuh zih shuhn) *n.*
a formal inquiry or discussion
Synonyms: dialogue, dissertation, speech

RESOLVE (rih sahlv) *v.* **-ing,-ed.**
to determine or to make a firm decision about
Synonyms: solve, decide

ERADICATE (ih raad ih kayt) *v.* **-ing,-ed.**
to erase or wipe out
Synonyms: uproot, abolish, eliminate, annihilate

MELANCHOLY (mehl uhn kahl ee) *n.*
sadness, depression
Synonyms: dejection, despondency, woe, sorrow

SALUTATION (saal yoo tay shuhn) *n.*
greeting
Synonyms: salute, regards, welcome, hello

CHAPTER I

Day after day, week after week passed away on my return to Geneva; and I could not collect the courage to recommence my work. I feared the **vengeance** of the disappointed fiend, yet I was unable to overcome my **repugnance** to the task which was **enjoined** me. I found that I could not compose a female without again devoting several months to **profound** study and laborious **disquisition**. I had heard of some discoveries having been made by an English philosopher, the knowledge of which was material to my success, and I sometimes thought of obtaining my father's consent to visit England for this purpose; but I clung to every pretence of delay, and could not **resolve** to interrupt my returning tranquillity. My health, which had hitherto declined, was now much restored; and my spirits, when unchecked by the memory of my unhappy promise, rose proportionably. My father saw this change with pleasure, and he turned his thoughts towards the best method of **eradicating** the remains of my **melancholy**, which every now and then would return by fits, and with a devouring blackness overcast the approaching sunshine. At these moments I took refuge in the most perfect solitude. I passed whole days on the lake alone in a little boat, watching the clouds, and listening to the rippling of the waves, silent and listless. But the fresh air and bright sun seldom failed to restore me to some degree of composure; and, on my return, I met the **salutations** of my friends with a readier smile and a more cheerful heart.

It was after my return from one of these rambles that my father, calling me aside, thus addressed me:

CONJECTURE (kuhn jehk shuhr) *n.*
speculation, prediction
Synonyms: postulation, hypothesis, supposition, guess

CONJURE (kahn juhr) *v.* **-ing,-ed.**
to call on or beg solemnly; to affect or effect as if by magic; to bring to mind
Synonyms: entreat, implore, rouse, recollect

POIGNANT (poy nyaant) *adj.*
emotionally moving
Synonyms: stirring, touching, pathetic, piquant

DISSIPATE (dihs uh payt) *v.* **-ing,-ed.**
to scatter; to pursue pleasure to excess
Synonyms: carouse, squander, consume; disperse, dissolve

SOLEMNIZATION (sah luhm nih zay shuhn) *n.*
celebration
Synonyms: commemoration, ceremony, recognition

"I am happy to remark, my dear son, that you have resumed your former pleasures, and seem to be returning to yourself. And yet you are still unhappy, and still avoid our society. For some time I was lost in **conjecture** as to the cause of this; but yesterday an idea struck me, and if it is well founded, I **conjure** you to avow it. Reserve on such a point would be not only useless, but draw down treble misery on us all."

I trembled violently at this exordium, and my father continued—

"I confess, my son, that I have always looked forward to your marriage with your cousin as the tie of our domestic comfort, and the stay of my declining years. You were attached to each other from your earliest infancy; you studied together, and appeared, in dispositions and tastes, entirely suited to one another. But so blind is the experience of man, that what I conceived to be the best assistance to my plan may have entirely destroyed it. You, perhaps, regard her as your sister, without any wish that she might become your wife. Nay, you may have met with another whom you may love; and, considering yourself as bound in honour to your cousin, this struggle may occasion the **poignant** misery which you appear to feel."

"My dear father, re-assure yourself. I love my cousin tenderly and sincerely. I never saw any woman who excited, as Elizabeth does, my warmest admiration and affection. My future hopes and prospects are entirely bound up in the expectation of our union."

"The expression of your sentiments on this subject, my dear Victor, gives me more pleasure than I have for some time experienced. If you feel thus, we shall assuredly be happy, however present events may cast a gloom over us. But it is this gloom, which appears to have taken so strong a hold of your mind, that I wish to **dissipate**. Tell me, therefore, whether you object to an immediate **solemnization** of the marriage. We have been

INFIRMITY (ihn fuhr mih tee) *n.*
disease, ailment
Synonyms: weakness, frailty, infirmity, illness, affliction

CANDOUR or CANDOR (kaan dohr) *n.*
honest expression
Synonyms: frankness, sincerity, bluntness

CONJURE (kahn juhr) *v.* **-ing,-ed.**
to call on or beg solemnly; to affect or effect as if by magic; to bring to mind
Synonyms: entreat, implore, rouse, recollect

MULTITUDE (muhl tuh tood) *n.*
the state of being many; a great number
Synonyms: mass, myriad, slew, crowd

SOLEMN (sah luhm) *adj.*
deeply serious; somberly impressive
Synonyms: dignified, earnest, ceremonial

IMPEND (ihm pehnd) *v.* **-ing,-ed.**
to hover threateningly; to be about to occur
Synonyms: loom, near, progress, meet

IMPOSE (ihm pohz) *v.* **-ing,-ed.**
to inflict, force upon
Synonyms: dictate, decree, demand, ordain, prescribe

DILATORY (dihl uh tohr ee) *adj.*
slow, tending to delay
Synonyms: sluggish, tardy, unhurried

unfortunate, and recent events have drawn us from that every-day tranquillity befitting my years and **infirmities**. You are younger; yet I do not suppose, possessed as you are of a competent fortune, that an early marriage would at all interfere with any future plans of honour and utility that you may have formed. Do not suppose, however, that I wish to dictate happiness to you, or that a delay on your part would cause me any serious uneasiness. Interpret my words with **candour**, and answer me, I **conjure** you, with confidence and sincerity."

I listened to my father in silence, and remained for some time incapable of offering any reply. I revolved rapidly in my mind a **multitude** of thoughts, and endeavoured to arrive at some conclusion. Alas! To me the idea of an immediate union with my cousin was one of horror and dismay. I was bound by a **solemn** promise, which I had not yet fulfilled, and dared not break; or, if I did, what manifold miseries might not **impend** over me and my devoted family! Could I enter into a festival with this deadly weight yet hanging round my neck, and bowing me to the ground. I must perform my engagement, and let the monster depart with his mate, before I allowed myself to enjoy the delight of a union from which I expected peace.

I remembered also the necessity **imposed** upon me of either journeying to England, or entering into a long correspondence with those philosophers of that country, whose knowledge and discoveries were of indispensable use to me in my present undertaking. The latter method of obtaining the desired intelligence was **dilatory** and unsatisfactory. Besides, any variation was agreeable to me, and I was delighted with the idea of spending a year or two in change of scene and variety of occupation, in absence from my family, during which period some event might happen which would restore me to them in peace and happiness. My promise might be fulfilled, and the monster have departed; or some

ENTREATY (ehn tree tee) *n.*
a plea or request
Synonyms: imploration, prayer, petition

INDUCE (ihn doos) (ihn dyoos) *v.* **-ing,-ed.**
to persuade; bring about
Synonyms: prevail, convince, lead, effect, occasion

COMPLY (kuhm plie) *v.* **-ing,-ed.**
to yield or agree, to go along with
Synonyms: accord, submit, acquiesce, obey, respect

INDULGENT (ihn duhl jehnt) *adj.*
lenient, tolerant
Synonyms: gratifying, pleasing

FORBEAR (fohr bayr) *v.* **-ing,-bore.**
to refrain or resist
Synonyms: avoid

DEJECTION (dih jehk shuhn) *n.*
a state of depression or melancholy
Synonyms: grief, sadness, low spirits

AGITATION (aa gih tay shuhn) *n.*
commotion, excitement; uneasiness
Synonyms: disturbance, restlessness, anxiety, fluster, disquiet

EXASPERATE (ihg zaas puhr ayt) *v.* **-ing,-ed.**
irritate
Synonyms: frustrate, annoy, vex, pique

accident might occur to destroy him, and put an end to my slavery for ever.

These feelings dictated my answer to my father. I expressed a wish to visit England; but, concealing the true reasons of this request, I clothed my desires under the guise of wishing to travel and see the world before I sat down for life within the walls of my native town.

I urged my **entreaty** with earnestness, and my father was easily **induced** to **comply**; for a more **indulgent** and less dictatorial parent did not exist upon earth. Our plan was soon arranged. I should travel to Strassburg, where Clerval would join me. Some short time would be spent in the towns of Holland, and our principal stay would be in England. We should return by France; and it was agreed that the tour should occupy the space of two years.

My father pleased himself with the reflection, that my union with Elizabeth should take place immediately on my return to Geneva. "These two years," said he, "will pass swiftly, and it will be the last delay that will oppose itself to your happiness. And, indeed, I earnestly desire that period to arrive, when we shall all be united, and neither hopes or fears arise to disturb our domestic calm."

"I am content," I replied, "with your arrangement. By that time we shall both have become wiser, and I hope happier, than we at present are." I sighed; but my father kindly **forbore** to question me further concerning the cause of my **dejection**. He hoped that new scenes, and the amusement of travelling, would restore my tranquillity.

I now made arrangements for my journey; but one feeling haunted me, which filled me with fear and **agitation**. During my absence I should leave my friends unconscious of the existence of their enemy, and unprotected from his attacks, **exasperated** as he might be by my departure. But he had promised to follow me wherever I might go; and would he not accompany me to England? This imagination was dreadful in itself, but soothing, inasmuch as it supposed the safety of my friends. I was

INTIMATE (ihn tuh mayt) *v.* **-ing,-ed.**
to suggest or give a clue
Synonyms: implicate, allude, insinuate

MACHINATION (mahk uh nay shuhn) *n.*
plot or scheme
Synonyms: conspiracy, intrigue, design, cabal

EXILE (ehg ziel) (ehk siel) *n.*
1. the state or period of time where one is forced or volunteers to live outside of their country of origin
Synonyms: banishment, displacement, ostracism
2. one who lives outside of his native country
Synonyms: fugitive, deportee, outcast, refugee

ENTREAT (ehn treet) *v.* **-ing,-ed.**
to plead, beg
Synonyms: beseech, implore, importune, request, petition

RESOLVE (rih sahlv) *v.* **-ing,-ed.**
to determine or to make a firm decision about
Synonyms: solve, decide

LISTLESS (lihst lihs) *adj.*
lacking energy and enthusiasm
Synonyms: lethargic, sluggish, languid, fainéant, indolent

INDOLENCE (ihn duh luhnts) *n.*
habitual laziness, idleness
Synonyms: sloth, languor, lethargy, sluggishness

TRAVERSE (truh vuhrs) (traa vuhrs) *v.* **-ing,-ed.**
to travel or travel across; to turn or move laterally
Synonyms: cross, travel, intersect, pass through

DESPONDING (dih spahn dihng) *adj.*
feeling discouraged and dejected
Synonyms: sad, depressed, desolate, dejected, forlorn

agonized with the idea of the possibility that the reverse of this might happen. But through the whole period during which I was the slave of my creature, I allowed myself to be governed by the impulses of the moment; and my present sensations strongly **intimated** that the fiend would follow me, and exempt my family from the danger of his **machinations**.

It was in the latter end of August that I departed, to pass two years of **exile**. Elizabeth approved of the reasons of my departure, and only regretted that she had not the same opportunities of enlarging her experience, and cultivating her understanding. She wept, however, as she bade me farewell, and **entreated** me to return happy and tranquil. "We all," said she, "depend upon you; and if you are miserable, what must be our feelings?"

I threw myself into the carriage that was to convey me away, hardly knowing whither I was going, and careless of what was passing around. I remembered only, and it was with a bitter anguish that I reflected on it, to order that my chemical instruments should be packed to go with me. For I **resolved** to fulfil my promise while abroad, and return, if possible, a free man. Filled with dreary imaginations, I passed through many beautiful and majestic scenes; but my eyes were fixed and unobserving. I could only think of the bourne of my travels, and the work which was to occupy me whilst they endured.

After some days spent in **listless indolence**, during which I **traversed** many leagues, I arrived at Strasburgh, where I waited two days for Clerval. He came. Alas, how great was the contrast between us! He was alive to every new scene; joyful when he saw the beauties of the setting sun, and more happy when he beheld it rise, and recommence a new day. He pointed out to me the shifting colours of the landscape, and the appearances of the sky. "This is what it is to live," he cried. "Now I enjoy existence! But you, my dear Frankenstein, wherefore are you **desponding** and sorrowful?" In truth, I was occupied by

PRECIPICE (prehs ih pihs) *n.*
edge, steep overhang
Synonyms: crag, cliff, brink

VARIEGATED (vaar ee uh gayt ehd) *adj.*
varied; marked with different colors
Synonyms: motley, pied, diversified

MEANDERING (mee aan duhr ihng) *adj.*
wandering aimlessly
Synonyms: rambling, roaming, roving, straying

AGITATE (aa gih tayt) *v.* **-ing,-ed.**
to upset or excite; to make uneasy
Synonyms: disturb, fluster, bother

gloomy thoughts, and neither saw the descent of the evening star, nor the golden sun-rise reflected in the Rhine. And you, my friend, would be far more amused with the journal of Clerval, who observed the scenery with an eye of feeling and delight, than to listen to my reflections. I, a miserable wretch, haunted by a curse that shut up every avenue to enjoyment.

We had agreed to descend the Rhine in a boat from Strassburg to Rotterdam, whence we might take shipping for London. During this voyage, we passed by many willowy islands, and saw several beautiful towns. We stayed a day at Manheim, and, on the fifth from our departure from Strassburg, arrived at Mayence. The course of the Rhine below Mayence becomes much more picturesque. The river descends rapidly, and winds between hills, not high, but steep, and of beautiful forms. We saw many ruined castles standing on the edges of **precipices**, surrounded by black woods, high and inaccessible. This part of the Rhine, indeed, presents a singularly **variegated** landscape. In one spot you view rugged hills, ruined castles overlooking tremendous **precipices**, with the dark Rhine rushing beneath; and, on the sudden turn of a promontory, flourishing vineyards, with green sloping banks, and a **meandering** river, and populous towns, occupy the scene.

We travelled at the time of the vintage, and heard the song of the labourers, as we glided down the stream. Even I, depressed in mind, and my spirits continually **agitated** by gloomy feelings, even I was pleased. I lay at the bottom of the boat, and, as I gazed on the cloudless blue sky, I seemed to drink in a tranquillity to which I had long been a stranger. And if these were my sensations, who can describe those of Henry? He felt as if he had been transported to Fairy-land, and enjoyed a happiness seldom tasted by man. "I have seen," he said, "the most beautiful scenes of my own country; I have visited the lakes of Lucerne and Uri, where the snowy

VERDANT (<u>vuhr</u> dnt) *adj.*
green with vegetation; inexperienced
Synonyms: grassy, leafy, wooded

AGITATE (<u>aa</u> gih tayt) *v.* **-ing,-ed.**
to upset or excite; to make uneasy
Synonyms: disturb, fluster, bother

TEMPEST (<u>tehm</u> pehst) *n.*
a violent and windy storm
Synonyms: inclemency, turbulence, torrent

PRECIPICE (<u>prehs</u> ih pihs) *n.*
edge, steep overhang
Synonyms: crag, cliff, brink

EMINENTLY (<u>ehm</u> uh nuhnt lee) *adv.*
remarkably, outstandingly
Synonyms: famously, prominently, importantly, illustriously

CHASTEN (<u>chay</u> sehn) *v.* **-ing,-ed.**
to subdue or restrain
Synonyms: tame, moderate, temper

ARDENT (<u>ahr</u> dihnt) *adj.*
passionate, enthusiastic, fervent
Synonyms: intense, vehement, fervid

ARDOUR or ARDOR (<u>ahr</u> duhr) *n.*
passion, enthusiasm
Synonyms: intensity, vehemence

mountains descend almost perpendicularly to the water, casting black and impenetrable shades, which would cause a gloomy and mournful appearance, were it not for the most **verdant** islands that relieve the eye by their gay appearance; I have seen this lake **agitated** by a **tempest**, when the wind tore up whirlwinds of water, and gave you an idea of what the water-spout must be on the great ocean, and the waves dash with fury the base of the mountain, where the priest and his mistress were overwhelmed by an avalanche, and where their dying voices are still said to be heard amid the pauses of the nightly wind; I have seen the mountains of La Valais, and the Pays de Vaud—but this country, Victor, pleases me more than all those wonders. The mountains of Switzerland are more majestic and strange; but there is a charm in the banks of this divine river, that I never before saw equalled. Look at that castle which overhangs yon **precipice**; and that also on the island, almost concealed amongst the foliage of those lovely trees; and now that group of labourers coming from among their vines; and that village half-hid in the recess of the mountain. Oh, surely, the spirit that inhabits and guards this place has a soul more in harmony with man, than those who pile the glacier, or retire to the inaccessible peaks of the mountains of our own country."

Clerval! Beloved friend! Even now it delights me to record your words, and to dwell on the praise of which you are so **eminently** deserving. He was a being formed in the "very poetry of nature." His wild and enthusiastic imagination was **chastened** by the sensibility of his heart. His soul overflowed with **ardent** affections, and his friendship was of that devoted and wondrous nature that the worldly-minded teach us to look for only in the imagination. But even human sympathies were not sufficient to satisfy his eager mind. The scenery of external nature, which others regard only with admiration, he loved with **ardour**:

REPLETE (rih <u>pleet</u>) *adj.*
abundantly supplied
Synonyms: abounding, satiated, gorged, stuffed, full

CONSOLE (kuhn <u>sohl</u>) *v.* **-ing,-ed.**
to alleviate grief and raise the spirits of, provide solace
Synonyms: relieve, comfort, soothe

RESOLVE (<u>rih</u> sahlv) *v.* **-ing,-ed.**
to determine or to make a firm decision about
Synonyms: solve, decide

> The sounding <u>cataract</u>
> Haunted *him* like a passion: the tall rock,
> The mountain, and the deep and gloomy wood,
> Their colours and their forms, were then to him
> An appetite; a feeling, and a love,
> That had no need of a remoter charm,
> By thought supplied, or any interest
> Unborrowed from the eye.

And where does he now exist? Is this gentle and lovely being lost for ever? Has this mind so **replete** with ideas, imaginations fanciful and magnificent, which formed a world, whose existence depended on the life of its creator; has this mind perished? Does it now only exist in my memory? No, it is not thus; your form so divinely wrought, and beaming with beauty, has decayed, but your spirit still visits and **consoles** your unhappy friend.

Pardon this gush of sorrow; these ineffectual words are but a slight tribute to the unexampled worth of Henry, but they soothe my heart, overflowing with the anguish which his remembrance creates. I will proceed with my tale.

Beyond Cologne we descended to the plains of Holland; and we **resolved** to post the remainder of our way; for the wind was contrary, and the stream of the river was too gentle to aid us.

Our journey here lost the interest arising from beautiful scenery; but we arrived in a few days at Rotterdam, whence we proceeded by sea to England. It was on a clear morning, in the latter days of December, that I first saw the white cliffs of Britain. The banks of the Thames presented a new scene; they were flat, but fertile, and almost every town was marked by the remembrance of some story. We saw Tilbury Fort, and remembered the Spanish Armada; Gravesend, Woolwich, and Greenwich, places which I had heard of even in my country.

AVAIL (uh vayl) *v.* **-ing,-ed.**
to be of use or advantage to; to result in; to make use of
Synonyms: benefit, profit, serve, suffice

BLIGHT (bliet) *n.*
something that hinders growth or impedes progress and prosperity; affliction, destruction
Synonyms: damage, plague, ruin

PROFOUND (pruh fownd) (proh fownd) *adj.*
having intellectual depth; difficult to understand; extending far below the surface; all encompassing
Synonyms: deep, intellectual, shrewd, thoughtful

TRANSITORY (traan sih tohr ee) *adj.*
short-lived, existing only briefly
Synonyms: transient, ephemeral, fleeting, fugitive, momentary

INSURMOUNTABLE (ihn suhr mownt uh buhl) *adj.*
unable to be conquered or overcome
Synonyms: unsurpassable, insuperable, impossible, hopeless, unbeatable

At length we saw the numerous steeples of London, St. Paul's towering above all, and the Tower famed in English history.

CHAPTER II

London was our present point of rest; we determined to remain several months in this wonderful and celebrated city. Clerval desired the intercourse of the men of genius and talent who flourished at this time; but this was with me a secondary object; I was principally occupied with the means of obtaining the information necessary for the completion of my promise, and quickly **availed** myself of the letters of introduction that I had brought with me, addressed to the most distinguished natural philosophers.

If this journey had taken place during my days of study and happiness, it would have afforded me inexpressible pleasure. But a **blight** had come over my existence, and I only visited these people for the sake of the information they might give me on the subject in which my interest was so terribly **profound**. Company was irksome to me; when alone, I could fill my mind with the sights of heaven and earth; the voice of Henry soothed me, and I could thus cheat myself into a **transitory** peace. But busy uninteresting joyous faces brought back despair to my heart. I saw an **insurmountable** barrier placed between me and my fellow-men; this barrier was sealed with the blood of William and Justine; and to reflect on the events connected with those names filled my soul with anguish.

But in Clerval I saw the image of my former self; he was inquisitive, and anxious to gain experience and instruction. The difference of manners which he observed was to him an inexhaustible source of instruction and

DEJECTED (dih jehk tehd) *adj.*
depressed or melancholy
Synonyms: grief-stricken, sad, low in spirits

MIEN (meen) *n.*
characteristics expressive of attitude or personality
Synonyms: manner, demeanor, expression, style

ALLEGE (uh lehj) *v.* **-ing,-ed.**
to charge, claim
Synonyms: assert, contend, declare

ALLUSION (uh loo zhuhn) *n.*
indirect reference
Synonyms: intimation, suggestion

PALPITATE (paal pih tayt) *v.* **-ing,-ed.**
to beat rapidly and strongly
Synonyms: flutter, pound, pulsate, throb

ALLUREMENT (uh lohr mehnt) *n.*
enticement by charm; attraction
Synonyms: lure, temptation, appeal

INDUCE (ihn doos) (ihn dyoos) *v.* **-ing,-ed.**
to persuade; bring about
Synonyms: prevail, convince, lead, effect, occasion

ABHORRED (uhb hohr ehd) *adj.*
loathed, detested
Synonyms: hated, condemned, abominated, execrated, despised

EXPIRATION (ehk spuhr ay shuhn) *n.*
1. an end or ending; death
Synonyms: termination, conclusion, cessation
2. the action of breathing out
Synonyms: exhalation, inhalation

RESOLVE (rih sahlv) *v.* **-ing,-ed.**
to determine or to make a firm decision about
Synonyms: solve, decide

OBSCURE (uhb skyoor) *adj.*
dim, unclear; not well known
Synonyms: dark, faint, remote, dim, minor

amusement. He was for ever busy; and the only check to his enjoyments was my sorrowful and **dejected mien**. I tried to conceal this as much as possible, that I might not debar him from the pleasures natural to one who was entering on a new scene of life, undisturbed by any care or bitter recollection. I often refused to accompany him, **alleging** another engagement, that I might remain alone. I now also began to collect the materials necessary for my new creation, and this was to me like the torture of single drops of water continually falling on the head. Every thought that was devoted to it was an extreme anguish, and every word that I spoke in **allusion** to it caused my lips to quiver, and my heart to **palpitate**.

After passing some months in London, we received a letter from a person in Scotland, who had formerly been our visitor at Geneva. He mentioned the beauties of his native country, and asked us if those were not sufficient **allurements** to **induce** us to prolong our journey as far north as Perth, where he resided. Clerval eagerly desired to accept this invitation; and I, although I **abhorred** society, wished to view again mountains and streams, and all the wondrous works with which Nature adorns her chosen dwelling-places.

We had arrived in England at the beginning of December, and it was now February. We accordingly determined to commence our journey towards the north at the **expiration** of another month. In this expedition we did not intend to follow the great road to Edinburgh, but to visit Windsor, Oxford, Matlock, and the Cumberland lakes, **resolving** to arrive at the completion of this tour about the end of July. I packed my chemical instruments, and the materials I had collected, **resolving** to finish my labours in some **obscure** nook in the northern highlands of Scotland.

We quitted London on the 27th of March, and remained a few days at Windsor, rambling in its beautiful forest. This was a new scene to us mountaineers; the

AMIABLE (ay mee uh buhl) *adj.*
friendly, pleasant, likable
Synonyms: affable, convivial, amicable, agreeable, genial

INSOLENT (ihn suh luhnt) *adj.*
insulting and arrogant
Synonyms: audacious, rude, presumptuous, impertinent

VERDURE (vuhr juhr) *n.*
lush vegetation
Synonyms: grass, greenery, growth

PLACID (plaa sihd) *adj.*
calm
Synonyms: tranquil, serene, peaceful, complacent

ENNUI (ahn wee) (ahn wee) *n.*
boredom, lack of interest and energy
Synonyms: tedium, listlessness, world-weariness

SUBLIME (suh bliem) *adj.*
awe-inspiring; of high spiritual or moral value
Synonyms: noble, majestic, supreme, ideal

ABHORRENT (uhb hohr ehnt) *adj.*
loathsome, disgusting
Synonyms: hateful, condemnable, repellant, destestable

majestic oaks, the quantity of game, and the herds of stately deer, were all novelties to us.

From thence we proceeded to Oxford. As we entered this city, our minds were filled with the remembrance of the events that had been transacted there more than a century and a half before. It was here that Charles I had collected his forces. This city had remained faithful to him, after the whole nation had forsaken his cause to join the standard of parliament and liberty. The memory of that unfortunate king, and his companions, the **amiable** Falkland, the **insolent** Goring, his queen, and son, gave a peculiar interest to every part of the city, which they might be supposed to have inhabited. The spirit of elder days found a dwelling here, and we delighted to trace its footsteps. If these feelings had not found an imaginary gratification, the appearance of the city had yet in itself sufficient beauty to obtain our admiration. The colleges are ancient and picturesque; the streets are almost magnificent; and the lovely Isis, which flows beside it through meadows of exquisite **verdure**, is spread forth into a **placid** expanse of waters, which reflects its majestic assemblage of towers, and spires, and domes, embosomed among aged trees.

I enjoyed this scene; and yet my enjoyment was embittered both by the memory of the past, and the anticipation of the future. I was formed for peaceful happiness. During my youthful days discontent never visited my mind; and if I was ever overcome by **ennui**, the sight of what is beautiful in nature, or the study of what is excellent and **sublime** in the productions of man, could always interest my heart, and communicate elasticity to my spirits. But I am a blasted tree; the bolt has entered my soul; and I felt then that I should survive to exhibit, what I shall soon cease to be—a miserable spectacle of wrecked humanity, pitiable to others, and **abhorrent** to myself.

We passed a considerable period at Oxford, rambling

ANIMATING (aa nih mayt ihng) *adj.*

1. exciting

   Synonyms: inspiring, interesting, encouraging

2. lively or filled with life

   Synonyms: alive, awakening, enlivening

ILLUSTRIOUS (ih luhs tree uhs) *adj.*

famous, renowned

Synonyms: noted, celebrated, eminent, famed, notable

DEBASING (dih bays ihng) *adj.*

degrading or low in quality or stature

Synonyms: demeaning, denigrating, defiling

DISPOSE (dih spohz) *v.* **-ing,-ed.**

to deal with or settle; to put in place; to give tendency to

Synonyms: prepare, adjust, decide

CONTRIVE (kuhn triev) *v.* **-ing,-ed.**

to devise, plan, or manage; to form in an artistic manner

Synonyms: concoct, create, scheme, design

among its environs, and endeavouring to identify every spot which might relate to the most **animating** epoch of English history. Our little voyages of discovery were often prolonged by the successive objects that presented themselves. We visited the tomb of the **illustrious** Hampden, and the field on which that patriot fell. For a moment my soul was elevated from its **debasing** and miserable fears to contemplate the divine ideas of liberty and self-sacrifice, of which these sights were the monuments and the remembrancers. For an instant I dared to shake off my chains, and look around me with a free and lofty spirit; but the iron had eaten into my flesh, and I sank again, trembling and hopeless, into my miserable self.

We left Oxford with regret, and proceeded to Matlock, which was our next place of rest. The country in the neighbourhood of this village resembled, to a greater degree, the scenery of Switzerland; but every thing is on a lower scale, and the green hills want the crown of distant white Alps, which always attend on the piny mountains of my native country. We visited the wondrous cave, and the little cabinets of natural history, where the curiosities are **disposed** in the same manner as in the collections at Servox and Chamounix. The latter name made me tremble, when pronounced by Henry; and I hastened to quit Matlock, with which that terrible scene was thus associated.

From Derby still journeying northward, we passed two months in Cumberland and Westmoreland. I could now almost fancy myself among the Swiss mountains. The little patches of snow which yet lingered on the northern sides of the mountains, the lakes, and the dashing of the rocky streams, were all familiar and dear sights to me. Here also we made some acquaintances, who almost **contrived** to cheat me into happiness. The delight of Clerval was proportionably greater than mine; his mind expanded in the company of men of talent, and he found in his own nature greater capacities and resources

REPOSE (rih pohz) *n.*
relaxation, leisure
Synonyms: calmness, tranquility, rest, ease, idleness

FORSAKE (fohr sayk) *v.* **-ing,-sook.**
to abandon, withdraw from
Synonyms: desert, renounce, leave, quit

NEGLECT (neh glehkt) *v.* **-ing,-ed.**
to ignore or disregard, to be negligent
Synonyms: overlook, skimp

VENGEANCE (vehn juhns) *n.*
punishment inflicted in retaliation; vehemence
Synonyms: revenge, repayment, wrath

ASCERTAIN (aa suhr tayn) *v.* **-ing,-ed.**
to determine, discover, make certain of
Synonyms: verify, calculate, detect

EXPEDITE (ehk spuh diet) *v.* **-ing,-ed.**
to execute promptly; to accelerate the progress of; to dispatch
Synonyms: rush, quicken, urge, advance

REMISSNESS (rih mihss nihs) *n.*
negligence in the performance of work or duty
Synonyms: unwillingness, tardiness, idleness

LANGUID (laang gwihd) *adj.*
lacking energy, indifferent, slow
Synonyms: weak, listless, lackadaisical, sluggish, fainéant

than he could have imagined himself to have possessed while he associated with his inferiors. "I could pass my life here," said he to me, "and among these mountains I should scarcely regret Switzerland and the Rhine."

But he found that a traveller's life is one that includes much pain amidst its enjoyments. His feelings are for ever on the stretch; and when he begins to sink into **repose**, he finds himself obliged to quit that on which he rests in pleasure for something new, which again engages his attention, and which also he **forsakes** for other novelties.

We had scarcely visited the various lakes of Cumberland and Westmoreland, and conceived an affection for some of the inhabitants, when the period of our appointment with our Scotch friend approached, and we left them to travel on. For my own part I was not sorry. I had now **neglected** my promise for some time, and I feared the effects of the daemon's disappointment. He might remain in Switzerland, and wreak his **vengeance** on my relatives. This idea pursued me, and tormented me at every moment from which I might otherwise have snatched **repose** and peace. I waited for my letters with feverish impatience. If they were delayed, I was miserable, and overcome by a thousand fears; and when they arrived, and I saw the superscription of Elizabeth or my father, I hardly dared to read and **ascertain** my fate. Sometimes I thought that the fiend followed me, and might **expedite** my **remissness** by murdering my companion. When these thoughts possessed me, I would not quit Henry for a moment, but followed him as his shadow, to protect him from the fancied rage of his destroyer. I felt as if I had committed some great crime, the consciousness of which haunted me. I was guiltless, but I had indeed drawn down a horrible curse upon my head, as mortal as that of crime.

I visited Edinburgh with **languid** eyes and mind; and yet that city might have interested the most unfortunate being. Clerval did not like it so well as Oxford; for the

ANTIQUITY (aan <u>tih</u> kwih tee) *n.*
the quality of being very old
Synonyms: ancientness, history, antiqueness

COMPENSATE (<u>kahm</u> pehn sayt) *v.* **-ing,-ed.**
to repay or reimburse
Synonyms: indemnify, recompense, balance

ENTREAT (ehn <u>treet</u>) *v.* **-ing,-ed.**
to plead, beg
Synonyms: beseech, implore, importune, request, petition

CONGENIAL (kuhn <u>jee</u> nee uhl) (kuhn <u>jeen</u> yuhl) *adj.*
similar in tastes and habits; having a pleasant disposition
Synonyms: affable, pleasurable, amiable, personable, agreeable

DISSUADE (dih <u>swayd</u>) *v.* **-ing,-ed.**
to persuade someone to alter original intentions
Synonyms: discourage, deter

REMONSTRATE (reh <u>mahn</u> strayt) *v.* **-ing,-ed.**
to present and urge reasons in opposition; to say or plead in protest
Synonyms: challenge, resist, dispute

RESOLUTION (reh suh <u>loo</u> shun) *n.*
firm determination; a formal decision
Synonyms: firmness, intention, resolve

TRAVERSE (truh <u>vuhrs</u>) (traa <u>vuhrs</u>) *v.* **-ing,-ed.**
to travel or travel across; to turn or move laterally
Synonyms: cross, travel, intersect, pass through

REMOTE (rih <u>moht</u>) *adj.*
distant, isolated
Synonyms: far, removed, aloof

antiquity of the latter city was more pleasing to him. But the beauty and regularity of the new town of Edinburgh, its romantic castle, and its environs, the most delightful in the world, Arthur's Seat, St. Bernard's Well, and the Pentland Hills, **compensated** him for the change, and filled him with cheerfulness and admiration. But I was impatient to arrive at the termination of my journey.

We left Edinburgh in a week, passing through Coupar, St. Andrews, and along the banks of the Tay, to Perth, where our friend expected us. But I was in no mood to laugh and talk with strangers, or enter into their feelings or plans with the good humour expected from a guest; and accordingly I told Clerval that I wished to make the tour of Scotland alone. "Do you," said I, "enjoy yourself, and let this be our rendezvous. I may be absent a month or two; but do not interfere with my motions, I **entreat** you. Leave me to peace and solitude for a short time; and when I return, I hope it will be with a lighter heart, more **congenial** to your own temper."

Henry wished to **dissuade** me; but, seeing me bent on this plan, ceased to **remonstrate**. He **entreated** me to write often. "I had rather be with you," he said, "in your solitary rambles, than with these Scotch people, whom I do not know. Hasten then, my dear friend, to return, that I may again feel myself somewhat at home, which I cannot do in your absence."

Having parted from my friend, I determined to visit some remote spot of Scotland, and finish my work in solitude. I did not doubt but that the monster followed me, and would discover himself to me when I should have finished, that he might receive his companion.

With this **resolution I traversed** the northern highlands, and fixed on one of the **remotest** of the Orkneys as the scene of my labours. It was a place fitted for such a work, being hardly more than a rock, whose high sides were continually beaten upon by the waves. The soil was barren, scarcely affording pasture for a few miserable cows,

GAUNT (gawnt) *adj.*
thin and bony
Synonyms: lean, spare, skinny, scrawny, lank

INDULGE (ihn duhlj) *v.* **-ing,-ed.**
to give in to a craving or desire
Synonyms: humor, gratify, allow, pamper

LUXURY (luhg zhoor ee) *n.*
an elegant thing; opulence and exorbitance
Synonyms: extra, extravagance, nonessential

PROCURE (proh kyoor) *v.* **-ing,-ed.**
to obtain
Synonyms: acquire, secure, get, gain

SQUALIDNESS (skwa lihd nehs) *n.*
filth or poverty; moral repulsion
Synonyms: foulness, nastiness, wretchedness

PENURY (pehn yuh ree) *n.*
extreme poverty
Synonyms: destitution, beggary, need, privation

SQUALID (skwa lihd) *adj.*
filthy; morally repulsive
Synonyms: dirty, foul, nasty, wretched, sordid

PITTANCE (pih tehnts) *n.*
a small portion, amount, or wage
Synonyms: ration, trace, bit, insufficiency

MONOTONOUS (muh nah tuh nihs) *adj.*
repetitive, unvaried
Synonyms: recurrent, tedious, boring, dull

DESOLATE (deh soh liht) *adj.*
showing the effects of abandonment or neglect; devoid of warmth or comfort
Synonyms: barren, bleak, forsaken, vacant

APPALLING (uh pahl lihng) *adj.*
overcome with shock or dismay
Synonyms: horrifying, dreadful, ghastly, awful

TUMULT (tuh muhlt) *n.*
state of confusion; agitation
Synonyms: disturbance, turmoil, din, commotion, chaos

and oatmeal for its inhabitants, which consisted of five persons, whose **gaunt** and scraggy limbs gave tokens of their miserable fare. Vegetables and bread, when they **indulged** in such **luxuries**, and even fresh water, were to be **procured** from the main land, which was about five miles distant.

On the whole island there were but three miserable huts, and one of these was vacant when I arrived. This I hired. It contained but two rooms, and these exhibited all the **squalidness** of the most miserable **penury**. The thatch had fallen in, the walls were unplastered, and the door was off its hinges. I ordered it to be repaired, bought some furniture, and took possession; an incident which would, doubtless, have occasioned some surprise, had not all the senses of the cottagers been benumbed by want and **squalid** poverty. As it was, I lived ungazed at and unmolested, hardly thanked for the **pittance** of food and clothes which I gave; so much does suffering blunt even the coarsest sensations of men.

In this retreat I devoted the morning to labour; but in the evening, when the weather permitted, I walked on the stony beach of the sea, to listen to the waves as they roared, and dashed at my feet. It was a **monotonous**, yet ever-changing scene. I thought of Switzerland; it was far different from this **desolate** and **appalling** landscape. Its hills are covered with vines, and its cottages are scattered thickly in the plains. Its fair lakes reflect a blue and gentle sky; and, when troubled by the winds, their **tumult** is but as the play of a lively infant, when compared to the roarings of the giant ocean.

In this manner I distributed my occupations when I first arrived; but, as I proceeded in my labour, it became every day more horrible and irksome to me. Sometimes I could not prevail on myself to enter my laboratory for several days; and at other times I toiled day and night in order to complete my work. It was indeed a filthy process in which I was engaged. During my first experiment, a

DETESTABLE (dee tehst uh buhl) *adj.*
deserving of intense and violent hatred
Synonyms: disgusting, despicable, loathsome

IMMERSE (ih muhrs) *v.* **-ing,-ed.**
to bathe, dip; to engross, preoccupy
Synonyms: douse, dunk, submerge, engage, absorb

TREMULOUS (treh myoo luhs) *adj.*
trembling, quivering; fearful, timid
Synonyms: shaking, palsied, timorous, anxious

OBSCURE (uhb skyoor) *adj.*
dim, unclear; not well known
Synonyms: dark, faint, remote, dim, minor

FOREBODING (fohr boh dihng) *n.*
an omen, prediction, or presentiment of upcoming evil
Synonyms: anxiety, dread, premonition, augury

UNREMITTING (uhn rih mih ting) *adj.*
never lessening, persistent
Synonyms: incessant, continued, persevering

BARBARITY (bahr baa rih tee) *n.*
lack of culture or refinement; merciless cruelty
Synonyms: savagery, vulgarity, inhumanity

DESOLATE (deh suh layt) *v.* **-ing,-ed.**
to lay waste or make wretched; to deprive of inhabitants
Synonyms: destroy, devastate, pillage, plunder

REMORSE (rih mohrs) *n.*
a gnawing distress arising from a sense of guilt
Synonyms: anguish, ruefulness, shame, penitence

kind of enthusiastic frenzy had blinded me to the horror of my employment; my mind was intently fixed on the sequel of my labour, and my eyes were shut to the horror of my proceedings. But now I went to it in cold blood, and my heart often sickened at the work of my hands.

Thus situated, employed in the most **detestable** occupation, **immersed** in a solitude where nothing could for an instant call my attention from the actual scene in which I was engaged, my spirits became unequal; I grew restless and nervous. Every moment I feared to meet my persecutor. Sometimes I sat with my eyes fixed on the ground, fearing to raise them lest they should encounter the object that I so much dreaded to behold. I feared to wander from the sight of my fellow-creatures, lest when alone he should come to claim his companion.

In the mean time I worked on, and my labour was already considerably advanced. I looked towards its completion with a **tremulous** and eager hope, which I dared not trust myself to question, but which was intermixed with **obscure forebodings** of evil, that made my heart sicken in my bosom.

CHAPTER III

I sat one evening in my laboratory; the sun had set, and the moon was just rising from the sea; I had not sufficient light for my employment, and I remained idle, in a pause of consideration of whether I should leave my labour for the night, or hasten its conclusion by an **unremitting** attention to it. As I sat, a train of reflection occurred to me, which led me to consider the effects of what I was now doing. Three years before I was engaged in the same manner, and had created a fiend whose unparalleled **barbarity** had **desolated** my heart, and filled it for ever with the bitterest **remorse**. I was now about to form

MALIGNANT (muh lihg nehnt) *adj.*
evil in influence of effect; aggressively malicious; tending to produce death
Synonyms: deadly, destructive, poisonous

COMPLY (kuhm plie) *v.* **-ing,-ed.**
to yield or agree, to go along with
Synonyms: accord, submit, acquiesce, obey, respect

LOATHE (lohth) *v.* **-ing,-ed.**
to abhor, despise, hate
Synonyms: abominate, execrate, detest, condemn

DEFORMITY (dih fohr mih tee) *n.*
disfigurement, the state of being misshapen
Synonyms: contortion, malformation, disproportion

ABHORRENCE (uhb hohr ehnts) *n.*
loathing, detestation
Synonyms: hatred, condemnation, abomination, execration

EXASPERATE (ihg zaas puhr ayt) *v.* **-ing,-ed.**
irritate
Synonyms: frustrate, annoy, vex, pique

PROVOCATION (proh vah kay shuhn) *n.*
something that provokes a response, e.g., anger or disagreement
Synonyms: controversy, stimulation, contention

PROPAGATE (prah puh gayt) *v.* **-ing,-ed.**
to spread or proliferate; to breed
Synonyms: distribute, circulate, disseminate, reproduce, procreate

PRECARIOUS (prih caa ree uhs) *adj.*
uncertain
Synonyms: insecure, unstable, hazardous, perilous

LOITER (loy tuhr) *v.* **-ing,-ed.**
to stand around idly
Synonyms: linger, delay, dawdle

another being, of whose dispositions I was alike ignorant; she might become ten thousand times more **malignant** than her mate, and delight, for its own sake, in murder and wretchedness. He had sworn to quit the neighbourhood of man, and hide himself in deserts; but she had not; and she, who in all probability was to become a thinking and reasoning animal, might refuse to **comply** with a compact made before her creation. They might even hate each other; the creature who already lived **loathed** his own **deformity**, and might he not conceive a greater **abhorrence** for it when it came before his eyes in the female form? She also might turn with disgust from him to the superior beauty of man; she might quit him, and he would be again alone, **exasperated** by the fresh **provocation** of being deserted by one of his own species.

Even if they were to leave Europe, and inhabit the deserts of the New World, yet one of the first results of those sympathies for which the daemon thirsted would be children, and a race of devils would be **propagated** upon the earth, who might make the very existence of the species of man a condition **precarious** and full of terror. Had I a right, for my own benefit, to inflict this curse upon everlasting generations? I had before been moved by the sophisms of the being I had created; I had been struck senseless by his fiendish threats. But now, for the first time, the wickedness of my promise burst upon me; I shuddered to think that future ages might curse me as their pest, whose selfishness had not hesitated to buy its own peace at the price perhaps of the existence of the whole human race.

I trembled, and my heart failed within me; when, on looking up, I saw, by the light of the moon, the daemon at the casement. A ghastly grin wrinkled his lips as he gazed on me, where I sat fulfilling the task which he had allotted to me. Yes, he had followed me in my travels; he had **loitered** in forests, hid himself in caves, or taken refuge in wide and desert heaths; and he now came to mark my progress, and claim the fulfilment of my promise.

COUNTENANCE (kown tuh nuhns) *n.*
appearance, facial expression
Synonyms: face, features, visage

MALICE (maal ihs) *n.*
animosity, spite, hatred
Synonyms: malevolence, cruelty, enmity, rancor, hostility

TREACHERY (treh chuhr ee) *n.*
betrayal of trust, deceit
Synonyms: perfidy, treason, disloyalty, falseness, infidelity

SOLEMN (sah luhm) *adj.*
deeply serious; somberly impressive
Synonyms: dignified, earnest, ceremonial

DISSIPATE (dihs uh payt) *v.* **-ing,-ed.**
to scatter; to pursue pleasure to excess
Synonyms: carouse, squander, consume; disperse, dissolve

REVERIE (rehv uh ree) *n.*
a daydream
Synonyms: dream, absorption, muse, meditation

REPOSE (rih pohz) *v.* **-ing,-ed.**
1. to relax or rest; to lie dead
Synonyms: sleep, slumber
2. to place (trust) or to count on
Synonyms: entrust, invest, place

PROFUNDITY (pruh fuhn dih tee) *n.*
intellectual depth; great depth
Synonyms: intellect, shrewdness; extent, intensity

IMPENDING (ihm pehn dihng) *adj.*
hovering threateningly; about to occur, approaching
Synonyms: looming, ominous, forthcoming

As I looked on him, his **countenance** expressed the utmost extent of **malice** and **treachery**. I thought with a sensation of madness on my promise of creating another like to him, and, trembling with passion, tore to pieces the thing on which I was engaged. The wretch saw me destroy the creature on whose future existence he depended for happiness, and, with a howl of devilish despair and revenge, withdrew.

I left the room, and, locking the door, made a **solemn** vow in my own heart never to resume my labours; and then, with trembling steps, I sought my own apartment. I was alone; none were near me to **dissipate** the gloom, and relieve me from the sickening oppression of the most terrible **reveries**.

Several hours passed, and I remained near my window gazing on the sea; it was almost motionless, for the winds were hushed, and all nature **reposed** under the eye of the quiet moon. A few fishing vessels alone specked the water, and now and then the gentle breeze wafted the sound of voices, as the fishermen called to one another. I felt the silence, although I was hardly conscious of its extreme **profundity** until my ear was suddenly arrested by the paddling of oars near the shore, and a person landed close to my house.

In a few minutes after, I heard the creaking of my door, as if some one endeavoured to open it softly. I trembled from head to foot; I felt a presentiment of who it was, and wished to rouse one of the peasants who dwelt in a cottage not far from mine; but I was overcome by the sensation of helplessness, so often felt in frightful dreams, when you in vain endeavour to fly from an **impending** danger, and was rooted to the spot.

Presently I heard the sound of footsteps along the passage; the door opened, and the wretch whom I dreaded appeared. Shutting the door, he approached me, and said, in a smothered voice—

"You have destroyed the work which you began; what

DEFORMITY (dih fohr mih tee) *n.*
disfigurement, the state of being misshapen
Synonyms: contortion, malformation, disproportion

CONDESCENSION (kahn dih sehn shuhn) *n.*
an attitude of superiority
Synonyms: patronization, superiority, smugness

RESOLUTION (reh suh loo shuhn) *n.*
a firm decision
Synonyms: determination, will, explanation

EXASPERATE (ihg zaas puhr ayt) *v.* **-ing,-ed.**
irritate
Synonyms: frustrate, annoy, vex, pique

REQUITE (rih kwiet) *v.* **-ing,-ed.**
to return or repay
Synonyms: reciprocate, avenge, compensate, reimburse, recompense

DETESTATION (dee tehs tay shuhn) *n.*
intense and violent hatred
Synonyms: hate, disgust, loathing, abhorrence

RAVISH (raa vihsh) *v.* **-ing,-ed.**
to overcome with emotion; to seize and take away through violence
Synonyms: enchant, captivate, enthrall; assault

GROVEL (grah vuhl) *v.* **-ing,-ed.**
to humble oneself in a demeaning way
Synonyms: cringe, fawn, kowtow, toady, bootlick

is it that you intend? Do you dare to break your promise? I have endured toil and misery. I left Switzerland with you; I crept along the shores of the Rhine, among its willow islands, and over the summits of its hills. I have dwelt many months in the heaths of England, and among the deserts of Scotland. I have endured incalculable fatigue, and cold, and hunger; do you dare destroy my hopes?"

"Begone! I do break my promise; never will I create another like yourself, equal in **deformity** and wickedness."

"Slave, I before reasoned with you, but you have proved yourself unworthy of my **condescension**. Remember that I have power; you believe yourself miserable, but I can make you so wretched that the light of day will be hateful to you. You are my creator, but I am your master—obey!"

"The hour of my weakness is past, and the period of your power is arrived. Your threats cannot move me to do an act of wickedness; but they confirm me in a **resolution** of not creating you a companion in vice. Shall I, in cool blood, set loose upon the earth a daemon, whose delight is in death and wretchedness? Begone! I am firm, and your words will only **exasperate** my rage."

The monster saw my determination in my face, and gnashed his teeth in the impotence of anger. "Shall each man," cried he, "find a wife for his bosom, and each beast have his mate, and I be alone? I had feelings of affection, and they were **requited** by **detestation** and scorn. Man, you may hate; but beware! Your hours will pass in dread and misery, and soon the bolt will fall which must **ravish** from you your happiness for ever. Are you to be happy, while I **grovel** in the intensity of my wretchedness? You can blast my other passions; but revenge remains—revenge, henceforth dearer than light or food! I may die; but first you, my tyrant and tormentor, shall curse the sun that gazes on your misery. Beware; for I am fearless, and therefore powerful. I will

WILINESS (wie lee nehs) *n.*
cleverness, deception
Synonyms: cunning, slyness, trickery, craftiness

REPENT (rih pehnt) *v.* **-ing,-ed.**
to regret a past action
Synonyms: rue, atone, apologize

MALICE (maal ihs) *n.*
animosity, spite, hatred
Synonyms: malevolence, cruelty, enmity, rancor

RESOLUTION (reh suh loo shun) *n.* ***See page 312.***

INEXORABLE (ihn ehk suhr uh buhl) *adj.*
inflexible, unyielding
Synonyms: adamant, obdurate, relentless

ELUDE (ih lood) *v.* **-ing,-ed.**
escape, avoid
Synonyms: evade, dodge

PRECIPITATION (preh sih puh tay shuhn) *n.*
sudden and unexpected haste
Synonyms: abruptness, recklessness, rashness

PRECIPITATE (preh sih puh tayt) *v.* **-ing,-ed.**
1. to throw, usually from a great height
Synonyms: hurl, fall, rush
2. to bring about abruptly
Synonyms: speed, launch, accelerate, quicken

PERTURBED (puhr tuhrb) *adj.*
disturbed and upset
Synonyms: bothered, annoyed, distressed, confused

CONJURE (kahn juhr) *v.* **-ing,-ed.**
to call on or beg solemnly; to affect or effect as if by magic; to bring to mind
Synonyms: entreat, implore, rouse, recollect

INSATIATE (ihn say shee iht) *adj.*
unable to be satisfied
Synonyms: insatiable, greedy, ravenous, gluttonous

BARBAROUSLY (baar buh ruhs lee) *adv.*
without culture or refinement; with merciless cruelty
Synonyms: savagely, vulgarly, inhumanely

RESOLVE (rih sahlv) *v.* **-ing,-ed.** ***See page 290.***

watch with the **wiliness** of a snake, that I may sting with its venom. Man, you shall **repent** of the injuries you inflict."

"Devil, cease; and do not poison the air with these sounds of **malice**. I have declared my **resolution** to you, and I am no coward to bend beneath words. Leave me; I am **inexorable**."

"It is well. I go; but remember, I will be with you on your wedding-night."

I started forward, and exclaimed, "Villain! Before you sign my death-warrant, be sure that you are yourself safe."

I would have seized him; but he **eluded** me, and quitted the house with **precipitation**. In a few moments I saw him in his boat, which shot across the waters with an arrowy swiftness, and was soon lost amidst the waves.

All was again silent; but his words rung in my ears. I burned with rage to pursue the murderer of my peace, and **precipitate** him into the ocean. I walked up and down my room hastily and **perturbed**, while my imagination **conjured** up a thousand images to torment and sting me. Why had I not followed him, and closed with him in mortal strife? But I had suffered him to depart, and he had directed his course towards the main land. I shuddered to think who might be the next victim sacrificed to his **insatiate** revenge. And then I thought again of his words—"*I will be with you on your wedding-night.*" That then was the period fixed for the fulfilment of my destiny. In that hour I should die, and at once satisfy and extinguish his **malice**. The prospect did not move me to fear; yet when I thought of my beloved Elizabeth, of her tears and endless sorrow, when she should find her lover so **barbarously** snatched from her, tears, the first I had shed for many months, streamed from my eyes, and I **resolved** not to fall before my enemy without a bitter struggle.

The night passed away, and the sun rose from the

CONTENTION (kuhn <u>tehn</u> shuhn) *n.*
quarrel, disagreement; state of belligerence
Synonyms: argument, assertion

INSUPERABLE (ihn <u>soo</u> puhr uh buhl) *adj.*
insurmountable, unconquerable
Synonyms: unbeatable, undefeatable, invincible

AGITATED (<u>aa</u> gih tay tihd) *adj.*
upset or uneasy
Synonyms: disturbed, flustered, bothered

RAVENOUS (<u>raa</u> vehn uhs) *adj.*
extremely hungry
Synonyms: voracious, gluttonous, rapacious, predatory, famished

ENTREAT (ehn <u>treet</u>) *v.* **-ing,-ed.**
to plead, beg
Synonyms: beseech, implore, importune, request, petition

EXPIRATION (ehk spuhr <u>ay</u> shuhn) *n.*
1. an end or ending; death
Synonyms: termination, conclusion, cessation
2. the action of breathing out
Synonyms: exhalation, inhalation

ocean; my feelings became calmer, if it may be called calmness, when the violence of rage sinks into the depths of despair. I left the house, the horrid scene of the last night's **contention**, and walked on the beach of the sea, which I almost regarded as an **insuperable** barrier between me and my fellow-creatures; nay, a wish that such should prove the fact stole across me. I desired that I might pass my life on that barren rock, wearily it is true, but uninterrupted by any sudden shock of misery. If I returned, it was to be sacrificed, or to see those whom I most loved die under the grasp of a daemon whom I had myself created.

I walked about the isle like a restless spectre, separated from all it loved, and miserable in the separation. When it became noon, and the sun rose higher, I lay down on the grass, and was overpowered by a deep sleep. I had been awake the whole of the preceding night, my nerves were **agitated**, and my eyes inflamed by watching and misery. The sleep into which I now sunk refreshed me; and when I awoke, I again felt as if I belonged to a race of human beings like myself, and I began to reflect upon what had passed with greater composure; yet still the words of the fiend rung in my ears like a death-knell, they appeared like a dream, yet distinct and oppressive as a reality.

The sun had far descended, and I still sat on the shore, satisfying my appetite, which had become **ravenous**, with an oaten cake, when I saw a fishing-boat land close to me, and one of the men brought me a packet; it contained letters from Geneva, and one from Clerval, **entreating** me to join him. He said that nearly a year had elapsed since we had quitted Switzerland, and France was yet unvisited. He **entreated** me, therefore, to leave my solitary isle, and meet him at Perth, in a week from that time, when we might arrange the plan of our future proceedings. This letter in a degree recalled me to life, and I determined to quit my island at the **expiration** of two days.

Yet, before I departed, there was a task to perform, on

ODIOUS (<u>oh</u> dee uhs) *adj.*
hateful, contemptible
Synonyms: detestable, obnoxious, offensive, repellent, loathsome

AVERT (uh <u>vuhrt</u>) *v.* **-ing,-ed.**
to turn away; avoid
Synonyms: deter, forestall, preclude, deflect, parry

RESOLVE (rih <u>sahlv</u>) *v.* **-ing,-ed.**
to determine or to make a firm decision about
Synonyms: solve, decide

BASE (bays) *adj.*
lacking qualities of higher mind or spirit
Synonyms: vulgar, corrupt, immoral, menial

ATROCIOUS (uh <u>troh</u> shuhs) *adj.*
revolting, shockingly bad, wicked
Synonyms: horrible, appalling, deplorable, direful

BANISH (<u>baan</u> ish) *v.* **-ing,-ed.**
to force to leave, exile
Synonyms: expel, deport

which I shuddered to reflect. I must pack my chemical instruments; and for that purpose I must enter the room which had been the scene of my **odious** work, and I must handle those utensils, the sight of which was sickening to me. The next morning, at day-break, I summoned sufficient courage, and unlocked the door of my laboratory. The remains of the half-finished creature, whom I had destroyed, lay scattered on the floor, and I almost felt as if I had mangled the living flesh of a human being. I paused to collect myself, and then entered the chamber. With trembling hand I conveyed the instruments out of the room; but I reflected that I ought not to leave the relics of my work to excite the horror and suspicion of the peasants, and I accordingly put them into a basket, with a great quantity of stones, and laying them up, determined to throw them into the sea that very night; and in the mean time I sat upon the beach, employed in cleaning and arranging my chemical apparatus.

Nothing could be more complete than the alteration that had taken place in my feelings since the night of the appearance of the daemon. I had before regarded my promise with a gloomy despair, as a thing that, with whatever consequences, must be fulfilled; but I now felt as if a film had been taken from before my eyes, and that I, for the first time, saw clearly. The idea of renewing my labours did not for one instant occur to me; the threat I had heard weighed on my thoughts, but I did not reflect that a voluntary act of mine could **avert** it. I had **resolved** in my own mind, that to create another like the fiend I had first made would be an act of the **basest** and most **atrocious** selfishness; and I **banished** from my mind every thought that could lead to a different conclusion.

Between two and three in the morning the moon rose; and I then, putting my basket aboard a little skiff, sailed out about four miles from the shore. The scene was perfectly solitary. A few boats were returning towards land, but I sailed away from them. I felt as if I was about the

RESOLVE (rih <u>sahlv</u>) *v.* **-ing,-ed.**
to determine or to make a firm decision about
Synonyms: solve, decide

OBSCURE (uhb <u>skyoor</u>) *adj.*
dim, unclear; not well known
Synonyms: dark, faint, remote, dim, minor

commission of a dreadful crime, and avoided with shuddering anxiety any encounter with my fellow-creatures. At one time the moon, which had before been clear, was suddenly overspread by a thick cloud, and I took advantage of the moment of darkness, and cast my basket into the sea; I listened to the gurgling sound as it sunk, and then sailed away from the spot. The sky became clouded; but the air was pure, although chilled by the north-east breeze that was then rising. But it refreshed me, and filled me with such agreeable sensations, that I **resolved** to prolong my stay on the water, and fixing the rudder in a direct position, stretched myself at the bottom of the boat. Clouds hid the moon, every thing was **obscure**, and I heard only the sound of the boat, as its keel cut through the waves; the murmur lulled me, and in a short time I slept soundly.

I do not know how long I remained in this situation, but when I awoke I found that the sun had already mounted considerably. The wind was high, and the waves continually threatened the safety of my little skiff. I found that the wind was north-east, and must have driven me far from the coast from which I had embarked. I endeavoured to change my course, but quickly found that if I again made the attempt the boat would be instantly filled with water. Thus situated, my only resource was to drive before the wind. I confess that I felt a few sensations of terror. I had no compass with me, and was so little acquainted with the geography of this part of the world that the sun was of little benefit to me. I might be driven into the wide Atlantic, and feel all the tortures of starvation, or be swallowed up in the immeasurable waters that roared and buffeted around me. I had already been out many hours, and felt the torment of a burning thirst, a prelude to my other sufferings. I looked on the heavens, which were covered by clouds that flew before the wind only to be replaced by others. I looked upon the sea, it was to be my grave. "Fiend," I

REVERIE (rehv uh ree) *n.*
a daydream
Synonyms: dream, absorption, muse, meditation

MUTABLE (myoo tuh buhl) *adj.*
changeable, inconsistent
Synonyms: inconstant, impermanent

DEBILITY (dih bih lih tee) *n.*
weakness
Synonyms: devitalization, enervation, exhaustion

RESOLVE (rih sahlv) *v.* **-ing,-ed.**
to determine or to make a firm decision about
Synonyms: solve, decide

PROCURE (proh kyoor) *v.* **-ing,-ed.**
to obtain
Synonyms: acquire, secure, get, gain

exclaimed, "your task is already fulfilled!" I thought of Elizabeth, of my father, and of Clerval; and sunk into a **reverie**, so despairing and frightful, that even now, when the scene is on the point of closing before me for ever, I shudder to reflect on it.

Some hours passed thus; but by degrees, as the sun declined towards the horizon, the wind died away into a gentle breeze, and the sea became free from breakers. But these gave place to a heavy swell; I felt sick, and hardly able to hold the rudder, when suddenly I saw a line of high land towards the south.

Almost spent, as I was by fatigue, and the dreadful suspense I endured for several hours, this sudden certainty of life rushed like a flood of warm joy to my heart, and tears gushed from my eyes.

How **mutable** are our feelings, and how strange is that clinging love we have of life even in the excess of misery! I constructed another sail with a part of my dress, and eagerly steered my course towards the land. It had a wild and rocky appearance; but as I approached nearer, I easily perceived the traces of cultivation. I saw vessels near the shore, and found myself suddenly transported back to the neighbourhood of civilized man. I eagerly traced the windings of the land, and hailed a steeple which I at length saw issuing from behind a small promontory. As I was in a state of extreme **debility**, I **resolved** to sail directly towards the town as a place where I could most easily **procure** nourishment. Fortunately I had money with me. As I turned toward the promontory, I perceived a small neat town and a good harbour, which I entered, my heart bounding with joy at my unexpected escape.

As I was occupied in fixing the boat and arranging the sails, several people crowded towards the spot. They seemed very much surprised at my appearance; but, instead of offering me any assistance, whispered together with gestures that at any other time might have produced in me a slight sensation of alarm. As it was, I merely

DISCONCERTED (dihs kuhn suhr tehd) *adj.*
confused; discomposed
Synonyms: frustrated, ruffled, disturbed

COUNTENANCE (kown tuh nuhns) *n.*
appearance, facial expression
Synonyms: face, features, visage

MAGISTRATE (maa juh strayt) *n.*
an official who can administrate laws
Synonyms: judge, arbiter, authority, marshal

remarked that they spoke English; and I therefore addressed them in that language. "My good friends," said I, "will you be so kind as to tell me the name of this town, and inform me where I am?"

"You will know that soon enough," replied a man with a gruff voice. "Maybe you have come to a place that will not prove much to your taste, but you will not be consulted as to your quarters, I promise you."

I was exceedingly surprised on receiving so rude an answer from a stranger; and I was also **disconcerted** on perceiving the frowning and angry **countenances** of his companions. "Why do you answer me so roughly?" I replied. "Surely it is not the custom of Englishmen to receive strangers so inhospitably."

"I do not know," said the man, "what the custom of the English may be, but it is the custom of the Irish to hate villains."

While this strange dialogue continued, I perceived the crowd to rapidly increase. Their faces expressed a mixture of curiosity and anger, which annoyed, and in some degree alarmed me. I inquired the way to the inn; but no one replied. I then moved forward, and a murmuring sound arose from the crowd as they followed and surrounded me; when an ill-looking man approaching tapped me on the shoulder, and said, "Come, Sir, you must follow me to Mr. Kirwin's, to give an account of yourself."

"Who is Mr. Kirwin? Why am I to give an account of myself? Is not this a free country?"

"Aye, sir, free enough for honest folks. Mr. Kirwin is a **magistrate**; and you are to give an account of the death of a gentleman who was found murdered here last night."

This answer startled me; but I presently recovered myself. I was innocent; that could easily be proved. Accordingly I followed my conductor in silence, and was led to one of the best houses in the town. I was ready to

POLITIC (pah luh tihk) *adj.*
discreet, tactful
Synonyms: prudent, artful, diplomatic, judicious, cunning

DEBILITY (dih bih lih tee) *n.*
weakness
Synonyms: devitalization, enervation, exhaustion

CONSTRUE (kuhn stroo) *v.* **-ing,-ed.**
to explain or interpret
Synonyms: analyze, translate

APPREHENSION (aa prih hehn shuhn) *n.*
1. suspicion or fear of future or unknown evil
Synonyms: mistrust, uneasiness
2. a legal seizure
Synonym: arrest

CALAMITY (kuh laam ih tee) *n.*
state of despair, misfortune
Synonyms: disaster, cataclysm

IGNOMINY (ihg nuh mih nee) *n.*
disgrace and dishonor
Synonyms: degradation, debasement, shame

FORTITUDE (fohr tih tood) *n.*
strength, stamina
Synonyms: endurance, hardiness, toughness, courage

MAGISTRATE (maa juh strayt) *n.*
an official who can administrate laws
Synonyms: judge, arbiter, authority, marshal

BENEVOLENT (buh neh vuh luhnt) *adj.*
kind, compassionate
Synonyms: charitable, altruistic, beneficent, generous

DEPOSE (dih pohs) *v.* **-ing,-ed.**
to testify; to remove from a high position
Synonyms: swear; unseat, dethrone, overthrow

sink from fatigue and hunger; but, being surrounded by a crowd, I thought it **politic** to rouse all my strength, that no physical **debility** might be **construed** into **apprehension** or conscious guilt. Little did I then expect the **calamity** that was in a few moments to overwhelm me, and extinguish in horror and despair all fear of **ignominy** or death.

I must pause here; for it requires all my **fortitude** to recall the memory of the frightful events which I am about to relate, in proper detail, to my recollection.

CHAPTER IV

I was soon introduced into the presence of the **magistrate**, an old **benevolent** man, with calm and mild manners. He looked upon me, however, with some degree of severity; and then, turning towards my conductors, he asked who appeared as witnesses on this occasion.

About half a dozen men came forward; and one being selected by the **magistrate**, he **deposed**, that he had been out fishing the night before with his son and brother-in-law, Daniel Nugent, when, about ten o'clock, they observed a strong northerly blast rising, and they accordingly put in for port. It was a very dark night, as the moon had not yet risen; they did not land at the harbour, but, as they had been accustomed, at a creek about two miles below. He walked on first, carrying a part of the fishing tackle, and his companions followed him at some distance. As he was proceeding along the sands, he struck his foot against something, and fell all his length on the ground. His companions came up to assist him; and, by the light of their lantern, they found that he had fallen on the body of a man, who was to all appearance dead. Their first <u>supposition</u> was, that it was the corpse of some person who had been drowned, and was thrown on shore by the waves; but, upon examination, they found

DEPOSITION (deh puh zih shuhn) *n.*
a testimony under oath that has been written down
Synonyms: affidavit, attestation

AGITATED (aa gih tay tihd) *adj.*
upset or uneasy
Synonyms: disturbed, flustered, bothered

MAGISTRATE (maa juh strayt) *n.*
an official who can administrate laws
Synonyms: judge, arbiter, authority, marshal

AUGURY (aw gyuh ree) (aw guh ree) *n.*
prophecy, prediction of events
Synonyms: omen, auspices, portent, harbinger, presage

DEPOSE (dih pohs) *v.* **-ing,-ed.**
to testify; to remove from a high position
Synonyms: swear; unseat, dethrone, overthrow

that the clothes were not wet, and even that the body was not then cold. They instantly carried it to the cottage of an old woman near the spot, and endeavoured, but in vain, to restore it to life. He appeared to be a handsome young man, about five and twenty years of age. He had apparently been strangled; for there was no sign of any violence, except the black mark of fingers on his neck.

The first part of this **deposition** did not in the least interest me; but when the mark of the fingers was mentioned, I remembered the murder of my brother, and felt myself extremely **agitated**; my limbs trembled, and a mist came over my eyes, which obliged me to lean on a chair for support. The **magistrate** observed me with a keen eye, and of course drew an unfavourable **augury** from my manner.

The son confirmed his father's account. But when Daniel Nugent was called, he swore positively that just before the fall of his companion he saw a boat, with a single man in it, at a short distance from the shore; and, as far as he could judge by the light of a few stars, it was the same boat in which I had just landed.

A woman **deposed** that she lived near the beach, and was standing at the door of her cottage, waiting for the return of the fishermen, about an hour before she heard of the discovery of the body, when she saw a boat, with only one man in it, push off from that part of the shore where the corpse was afterwards found.

Another woman confirmed the account of the fishermen having brought the body into her house; it was not cold. They put it into a bed, and rubbed it; and Daniel went to the town for an apothecary, but life was quite gone.

Several other men were examined concerning my landing; and they agreed, that, with the strong north wind that had arisen during the night, it was very probable that I had beaten about for many hours, and had been obliged to return nearly to the same spot from which I had departed.

INTERMENT (ihn tuhr mehnt) *n.*
burial
Synonyms: entombment, inhumation

AGITATION (aa gih tay shuhn) *n.*
commotion, excitement; uneasiness
Synonyms: disturbance, restlessness, anxiety, fluster, disquiet

MAGISTRATE (maa juh strayt) *n.*
an official who can administrate laws
Synonyms: judge, arbiter, authority, marshal

PARCHED (pahrchd) *adj.*
extremely thirsty; shriveled
Synonyms: dehydrated, desiccated, scorched

MACHINATION (mahk uh nay shuhn) *n.*
plot or scheme
Synonyms: conspiracy, intrigue, design, cabal

BENEFACTOR (behn uh faak tohr) *n.*
someone giving aid or money
Synonyms: contributor, backer, donor, patron

Besides, they observed that it appeared that I had brought the body from another place, and it was likely, that as I did not appear to know the shore, I might have put it into the harbour ignorant of the distance of the town of——from the place where I had deposited the corpse.

Mr. Kirwin, on hearing this evidence, desired that I should be taken into the room where the body lay for **interment** that it might be observed what effect the sight of it would produce upon me. This idea was probably suggested by the extreme **agitation** I had exhibited when the mode of the murder had been described. I was accordingly conducted, by the **magistrate** and several other persons, to the inn. I could not help being struck by the strange coincidences that had taken place during this eventful night; but, knowing that I had been conversing with several persons on the island I had inhabited about the time that the body had been found, I was perfectly tranquil as to the consequences of the affair.

I entered the room where the corpse lay, and was led up to the coffin. How can I describe my sensations on beholding it? I feel yet **parched** with horror, nor can I reflect on that terrible moment without shuddering and agony, that faintly reminds me of the anguish of the recognition. The trial, the presence of the **magistrate** and witnesses, passed like a dream from my memory, when I saw the lifeless form of Henry Clerval stretched before me. I gasped for breath; and, throwing myself on the body, I exclaimed, "Have my murderous **machinations** deprived you also, my dearest Henry, of life? Two I have already destroyed; other victims await their destiny—but you, Clerval, my friend, my **benefactor.**"

The human frame could no longer support the agonizing suffering that I endured, and I was carried out of the room in strong convulsions.

A fever succeeded to this. I lay for two months on the point of death. My ravings, as I afterwards heard, were frightful; I called myself the murderer of William, of

ENTREAT (ehn treet) *v.* **-ing,-ed.**
to plead, beg
Synonyms: beseech, implore, importune, request, petition

DOTING (doht ihng) *adj.*
indulgent; extremely or extravagantly loving
Synonyms: adoring, cherishing, spoiling

SQUALIDNESS (skwa lihd nehs) *n.*
filth or poverty; moral repulsion
Synonyms: foulness, nastiness, wretchedness

COUNTENANCE (kown tuh nuhns) *n.*
appearance, facial expression
Synonyms: face, features, visage

INDIFFERENCE (ihn dihf ruhnts) (ihn dihf uhr uhnts) *n.*
lack of interest; carelessness or negligence
Synonyms: detachment, disinterest, apathy, unconcern

Justine, and of Clerval. Sometimes I **entreated** my attendants to assist me in the destruction of the fiend by whom I was tormented; and, at others, I felt the fingers of the monster already grasping my neck, and screamed aloud with agony and terror. Fortunately, as I spoke my native language, Mr. Kirwin alone understood me; but my gestures and bitter cries were sufficient to affright the other witnesses.

Why did I not die? More miserable than man ever was before, why did I not sink into forgetfulness and rest? Death snatches away many blooming children, the only hopes of their **doting** parents. How many brides and youthful lovers have been one day in the bloom of health and hope, and the next a prey for worms and the decay of the tomb! Of what materials was I made, that I could thus resist so many shocks, which, like the turning of the wheel, continually renewed the torture.

But I was doomed to live; and, in two months, found myself as awaking from a dream, in a prison, stretched on a wretched bed, surrounded by gaolers, turnkeys, bolts, and all the miserable apparatus of a dungeon. It was morning, I remember, when I thus awoke to understanding. I had forgotten the particulars of what had happened, and only felt as if some great misfortune had suddenly overwhelmed me; but when I looked around, and saw the barred windows, and the **squalidness** of the room in which I was, all flashed across my memory, and I groaned bitterly.

This sound disturbed an old woman who was sleeping in a chair beside me. She was a hired nurse, the wife of one of the turnkeys, and her **countenance** expressed all those bad qualities which often characterize that class. The lines of her face were hard and rude, like that of persons accustomed to see without sympathizing in sights of misery. Her tone cxpressed her entire **indifference**; she addressed me in English, and the voice struck me as one that I had heard during my sufferings:

LOATHING (lohth ing) *n.*
hatred or great dislike
Synonyms: detestation, abhorrence

LANGUID (laang gwihd) *adj.*
lacking energy, indifferent, slow
Synonyms: weak, listless, lackadaisical, sluggish, fainéant

VISAGE (vih sihj) *n.*
the appearance of a person or place
Synonyms: expression, look, style, manner

ARDENTLY (ahr dihnt lee) *adv.*
passionately, enthusiastically, fervently
Synonyms: intensely, vehemently

"Are you better now, sir?" said she.

I replied in the same language, with a feeble voice, "I believe I am; but if it be all true, if indeed I did not dream, I am sorry that I am still alive to feel this misery and horror."

"For that matter," replied the old woman, "if you mean about the gentleman you murdered, I believe that it were better for you if you were dead, for I fancy it will go hard with you; but you will be hung when the next sessions come on. However, that's none of my business, I am sent to nurse you, and get you well; I do my duty with a safe conscience, it were well if every body did the same."

I turned with **loathing** from the woman who could utter so unfeeling a speech to a person just saved, on the very edge of death; but I felt **languid**, and unable to reflect on all that had passed. The whole series of my life appeared to me as a dream; I sometimes doubted if indeed it were all true, for it never presented itself to my mind with the force of reality.

As the images that floated before me became more distinct, I grew feverish; a darkness pressed around me; no one was near me who soothed me with the gentle voice of love; no dear hand supported me. The physician came and prescribed medicines, and the old woman prepared them for me; but utter carelessness was visible in the first, and the expression of brutality was strongly marked in the **visage** of the second. Who could be interested in the fate of a murderer, but the hangman who would gain his fee?

These were my first reflections; but I soon learned that Mr. Kirwin had shown me extreme kindness. He had caused the best room in the prison to be prepared for me (wretched indeed was the best); and it was he who had provided a physician and a nurse. It is true, he seldom came to see me; for, although he **ardently** desired to relieve the sufferings of every human creature, he did not wish to be present at the agonies and miserable ravings of

NEGLECT (neh glehkt) *v.* **-ing,-ed.**
to ignore or disregard, to be negligent
Synonyms: overlook, skimp

LIVID (lih vihd) *adj.*
discolored from a bruise; pale; reddened with anger
Synonyms: furious, ashen, pallid, black-and-blue

REPLETE (rih pleet) *adj.*
abundantly supplied
Synonyms: abounding, satiated, gorged, stuffed, full

COUNTENANCE (kown tuh nuhns) *n.*
appearance, facial expression
Synonyms: face, features, visage

MELANCHOLY (mehl uhn kahl ee) *adj.*
sad, gloomy
Synonyms: depressed, despondent, woeful, sorrowful

a murderer. He came, therefore, sometimes to see that I was not **neglected**; but his visits were short, and at long intervals.

One day, when I was gradually recovering, I was seated in a chair, my eyes half open, and my cheeks **livid** like those in death, I was overcome by gloom and misery, and often reflected I had better seek death than remain miserably pent up only to be let loose in a world **replete** with wretchedness. At one time I considered whether I should not declare myself guilty, and suffer the penalty of the law, less innocent than poor Justine had been. Such were my thoughts, when the door of my apartment was opened, and Mr. Kirwin entered. His **countenance** expressed sympathy and compassion; he drew a chair close to mine, and addressed me in French—

"I fear that this place is very shocking to you; can I do anything to make you more comfortable?"

"I thank you; but all that you mention is nothing to me. On the whole earth there is no comfort which I am capable of receiving."

"I know that the sympathy of a stranger can be but of little relief to one borne down as you are by so strange a misfortune. But you will, I hope, soon quit this **melancholy** abode; for, doubtless, evidence can easily be brought to free you from the criminal charge."

"That is my least concern. I have, by a course of strange events, become the most miserable of mortals. Persecuted and tortured as I am and have been, can death be any evil to me?"

"Nothing indeed could be more unfortunate and agonizing than the strange chances that have lately occurred. You were thrown, by some surprising accident, on this shore, renowned for its hospitality, seized immediately, and charged with murder. The first sight that was presented to your eyes was the body of your friend, murdered in so unaccountable a manner, and placed, as it were, by some fiend across your path."

AGITATION (aa gih tay shuhn) *n.*
commotion, excitement; uneasiness
Synonyms: disturbance, restlessness, anxiety, fluster, disquiet

RETROSPECT (reh truh spehkt) *n.*
a review or mediation on the past or past events
Synonyms: remembrance, reminiscence

COUNTENANCE (kown tuh nuhns) *n.*
appearance, facial expression
Synonyms: face, features, visage

LAMENT (luh mehnt) *v.* **-ing,-ed.**
to deplore, grieve
Synonyms: mourn, sorrow, regret, bewail

INCITEMENT (ihn siet mehnt) *n.*
provocation, incentive, motive
Synonyms: spur, impulse, encouragement

COMPLY (kuhm plie) *v.* **-ing,-ed.**
to yield or agree, to go along with
Synonyms: accord, submit, acquiesce, obey, respect

PRESUMPTION (pree suhmp shuhn) *n.*
1. probable evidence
Synonyms: grounds, suspicion, likelihood
2. bold arrogance or rude behavior
Synonyms: audacity, frontery, nerve

REPUGNANCE (rih puhg nehnts) *n.*
strong dislike, distaste, or antagonism; an instance of contradiction or inconsistency
Synonyms: repulsion, hatred, aversion

As Mr. Kirwin said this, notwithstanding the **agitation** I endured on this **retrospect** of my sufferings, I also felt considerable surprise at the knowledge he seemed to possess concerning me. I suppose some astonishment was exhibited in my **countenance**; for Mr. Kirwin hastened to say—

"It was not until a day or two after your illness that I thought of examining your dress, that I might discover some trace by which I could send to your relations an account of your misfortune and illness. I found several letters, and, among others, one which I discovered from its commencement to be from your father. I instantly wrote to Geneva; nearly two months have elapsed since the departure of my letter. But you are ill; even now you tremble. You are unfit for **agitation** of any kind."

"This suspense is a thousand times worse than the most horrible event. Tell me what new scene of death has been acted, and whose murder I am now to **lament**."

"Your family is perfectly well," said Mr. Kirwin, with gentleness, "and someone, a friend, has come to visit you."

I know not by what chain of thought the idea presented itself, but it instantly darted into my mind that the murderer had come to mock at my misery, and taunt me with the death of Clerval, as a new **incitement** for me to **comply** with his hellish desires. I put by hand before my eyes, and cried out in agony—

"Oh! Take him away! I cannot see him; for God's sake, do not let him enter!"

Mr. Kirwin regarded me with a troubled **countenance**. He could not help regarding my exclamation as a **presumption** of my guilt, and said, in rather a severe tone, "I should have thought, young man, that the presence of your father would have been welcome, instead of inspiring such violent **repugnance**."

"My father!" cried I, while every feature and every muscle was relaxed from anguish to pleasure. "Is my

MAGISTRATE (maa juh strayt) *n.*
an official who can administrate laws
Synonyms: judge, arbiter, authority, marshal

BENEVOLENCE (buh neh vuh luhnts) *n.*
kindness, compassion
Synonyms: charity, altruism, generosity

DESPONDING (dih spahn dihng) *adj.*
feeling discouraged and dejected
Synonyms: sad, depressed, desolate, dejected, forlorn

AGITATION (aa gih tay shuhn) *n.*
commotion, excitement; uneasiness
Synonyms: disturbance, restlessness, anxiety, fluster, disquiet

PRECARIOUS (prih caa ree uhs) *adj.*
uncertain
Synonyms: insecure, unstable, hazardous, perilous

MELANCHOLY (mehl uhn kahl ee) *n.*
sadness, depression
Synonyms: dejection, despondency, woe, sorrow

DISSIPATE (dihs uh payt) *v.* **-ing,-ed.**
to scatter; to pursue pleasure to excess
Synonyms: carouse, squander, consume; disperse, dissolve

father, indeed, here? How kind, how very kind. But where is he, why does he not hasten to me?"

My change of manner surprised and pleased the **magistrate**; perhaps he thought that my former exclamation was a momentary return of delirium, and now he instantly resumed his former **benevolence**. He rose, and quitted the room with my nurse, and in a moment my father entered it.

Nothing, at this moment, could have given me greater pleasure than the arrival of my father. I stretched out my hand to him, and cried,

"Are you then safe—and Elizabeth—and Ernest?"

My father calmed me with assurances of their welfare, and endeavoured, by dwelling on these subjects so interesting to my heart, to raise my **desponding** spirits; but he soon felt that a prison cannot be the abode of cheerfulness. "What a place is this that you inhabit, my son!" said he, looking mournfully at the barred windows, and wretched appearance of the room. "You travelled to seek happiness, but a fatality seems to pursue you. And poor Clerval—"

The name of my unfortunate and murdered friend was an **agitation** too great to be endured in my weak state; I shed tears.

"Alas! Yes, my father," replied I, "some destiny of the most horrible kind hangs over me, and I must live to fulfil it, or surely I should have died on the coffin of Henry."

We were not allowed to converse for any length of time, for the **precarious** state of my health rendered every precaution necessary that could insure tranquillity. Mr. Kirwin came in, and insisted that my strength should not be exhausted by too much exertion. But the appearance of my father was to me like that of my good angel, and I gradually recovered my health.

As my sickness quitted me, I was absorbed by a gloomy and black **melancholy**, that nothing could **dissipate**. The image of Clerval was for ever before me,

AGITATION (aa gih tay shuhn) *n.*
commotion, excitement; uneasiness
Synonyms: disturbance, restlessness, anxiety, fluster, disquiet

DETESTED (dee tehst ehd) (dih tehst ehd) *adj.*
intensely and violently hated
Synonyms: hated, disliked, loathed

EXECUTE (ehk sih kyoot) *v.* **-ing,-ed.**
1. to carry out fully; to make or produce
Synonyms: accomplish, achieve, perform
2. to put to death by penalty of crime
Synonyms: kill, punish, murder

ENRAPTURE (ehn raap chuhr) *v.* **-ing,-ed.**
to absorb deeply; to fill with delight
Synonyms: engross, enthrall, move, entrance, ravish

VEXATION (vehk zay shuhn) *n.*
irritation, annoyance; confusion, puzzlement
Synonyms: bother, plague, affliction

LANGUISH (laan gwihsh) *v.* **-ing,-ed.**
to lose strength or become weak
Synonyms: wither, fade, droop, slow, deteriorate

ghastly and murdered. More than once the **agitation** into which these reflections threw me made my friends dread a dangerous relapse. Alas! Why did they preserve so miserable and **detested** a life? It was surely that I might fulfil my destiny, which is now drawing to a close. Soon, oh, very soon, will death extinguish these throbbings, and relieve me from the mighty weight of anguish that bears me to the dust; and, in **executing** the award of justice, I shall also sink to rest. Then the appearance of death was distant, although the wish was ever present to my thoughts; and I often sat for hours motionless and speechless, wishing for some mighty revolution that might bury me and my destroyer in its ruins.

The season of the assizes approached. I had already been three months in prison; and although I was still weak, and in continual danger of a relapse, I was obliged to travel nearly a hundred miles to the county-town, where the court was held. Mr. Kirwin charged himself with every care of collecting witnesses, and arranging my defence. I was spared the disgrace of appearing publicly as a criminal, as the case was not brought before the court that decides on life and death. The grand jury rejected the bill, on its being proved that I was on the Orkney Islands at the hour the body of my friend was found, and a fortnight after my removal I was liberated from prison.

My father was **enraptured** on finding me freed from the **vexations** of a criminal charge, that I was again allowed to breathe the fresh atmosphere, and allowed to return to my native country. I did not participate in these feelings; for to me the walls of a dungeon or a palace were alike hateful. The cup of life was poisoned for ever; and although the sun shone upon me, as upon the happy and gay of heart, I saw around me nothing but a dense and frightful darkness, penetrated by no light but the glimmer of two eyes that glared upon me. Sometimes they were the expressive eyes of Henry, **languishing** in death,

MELANCHOLY (mehl uhn kahl ee) *adj.*
sad, depressing
Synonyms: dejected, despondent, woeful, sorrowful

TORPOR (tohr puhr) *n.*
lethargy or sluggishness; dormancy
Synonyms: hibernation, apathy, inactivity, inertia

LOATHE (lohth) *v.* **-ing,-ed.**
to abhor, despise, hate
Synonyms: abominate, execrate, detest, condemn

VIGILANCE (vih juh lehnts) *n.*
attention, watchfulness
Synonyms: alertness, awareness, care

RESTRAIN (rih strayn) *v.* **-ing,-ed.**
to control, repress, restrict
Synonyms: hamper, bridle, curb, check

MACHINATION (mahk uh nay shuhn) *n.*
plot or scheme
Synonyms: conspiracy, intrigue, design, cabal

ACCEDE (aak seed) *v.* **-ing,-ed.**
to express approval; agree to
Synonyms: assent, acquiesce, consent, concur

the dark orbs nearly covered by the lids, and the long black lashes that fringed them; sometimes it was the watery clouded eyes of the monster, as I first saw them in my chamber at Ingolstadt.

My father tried to awaken in me the feelings of affection. He talked of Geneva, which I should soon visit—of Elizabeth and Ernest; but these words only drew deep groans from me. Sometimes, indeed, I felt a wish for happiness; and thought, with **melancholy** delight, of my beloved cousin; or longed, with a devouring *maladie du pays*, to see once more the blue lake and rapid Rhone, that had been so dear to me in early childhood. But my general state of feeling was a **torpor**, in which a prison was as welcome a residence as the divinest scene in nature; and these fits were seldom interrupted, but by paroxysms of anguish and despair. At these moments I often endeavoured to put an end to the existence I **loathed**; and it required unceasing attendance and **vigilance** to **restrain** me from committing some dreadful act of violence.

I remember, as I quitted the prison, I heard one of the men say, "He may be innocent of the murder, but he has certainly a bad conscience." These words struck me. A bad conscience! Yes, surely I had one. William, Justine, and Clerval had died through my infernal **machinations**; "And whose death," cried I, "is to finish the tragedy? Ah! My father, do not remain in this wretched country; take me where I may forget myself, my existence, and all the world."

My father easily **acceded** to my desire; and, after having taken leave of Mr. Kirwin, we hastened to Dublin. I felt as if I was relieved from a heavy weight, when the packet sailed with a fair wind from Ireland, and I had quitted for ever the country which had been to me the scene of so much misery.

It was midnight. My father slept in the cabin; and I lay on the deck, looking at the stars, and listening to the

DETESTED (dee tehst ehd) (dih tehst ehd) *adj.*
intensely and violently hated
Synonyms: hated, disliked, loathed

PROFOUNDLY (pruh fownd lee) (proh fownd lee) *adv.*
with deep intellect; deeply, extremely
Synonyms: shrewdly; greatly, intensely

RESPITE (reh spiht) *n.*
interval of relief
Synonyms: rest, pause, intermission, recess, suspension

dashing of the waves. I hailed the darkness that shut Ireland from my sight, and my pulse beat with a feverish joy, when I reflected that I should soon see Geneva. The past appeared to me in the light of a frightful dream; yet the vessel in which I was, the wind that blew me from the **detested** shore of Ireland, and the sea which surrounded me, told me too forcibly that I was deceived by no vision, and that Clerval, my friend and dearest companion, had fallen a victim to me and the monster of my creation. I repassed, in my memory, my whole life; my quiet happiness while residing with my family in Geneva, the death of my mother, and my departure for Ingolstadt. I remembered, shuddering, the mad enthusiasm that hurried me on to the creation of my hideous enemy, and I called to mind the night during which he first lived. I was unable to pursue the train of thought; a thousand feelings pressed upon me, and I wept bitterly.

Ever since my recovery from the fever I had been in the custom of taking every night a small quantity of laudanum; for it was by means of this drug only that I was enabled to gain the rest necessary for the preservation of life. Oppressed by the recollection of my various misfortunes, I now took a double dose, and soon slept **profoundly**. But sleep did not afford me **respite** from thought and misery; my dreams presented a thousand objects that scared me. Towards morning I was possessed by a kind of nightmare; I felt the fiend's grasp in my neck, and could not free myself from it; groans and cries rung in my ears. My father, who was watching over me, perceiving my restlessness, awoke me, and pointed to the port of Holyhead, which we were now entering.

RESOLVE (rih sahlv) *v.* **-ing,-ed.**
to determine or to make a firm decision about
Synonyms: solve, decide

UNREMITTING (uhn rih mih ting) *adj.*
never lessening, persistent
Synonyms: incessant, continued, persevering

OBSTINATE (ahb stih nuht) *adj.*
stubborn
Synonyms: headstrong, stiff-necked, bullheaded, pigheaded, mulish

DEGRADATION (day greh day shuhn) *n.*
the act of falling in rank or status; the act of losing moral or intellectual character
Synonyms: abasement, demotion, disgrace, shame

FUTILITY (fyoo tihl ih tee) *n.*
uselessness; lack of importance
Synonyms: worthlessness, waste

DEGRADE (dih grayd) (dee grayd) *v.* **-ing,-ed.**
to lower in rank or status; to drag down in moral or intellectual character
Synonyms: shame, demean, dishonor, weaken

CONVALESCENCE (kahn vuhl ehs uhns) *n.*
a gradual recovery after an illness
Synonyms: healing, recuperation

CHAPTER V

We had **resolved** not to go to London, but to cross the country to Portsmouth, and thence to embark for Havre. I preferred this plan principally because I dreaded to see again those places in which I had enjoyed a few moments of tranquillity with my beloved Clerval. I thought with horror of seeing again those persons whom we had been accustomed to visit together, and who might make inquiries concerning an event, the very remembrance of which made me again feel the pang I endured when I gazed on his lifeless form in the inn at——.

As for my father, his desires and exertions were bounded to seeing me restored to health and peace of mind. His tenderness and attentions were **unremitting**; my grief and gloom were **obstinate**, but he would not despair. Sometimes he thought that I felt deeply the **degradation** of being obliged to answer a charge of murder, and he endeavoured to prove to me the **futility** of pride.

"Alas! My father," said I, "how little do you know me. Human beings, their feelings and passions, would indeed be **degraded**, if such a wretch as I felt pride. Justine, poor unhappy Justine, was as innocent as I, and she suffered the same charge; she died for it; and I am the cause of this—I murdered her. William, Justine, and Henry—they all died by my hands."

My father had often, during my imprisonment, heard me make the same assertion; when I thus accused myself, he sometimes seemed to desire an explanation, and at others he appeared to consider it as caused by delirium, and that during my illness, some idea of this kind had presented itself to my imagination, the remembrance of which I preserved in my **convalescence**. I avoided

ENTREAT (ehn treet) *v.* **-ing,-ed.**
to plead, beg
Synonyms: beseech, implore, importune, request, petition

MACHINATION (mahk uh nay shuhn) *n.*
plot or scheme
Synonyms: conspiracy, intrigue, design, cabal

DERANGED (dih raynjd) *adj.*
disturbed and disordered; insane
Synonyms: disarranged, maddening, confounded

ALLUDE (uh lood) *v.* **-ing,-ed.**
to make an indirect reference
Synonyms: intimate, suggest, refer, indicate, hint

INCOHERENT (ihn koh heer uhnt) *adj.*
unable to be understood; unintelligible, incomprehensible
Synonyms: disorderly, illogical, inconsistent

IMPERIOUS (ihm pihr ee uhs) *adj.*
arrogantly self-assured, domineering, overbearing
Synonyms: authoritarian, despotic

DETAIN (dih tayn) (dee tayn) *v.* **-ing,-ed.**
to hold as if in custody; to restrain from continuing on
Synonyms: arrest, confine, nab, hinder

explanation, and maintained a continual silence concerning the wretch I had created. I had a feeling that I should be supposed mad, and this for ever chained my tongue, when I would have given the whole world to have confided the fatal secret.

Upon this occasion my father said, with an expression of unbounded wonder, "What do you mean, Victor? Are you mad? My dear son, I **entreat** you never to make such an assertion again."

"I am not mad," I cried energetically. "The sun and the heavens, who have viewed my operations, can bear witness of my truth. I am the assassin of those most innocent victims; they died by my **machinations**. A thousand times would I have shed my own blood, drop by drop, to have saved their lives; but I could not, my father, indeed I could not sacrifice the whole human race."

The conclusion of this speech convinced my father that my ideas were **deranged**, and he instantly changed the subject of our conversation, and endeavoured to alter the course of my thoughts. He wished as much as possible to obliterate the memory of the scenes that had taken place in Ireland, and never **alluded** to them, or suffered me to speak of my misfortunes.

As time passed away I became more calm. Misery had her dwelling in my heart, but I no longer talked in the same **incoherent** manner of my own crimes; sufficient for me was the consciousness of them. By the utmost self-violence, I curbed the **imperious** voice of wretchedness, which sometimes desired to declare itself to the whole world; and my manners were calmer and more composed than they had ever been since my journey to the sea of ice.

We arrived at Havre on the 8th of May, and instantly proceeded to Paris, where my father had some business which **detained** us a few weeks. In this city, I received the following letter from Elizabeth:

FORMIDABLE (fohr mih duh buhl) (fohr mih duh buhl) *adj.*
fearsome, daunting
Synonyms: difficult, tough, alarming, admirable

COUNTENANCE (kown tuh nuhns) *n.*
appearance, facial expression
Synonyms: face, features, visage

DEVOID (dih voyd) *adj.*
being without
Synonyms: destitute, empty, vacant, null, bare

AUGMENT (awg mehnt) *v.* **-ing,-ed.**
to expand, extend
Synonyms: enhance, compound, increase, enlarge, inflate

"*To Victor Frankenstein.*

"My dearest Friend,

"It gave me the greatest pleasure to receive a letter from my uncle dated at Paris; you are no longer at a **formidable** distance, and I may hope to see you in less than a fortnight. My poor cousin, how much you must have suffered! I expect to see you looking even more ill than when you quitted Geneva. This winter has been passed most miserably, tortured as I have been by anxious suspense; yet I hope to see peace in your **countenance**, and to find that your heart is not totally **devoid** of comfort and tranquillity.

"Yet I fear that the same feelings now exist that made you so miserable a year ago, even perhaps **augmented** by time. I would not disturb you at this period, when so many misfortunes weigh upon you; but a conversation that I had with my uncle previous to his departure renders some explanation necessary before we meet.

"Explanation! You may possibly say; what can Elizabeth have to explain? If you really say this, my questions are answered, and I have no more to do than to sign myself your affectionate cousin. But you are distant from me, and it is possible that you may dread, and yet be pleased with this explanation; and, in a probability of this being the case, I dare not any longer postpone writing what, during your absence, I have often wished to express to you, but have never had the courage to begin.

"You well know, Victor, that our union had been the favourite plan of your parents ever since our infancy. We were told this when young, and taught to look forward to it as an event that would certainly take place. We were affectionate playfellows during childhood, and, I believe, dear and valued friends to one another as we grew older. But as brother and sister often entertain a lively affection towards each other, without desiring a more intimate union, may not such also be our case? Tell me, dearest

CONJURE (kahn juhr) *v.* **-ing,-ed.**
to call on or beg solemnly; to affect or effect as if by magic; to bring to mind
Synonyms: entreat, implore, rouse, recollect

INCLINATION (ihn cluh nay shuhn) *n.*
tendency toward
Synonyms: leaning, trend, preference, disposition, propensity

STIFLE (stie fuhl) *v.* **-ing,-ed.**
to smother or suffocate; suppress
Synonyms: repress, strangle, throttle

Victor. Answer me, I **conjure** you, by our mutual happiness, with simple truth—Do you not love another?

"You have travelled; you have spent several years of your life at Ingolstadt; and I confess to you, my friend, that when I saw you last autumn so unhappy, flying to solitude, from the society of every creature, I could not help supposing that you might regret our connection, and believe yourself bound in honour to fulfil the wishes of your parents, although they opposed themselves to your **inclinations**. But this is false reasoning. I confess to you, my cousin, that I love you, and that in my airy dreams of futurity you have been my constant friend and companion. But it is your happiness I desire as well as my own, when I declare to you, that our marriage would render me eternally miserable, unless it were the dictate of your own free choice. Even now I weep to think that, borne down as you are by the cruelest misfortunes, you may **stifle**, by the word *honour*, all hope of that love and happiness which would alone restore you to yourself. I, who have so interested an affection for you, may increase your miseries ten-fold, by being an obstacle to your wishes. Ah, Victor, be assured that your cousin and playmate has too sincere a love for you not to be made miserable by this <u>supposition</u>. Be happy, my friend; and if you obey me in this one request, remain satisfied that nothing on earth will have the power to interrupt my tranquillity.

"Do not let this letter disturb you; do not answer it to-morrow, or the next day, or even until you come, if it will give you pain. My uncle will send me news of your health; and if I see but one smile on your lips when we meet, occasioned by this or any other exertion of mine, I shall need no other happiness.

"Elizabeth Lavenza.

"*Geneva, May 18th, 17—.*"

CONSOLE (kuhn sohl) *v.* **-ing,-ed.**
to alleviate grief and raise the spirits of, provide solace
Synonyms: relieve, comfort, soothe

CONSUMMATE (kahn suh mayt) *v.* **-ing,-ed.**
to accomplish or complete
Synonyms: conclude, fulfill, achieve, perfect

VANQUISH (vaan kwihsh) *v.* **-ing,-ed.**
to conquer, defeat
Synonyms: subjugate, overcome, subdue, suppress, trounce

REMORSE (rih mohrs) *n.*
a gnawing distress arising from a sense of guilt
Synonyms: anguish, ruefulness, shame, penitence

EXECUTE (ehk sih kyoot) *v.* **-ing,-ed.**
1. to carry out fully; to make or produce
Synonyms: accomplish, achieve, perform
2. to put to death by penalty of crime
Synonyms: kill, punish, murder

SATIATE (say shee ayt) *v.* **-ing,-ed.**
to satisfy
Synonyms: sate, cloy, glut, gorge, surfeit

ENUNCIATION (ih nuhn see ay shuhn) (ee nuhn see ay shuhn) *n.*
clear pronunciation; accentuation of words
Synonyms: articulation, emphasis, inflection

RESOLVE (rih sahlv) *v.* **-ing,-ed.**
to determine or to make a firm decision about
Synonyms: solve, decide

CONDUCE (kuhn doos) (kuhn dyoos) *v.* **-ing,-ed.**
to lead to a particular and usually desirable outcome
Synonyms: contribute, advance, direct, produce

ADVERSARY (aad vuhr saa ree) *n.*
an opponent or enemy
Synonyms: antagonist, foe, opposition

This letter revived in my memory what I had before forgotten, the threat of the fiend—"*I will be with you on your wedding night!*" Such was my sentence, and on that night would the daemon employ every art to destroy me, and tear me from the glimpse of happiness which promised partly to **console** my sufferings. On that night he had determined to **consummate** his crimes by my death. Well, be it so; a deadly struggle would then assuredly take place, in which if he was victorious, I should be at peace, and his power over me be at an end. If he were **vanquished**, I should be a free man. Alas! What freedom? Such as the peasant enjoys when his family have been massacred before his eyes, his cottage burnt, his lands laid waste, and he is turned adrift, homeless, pennyless, and alone, but free. Such would be my liberty, except that in my Elizabeth I possessed a treasure, alas, balanced by those horrors of **remorse** and guilt, which would pursue me until death.

Sweet and beloved Elizabeth! I read and re-read her letter, and some softened feelings stole into my heart, and dared to whisper paradisaical dreams of love and joy; but the apple was already eaten, and the angel's arm bared to drive me from all hope. Yet I would die to make her happy. If the monster **executed** his threat, death was inevitable; yet, again, I considered whether my marriage would hasten my fate. My destruction might indeed arrive a few months sooner; but if my torturer should suspect that I postponed it, influenced by his menaces, he would surely find other, and perhaps more dreadful means of revenge. He had vowed *to be with me on my wedding night*, yet he did not consider that threat as binding him to peace in the mean time; for, as if to show me that he was not yet **satiated** with blood, he had murdered Clerval immediately after the **enunciation** of his threats. I **resolved**, therefore, that if my immediate union with my cousin would **conduce** either to hers or my father's happiness, my **adversary's** designs against my life should not retard it a single hour.

CONSECRATE (kahn suh krayt) *v.* **-ing,-ed.**
to declare sacred; dedicate to a worship
Synonyms: sanctify, devote

CONJURE (kahn juhr) *v.* **-ing,-ed.**
to call on or beg solemnly; to affect or effect as if by magic; to bring to mind
Synonyms: entreat, implore, rouse, recollect

ALLUDE (uh lood) *v.* **-ing,-ed.**
to make an indirect reference
Synonyms: intimate, suggest, refer, indicate, hint

ENTREAT (ehn treet) *v.* **-ing,-ed.**
to plead, beg
Synonyms: beseech, implore, importune, request

COMPLY (kuhm plie) *v.* **-ing,-ed.**
to yield or agree, to go along with
Synonyms: accord, submit, acquiesce, obey, respect

EMACIATED (ih may shee ay tihd) *adj.*
very thin due to hunger or disease; feeble
Synonyms: bony, gaunt, haggard, skeletal

VIVACITY (vih vahs ih tee) *n.*
liveliness, spiritedness
Synonyms: vibrance, zest

DESPONDENT (dih spahn duhnt) *adj.*
feeling discouraged and dejected
Synonyms: sad, depressed, desolate, dejected, forlorn

MULTITUDE (muhl tuh tood) *n.*
the state of being many; a great number
Synonyms: mass, myriad, slew, crowd

TORPOR (tohr puhr) *n.*
lethargy or sluggishness; dormancy
Synonyms: hibernation, apathy, inactivity, inertia

REMONSTRATE (reh mahn strayt) *v.* **-ing,-ed.**
to present and urge reasons in opposition; to say or plead in protest
Synonyms: challenge, resist, dispute

In this state of mind I wrote to Elizabeth. My letter was calm and affectionate. "I fear, my beloved girl," I said, "little happiness remains for us on earth; yet all that I may one day enjoy is concentered in you. Chase away your idle fears; to you alone do I **consecrate** my life, and my endeavours for contentment. I have one secret, Elizabeth, a dreadful one; when revealed to you, it will chill your frame with horror, and then, far from being surprised at my misery, you will only wonder that I survive what I have endured. I will confide this tale of misery and terror to you the day after our marriage shall take place; for, my sweet cousin, there must be perfect confidence between us. But until then, I **conjure** you, do not mention or **allude** to it. This I most earnestly **entreat**, and I know you will **comply**."

In about a week after the arrival of Elizabeth's letter, we returned to Geneva. My cousin welcomed me with warm affection; yet tears were in her eyes, as she beheld my **emaciated** frame and feverish cheeks. I saw a change in her also. She was thinner, and had lost much of that heavenly **vivacity** that had before charmed me; but her gentleness, and soft looks of compassion, made her a more fit companion for one blasted and miserable as I was.

The tranquillity which I now enjoyed did not endure. Memory brought madness with it; and when I thought on what had passed, a real insanity possessed me; sometimes I was furious, and burnt with rage, sometimes low and **despondent**. I neither spoke nor looked, but sat motionless, bewildered by the **multitude** of miseries that overcame me.

Elizabeth alone had the power to draw me from these fits; her gentle voice would soothe me when transported by passion, and inspire me with human feelings when sunk in **torpor**. She wept with me, and for me. When reason returned, she would **remonstrate**, and endeavour to inspire me with resignation. Ah! It is well for the

REMORSE (rih mohrs) *n.*
a gnawing distress arising from a sense of guilt
Synonyms: anguish, ruefulness, shame, penitence

LUXURY (luhg zhoor ee) *n.*
an elegant thing; opulence and exorbitance
Synonyms: extra, extravagance, nonessential

INDULGE (ihn duhlj) *v.* **-ing,-ed.**
to give in to a craving or desire
Synonyms: humor, gratify, allow, pamper

CONSECRATE (kahn suh krayt) *v.* **-ing,-ed.**
to declare sacred; dedicate to a worship
Synonyms: sanctify, devote

OMNIPOTENT (ahm nihp uh tuhnt) *adj.*
having unlimited or universal power, authority, or force; all-powerful
Synonyms: divine, godlike, supreme, almighty

INVINCIBLE (ihn vihn suh buhl) *adj.*
invulnerable, unbeatable
Synonyms: unconquerable, insuperable

COUNTENANCE (kown tuh nuhns) *n.*
appearance, facial expression
Synonyms: face, features, visage

ADVERSARY (aad vuhr saa ree) *n.*
an opponent or enemy
Synonyms: antagonist, foe, opposition

BANISH (baan ish) *v.* **-ing,-ed.**
to force to leave, exile
Synonyms: expel, deport

unfortunate to be resigned, but for the guilty there is no peace. The agonies of **remorse** poison the **luxury** there is otherwise sometimes found in **indulging** the excess of grief.

Soon after my arrival my father spoke of my immediate marriage with my cousin. I remained silent.

"Have you, then, some other attachment?"

"None on earth. I love Elizabeth, and look forward to our union with delight. Let the day therefore be fixed; and on it I will **consecrate** myself, in life or death, to the happiness of my cousin."

"My dear Victor, do not speak thus. Heavy misfortunes have befallen us; but let us only cling closer to what remains, and transfer our love for those whom we have lost to those who yet live. Our circle will be small, but bound close by the ties of affection and mutual misfortune. And when time shall have softened your despair, new and dear objects of care will be born to replace those of whom we have been so cruelly deprived."

Such were the lessons of my father. But to me the remembrance of the threat returned. Nor can you wonder, that, **omnipotent** as the fiend had yet been in his deeds of blood, I should almost regard him as **invincible**; and that when he had pronounced the words, "*I shall be with you on your wedding night*," I should regard the threatened fate as unavoidable. But death was no evil to me, if the loss of Elizabeth were balanced with it; and I therefore, with a contented and even cheerful **countenance**, agreed with my father, that if my cousin would consent, the ceremony should take place in ten days, and thus put, as I imagined, the seal to my fate.

Great God! If for one instant I had thought what might be the hellish intention of my fiendish **adversary**, I would rather have **banished** myself for ever from my native country, and wandered a friendless outcast over the earth, than have consented to this miserable marriage. But, as if possessed of magic powers, the monster had blinded me to his real intentions; and when I

PROPHETIC (pruh feh tihk) *adj.*
foretelling events
Synonyms: visionary, foreshadowing, portentous

COUNTENANCE (kown tuh nuhns) *n.*
appearance, facial expression
Synonyms: face, features, visage

PLACID (plaa sihd) *adj.*
calm
Synonyms: tranquil, serene, peaceful, complacent

TANGIBLE (taan juh buhl) *adj.*
able to be sensed, perceptible, measurable
Synonyms: palpable, real, concrete, factual, corporeal

DISSIPATE (dihs uh payt) *v.* **-ing,-ed.**
to scatter; to pursue pleasure to excess
Synonyms: carouse, squander, consume; disperse, dissolve

SOLEMNIZATION (sah luhm nih zay shuhn) *n.*
celebration
Synonyms: commemoration, ceremony, recognition

thought that I prepared only my own death, I hastened that of a far dearer victim.

As the period fixed for our marriage drew nearer, whether from cowardice or a **prophetic** feeling, I felt my heart sink within me. But I concealed my feelings by an appearance of hilarity, that brought smiles and joy to the **countenance** of my father, but hardly deceived the ever-watchful and nicer eye of Elizabeth. She looked forward to our union with **placid** contentment, not unmingled with a little fear, which past misfortunes had impressed, that what now appeared certain and **tangible** happiness, might soon **dissipate** into an airy dream, and leave no trace but deep and everlasting regret.

Preparations were made for the event; congratulatory visits were received; and all wore a smiling appearance. I shut up, as well as I could, in my own heart the anxiety that preyed there, and entered with seeming earnestness into the plans of my father, although they might only serve as the decorations of my tragedy. A house was purchased for us near Cologny, by which we should enjoy the pleasures of the country, and yet be so near Geneva as to see my father every day; who would still reside within the walls, for the benefit of Ernest, that he might follow his studies at the schools.

In the mean time I took every precaution to defend my person, in case the fiend should openly attack me. I carried pistols and a dagger constantly about me, and was ever on the watch to prevent artifice; and by these means gained a greater degree of tranquillity. Indeed, as the period approached, the threat appeared more as a delusion, not to be regarded as worthy to disturb my peace, while the happiness I hoped for in my marriage wore a greater appearance of certainty, as the day fixed for its **solemnization** drew nearer, and I heard it continually spoken of as an occurrence which no accident could possibly prevent.

Elizabeth seemed happy; my tranquil demeanour

MELANCHOLY (mehl uhn kahl ee) *adj.*
sad, gloomy
Synonyms: depressed, despondent, woeful, sorrowful

PERVADE (puhr vayd) *v.* **-ing,-ed.**
to become diffused throughout every part of
Synonyms: spread, permeate, infuse, penetrate

MELANCHOLY (mehl uhn kahl ee) *n.*
sadness, depression
Synonyms: dejection, despondency, woe, sorrow

DIFFIDENCE (dih fih duhns) (dih fih dehns) *n.*
shyness, lack of confidence
Synonyms: timidity, reticence

RESOLVE (rih sahlv) *v.* **-ing,-ed.**
to determine or to make a firm decision about
Synonyms: solve, decide

SURMOUNT (suhr mownt) *v.* **-ing,-ed.**
to conquer, overcome
Synonyms: clear, hurdle, leap, surpass, exceed

EMULATE (ehm yuh layt) *v.* **-ing,-ed.**
to copy, imitate
Synonyms: compete, rival, vie, ape

INSURMOUNTABLE (ihn suhr mownt uh buhl) *adj.*
impossible, unable to be overcome
Synonyms: unachievable, insuperable, unattainable

contributed greatly to calm her mind. But on the day that was to fulfill my wishes and my destiny, she was **melancholy**, and a presentiment of evil **pervaded** her; and perhaps also she thought of the dreadful secret, which I had promised to reveal to her the following day. My father was in the mean time overjoyed, and, in the bustle of preparation, only observed in the **melancholy** of his niece the **diffidence** of a bride.

After the ceremony was performed, a large party assembled at my father's; but it was agreed that Elizabeth and I should pass the afternoon and night at Evian, and return to Cologny the next morning. As the day was fair, and the wind favourable, we **resolved** to go by water.

Those were the last moments of my life during which I enjoyed the feeling of happiness. We passed rapidly along. The sun was hot, but we were sheltered from its rays by a kind of canopy, while we enjoyed the beauty of the scene, sometimes on one side of the lake, where we saw Mont Saleve, the pleasant banks of Montalegre, and at a distance, **surmounting** all, the beautiful Mont Blanc, and the assemblage of snowy mountains that in vain endeavour to **emulate** her; sometimes coasting the opposite banks, we saw the mighty Jura opposing its dark side to the ambition that would quit its native country, and an almost **insurmountable** barrier to the invader who should wish to enslave it.

I took the hand of Elizabeth. "You are sorrowful, my love. Ah! If you knew what I have suffered, and what I may yet endure, you would endeavour to let me taste the quiet, and freedom from despair, that this one day at least permits me to enjoy."

"Be happy, my dear Victor," replied Elizabeth. "There is, I hope, nothing to distress you; and be assured that if a lively joy is not painted in my face, my heart is contented. Something whispers to me not to depend too much on the prospect that is opened before us; but I will not listen to such a sinister voice. Observe how fast we

OBSCURE (uhb skyoor) *v.* **-ing,-ed.**
to make dim or unclear
Synonyms: darken, block, conceal, hide, shade

INNUMERABLE (ih noo muhr uh buhl) (ih nyoo muhr uh buhl) *adj.*
too many to be counted
Synonyms: incalculable, immeasurable, infinite, inestimable

SERENE (suh reen) *adj.*
calm, peaceful
Synonyms: tranquil, composed, content

DIVERT (die vuhrt) *v.* **-ing,-ed.**
to distract, to move in different directions from a particular point
Synonyms: deviate, separate

MELANCHOLY (mehl uhn kahl ee) *adj.*
sad, gloomy
Synonyms: depressed, despondent, woeful, sorrowful

FLUCTUATE (fluhk choo ayt) *v.* **-ing,-ed.**
to alternate, waver
Synonyms: swing, oscillate, vary, undulate

REVERIE (rehv uh ree) *n.*
a daydream
Synonyms: dream, absorption, muse, meditation

TRANSITORY (traan sih tohr ee) *adj.*
short-lived, existing only briefly
Synonyms: transient, ephemeral, fleeting, fugitive, momentary

move along, and how the clouds which sometimes **obscure**, and sometimes rise above the dome of Mont Blanc, render this scene of beauty still more interesting. Look also at the **innumerable** fish that are swimming in the clear waters, where we can distinguish every pebble that lies at the bottom. What a divine day! How happy and **serene** all nature appears!"

Thus Elizabeth endeavoured to **divert** her thoughts and mine from all reflection upon **melancholy** subjects. But her temper was **fluctuating**; joy for a few instants shone in her eyes, but it continually gave place to distraction and **reverie**.

The sun sunk lower in the heavens; we passed the river Drance, and observed its path through the chasms of the higher, and the glens of the lower hills. The Alps here come closer to the lake, and we approached the amphitheatre of mountains which forms its eastern boundary. The spire of Evian shone under the woods that surrounded it, and the range of mountain above mountain by which it was overhung.

The wind, which had hitherto carried us along with amazing rapidity, sunk at sunset to a light breeze; the soft air just ruffled the water, and caused a pleasant motion among the trees as we approached the shore, from which it wafted the most delightful scent of flowers and hay. The sun sunk beneath the horizon as we landed; and as I touched the shore, I felt those cares and fears revive, which soon were to clasp me, and cling to me for ever.

CHAPTER VI

It was eight o'clock when we landed; we walked for a short time on the shore, enjoying the **transitory** light, and then retired to the inn, and contemplated the lovely scene

OBSCURE (uhb skyoor) *v.* **-ing,-ed.**
to make dim or unclear
Synonyms: darken, block, conceal, hide, shade

RESOLVE (rih sahlv) *v.* **-ing,-ed.**
to determine or to make a firm decision about
Synonyms: solve, decide

IMPENDING (ihm pehn dihng) *adj.*
hovering threateningly; about to occur, approaching
Synonyms: looming, ominous, forthcoming

ADVERSARY (aad vuhr saa ree) *n.*
an opponent or enemy
Synonyms: antagonist, foe, opposition

AGITATION (aa gih tay shuhn) *n.*
commotion, excitement; uneasiness
Synonyms: disturbance, restlessness, anxiety

AGITATE (aa gih tayt) *v.* **-ing,-ed.**
to upset or excite; to make uneasy
Synonyms: disturb, fluster, bother

ENTREAT (ehn treet) *v.* **-ing,-ed.**
to plead, beg
Synonyms: beseech, implore, importune, request

CONJECTURE (kuhn jehk shuhr) *v.* **-ing,-ed.**
to infer, predict, guess
Synonyms: postulate, hypothesize, suppose, surmise

EXECUTION (ehk sih kyoo shuhn) *n.*
1. the act of performing or carrying out a task
   Synonyms: accomplishment, achievement
2. the act of putting to death
   Synonyms: killing, capital punishment, murder

of waters, woods, and mountains, **obscured** in darkness, yet still displaying their black outlines.

The wind, which had fallen in the south, now rose with great violence in the west. The moon had reached her summit in the heavens, and was beginning to descend; the clouds swept across it swifter than the flight of the vulture, and dimmed her rays, while the lake reflected the scene of the busy heavens, rendered still busier by the restless waves that were beginning to rise. Suddenly a heavy storm of rain descended.

I had been calm during the day; but so soon as night **obscured** the shapes of objects, a thousand fears arose in my mind. I was anxious and watchful, while my right hand grasped a pistol which was hidden in my bosom. Every sound terrified me; but I **resolved** that I would sell my life dearly, and not relax the **impending** conflict until my own life, or that of my **adversary**, were extinguished.

Elizabeth observed my **agitation** for some time in timid and fearful silence; at length she said, "What is it that **agitates** you, my dear Victor? What is it you fear?"

"Oh! Peace, peace, my love," replied I, "this night, and all will be safe. But this night is dreadful, very dreadful."

I passed an hour in this state of mind, when suddenly I reflected how dreadful the combat which I momentarily expected would be to my wife, and I earnestly **entreated** her to retire, **resolving** not to join her until I had obtained some knowledge as to the situation of my enemy.

She left me, and I continued some time walking up and down the passages of the house, and inspecting every corner that might afford a retreat to my **adversary**. But I discovered no trace of him, and was beginning to **conjecture** that some fortunate chance had intervened to prevent the **execution** of his menaces; when suddenly I heard a shrill and dreadful scream. It came from the room into which Elizabeth had retired. As I heard it, the whole truth rushed into my mind, my arms dropped, the motion of every muscle and fibre was suspended; I could

EXPIRE (ehk spier) *v.* **-ing,-ed.**
to come to an end; die; breathe out
Synonyms: terminate; exhale

INANIMATE (ihn aan ih miht) *adj.*
not alive, lacking energy
Synonyms: dead, lifeless, dull, inactive, soulless

OBSTINATE (ahb stih nuht) *adj.*
stubborn
Synonyms: headstrong, stiff-necked, bullheaded, pigheaded, mulish

COUNTENANCE (kown tuh nuhns) *n.*
appearance, facial expression
Synonyms: face, features, visage

ARDOUR or ARDOR (ahr duhr) *n.*
passion, enthusiasm
Synonyms: intensity, vehemence

LANGUOR (laang guhr) (laang uhr) *n.*
lack of energy, indifference, slowness
Synonyms: weakness, listlessness, sluggishness

ABHORRED (uhb hohr ehd) *adj.*
loathed, detested
Synonyms: hated, condemned, abominated, execrated, despised

feel the blood trickling in my veins, and tingling in the extremities of my limbs. This state lasted but for an instant; the scream was repeated, and I rushed into the room.

Great God! Why did I not then **expire**! Why am I here to relate the destruction of the best hope, and the purest creature of earth? She was there, lifeless and **inanimate**, thrown across the bed, her head hanging down, and her pale and distorted features half covered by her hair. Every where I turn I see the same figure—her bloodless arms and relaxed form flung by the murderer on its bridal bier. Could I behold this, and live? Alas! Life is **obstinate**, and clings closest where it is most hated. For a moment only did I lose recollection; I fainted.

When I recovered, I found myself surrounded by the people of the inn; their **countenances** expressed a breathless terror. But the horror of others appeared only as a mockery, a shadow of the feelings that oppressed me. I escaped from them to the room where lay the body of Elizabeth, my love, my wife, so lately living, so dear, so worthy. She had been moved from the posture in which I had first beheld her; and now, as she lay, her head upon her arm, and a handkerchief thrown across her face and neck, I might have supposed her asleep. I rushed towards her, and embraced her with **ardour**; but the deathly **languor** and coldness of the limbs told me, that what I now held in my arms had ceased to be the Elizabeth whom I had loved and cherished. The murderous mark of the fiend's grasp was on her neck, and the breath had ceased to issue from her lips.

While I still hung over her in the agony of despair, I happened to look up. The windows of the room had before been darkened; and I felt a kind of panic on seeing the pale yellow light of the moon illuminate the chamber. The shutters had been thrown back; and, with a sensation of horror not to be described, I saw at the open window a figure, the most hideous and **abhorred**. A grin

ELUDE (ih lood) *v.* **-ing,-ed.**
escape, avoid
Synonyms: evade, dodge

CONJURE (kahn juhr) *v.* **-ing,-ed.**
to call on or beg solemnly; to affect or effect as if by magic; to bring to mind
Synonyms: entreat, implore, rouse, recollect

PARCHED (pahrchd) *adj.*
extremely thirsty; shriveled
Synonyms: dehydrated, desiccated, scorched

EXECUTION (ehk sih kyoo shuhn) *n.*
1. the act of performing or carrying out a task
Synonyms: accomplishment, achievement
2. the act of putting to death
Synonyms: killing, capital punishment, murder

MALIGNITY (muh lihg nih tee) *n.*
evil or aggressive malice; something that produces death
Synonyms: malevolence, bitterness, resentment

RESOLVE (rih sahlv) *v.* **-ing,-ed.**
to determine or to make a firm decision about
Synonyms: solve, decide

PROCURE (proh kyoor) *v.* **-ing,-ed.**
to obtain
Synonyms: acquire, secure, get, gain

TORRENT (tawr rehnt) *n.*
a turbulent, fast-flowing stream
Synonyms: outpouring, deluge, flood

was on the face of the monster; he seemed to jeer, as with his fiendish finger he pointed towards the corpse of my wife. I rushed towards the window, and drawing a pistol from my bosom, shot; but he **eluded** me, leaped from his station, and, running with the swiftness of lightning, plunged into the lake.

The report of the pistol brought a crowd into the room. I pointed to the spot where he had disappeared, and we followed the track with boats; nets were cast, but in vain. After passing several hours, we returned hopeless, most of my companions believing it to have been a form **conjured** by my fancy. After having landed, they proceeded to search the country, parties going in different directions among the woods and vines.

I did not accompany them; I was exhausted. A film covered my eyes, and my skin was **parched** with the heat of fever. In this state I lay on a bed, hardly conscious of what had happened; my eyes wandered round the room, as if to seek something that I had lost.

At length I remembered that my father would anxiously expect the return of Elizabeth and myself, and that I must return alone. This reflection brought tears into my eyes, and I wept for a long time; but my thoughts rambled to various subjects, reflecting on my misfortunes, and their cause. I was bewildered in a cloud of wonder and horror. The death of William, the **execution** of Justine, the murder of Clerval, and lastly of my wife; even at that moment I knew not that my only remaining friends were safe from the **malignity** of the fiend; my father even now might be writhing under his grasp, and Ernest might be dead at his feet. This idea made me shudder, and recalled me to action. I started up, and **resolved** to return to Geneva with all possible speed.

There were no horses to be **procured**, and I must return by the lake; but the wind was unfavourable, and the rain fell in **torrents**. However, it was hardly morning, and I might reasonably hope to arrive by night. I hired men

AGITATION (aa gih tay shuhn) *n.*
commotion, excitement; uneasiness
Synonyms: disturbance, restlessness, anxiety

ACME (aak mee) *n.*
highest point; summit
Synonyms: apex, crown, peak, pinnacle, zenith

TEDIOUS (tee dee uhs) *adj.*
tiresome because of length or dullness
Synonyms: dull, fatiguing, unexciting, wearisome

DESOLATE (deh soh liht) *adj.*
showing the effects of abandonment or neglect; devoid of warmth or comfort
Synonyms: barren, bleak, forsaken, vacant

VENERABLE (veh nehr uh buhl) *adj.*
respected because of age
Synonyms: respectable, distinguished, elderly

DOTE (doht) *v.* **-ing,-ed.**
to lavish attention, love to excess
Synonyms: adore, cherish, spoil

to row, and took an oar myself, for I had always experienced relief from mental torment in bodily exercise. But the overflowing misery I now felt, and the excess of **agitation** that I endured, rendered me incapable of any exertion. I threw down the oar; and, leaning my head upon my hands, gave way to every gloomy idea that arose. If I looked up, I saw the scenes which were familiar to me in my happier time, and which I had contemplated but the day before in the company of her who was now but a shadow and a recollection. Tears streamed from my eyes. The rain had ceased for a moment, and I saw the fish play in the waters as they had done a few hours before; they had then been observed by Elizabeth. Nothing is so painful to the human mind as a great and sudden change. The sun might shine, or the clouds might lower; but nothing could appear to me as it had done the day before. A fiend had snatched from me every hope of future happiness. No creature had ever been so miserable as I was; so frightful an event is single in the history of man.

But why should I dwell upon the incidents that followed this last overwhelming event. Mine has been a tale of horrors; I have reached their **acme**, and what I must now relate can but be **tedious** to you. Know that, one by one, my friends were snatched away; I was left **desolate**. My own strength is exhausted; and I must tell, in a few words, what remains of my hideous narration.

I arrived at Geneva. My father and Ernest yet lived; but the former sunk under the tidings that I bore. I see him now, excellent and **venerable** old man! His eyes wandered in vacancy, for they had lost their charm and their delight—his niece, his more than daughter, whom he **doted** on with all that affection which a man feels, who, in the decline of life, having few affections, clings more earnestly to those that remain. Cursed, cursed be the fiend that brought misery on his grey hairs, and doomed him to waste in wretchedness! He could not live under the horrors that were accumulated around him; an

APOPLECTIC (aa puh <u>plehk</u> tihk) *adj.*
relating to, showing symptoms of, or causing stroke
Synonyms: motionless, numb, petrified

MELANCHOLY (<u>mehl</u> uhn kahl ee) *n.*
sadness, depression
Synonyms: dejection, despondency, woe, sorrow

ARDENTLY (<u>ahr</u> dihnt lee) *adv.*
passionately, enthusiastically, fervently
Synonyms: intensely, vehemently, fervidly

APPREHENSION (aa prih <u>hehn</u> shuhn) *n.*
1. a legal seizure
Synonym: arrest
2. suspicion or fear of future or unknown evil
Synonyms: mistrust, uneasiness

MAGISTRATE (<u>maa</u> juh strayt) *n.*
an official who can administrate laws
Synonyms: judge, arbiter, authority, marshal

DEPOSITION (deh puh <u>zih</u> shun) *n.*
a testimony under oath that has been written down
Synonyms: affidavit, attestation

apoplectic fit was brought on, and in a few days he died in my arms.

What then became of me? I know not; I lost sensation, and chains and darkness were the only objects that pressed upon me. Sometimes, indeed, I dreamt that I wandered in flowery meadows and pleasant vales with the friends of my youth; but awoke, and found myself in a dungeon. **Melancholy** followed, but by degrees I gained a clear conception of my miseries and situation, and was then released from my prison. For they had called me mad; and during many months, as I understood, a solitary cell had been my habitation.

But liberty had been a useless gift to me had I not, as I awakened to reason, at the same time awakened to revenge. As the memory of past misfortunes pressed upon me, I began to reflect on their cause—the monster whom I had created, the miserable daemon whom I had sent abroad into the world for my destruction. I was possessed by a maddening rage when I thought of him, and desired and **ardently** prayed that I might have him within my grasp to wreak a great and signal revenge on his cursed head.

Nor did my hate long confine itself to useless wishes; I began to reflect on the best means of securing him; and for this purpose, about a month after my release, I repaired to a criminal judge in the town, and told him that I had an accusation to make; that I knew the destroyer of my family; and that I required him to exert his whole authority for the **apprehension** of the murderer.

The **magistrate** listened to me with attention and kindness. "Be assured, sir," said he, "no pains or exertions on my part shall be spared to discover the villain."

"I thank you," replied I. "Listen, therefore, to the **deposition** that I have to make. It is indeed a tale so strange, that I should fear you would not credit it, were there not something in truth which, however wonderful,

RESOLUTION (reh suh loo shuhn) *n.*
a firm decision
Synonyms: determination, will, explanation

PROVISIONALLY (pruh vih zhuhn uh lee) *adv.*
with the readiness to deal with a need or contingency
Synonyms: temporarily, conditionally

RECONCILE (reh kuhn siel) *v.* **-ing,-ed.**
1. to bring to accept
Synonyms: resign, submit, placate, pacify, appease
2. to resolve a dispute
Synonyms: agree, accommodate, rectify, reunite

DEVIATE (dee vee ayt) *v.* **-ing,-ed.**
to stray, wander
Synonyms: diverge, dissent, digress, disagree, divert

INVECTIVE (ihn vehk tihv) *n.*
abusive language
Synonyms: vituperation, denunciation, revilement

MAGISTRATE (maa juh strayt) *n.*
an official who can administrate laws
Synonyms: judge, arbiter, authority, marshal

INCREDULOUS (ihn krehj uh luhs) *adj.*
skeptical, doubtful
Synonyms: disbelieving, suspicious

COUNTENANCE (kown tuh nuhns) *n.*
appearance, facial expression
Synonyms: face, features, visage

EXECUTION (ehk sih kyoo shuhn) *n.* ***See page 372.***

INCREDULITY (ihn kreh doo lih tee) *n.*
skepticism, doubt
Synonyms: disbelief, suspicion

TRAVERSE (truh vuhrs) (traa vuhrs) *v.* **-ing,-ed.**
to travel or travel across; to turn or move laterally
Synonyms: cross, travel, intersect, pass through

CONJECTURE (kuhn jehk shuhr) *v.* **-ing,-ed.**
to infer, predict, guess
Synonyms: postulate, hypothesize, suppose, surmise

forces conviction. The story is too connected to be mistaken for a dream, and I have no motive for falsehood." My manner, as I thus addressed him, was impressive, but calm; I had formed in my own heart a **resolution** to pursue my destroyer to death; and this purpose quieted my agony, and **provisionally reconciled** me to life. I now related my history briefly, but with firmness and precision, marking the dates with accuracy, and never **deviating** into **invective** or exclamation.

The **magistrate** appeared at first perfectly **incredulous**, but as I continued he became more attentive and interested; I saw him sometimes shudder with horror, at others a lively surprise, unmingled with disbelief, was painted on his **countenance**.

When I had concluded my narration, I said, "This is the being whom I accuse, and for whose detection and punishment I call upon you to exert your whole power. It is your duty as a **magistrate**, and I believe and hope that your feelings as a man will not revolt from the **execution** of those functions on this occasion."

This address caused a considerable change in the physiognomy of my auditor. He had heard my story with that half kind of belief that is given to a tale of spirits and supernatural events; but when he was called upon to act officially in consequence, the whole tide of his **incredulity** returned. He, however, answered mildly, "I would willingly afford you every aid in your pursuit; but the creature of whom you speak appears to have powers which would put all my exertions to defiance. Who can follow an animal which can **traverse** the sea of ice, and inhabit caves and dens, where no man would venture to intrude? Besides, some months have elapsed since the commission of his crimes, and no one can **conjecture** to what placc he has wandered, or what region he may now inhabit."

"I do not doubt that he hovers near the spot which I inhabit; and if he has indeed taken refuge in the Alps, he

MAGISTRATE (maa juh strayt) *n.*
an official who can administrate laws
Synonyms: judge, arbiter, authority, marshal

IMPRACTICABLE (ihm praak tihk uh buhl) *adj.*
impossible; impassable
Synonyms: insane, imprudent, absurd

AVAIL (uh vayl) *n.*
use or advantage
Synonyms: benefit, service, usefulness

AGITATION (aa gih tay shuhn) *n.*
commotion, excitement; uneasiness
Synonyms: disturbance, restlessness, anxiety, fluster, disquiet

HAUGHTY (haw tee) (hah tee) *adj.*
arrogant and condescending
Synonyms: proud, disdainful, supercilious, scornful, vainglorious

REVERT (rih vuhrt) *v.* **-ing,-ed.**
to backslide, regress
Synonyms: return, recur, degenerate, deteriorate

may be hunted like the chamois, and destroyed as a beast of prey. But I perceive your thoughts. You do not credit my narrative, and do not intend to pursue my enemy with the punishment which is his desert."

As I spoke, rage sparkled in my eyes; the **magistrate** was intimidated. "You are mistaken," said he, "I will exert myself; and if it is in my power to seize the monster, be assured that he shall suffer punishment proportionate to his crimes. But I fear, from what you have yourself described to be his properties, that this will prove **impracticable**, and that, while every proper measure is pursued, you should endeavour to make up your mind to disappointment."

"That cannot be; but all that I can say will be of little **avail**. My revenge is of no moment to you; yet, while I allow it to be a vice, I confess that it is the devouring and only passion of my soul. My rage is unspeakable, when I reflect that the murderer, whom I have turned loose upon society, still exists. You refuse my just demand. I have but one resource; and I devote myself, either in my life or death, to his destruction."

I trembled with excess of **agitation** as I said this; there was a frenzy in my manner, and something, I doubt not, of that **haughty** fierceness, which the martyrs of old are said to have possessed. But to a Genevan **magistrate**, whose mind was occupied by far other ideas than those of devotion and heroism, this elevation of mind had much the appearance of madness. He endeavoured to soothe me as a nurse does a child, and **reverted** to my tale as the effects of delirium.

"Man," I cried, "how ignorant art thou in thy pride of wisdom! Cease; you know not what it is you say."

I broke from the house angry and disturbed, and retired to meditate on some other mode of action.

ENDOW (ehn dow) *v.* **-ing,-ed.**
to furnish with an income or grant; to provide with something naturally or freely
Synonyms: bestow, donate, empower, grant, support

RESOLUTION (reh suh loo shuhn) *n.*
a firm decision
Synonyms: determination, will, explanation

ADVERSITY (aad vuhr sih tee) *n.*
hardship
Synonyms: suffering, distress, tribulation

TRAVERSE (truh vuhrs) (traa vuhrs) *v.* **-ing,-ed.**
to travel or travel across; to turn or move laterally
Synonyms: cross, travel, intersect, pass through

BARBAROUS (baar buh ruhs) *adj.*
lacking culture or refinement; mercilessly cruel
Synonyms: savage, vulgar, inhumane

ADVERSARY (aad vuhr saa ree) *n.*
an opponent or enemy
Synonyms: antagonist, foe, opposition

REPOSE (rih pohz) *v.* **-ing,-ed.**
1. to relax or rest; to lie dead
Synonyms: sleep, slumber
2. to place (trust) or to count on
Synonyms: entrust, invest, place

AGITATED (aa gih tay tihd) *adj.*
upset or uneasy
Synonyms: disturbed, flustered, bothered

SOLEMN (sah luhm) *adj.*
deeply serious; somberly impressive
Synonyms: dignified, earnest, ceremonial

AFFECTING (uh fehk tihng) *adj.*
1. emotionally touching
Synonyms: moving, inspiring, stirring, upsetting
2. able to influence or cause a change in
Synonyms: changing, altering, transforming

CHAPTER VII

My present situation was one in which all voluntary thought was swallowed up and lost. I was hurried away by fury; revenge alone **endowed** me with strength and composure; it modelled my feelings, and allowed me to be calculating and calm, at periods when otherwise delirium or death would have been my portion.

My first **resolution** was to quit Geneva for ever; my country, which, when I was happy and beloved, was dear to me, now, in my **adversity**, became hateful. I provided myself with a sum of money, together with a few jewels which had belonged to my mother, and departed.

And now my wanderings began, which are to cease but with life. I have **traversed** a vast portion of the earth, and have endured all the hardships which travellers, in deserts and **barbarous** countries, are wont to meet. How I have lived I hardly know; many times have I stretched my failing limbs upon the sandy plain, and prayed for death. But revenge kept me alive; I dared not die, and leave my **adversary** in being.

When I quitted Geneva, my first labour was to gain some clue by which I might trace the steps of my fiendish enemy. But my plan was unsettled; and I wandered many hours around the confines of the town, uncertain what path I should pursue. As night approached, I found myself at the entrance of the cemetery where William, Elizabeth, and my father, **reposed**. I entered it, and approached the tomb which marked their graves. Every thing was silent, except the leaves of the trees, which were gently **agitated** by the wind; the night was nearly dark; and the scene would have been **solemn** and **affecting** even to an uninterested observer. The spirits of the departed seemed to flit around, and to cast a

EXECUTE (ehk sih kyoot) *v.* **-ing,-ed.**
1. to carry out fully; to make or produce
   Synonyms: accomplish, achieve, perform
2. to put to death by penalty of crime
   Synonyms: kill, punish, murder

VENGEANCE (vehn juhns) *n.*
punishment inflicted in retaliation; vehemence
Synonyms: revenge, repayment, wrath

SOLEMNITY (suh lehm nih tee) *n.*
dignified seriousness
Synonyms: ceremoniousness, formality, observance

ABHORRED (uhb hohr ehd) *adj.*
loathed, detested
Synonyms: hated, condemned, abominated, execrated, despised

AUDIBLE (aw dih buhl) *adj.*
capable of being heard
Synonyms: detectable, perceptible

shadow, which was felt but seen not, around the head of the mourner.

The deep grief which this scene had at first excited quickly gave way to rage and despair. They were dead, and I lived; their murderer also lived, and to destroy him I must drag out my weary existence. I knelt on the grass, and kissed the earth, and with quivering lips exclaimed, "By the sacred earth on which I kneel, by the shades that wander near me, by the deep and eternal grief that I feel, I swear; and by thee, O Night, and by the spirits that preside over thee, I swear to pursue the daemon, who caused this misery, until he or I shall perish in mortal conflict. For this purpose I will preserve my life—to **execute** this dear revenge, will I again behold the sun, and tread the green herbage of earth, which otherwise should vanish from my eyes for ever. And I call on you, spirits of the dead; and on you, wandering ministers of **vengeance**, to aid and conduct me in my work. Let the cursed and hellish monster drink deep of agony; let him feel the despair that now torments me."

I had begun my adjuration with **solemnity**, and an awe which almost assured me that the shades of my murdered friends heard and approved my devotion; but the furies possessed me as I concluded, and rage choked my utterance.

I was answered through the stillness of night by a loud and fiendish laugh. It rung on my ears long and heavily; the mountains re-echoed it, and I felt as if all hell surrounded me with mockery and laughter. Surely in that moment I should have been possessed by frenzy, and have destroyed my miserable existence, but that my vow was heard, and that I was reserved for **vengeance**. The laughter died away when a well-known and **abhorred** voice, apparently close to my ear, addressed me in an **audible** whisper, "I am satisfied, miserable wretch! You have determined to live, and I am satisfied."

I darted towards the spot from which the sound

ELUDE (ih lood) *v.* **-ing,-ed.**
escape, avoid
Synonyms: evade, dodge

APPARITION (aa puh rih shuhn) *n.*
an unexpected or unusual sight; a ghostly figure
Synonyms: ghost, illusion, spirit, specter

EXTRICATE (ehk strih kayt) *v.* **-ing,-ed.**
to free from, disentangle
Synonyms: disengage, untangle, release, disencumber

INSURMOUNTABLE (ihn suhr mownt uh buhl) *adj.*
unable to be conquered or overcome
Synonyms: unsurpassable, insuperable, impossible, hopeless, unbeatable

REPAST (rih paast) *n.*
meal or mealtime
Synonyms: feast, banquet

INVOKE (ihn vohk) *v.* **-ing,-ed.**
to call upon, request help
Synonyms: summon, solicit, conjure, evoke

PARCHED (pahrchd) *adj.*
extremely thirsty; shriveled
Synonyms: dehydrated, desiccated, scorched

proceeded, but the devil **eluded** my grasp. Suddenly the broad disk of the moon arose, and shone full upon his ghastly and distorted shape, as he fled with more than mortal speed.

I pursued him; and for many months this has been my task. Guided by a slight clue, I followed the windings of the Rhone, but vainly. The blue Mediterranean appeared; and, by a strange chance, I saw the fiend enter by night, and hide himself in a vessel bound for the Black Sea. I took my passage in the same ship; but he escaped, I know not how.

Amidst the wilds of Tartary and Russia, although he still evaded me, I have ever followed in his track. Sometimes the peasants, scared by this horrid **apparition**, informed me of his path; sometimes he himself, who feared that if I lost all trace I should despair and die, often left some mark to guide me. The snows descended on my head, and I saw the print of his huge step on the white plain. To you first entering on life, to whom care is new, and agony unknown, how can you understand what I have felt, and still feel? Cold, want, and fatigue, were the least pains which I was destined to endure; I was cursed by some devil, and carried about with me my eternal hell; yet still a spirit of good followed and directed my steps, and, when I most murmured, would suddenly **extricate** me from seemingly **insurmountable** difficulties. Sometimes, when nature, overcome by hunger, sunk under the exhaustion, a **repast** was prepared for me in the desert, that restored and inspirited me. The fare was indeed coarse, such as the peasants of the country ate; but I may not doubt that it was set there by the spirits that I had **invoked** to aid me. Often, when all was dry, the heavens cloudless, and I was **parched** by thirst, a slight cloud would bedim the sky, shed the few drops that revived me, and vanish.

I followed, when I could, the courses of the rivers; but the daemon generally avoided these, as it was here that

SUBSIST (suhb sihst) *v.* **-ing,-ed.**
to have existence; to nourish and take care of oneself
Synonyms: live, manage, survive, sustain

REPOSE (rih pohz) *v.* **-ing,-ed.**
1. to relax or rest; to lie dead
Synonyms: sleep, slumber
2. to place (trust) or to count on
Synonyms: entrust, invest, place

RAPTURE (raap chuhr) *n.*
deep absorption; ecstasy or extreme joy
Synonyms: exaltation, immersion

RETAIN (rih tayn) *v.* **-ing,-ed.**
to hold, keep possession of
Synonyms: withhold, reserve, maintain, remember

RESPITE (rih spiet) *n.*
interval of relief
Synonyms: rest, pause, intermission, recess

SUSTAIN (suh stayn) *v.* **-ing,-ed.**
to support, uphold; endure, undergo
Synonyms: maintain, prop, encourage, withstand

BENEVOLENT (buh neh vuh luhnt) *adj.*
kind, compassionate
Synonyms: charitable, altruistic, beneficent, good

COUNTENANCE (kown tuh nuhns) *n.* ***See page 378.***

VENGEANCE (vehn juhns) *n.* ***See page 384.***

ENJOIN (ehn joyn) *v.* **-ing,-ed.**
to urge, order, command; forbid or prohibit, as by judicial order
Synonyms: direct, instruct, charge; prohibit

ARDENT (ahr dihnt) *adj.*
passionate, enthusiastic, fervent
Synonyms: intense, vehement, fervid

INSTIGATE (ihn stih gayt) *v.* **-ing,-ed.**
to incite, urge, agitate
Synonyms: foment, goad, spark

LEGIBLE (leh juh buhl) *adj.*
readable
Synonyms: plain, clear

the population of the country chiefly collected. In other places human beings were seldom seen; and I generally **subsisted** on the wild animals that crossed my path. I had money with me, and gained the friendship of the villagers by distributing it, or bringing with me some food that I had killed, which, after taking a small part, I always presented to those who had provided me with fire and utensils for cooking.

My life, as it passed thus, was indeed hateful to me, and it was during sleep alone that I could taste joy. O blessed sleep! Often, when most miserable, I sank to **repose**, and my dreams lulled me even to **rapture**. The spirits that guarded me had provided these moments, or rather hours, of happiness, that I might **retain** strength to fulfill my pilgrimage. Deprived of this **respite**, I should have sunk under my hardships. During the day I was **sustained** and inspirited by the hope of night. In sleep I saw my friends, my wife, and my beloved country; again I saw the **benevolent countenance** of my father, heard the silver tones of my Elizabeth's voice, and beheld Clerval enjoying health and youth. Often, when wearied by a toilsome march, I persuaded myself that I was dreaming until night should come, and that I should then enjoy reality in the arms of my dearest friends. What agonizing fondness did I feel for them! How did I cling to their dear forms, as sometimes they haunted even my waking hours, and persuade myself that they still lived! At such moments, **vengeance** that burned within me died in my heart, and I pursued my path towards the destruction of the daemon, more as a task **enjoined** by heaven, as the mechanical impulse of some power of which I was unconscious, than as the **ardent** desire of my soul.

What his feelings were whom I pursued, I cannot know. Sometimes, indeed, he left marks in writing on the barks of the trees, or cut in stone, that guided me, and **instigated** my fury. "My reign is not yet over." (These words were **legible** in one of these inscriptions.) "You

IMPASSIVE (ihm pass ihv) *adj.*
emotionless
Synonyms: expressionless, stolid, cold, indifferent, placid

VENGEANCE (vehn juhns) *n.*
punishment inflicted in retaliation; vehemence
Synonyms: revenge, repayment, wrath

TEDIOUS (tee dee uhs) *adj.*
tiresome because of length or dullness
Synonyms: dull, fatiguing, unexciting, wearisome

PROCURE (proh kyoor) *v.* **-ing,-ed.**
to obtain
Synonyms: acquire, secure, get, gain

PERSEVERANCE (pehr suh veer ihns) *n.*
resolve, determination
Synonyms: persistence, tenacity, pertinacity, steadfastness

INVIGORATE (ihn vih guh rayt) *v.* **-ing,-ed.**
to give life or energy to
Synonyms: inspire, animate, enliven

RESOLVE (rih sahlv) *v.* **-ing,-ed.**
to determine or to make a firm decision about
Synonyms: solve, decide

UNABATED (uhn uh bay tehd) *adj.*
unstoppable, persistent
Synonyms: continuous, incessant, unremitting

FERVOUR or FERVOR (fuhr vuhr) *n.*
passion, intensity, zeal
Synonyms: vehemence, eagerness, enthusiasm

TRAVERSE (truh vuhrs) (traa vuhrs) *v.* **-ing,-ed.**
to travel or travel across; to turn or move laterally
Synonyms: cross, travel, intersect, pass through

live, and my power is complete. Follow me; I seek the everlasting ices of the north, where you will feel the misery of cold and frost, to which I am **impassive**. You will find near this place, if you follow not too tardily, a dead hare; eat, and be refreshed. Come on, my enemy; we have yet to wrestle for our lives; but many hard and miserable hours must you endure, until that period shall arrive."

Scoffing devil! Again do I vow **vengeance**; again do I devote thee, miserable fiend, to torture and death. Never will I omit my search, until he or I perish; and then with what ecstacy shall I join my Elizabeth, and those who even now prepare for me the reward of my **tedious** toil and horrible pilgrimage.

As I still pursued my journey northward, the snows thickened, and the cold increased in a degree almost too severe to support. The peasants were shut up in their hovels, and only a few of the most hardy ventured forth to seize the animals whom starvation had forced from their hiding places to seek for prey. The rivers were covered with ice, and no fish could be **procured**; and thus I was cut off from my chief article of maintenance.

The triumph of my enemy increased with the difficulty of my labours. One inscription that he left was in these words: "Prepare! Your toils only begin. Wrap yourself in furs, and provide food, for we shall soon enter upon a journey where your sufferings will satisfy my everlasting hatred."

My courage and **perseverance** were **invigorated** by these scoffing words; I **resolved** not to fail in my purpose; and, calling on heaven to support me, I continued with **unabated fervour** to **traverse** immense deserts, until the ocean appeared at a distance, and formed the utmost boundary of the horizon. Oh! How unlike it was to the blue seas of the south! Covered with ice, it was only to be distinguished from land by its superior wildness and ruggedness. The Greeks wept for joy when they beheld the Mediterranean from the hills of Asia, and hailed with

RAPTURE (raap chuhr) *n.*
deep absorption; ecstasy or extreme joy
Synonyms: exaltation, immersion

ADVERSARY (aad vuhr saa ree) *n.*
an opponent or enemy
Synonyms: antagonist, foe, opposition

GIBE or JIBE (jieb) *n.*
heckling, taunting remarks
Synonyms: ridicule, mockery, derision, jeer

PROCURE (proh kyoor) *v.* **-ing,-ed.**
to obtain
Synonyms: acquire, secure, get, gain

TRAVERSE (truh vuhrs) (traa vuhrs) *v.* **-ing,-ed.**
to travel or travel across; to turn or move laterally
Synonyms: cross, travel, intersect, pass through

CONJECTURE (kuhn jehk shuhr) *v.* **-ing,-ed.**
to infer, predict, guess
Synonyms: postulate, hypothesize, suppose, surmise

GENIAL (jeen yuhl) (jee nee uhl) *adj.*
favorable to growth or comfort; displaying or characterized by genius
Synonyms: good-natured, favorable, cordial, warm

VENGEANCE (vehn juhns) *n.*
punishment inflicted in retaliation; vehemence
Synonyms: revenge, repayment, wrath

rapture the boundary of their toils. I did not weep; but I knelt down, and, with a full heart, thanked my guiding spirit for conducting me in safety to the place where I hoped, notwithstanding my **adversary's gibe**, to meet and grapple with him.

Some weeks before this period I had **procured** a sledge and dogs, and thus **traversed** the snows with inconceivable speed. I know not whether the fiend possessed the same advantages; but I found that, as before I had daily lost ground in the pursuit, I now gained on him; so much so, that when I first saw the ocean, he was but one day's journey in advance, and I hoped to intercept him before he should reach the beach. With new courage, therefore, I pressed on, and in two days arrived at a wretched <u>hamlet</u> on the sea-shore. I inquired of the inhabitants concerning the fiend, and gained accurate information. A gigantic monster, they said, had arrived the night before, armed with a gun and many pistols; putting to flight the inhabitants of a solitary cottage, through fear of his terrific appearance. He had carried off their store of winter food, and, placing it in a sledge, to draw which he had seized on a numerous <u>drove</u> of trained dogs, he had harnessed them, and the same night, to the joy of the horror-struck villagers, had pursued his journey across the sea in a direction that led to no land; and they **conjectured** that he must speedily be destroyed by the breaking of the ice, or frozen by the eternal frosts.

On hearing this information, I suffered a temporary access of despair. He had escaped me; and I must commence a destructive and almost endless journey across the mountainous ices of the ocean, amidst cold that few of the inhabitants could long endure, and which I, the native of a **genial** and sunny climate, could not hope to survive. Yet at the idea that the fiend should live and be triumphant, my rage and **vengeance** returned, and, like a mighty tide, overwhelmed every other feeling. After a

REPOSE (rih pohz) *n.*
rest or relaxation, leisure
Synonyms: calmness, tranquility, rest, ease, idleness

INSTIGATE (ihn stih gayt) *v.* **-ing,-ed.**
to incite, urge, agitate
Synonyms: foment, goad, spark

PROVISION (pruh vih zhuhn) *n.*
a stock of needed materials or supplies; a measure taken to deal with a need or contingency
Synonyms: supplies, equipment, precaution

PROTRACTION (proh traak shuhn) *n.*
elongation, extension
Synonyms: lengthening, stretching

DESPONDENCY (dih spahn duhn see) *n.*
discouragement and dejection
Synonyms: sadness, depression, desolation, forlornness

DISENCUMBER (dihs ehn kuhm buhr) *v.* **-ing,-ed.**
to unburden or relieve
Synonyms: extricate, untangle, unload

slight **repose**, during which the spirits of the dead hovered round, and **instigated** me to toil and revenge, I prepared for my journey.

I exchanged my land sledge for one fashioned for the inequalities of the frozen ocean; and, purchasing a plentiful stock of **provisions**, I departed from land.

I cannot guess how many days have passed since then; but I have endured misery, which nothing but the eternal sentiment of a just retribution burning within my heart could have enabled me to support. Immense and rugged mountains of ice often barred up my passage, and I often heard the thunder of the ground sea, which threatened my destruction. But again the frost came, and made the paths of the sea secure.

By the quantity of **provision** which I had consumed I should guess that I had passed three weeks in this journey; and the continual **protraction** of hope, returning back upon the heart, often wrung bitter drops of **despondency** and grief from my eyes. Despair had indeed almost secured her prey, and I should soon have sunk beneath this misery; when once, after the poor animals that carried me had with incredible toil gained the summit of a sloping ice mountain, and one sinking under his fatigue died, I viewed the expanse before me with anguish, when suddenly my eye caught a dark speck upon the dusky plain. I strained my sight to discover what it could be, and uttered a wild cry of ecstacy when I distinguished a sledge, and the distorted proportions of a well-known form within. Oh! With what a burning gush did hope revisit my heart! Warm tears filled my eyes, which I hastily wiped away, that they might not intercept the view I had of the daemon; but still my sight was dimmed by the burning drops, until, giving way to the emotions that oppressed me, I wept aloud.

But this was not the time for delay; I **disencumbered** the dogs of their dead companion, gave them a plentiful portion of food; and, after an hour's rest, which was

OMINOUS (ah mihn uhs) *adj.*
menacing, threatening, indicating misfortune
Synonyms: inauspicious, unpropitious, sinister, dire, baleful

TUMULTUOUS (tuh muhl choo uhs) *adj.*
confusing or disorderly; agitated
Synonyms: disturbed, turbulent, chaotic, hectic

APPALLING (uh pahl lihng) *adj.*
overcome with shock or dismay
Synonyms: horrifying, dreadful, ghastly, awful

SUCCOUR or SUCCOR (suh kuhr) *n.*
relief; a thing that furnishes relief
Synonyms: aid, help, support

INDUCE (ihn doos) (ihn dyoos) *v.* **-ing,-ed.**
to persuade; bring about
Synonyms: prevail, convince, lead, effect, occasion

absolutely necessary, and yet which was bitterly irksome to me, I continued my route. The sledge was still visible; nor did I again lose sight of it, except at the moments when for a short time some ice rock concealed it with its intervening crags. I indeed perceptibly gained on it; and when, after nearly two days' journey, I beheld my enemy at no more than a mile distant, my heart bounded within me.

But now, when I appeared almost within grasp of my enemy, my hopes were suddenly extinguished, and I lost all trace of him more utterly than I had ever done before. A ground sea was heard; the thunder of its progress, as the waters rolled and swelled beneath me, became every moment more **ominous** and terrific. I pressed on, but in vain. The wind arose; the sea roared; and, as with the mighty shock of an earthquake, it split, and cracked with a tremendous and overwhelming sound. The work was soon finished. In a few minutes a **tumultuous** sea rolled between me and my enemy, and I was left drifting on a scattered piece of ice, that was continually lessening, and thus preparing for me a hideous death.

In this manner many **appalling** hours passed; several of my dogs died; and I myself was about to sink under the accumulation of distress, when I saw your vessel riding at anchor, and holding forth to me hopes of **succour** and life. I had no conception that vessels ever came so far north, and was astounded at the sight. I quickly destroyed part of my sledge to construct oars; and by these means was enabled, with infinite fatigue, to move my ice-raft in the direction of your ship. I had determined, if you were going southward, still to trust myself to the mercy of the seas, rather than abandon my purpose. I hoped to **induce** you to grant me a boat with which I could still pursue my enemy. But your direction was northward. You took me on board when my vigour was exhausted, and I should soon have sunk under my multiplied hardships into a death, which I still dread, for my task is unfulfilled.

VENGEANCE (<u>vehn</u> juhns) *n.*
punishment inflicted in retaliation; vehemence
Synonyms: revenge, repayment, wrath

ELOQUENT (<u>eh</u> luh kwuhnt) *adj.*
persuasive and effective (often used to describe speech)
Synonyms: expressive, fluent

TREACHERY (<u>treh</u> chuhr ee) *n.*
betrayal of trust, deceit
Synonyms: perfidy, treason, disloyalty, falseness, infidelity

MALICE (<u>maal</u> ihs) *n.*
animosity, spite, hatred
Synonyms: malevolence, cruelty, enmity, rancor, hostility

CONGEAL (kuhn <u>jeel</u>) *v.* **-ing,-ed.**
to become thick or solid; to make rigid
Synonyms: jell, coagulate, clot

REPLETE (rih <u>pleet</u>) *adj.*
abundantly supplied
Synonyms: abounding, satiated, gorged, stuffed, full

INDIGNATION (ihn dihg <u>nay</u> shun) *n.*
anger caused by something mean or unjust
Synonyms: fury, ire, wrath

COUNTENANCE (<u>kown</u> tuh nuhns) *n.*
appearance, facial expression
Synonyms: face, features, visage

SUPPRESS (suh <u>prehs</u>) *v.* **-ing,-ed.**
to hold back, restrain
Synonyms: subdue, stifle, muffle, quell, curb

AGITATION (aa gih <u>tay</u> shuhn) *n.*
commotion, excitement; uneasiness
Synonyms: disturbance, restlessness, anxiety

IMPRECATION (ihm prih <u>kay</u> shuhn) *n.*
curse
Synonyms: execration, anathema, malediction

Oh! When will my guiding spirit, in conducting me to the daemon, allow me the rest I so much desire; or must I die, and he yet live? If I do, swear to me, Walton, that he shall not escape; that you will seek him, and satisfy my **vengeance** in his death. Yet, do I dare ask you to undertake my pilgrimage, to endure the hardships that I have undergone? No; I am not so selfish. Yet, when I am dead, if he should appear; if the ministers of **vengeance** should conduct him to you, swear that he shall not live—swear that he shall not triumph over my accumulated woes, and live to make another such a wretch as I am. He is **eloquent** and persuasive; and once his words had even power over my heart. But trust him not. His soul is as hellish as his form, full of **treachery** and fiend-like **malice**. Hear him not; call on the names of William, Justine, Clerval, Elizabeth, my father, and of the wretched Victor, and thrust your sword into his heart. I will hover near, and direct the steel aright.

Walton, in continuation.

August 26th, 17—.

You have read this strange and terrific story, Margaret; and do you not feel your blood **congealed** with horror, like that which even now curdles mine? Sometimes, seized with sudden agony, he could not continue his tale; at others, his voice broken, yet piercing, uttered with difficulty the words so **replete** with agony. His fine and lovely eyes were now lighted up with **indignation**, now subdued to downcast sorrow, and quenched in infinite wretchedness. Sometimes he commanded his **countenance** and tones, and related the most horrible incidents with a tranquil voice, **suppressing** every mark of **agitation**; then, like a volcano bursting forth, his face would suddenly change to an expression of the wildest rage, as he shrieked out **imprecations** on his persecutor.

His tale is connected, and told with an appearance of

APPARITION (aa puh rih shuhn) *n.*
an unexpected or unusual sight; a ghostly figure
Synonyms: ghost, illusion, spirit, specter

AUGMENT (awg mehnt) *v.* **-ing,-ed.**
to expand, extend
Synonyms: enhance, compound, increase, enlarge

POSTERITY (pah steh ruh tee) *n.*
future generations; all of a person's descendants
Synonyms: progeny, offspring, line, lineage, heritage

DESTITUTE (dehs tih toot) (dehs tih tyoot) *adj.*
very poor, poverty-stricken
Synonyms: insolvent, impecunious, penurious, needy, broke

CONSOLATION (kahn suh lay shuhn) *n.*
something providing comfort or solace for a loss or hardship
Synonyms: condolence, solace

DERIVE (dih riev) *v.* **-ing,-ed.**
to obtain from a source
Synonyms: infer, deduce, arise

VENGEANCE (vehn juhns) *n.*
punishment inflicted in retaliation; vehemence
Synonyms: revenge, repayment, wrath

REMOTE (rih moht) *adj.*
distant, isolated
Synonyms: far, removed, aloof

SOLEMNITY (suh lehm nih tee) *n.*
dignified seriousness
Synonyms: ceremoniousness, formality, observance

REVERIE (rehv uh ree) *n.*
a daydream
Synonyms: dream, absorption, muse, meditation

the simplest truth; yet I own to you that the letters of Felix and Safie, which he showed me, and the **apparition** of the monster, seen from our ship, brought to me a greater conviction of the truth of his narrative than his asseverations, however earnest and connected. Such a monster has then really existence; I cannot doubt it; yet I am lost in surprise and admiration. Sometimes I endeavoured to gain from Frankenstein the particulars of his creature's formation; but on this point he was impenetrable.

"Are you mad, my friend?" said he, "or whither does your senseless curiosity lead you? Would you also create for yourself and the world a demoniacal enemy? Or to what do your questions tend? Peace, peace! Learn my miseries, and do not seek to increase your own."

Frankenstein discovered that I made notes concerning his history. He asked to see them, and then himself corrected and **augmented** them in many places, but principally in giving the life and spirit to the conversations he held with his enemy. "Since you have preserved my narration," said he, "I would not allow that a mutilated one should go down to **posterity**."

Thus has a week passed away, while I have listened to the strangest tale that ever imagination formed. My thoughts, and every feeling of my soul, have been drunk up by the interest for my guest, which this tale, and his own elevated and gentle manners have created. I wish to soothe him; yet can I counsel one so infinitely miserable, so **destitute** of every hope of **consolation**, to live? Oh, no! The only joy that he can now know will be when he composes his shattered feelings to peace and death. Yet he enjoys one comfort—the offspring of solitude and delirium. He believes, that, when in dreams he holds converse with his friends, and **derives** from that communion **consolation** for his miseries, or excitements to his **vengeance**, that they are not the creations of his fancy, but the real beings who visit him from the regions of a **remote** world. This faith gives a **solemnity** to his **reveries** that

IMPOSING (ihm pohz ihng) *adj.*
impressive in appearance; imperial
Synonyms: commanding, looming, grandiose

APPREHENSION (aa prih hehn shuhn) *n.*
suspicion or fear of future or unknown evil; the act of perceiving or comprehending; a legal seizure
Synonyms: fear, uneasiness, suspicion; arrest

ELOQUENCE (eh luh kwuhns) *n.*
persuasive and effective speech
Synonyms: expressiveness, fluency

PROSPERITY (prah speh ruh tee) *n.*
wealth or success
Synonyms: affluence, abundance, opulence

PROFOUND (pruh fownd) (proh fownd) *adj.*
having intellectual depth; difficult to understand; extending far below the surface; all encompassing
Synonyms: deep, intellectual, shrewd, thoughtful

ILLUSTRIOUS (ih luhs tree uhs) *adj.*
famous, renowned
Synonyms: noted, celebrated, eminent, famed, notable

ASPIRE (uh spier) *v.* **-ing,-ed.**
to have great hopes; to aim at a goal
Synonyms: intend, strive, purpose, resolve, expect

OMNIPOTENCE (ahm nihp uh tuhnts) *n.*
unlimited or universal power, authority, or force
Synonyms: divinity, mastery, supremecy

EXECUTE (ehk sih kyoot) *v.* **-ing,-ed.** ***See page 384.***

REVERIE (rehv uh ree) *n.*
a daydream
Synonyms: dream, absorption, muse, meditation

EXULT (ihg zuhlt) *v.* **-ing,-ed.**
to rejoice triumphantly
Synonyms: celebrate, cheer, glory

IMBUE (ihm byoo) *v.* **-ing,-ed.**
to infuse; dye, wet, moisten
Synonyms: charge, freight, impregnate, permeate

render them to me almost as **imposing** and interesting as truth.

Our conversations are not always confined to his own history and misfortunes. On every point of general literature he displays unbounded knowledge, and a quick and piercing **apprehension**. His **eloquence** is forcible and touching; nor can I hear him, when he relates a pathetic incident, or endeavours to move the passions of pity or love, without tears. What a glorious creature must he have been in the days of his **prosperity**, when he is thus noble and godlike in ruin. He seems to feel his own worth, and the greatness of his fall.

"When younger," said he, "I felt as if I were destined for some great enterprise. My feelings are **profound**; but I possessed a coolness of judgment that fitted me for **illustrious** achievements. This sentiment of the worth of my nature supported me, when others would have been oppressed; for I deemed it criminal to throw away in useless grief those talents that might be useful to my fellow-creatures. When I reflected on the work I had completed, no less a one than the creation of a sensitive and rational animal, I could not rank myself with the herd of common projectors. But this feeling, which supported me in the commencement of my career, now serves only to plunge me lower in the dust. All my speculations and hopes are as nothing; and, like the archangel who **aspired** to **omnipotence**, I am chained in an eternal hell. My imagination was vivid, yet my powers of analysis and application were intense; by the union of these qualities I conceived the idea, and **executed** the creation of a man. Even now I cannot recollect, without passion, my **reveries** while the work was incomplete. I trod heaven in my thoughts, now **exulting** in my powers, now burning with the idea of their effects. From my infancy I was **imbued** with high hopes and a lofty ambition; but how am I sunk! Oh! My friend, if you had known me as I once was, you would

DEGRADATION (day greh day shuhn) *n.*
the act of falling in rank or status; the act of losing moral or intellectual character
Synonyms: abasement, demotion, disgrace, shame

DESPONDENCY (dih spahn duhn see) *n.*
discouragement and dejection
Synonyms: sadness, depression, desolation

RECONCILE (reh kuhn siel) *v.* **-ing,-ed.**
1. to bring to accept
Synonyms: resign, submit, placate, pacify, appease
2. to resolve a dispute
Synonyms: agree, accommodate, rectify, reunite

REPULSE (rih puhls) *v.* **-ing,-ed.**
repel, fend off; sicken, disgust
Synonyms: rebuff, reject, parry; nauseate

ERADICATE (ih raad ih kayt) *v.* **-ing,-ed.**
to erase or wipe out
Synonyms: uproot, abolish, eliminate, annihilate

INTEGRITY (ihn tehg rih tee) *n.*
decency, honesty, wholeness
Synonyms: honor, probity, rectitude, virtue

MERIT (mehr iht) *n.*
high quality or excellence
Synonyms: virtue, credit

FRAUGHT (frawt) *adj.*
full of, accompanied by
Synonyms: filled, charged, loaded, replete

UTILITY (yoo tih lih tee) *n.*
usefulness, efficiency, functionality
Synonyms: practicality, convenience

not recognize me in this state of **degradation**. **Despondency** rarely visited my heart; a high destiny seemed to bear me on, until I fell, never, never again to rise."

Must I then lose this admirable being? I have longed for a friend; I have sought one who would sympathize with and love me. Behold, on these desert seas I have found such a one; but, I fear, I have gained him only to know his value, and lose him. I would **reconcile** him to life, but he **repulses** the idea.

"I thank you, Walton," he said, "for your kind intentions towards so miserable a wretch; but when you speak of new ties, and fresh affections, think you that any can replace those who are gone? Can any man be to me as Clerval was; or any woman another Elizabeth? Even where the affections are not strongly moved by any superior excellence, the companions of our childhood always possess a certain power over our minds, which hardly any later friend can obtain. They know our infantine dispositions, which, however they may be afterwards modified, are never **eradicated**; and they can judge of our actions with more certain conclusions as to the **integrity** of our motives. A sister or a brother can never, unless indeed such symptoms have been shown early, suspect the other of fraud or false dealing, when another friend, however strongly he may be attached, may, in spite of himself, be invaded with suspicion. But I enjoyed friends, dear not only through habit and association, but from their own **merits**; and, wherever I am, the soothing voice of my Elizabeth, and the conversation of Clerval, will be ever whispered in my ear. They are dead; and but one feeling in such a solitude can persuade me to preserve my life. If I were engaged in any high undertaking or design, **fraught** with extensive **utility** to my fellow-creatures, then could I live to fulfil it. But such is not my destiny; I must pursue and destroy the being to whom I gave existence; then my lot on earth will be fulfilled, and I may die."

ENCOMPASS (ehn kuhm puhs) *v.* **-ing,-ed.**
to include, cover, take in
Synonyms: surround, enclose, envelop, constitute, include

PERIL (pehr uhl) *n.*
danger; exposure to harmful risk
Synonyms: hazard, jeopardy

BESTOW (bih stoh) *v.* **-ing,-ed.**
to give as a gift
Synonyms: award, endow, donate, confer, present

APPALLING (uh pahl lihng) *adj.*
overcome with shock or dismay
Synonyms: horrifying, dreadful, ghastly, awful

AUGURY (aw gyuh ree) (aw guh ree) *n.*
prophecy, prediction of events
Synonyms: omen, auspices, portent, harbinger, presage

ELOQUENCE (eh luh kwuhns) *n.*
persuasive and effective speech
Synonyms: expressiveness, fluency

RESOLUTION (reh suh loo shun) *n.*
firm determination; a formal decision
Synonyms: firmness, intention, resolve

TRANSITORY (traan sih tohr ee) *adj.*
short-lived, existing only briefly
Synonyms: transient, ephemeral, fleeting, fugitive, momentary

September 2nd.

My beloved Sister,

I write to you, **encompassed** by **peril**, and ignorant whether I am ever doomed to see again dear England, and the dearer friends that inhabit it. I am surrounded by mountains of ice, which admit of no escape, and threaten every moment to crush my vessel. The brave fellows, whom I have persuaded to be my companions, look towards me for aid; but I have none to **bestow**. There is something terribly **appalling** in our situation, yet my courage and hopes do not desert me. We may survive; and if we do not, I will repeat the lessons of my Seneca, and die with a good heart.

Yet what, Margaret, will be the state of your mind? You will not hear of my destruction, and you will anxiously await my return. Years will pass, and you will have visitings of despair, and yet be tortured by hope. Oh! My beloved sister, the sickening failings of your heart-felt expectations are, in prospect, more terrible to me than my own death. But you have a husband, and lovely children; you may be happy. Heaven bless you, and make you so!

My unfortunate guest regards me with the tenderest compassion. He endeavours to fill me with hope; and talks as if life were a possession which he valued. He reminds me how often the same accidents have happened to other navigators, who have attempted this sea, and, in spite of myself, he fills me with cheerful **auguries**. Even the sailors feel the power of his **eloquence**. When he speaks, they no longer despair; he rouses their energies, and, while they hear his voice, they believe these vast mountains of ice are mole-hills, which will vanish before the **resolutions** of man. These feelings are **transitory**; each day's expectation delayed fills them with fear, and I almost dread a mutiny caused by this despair.

FORBEAR (fohr bayr) *v.* **-ing,-bore.**
to refrain or resist
Synonym: avoid

DESOLATION (deh suh lay shuhn) *n.*
barren wasteland; sadness, loneliness
Synonyms: bleakness, devastation, ruin; despair

WAN (wahn) *adj.*
sickly pale
Synonyms: ashen, pallid, blanched, pasty, sickly

COUNTENANCE (kown tuh nuhns) *n.*
appearance, facial expression
Synonyms: face, features, visage

LISTLESSLY (lihst lihs lee) *adv.*
without energy or enthusiasm
Synonyms: lethargically, sluggishly, languidly

IMMURE (ih myoor) *v.* **-ing,-ed.**
to enclose within; to build into a wall
Synonyms: confine, restrain, envelop

DISSIPATE (dihs uh payt) *v.* **-ing,-ed.**
to scatter; to pursue pleasure to excess
Synonyms: carouse, squander, consume; disperse, dissolve

SURMOUNT (suhr mownt) *v.* **-ing,-ed.**
to conquer, overcome
Synonyms: clear, hurdle, leap, surpass, exceed

SOLEMN (sah luhm) *adj.*
deeply serious; somberly impressive
Synonyms: dignified, earnest, ceremonial

September 5th.

A scene has just passed of such uncommon interest, that although it is highly probable that these papers may never reach you, yet I cannot **forbear** recording it.

We are still surrounded by mountains of ice, still in imminent danger of being crushed in their conflict. The cold is excessive, and many of my unfortunate comrades have already found a grave amidst this scene of **desolation**. Frankenstein has daily declined in health. A feverish fire still glimmers in his eyes; but he is exhausted, and, when suddenly roused to any exertion, he speedily sinks again into apparent lifelessness.

I mentioned in my last letter the fears I entertained of a mutiny. This morning, as I sat watching the **wan countenance** of my friend—his eyes half closed, and his limbs hanging **listlessly**—I was roused by half a dozen of the sailors, who desired admission into the cabin. They entered; and their leader addressed me. He told me that he and his companions had been chosen by the other sailors to come in deputation to me, to make me a demand, which, in justice, I could not refuse. We were **immured** in ice, and should probably never escape; but they feared that if, as was possible, the ice should **dissipate**, and a free passage be opened, I should be rash enough to continue my voyage, and lead them into fresh dangers, after they might happily have **surmounted** this. They desired, therefore, that I should engage with a **solemn** promise, that if the vessel should be freed, I would instantly direct my course southward.

This speech troubled me. I had not despaired; nor had I yet conceived the idea of returning, if set free. Yet could I, in justice, or even in possibility, refuse this demand? I hesitated before I answered; when Frankenstein, who had at first been silent, and, indeed, appeared hardly to have force enough to attend, now roused himself; his eyes sparkled, and his cheeks

PLACID (plaa sihd) *adj.*
calm
Synonyms: tranquil, serene, peaceful, complacent

FORTITUDE (fohr tih tood) *n.*
strength, stamina
Synonyms: endurance, hardiness, toughness, courage

BENEFACTOR (behn uh faak tohr) *n.*
someone giving aid or money
Synonyms: contributor, backer, donor, patron

PERIL (pehr uhl) *n.*
danger; exposure to harmful risk
Synonyms: hazard, jeopardy

MUTABLE (myoo tuh buhl) *adj.*
changeable, inconsistent
Synonyms: inconstant, impermanent

STIGMA (stihg mah) *n.*
mark of disgrace or inferiority
Synonyms: stain, blot, brand, taint

MODULATE (mah juh layt) *v.* **-ing,-ed.**
to pass gradually from one state to another; to tune to a key or pitch; to adjust or keep in proper measure
Synonyms: regulate, inflect, adjust

flushed with momentary vigour. Turning towards the men, he said—

"What do you mean? What do you demand of your captain? Are you then so easily turned from your design? Did you not call this a glorious expedition? And wherefore was it glorious? Not because the way was smooth and **placid** as a southern sea, but because it was full of dangers and terror; because, at every new incident, your **fortitude** was to be called forth, and your courage exhibited; because danger and death surrounded, and these dangers you were to brave and overcome. For this was it a glorious, for this was it an honourable undertaking. You were hereafter to be hailed as the **benefactors** of your species; your names adored, as belonging to brave men who encountered death for honour and the benefit of mankind. And now, behold, with the first imagination of danger, or, if you will, the first mighty and terrific trial of your courage, you shrink away, and are content to be handed down as men who had not strength enough to endure cold and **peril**; and so, poor souls, they were chilly, and returned to their warm fire-sides. Why, that requires not this preparation; ye need not have come thus far, and dragged your captain to the shame of a defeat, merely to prove yourselves cowards. Oh! Be men, or be more than men. Be steady to your purposes, and firm as a rock. This ice is not made of such stuff as your hearts might be; it is **mutable**, cannot withstand you, if you say that it shall not. Do not return to your families with the **stigma** of disgrace marked on your brows. Return as heroes who have fought and conquered, and who know not what it is to turn their backs on the foe."

He spoke this with a voice so **modulated** to the different feelings expressed in his speech, with an eye so full of lofty design and heroism, that can you wonder that these men were moved? They looked at one another, and were unable to reply. I spoke; I told them to retire, and consider of what had been said, that I would not lead them further

LANGUOR (laang guhr) (laang uhr) *n.*
lack of energy, indifference, slowness
Synonyms: weakness, listlessness, sluggishness

UTILITY (yoo tih lih tee) *n.*
usefulness, efficiency, functionality
Synonyms: practicality, convenience

DESPOND (dih spahnd) *v.* **-ing,-ed.**
to become discouraged or disheartened
Synonyms: despair, agonize, mope, grieve

PERIL (pehr uhl) *n.*
danger; exposure to harmful risk
Synonyms: hazard, jeopardy

TUMULTUOUS (tuh muhl choo uhs) *adj.*
confusing or disorderly; agitated
Synonyms: disturbed, turbulent, chaotic, hectic

north, if they strenuously desired the contrary; but that I hoped that, with reflection, their courage would return.

They retired, and I turned towards my friend; but he was sunk in **languor**, and almost deprived of life.

How all this will terminate, I know not; but I had rather die, than return shamefully, my purpose unfulfilled. Yet I fear such will be my fate; the men, unsupported by ideas of glory and honour, can never willingly continue to endure their present hardships.

September 7th.

The die is cast; I have consented to return, if we are not destroyed. Thus are my hopes blasted by cowardice and indecision; I come back ignorant and disappointed. It requires more philosophy than I possess, to bear this injustice with patience.

September 12th.

It is past; I am returning to England. I have lost my hopes of **utility** and glory—I have lost my friend. But I will endeavour to detail these bitter circumstances to you, my dear sister; and, while I am wafted towards England, and towards you, I will not **despond**.

September 9th, the ice began to move, and roarings like thunder were heard at a distance, as the islands split and cracked in every direction. We were in the most imminent **peril**; but, as we could only remain passive, my chief attention was occupied by my unfortunate guest, whose illness increased in such a degree, that he was entirely confined to his bed. The ice cracked behind us, and was driven with force towards the north; a breeze sprung from the west, and on the 11th the passage towards the south became perfectly free. When the sailors saw this, and that their return to their native country was apparently assured, a shout of **tumultuous**

TUMULT (tuh muhlt) *n.*
state of confusion; agitation
Synonyms: disturbance, turmoil, din, commotion, chaos

VENGEANCE (vehn juhns) *n.*
punishment inflicted in retaliation; vehemence
Synonyms: revenge, repayment, wrath

ENDOW (ehn dow) *v.* **-ing,-ed.**
to furnish with an income or grant; to provide with something naturally or freely
Synonyms: bestow, donate, empower, grant, support

EXTINCT (ihk stingkt) *adj.*
dead; no longer living or active
Synonyms: exterminated, eradicated, annihilated, eliminated, destroyed

ARDENT (ahr dihnt) *adj.*
passionate, enthusiastic, fervent
Synonyms: intense, vehement, fervid

ADVERSARY (aad vuhr saa ree) *n.*
an opponent or enemy
Synonyms: antagonist, foe, opposition

PARAMOUNT (paar uh mownt) *adj.*
supreme, dominant, primary
Synonyms: chief, commanding, primary

joy broke from them, loud and long-continued. Frankenstein, who was dozing, awoke, and asked the cause of the **tumult**. "They shout," I said, "because they will soon return to England."

"Do you then really return?"

"Alas, yes; I cannot withstand their demands. I cannot lead them unwillingly to danger, and I must return."

"Do so, if you will; but I will not. You may give up your purpose; but mine is assigned to me by heaven, and I dare not. I am weak; but surely the spirits who assist my **vengeance** will **endow** me with sufficient strength." Saying this, he endeavoured to spring from the bed, but the exertion was too great for him; he fell back, and fainted.

It was long before he was restored; and I often thought that life was entirely **extinct**. At length he opened his eyes, but he breathed with difficulty, and was unable to speak. The surgeon gave him a composing draught, and ordered us to leave him undisturbed. In the mean time he told me that my friend had certainly not many hours to live.

His sentence was pronounced; and I could only grieve, and be patient. I sat by his bed watching him; his eyes were closed, and I thought he slept; but presently he called to me in a feeble voice, and, bidding me come near, said, "Alas! The strength I relied on is gone; I feel that I shall soon die, and he, my enemy and persecutor, may still be in being. Think not, Walton, that in the last moments of my existence I feel that burning hatred, and **ardent** desire of revenge I once expressed, but I feel myself justified in desiring the death of my **adversary**. During these last days I have been occupied in examining my past conduct; nor do I find it blameable. In a fit of enthusiastic madness I created a rational creature, and was bound towards him, to assure, as far as was in my power, his happiness and well-being. This was my duty; but there was another still **paramount** to that. My duties towards my fellow-creatures had greater claims to my

MALIGNITY (muh lihg nih tee) *n.*
evil or aggressive malice; something that produces death
Synonyms: malevolence, bitterness, resentment

VENGEANCE (vehn juhns) *n.*
punishment inflicted in retaliation; vehemence
Synonyms: revenge, repayment, wrath

ACTUATE (aak chuh wayt) (aak shuh wayt) *v.* **-ing,-ed.**
to put into mechanical action; to move into action
Synonyms: animate, motivate, prompt

INDUCE (ihn doos) (ihn dyoos) *v.* **-ing,-ed.**
to persuade; bring about
Synonyms: prevail, convince, lead, effect, occasion

RENOUNCE (rih nowns) *v.* **-ing,-ed.**
to give up or reject a right, title, person, etc.
Synonyms: relinquish, disown, yield, resign, abandon

attention, because they included a greater proportion of happiness or misery. Urged by this view, I refused, and I did right in refusing, to create a companion for the first creature. He showed unparalleled **malignity** and selfishness in evil. He destroyed my friends; he devoted to destruction beings who possessed exquisite sensations, happiness, and wisdom; nor do I know where this thirst for **vengeance** may end. Miserable himself, that he may render no other wretched, he ought to die. The task of his destruction was mine, but I have failed. When **actuated** by selfish and vicious motives, I asked you to undertake my unfinished work; and I renew this request now, when I am only **induced** by reason and virtue.

"Yet I cannot ask you to **renounce** your country and friends to fulfill this task; and now, that you are returning to England, you will have little chance of meeting with him. But the consideration of these points, and the well-balancing of what you may esteem your duties, I leave to you; my judgment and ideas are already disturbed by the near approach of death. I dare not ask you to do what I think right, for I may still be misled by passion.

"That he should live to be an instrument of mischief disturbs me; in other respects this hour, when I momentarily expect my release, is the only happy one which I have enjoyed for several years. The forms of the beloved dead flit before me, and I hasten to their arms. Farewell, Walton! Seek happiness in tranquillity, and avoid ambition, even if it be only the apparently innocent one of distinguishing yourself in science and discoveries. Yet why do I say this? I have myself been blasted in these hopes, yet another may succeed."

His voice became fainter as he spoke; and at length, exhausted by his effort, he sunk into silence. About half an hour afterwards he attempted again to speak, but was unable; he pressed my hand feebly, and his eyes closed for ever, while the irradiation of a gentle smile passed away from his lips.

EXTINCTION (ihk <u>stingk</u> shuhn) *n.*
end of a living thing or species
Synonyms: extermination, eradication, annihilation, elimination, destruction

CONSOLATION (kahn suh <u>lay</u> shuhn) *n.*
something providing comfort or solace for a loss or hardship
Synonyms: condolence, solace

PORTEND (pohr <u>tehnd</u>) *v.* **-ing,-ed.**
to act as an omen or warning
Synonyms: predict, herald, indicate, forecast

UNCOUTH (uhn <u>kooth</u>) *adj.*
lacking in refinement; awkward and uncultivated in appearance or manner
Synonyms: clumsy, ungraceful, crude, unrefined

LOATHSOME (<u>lohth</u> suhm) *adj.*
abhorrent, hateful
Synonyms: offensive, disgusting

APPALLING (uh <u>pahl</u> lihng) *adj.*
overcome with shock or dismay
Synonyms: horrifying, dreadful, ghastly, awful

INSTIGATE (<u>ihn</u> stih gayt) *v.* **-ing,-ed.**
to incite, urge, agitate
Synonyms: foment, goad, spark

Margaret, what comment can I make on the untimely **extinction** of this glorious spirit? What can I say, that will enable you to understand the depth of my sorrow? All that I should express would be inadequate and feeble. My tears flow; my mind is overshadowed by a cloud of disappointment. But I journey towards England, and I may there find **consolation**.

I am interrupted. What do these sounds **portend**? It is midnight; the breeze blows fairly, and the watch on deck scarcely stir. Again; there is a sound as of a human voice, but hoarser; it comes from the cabin where the remains of Frankenstein still lie. I must arise, and examine. Good night, my sister.

Great God! What a scene has just taken place! I am yet dizzy with the remembrance of it. I hardly know whether I shall have the power to detail it; yet the tale which I have recorded would be incomplete without this final and wonderful catastrophe.

I entered the cabin, where lay the remains of my ill-fated and admirable friend. Over him hung a form which I cannot find words to describe; gigantic in stature, yet **uncouth** and distorted in its proportions. As he hung over the coffin, his face was concealed by long locks of ragged hair; but one vast hand was extended, in colour and apparent texture like that of a mummy. When he heard the sound of my approach, he ceased to utter exclamations of grief and horror, and sprung towards the window. Never did I behold a vision so horrible as his face, of such **loathsome**, yet **appalling** hideousness. I shut my eyes involuntarily, and endeavoured to recollect what were my duties with regard to this destroyer. I called on him to stay.

He paused, looking on me with wonder; and, again turning towards the lifeless form of his creator, he seemed to forget my presence, and every feature and gesture seemed **instigated** by the wildest rage of some uncontrollable passion.

CONSUMMATE (kahn suh mayt) *v.* **-ing,-ed.**
to accomplish or complete
Synonyms: conclude, fulfill, achieve, perfect

AVAIL (uh vayl) *v.* **-ing,-ed.**
to be of use or advantage to; to result in; to make use of
Synonyms: benefit, profit, serve, suffice

INCOHERENT (ihn koh heer uhnt) *adj.*
unable to be understood; unintelligible, incomprehensible
Synonyms: disorderly, illogical, inconsistent

REPROACH (rih prohch) *n.*
discredit; expressed disappointment or displeasure
Synonyms: blame, disgrace

RESOLUTION (reh suh loo shun) *n.*
firm determination; a formal decision
Synonyms: firmness, intention, resolve

TEMPEST (tehm pehst) *n.*
a violent and windy storm
Synonyms: inclemency, turbulence, torrent

REPENTANCE (rih pehnt ehnts) *n.*
guilt, remorse for one's past conduct
Synonyms: contrition, regret, penitence

SUPERFLUOUS (soo puhr floo uhs) *adj.*
extra, more than necessary
Synonyms: excess, spare, supernumerary, surplus

REMORSE (rih mohrs) *n.* ***See page 360.***

DIABOLICAL (die uh bahl ih kuhl) *adj.*
characteristic of the devil, devilish
Synonyms: cruel, heartless, ruthless, brutal

VENGEANCE (vehn juhns) *n.* ***See page 416.***

CONSUMMATION (kahn suh may shun) *n.*
fulfillment; ultimate goal or accomplishment
Synonyms: completion

EXECUTION (ek sih kyoo shuhn) *n.* ***See page 372.***

SUSCEPTIBLE (suh sehp tuh buhl) *adj.*
vulnerable, unprotected
Synonyms: sensitive, impressionable, prone, subject

ABHOR (uhb hohr) *v.* **-ing,-ed.**
to loathe, detest, despise
Synonyms: hate, condemn, abominate, execrate

"That is also my victim!" he exclaimed. "In his murder my crimes are **consummated**; the miserable series of my being is wound to its close! Oh, Frankenstein! Generous and self-devoted being! What does it **avail** that I now ask thee to pardon me? I, who irretrievably destroyed thee by destroying all thou lovedst. Alas! He is cold; he may not answer me."

His voice seemed suffocated; and my first impulses, which had suggested to me the duty of obeying the dying request of my friend, in destroying his enemy, were now suspended by a mixture of curiosity and compassion. I approached this tremendous being; I dared not again raise my looks upon his face—there was something so scaring and unearthly in his ugliness. I attempted to speak, but the words died away on my lips. The monster continued to utter wild and **incoherent** self-**reproaches**. At length I gathered **resolution** to address him, in a pause of the **tempest** of his passion. "Your **repentance**," I said, "is now **superfluous**. If you had listened to the voice of conscience, and heeded the stings of **remorse**, before you had urged your **diabolical vengeance** to this extremity, Frankenstein would yet have lived."

"And do you dream?" said the daemon. "Do you think that I was then dead to agony and **remorse**? He," he continued, pointing to the corpse, "he suffered not more in the **consummation** of the deed—oh! Not the ten-thousandth portion of the anguish that was mine during the lingering detail of its **execution**. A frightful selfishness hurried me on, while my heart was poisoned with **remorse**. Think ye that the groans of Clerval were music to my ears? My heart was fashioned to be **susceptible** to love and sympathy; and, when wrenched by misery to <u>vice</u> and hatred, it did not endure the violence of the change without torture, such as you cannot even imagine.

"After the murder of Clerval, I returned to Switzerland, heart-broken and overcome. I pitied Frankenstein, my pity amounted to horror; I **abhorred** myself. But when

INDULGENCE (ihn duhl jehns) *n.*
lenience, the act of giving into desires
Synonyms: gratification, tolerance, pampering

INDIGNATION (ihn dihg nay shun) *n.*
anger caused by something mean or unjust
Synonyms: fury, ire, wrath

INSATIABLE (ihn say shuh buhl) *adj.*
unable to be satisfied
Synonyms: insatiate, greedy, ravenous, gluttonous

VENGEANCE (vehn juhns) *n.* ***See page 416.***

RESOLVE (rih sahlv) *v.* **-ing,-ed.**
to determine or to make a firm decision about
Synonyms: solve, decide

DETEST (dee tehst) (dih tehst) *v.* **-ing,-ed.** ***See page 168.***

ADAPT (uh daapt) *v.* **-ing,-ed.**
to accommodate; adjust
Synonyms: conform, fit, reconcile

ELOQUENCE (eh luh kwuhns) *n.*
persuasive and effective speech
Synonyms: expressiveness, fluency

REKINDLE (ree kihn duhl) *v.* **-ing,-ed.**
to set fire to or ignite again; excite or inspire again
Synonyms: relight, spark, arouse, reawaken

DESOLATION (deh suh lay shuhn) *n.*
barren wasteland; sadness, loneliness
Synonyms: bleakness, devastation, ruin; despair

LAMENT (luh mehnt) *v.* **-ing,-ed.**
to deplore, grieve
Synonyms: mourn, sorrow, regret, bewail

HYPOCRITICAL (hih puh krih tih kuhl) *adj.*
claiming to have feelings or virtues that one doesn't have
Synonyms: fraudulent, deceitful, fake, phony

MALIGNITY (muh lihg nih tee) *n.* ***See page 416.***

PURPORT (puhr pohrt) *n.*
intention or purpose
Synonyms: importance, meaning

I discovered that he, the author at once of my existence and of its unspeakable torments, dared to hope for happiness; that while he accumulated wretchedness and despair upon me, he sought his own enjoyment in feelings and passions from the **indulgence** of which I was for ever barred, then impotent envy and bitter **indignation** filled me with an **insatiable** thirst for **vengeance**. I recollected my threat, and **resolved** that it should be accomplished. I knew that I was preparing for myself a deadly torture; but I was the slave, not the master of an impulse, which I **detested**, yet could not disobey. Yet when she died! Nay, then I was not miserable. I had cast off all feeling, subdued all anguish to riot in the excess of my despair. Evil thenceforth became my good. Urged thus far, I had no choice but to **adapt** my nature to an element which I had willingly chosen. The completion of my demoniacal design became an **insatiable** passion. And now it is ended; there is my last victim!"

I was at first touched by the expressions of his misery; yet when I called to mind what Frankenstein had said of his powers of **eloquence** and persuasion, and when I again cast my eyes on the lifeless form of my friend, **indignation** was **rekindled** within me. "Wretch!" I said, "it is well that you come here to whine over the **desolation** that you have made. You throw a torch into a pile of buildings, and when they are consumed you sit among the ruins, and **lament** the fall. **Hypocritical** fiend! If he whom you mourn still lived, still would he be the object, again would he become the prey of your accursed **vengeance**. It is not pity that you feel; you **lament** only because the victim of your **malignity** is withdrawn from your power."

"Oh, it is not thus—not thus," interrupted the being. "Yet such must be the impression conveyed to you by what appears to be the **purport** of my actions. Yet I seek not a fellow-feeling in my misery. No sympathy may I ever find. When I first sought it, it was the love of virtue,

LOATHING (lohth ing) *adj.*
hating or disliking
Synonyms: detesting, abhorring
ABHORRENCE (uhb hohr ehnts) *n.* ***See page 308.***
DEGRADE (dih grayd) *v.* **-ing,-ed.** ***See page 348.***
MALIGNITY (mah lihg nih tee) *n.* ***See page 416.***
SUBLIME (suh bliem) *adj.*
awe-inspiring; of high spiritual or moral value
Synonyms: noble, majestic, supreme, ideal
TRANSCENDENT (traan sehn daant) *adj.*
able to rise above or go beyond; supreme
Synonyms: surpassing, excellent, exceeding
MALIGNANT (muh lihg nehnt) *adj.*
evil in influence of effect; aggressively malicious; tending to produce death
Synonyms: deadly, destructive, poisonous
DESOLATION (deh soh lay shuhn) *n.* ***See page 422.***
ARDENT (ahr dihnt) *adj.* ***See page 414.***
SPURN (spuhrn) *v.* **-ing,-ed.**
to reject or refuse contemptuously; scorn
Synonyms: disdain, snub, ostracize, ignore, cut
CONTUMELY (kahn too muh lee) (kuhn too muh lee) *n.*
harsh language or treatment arising from haughtiness
Synonyms: rudeness, contempt, insolence, abuse
EXECRATE (ehk sih krayt) *v.* **-ing,-ed.**
to curse, to declare to be evil
Synonyms: hate, abhor, loathe
RUSTIC (ruh stihk) *adj.*
rural
Synonyms: bucolic, pastoral
VIRTUOUS (vuhr choo ihs) *adj.*
good, worthy, moral
Synonyms: exemplary, admirable, dutiful, righteous
IMMACULATE (ih maa kyuh luht) *adj.*
spotless; free from error
Synonyms: clean, pure, unstained

the feelings of happiness and affection with which my whole being overflowed, that I wished to be participated. But now, that virtue has become to me a shadow, and that happiness and affection are turned into bitter and **loathing** despair, in what should I seek for sympathy? I am content to suffer alone, while my sufferings shall endure. When I die, I am well satisfied that **abhorrence** and opprobrium should load my memory. Once my fancy was soothed with dreams of virtue, of fame, and of enjoyment. Once I falsely hoped to meet with beings, who, pardoning my outward form, would love me for the excellent qualities which I was capable of bringing forth. I was nourished with high thoughts of honour and devotion. But now vice has **degraded** me beneath the meanest animal. No crime, no mischief, no **malignity**, no misery, can be found comparable to mine. When I call over the frightful catalogue of my deeds, I cannot believe that I am he whose thoughts were once filled with **sublime** and **transcendent** visions of the beauty and the majesty of goodness. But it is even so; the fallen angel becomes a **malignant** devil. Yet even that enemy of God and man had friends and associates in his **desolation**; I am quite alone.

"You, who call Frankenstein your friend, seem to have a knowledge of my crimes and his misfortunes. But, in the detail which he gave you of them, he could not sum up the hours and months of misery which I endured, wasting in impotent passions. For whilst I destroyed his hopes, I did not satisfy my own desires. They were for ever **ardent** and craving; still I desired love and fellowship, and I was still **spurned**. Was there no injustice in this? Am I to be thought the only criminal, when all human kind sinned against me? Why do you not hate Felix, who drove his friend from his door with **contumely**? Why do you not **execrate** the **rustic** who sought to destroy the saviour of his child? Nay, these are **virtuous** and **immaculate** beings! I, the miserable and the

SPURN (spuhrn) *v.* **-ing,-ed.**
to reject or refuse contemptuously; scorn
Synonyms: disdain, snub, ostracize, ignore, cut

ABHORRENCE (uhb hohr ehnts) *n.*
loathing, detestation
Synonyms: hatred, condemnation, abomination, execration

EXECUTE (ehk sih kyoot) *v.* **-ing,-ed.**
1. to carry out fully; to make or produce
   Synonyms: accomplish, achieve, perform
2. to put to death by penalty of crime
   Synonyms: kill, punish, murder

CONSUMMATE (kahn suh mayt) *v.* **-ing,-ed.**
to accomplish or complete
Synonyms: conclude, fulfill, achieve, perfect

UNHALLOWED (uhn haa lohd) *adj.*
unholy; desecrated
Synonyms: profane, wicked

abandoned, am an abortion, to be **spurned** at, and kicked, and trampled on. Even now my blood boils at the recollection of this injustice.

"But it is true that I am a wretch. I have murdered the lovely and the helpless; I have strangled the innocent as they slept, and grasped to death his throat who never injured me or any other living thing. I have devoted my creator, the select specimen of all that is worthy of love and admiration among men, to misery; I have pursued him even to that irremediable ruin. There he lies, white and cold in death. You hate me; but your **abhorrence** cannot equal that with which I regard myself. I look on the hands which **executed** the deed; I think on the heart in which the imagination of it was conceived, and long for the moment when they will meet my eyes, when it will haunt my thoughts, no more.

"Fear not that I shall be the instrument of future mischief. My work is nearly complete. Neither yours nor any man's death is needed to **consummate** the series of my being, and accomplish that which must be done; but it requires my own. Do not think that I shall be slow to perform this sacrifice. I shall quit your vessel on the ice-raft which brought me hither, and shall seek the most northern extremity of the globe; I shall collect my funeral pile, and consume to ashes this miserable frame, that its remains may afford no light to any curious and **unhallowed** wretch, who would create such another as I have been. I shall die. I shall no longer feel the agonies which now consume me, or be the prey of feelings unsatisfied, yet unquenched. He is dead who called me into being; and when I shall be no more, the very remembrance of us both will speedily vanish. I shall no longer see the sun or stars, or feel the winds play on my cheeks. Light, feeling, and sense, will pass away; and in this condition must I find my happiness. Some years ago, when the images which this world affords first opened upon me, when I felt the cheering warmth of summer, and

CONSOLATION (kahn suh lay shuhn) *n.*
something providing comfort or solace for a loss or hardship
Synonyms: condolence, solace

REMORSE (rih mohrs) *n.*
a gnawing distress arising from a sense of guilt
Synonyms: anguish, ruefulness, shame, penitence

SATIATE (say shee ayt) *v.* **-ing,-ed.**
to satisfy
Synonyms: sate, cloy, glut, gorge, surfeit

EXTINCTION (ihk stingk shuhn) *n.*
end of a living thing or species
Synonyms: extermination, eradication, annihilation, elimination, destruction

SOLEMN (sah luhm) *adj.*
deeply serious; somberly impressive
Synonyms: dignified, earnest, ceremonial

EXTINCT (ihk stingkt) *adj.*
dead; no longer living or active
Synonyms: exterminated, eradicated, annihilated, eliminated, destroyed

ASCEND (uh sehnd) *v.* **-ing,-ed.**
to rise to another level or climb; move upward
Synonyms: elevate, escalate, hoist, lift, mount

EXULT (ihg zuhlt) *v.* **-ing,-ed.**
to rejoice triumphantly
Synonyms: celebrate, cheer, glory

CONFLAGRATION (kahn fluh gray shuhn) *n.*
big, destructive fire
Synonyms: blaze, holocaust, inferno

heard the rustling of the leaves and the chirping of the birds, and these were all to me, I should have wept to die; now it is my only **consolation**. Polluted by crimes, and torn by the bitterest **remorse**, where can I find rest but in death?

"Farewell! I leave you, and in you the last of human kind whom these eyes will ever behold. Farewell, Frankenstein! If thou wert yet alive, and yet cherished a desire of revenge against me, it would be better **satiated** in my life than in my destruction. But it was not so; thou didst seek my **extinction**, that I might not cause greater wretchedness; and if yet, in some mode unknown to me, thou hast not yet ceased to think and feel, thou desirest not my life for my own misery. Blasted as thou wert, my agony was still superior to thine; for the bitter sting of **remorse** may not cease to rankle in my wounds until death shall close them for ever.

"But soon," he cried, with sad and **solemn** enthusiasm, "I shall die, and what I now feel be no longer felt. Soon these burning miseries will be **extinct**. I shall **ascend** my funeral pile triumphantly, and **exult** in the agony of the torturing flames. The light of that **conflagration** will fade away; my ashes will be swept into the sea by the winds. My spirit will sleep in peace; or if it thinks, it will not surely think thus. Farewell."

He sprung from the cabin-window, as he said this, upon the ice-raft which lay close to the vessel. He was soon borne away by the waves, and lost in darkness and distance.

THE END

Glossary

The following words appear underlined throughout the text:

abode (uh bohd) *n.*
a home or house; a place to dwell

adjuration (aa juh ray shuhn) *n.*
an earnest appeal

affright (uh friet) *n.*
extreme terror or great fear

aiguille (ay gweel) *n.*
a pointed and rocky mountain peak

albatross (aal buh trahs) *n.*
a large web-footed bird of the southern hemisphere; an obstacle or burden

alight (uh liet) *v.* **-ing-ed.**
to settle or come to rest; to dismount

apothecary (uh pah thih keh ree) *n.*
someone who prepares and sells drugs and remedies

artifice (ahr tih fihs) *n.*
trickery or clever skill

asseveration (uh seh vuhr ay shuhn) *n.*
a serious declaration

assizes (uh sie zehs) *n.*
in England and Wales, a time of periodic court sessions

bauble (baw buhl) *n.*
an inexpensive ornament or piece of jewlery

bier (beer) *n.*
a portable stand for a coffin, used before burial

bourne (bohrn) *n.*
a goal or destination; a limit

buffet (buh fiht) *v.* **-ing.-ed.**
to hit or strike with forcc

cabriolet (kaa bree uh lay) *n.*
a one-horse carriage with two wheels

Glossary

cadence (kay dihns) *n.*
a progression of musical chords; rhythmic change of voice

canvass (kaan vuhs) *v.* **-ing,-ed.**
to examine thoroughly; scrutinize

casement (kays mehnt) *n.*
a window with hinged coverings that open outward

cataract (kaa tuh raakt) *n.*
a large waterfall or strong downpour

charnel (chahr nuhl) *adj.*
able to receive the dead; countaining dead bodies

chasm (kaa zuhm) *n.*
an abyss or gorge with very steep sides

communion (kuh myoon yihn) *n.*
the act of sharing feelings and thoughts

concenter (kuhn sehn tuhr) *v.* **-ing,-ed.**
to come together at a common point

cowardice (kow uhr dihs) *n.*
fear of danger or pain; lack of courage

death-knell (dehth nehl) *n.*
a bell toll that announces death

debar (dee bahr) *v.* **-ing,-ed.**
to exclude or forbid

demoniacal (dee muh nie uh kuhl) *adj.*
influenced by or resembling a devil or demon

deputation (deh pyuh tay shuhn) *n.*
a group of representatives

dictatorial (dihk tah tohr ee uhl) *adj.*
domineering or overbearing

disposition (dihs puh zih shuhn) *n.*
one's temperament or characteristic tendencies

draught (draaft) *n.*
a drink serving, usually alcoholic

drove (drohv) *n.*
a large group of animals or people travelling as a mass

Glossary

elasticity (ee laas tih sih tee) *n.*
flexibility; the ability to rebound from sadness

embitter (ehm bih tuhr) *v.* **-ing,-ed.**
to make upset or bitter

emblem (ehm bluhm) *n.*
a symbol

embosom (ehm buh suhm) *v.* **-ing,-ed.**
to shelter protectively; to hug or hold close

endue (ehn doo) *v.* **-ing,-ed.**
to give a quality to; to endow

ensue (ehn soo) *v.* **-ing,-ed.**
to follow afterward, to happen subsequently

exordium (ek zohr dee uhm) *n.*
an introduction, usually as part of a speech

fortnight (fohrt niet) *n.*
a two-week period of time

gale (gayl) *n.*
a strong wind or breeze

gaoler (jay luhr) *n.*
one who guards prisoners; a jailer

hamlet (haam leht) *n.*
a small village

heath (heeth) *n.*
a low-growing shrub

hovel (huh vuhl) *n.*
a small, crude hut or dwelling place

imbibe (ihm bieb) *v.* **-ing,-ed.**
1. to absorb into one's mind 2. to drink

impotence (ihm poh tehnts) *n.*
1. lack of strength; weakness 2. sterility

impotent (ihm poh tehnt) *adj.*
1. having little or no strength; weak 2. sterile

incantation (ihn kaan tay shuhn) *n.*
recitation of a charm or spell for a magical result

Glossary

incommode (ihn kuh mohd) *v.* **-ing,-ed.**
to disturb or inconvenience

infantine (ihn fehn tien) *adj.*
childish

intercourse (ihn tuhr cohrs) *n.*
communication between people

irksome (urk suhm) *adj.*
annoying or tedious

irradiation (ih ray dee ay shuhn) *n.*
brilliance of light

irremediable (ih rih mee dee uh buhl) *adj.*
unable to be fixed or cured; irreparable

laudanum (law duh nuhm) *n.*
a preparation of opium, once used for medical purposes

lichen (lie kihn) *n.*
a fungus that grows on rocks and dead trees

lustrous (luh struhs) *adj.*
shiny, glowing, and radiant

manacle (maan uh kuhl) *v.* **-ing,-ed.**
to restrain with handcuffs

manifold (maan ih fohld) *adj.*
multiple; having many forms

maw *n.*
the mouth of something vicious (i.e. animal, hell)

meed *n.*
a repayment or reward

minute (mie noot) *adj.*
very small or insignificant

minutiae (mih noo shee ee) *n. pl.*
small or trivial details

moralize (mohr uh liez) *v.* **-ing,-ed.**
to interpret or explain meanings of morals

mortification (mohr tih fih kay shuhn) n.
strong feelings of shame, humiliation and embarassment

nought (nawt) *n.*
nonexistence; nothing

offals (aw fuhl) *n. pl.*
wasted part of a butchered animal; garbage, leftovers

opprobrium (uh proh bree uhm) *n.*
extreme disgrace or dishonor

orb (ohrb) *n.*
1. a celestial body (moon or sun) 2. a spherical object

paradisaical (paa ruh dih say ih kuhl) *adj.*
relating to paradise; able to bring about happiness

paroxysm (puh rahk sihz uhm) *n.*
an outburst of passion or emotion; a convulsion

perambulation (puhr aam byuh lay shuhn) *n.*
the act of walking or strolling

perpendicularity (puhr pehn dih kyuh laar ih tee) *n.*
the quality of being vertical with relation to the horizon

physiognomy (fih zee ahg nuh mee) *n.*
characteristic facial features; the art of judging one's character from facial features

plait (playt) (plaat) *v.* **-ing,-ed.**
to braid, especially hair

portmanteau (pohrt maan toh) *n.*
a French word for a leather suitcase

presentiment (prih sehn tih mehnt) *n.*
the anticipation or sense that something may happen

promontory (prah muhn tohr ee) *n.*
a high, mountainous point that juts out into the sea

prophesy (prah fih sie) *v.* **-ing,-ed.**
to predict or foretell as if by divine inspiration

ramble (raam buhl) *n.* and *v.* **-ing,-ed.**
n. a leisurely stroll *v.* to walk aimlessly for pleasure

rankle (raang kuhl) *v.* **-ing,-ed.**
to irritate or inflame; to fester

recommence (reh kuh mehnts) *v.* **-ing.-ed.**
to begin again

rend (rehnd) *v.* **-ing,-ed.**
to tear or split into pieces

rendezvous (rahn day voo) *n.*
a special meeting or meeting place

requisition (reh kwih zih shuhn) *n.*
a request or a demand

ribband (rih behnd) *n.*
a narrow, flexible length of wood

sally (saal ee) *n.*
a witty remark; a lively outburst

scion (sie uhn) *n.*
a descendant or heir

scourge (skuhrj) *n.*
a source of severe suffering and devastation

scraggy (skraa gee) *adj.*
rough and irregular; scrawny

siroc (sih rahk) *n.*
a hot oppressive wind

slake (slayk) *v.* **-ing,-ed.**
to quench; to lessen a force or feeling

sophism (sohf ihz uhm) *n.*
a believable argument that is actually false

spectre or **specter** (spehk tuhr) *n.*
a ghost; something that haunts the mind

supposition (suh puh zih shuhn) *n.*
an assumption; a hypothesis based on little evidence

syndic (sihn dihk) *n.*
a government official in some European nations

toilsome (toyl suhm) *adj.*
laborious, grueling, exhausting

treble (treh buhl) *adj.*
triple

turnkey (tuhrn kee) *n.*
a jailer; the key keeper in a prison

viand (vie uhnd) *n.*
a food item

vice (vies) *n.*
an evil or undesirable practice or habit

vile (viel) *adj.*
wretched, offensive, disgusting

writhe (rieth) *v.* **-ing,-ed.**
to stuggle or suffer in pain

Index

A

Index

B

Index

C

D

E

F

G

H

I

Index

K-L

M

N

O

P

R

S

Index

T

U

V

W

Z